Aesop's Fables

OVER 2,000 years ago, a humble Greek slave won freedom and renown when he entertained the nobles in the court of powerful King Croesus with his fascinating and clever tales of animals who could talk like human beings. Because these fables were instructive as well as amusing, Croesus and his court probably learned more home truths from Aesop's narrative skill than from all the profound writings of the royal collection of philosophers.

Since then, Aesop's fables have become popular for their gaiety and wit. They rank among the finest, to be read and remembered by readers of all ages, and they offer an endless source of entertainment.

Generations of children have derived untold pleasure, wit, and wisdom from favorite stories like THE FOX AND THE GRAPES, THE HARE AND THE TORTOISE, and THE COUNTRY MOUSE AND THE TOWN MOUSE.

ILLUSTRATED BY WILLIAM K. PLUMMER

AESOP'S FABLES

COMPANION LIBRARY

PUBLISHERS Grosset & Dunlap NEW YORK

PRINTED IN THE UNITED STATES OF AMERICA

Alphabetical List of Fables

THE LIFE AND WORK OF AESOP

SOMETIME between the years 620 and 560 B.C. there came to the court of Croesus, last of the kings of Lydia in Asia Minor, a freedman known as Aesop. While still a slave of Iadmon on the island of Samos he had gained some local fame for himself and considerable prestige for his master as a narrator of tales about animals.

At any rate, the ex-slave's renown had preceded him when he arrived at Sardis to match wits with such exiled pundits as Solon of Athens and Thales of Miletus and the other sages and philosophers who had gathered at the court of the outstanding patron of learning of that time. There is no doubt that the former bondsman quickly grew in favor with Croesus as a result of his shrewd intelligence and native wit, plus a certain amount of well-directed flattery. It would be a mistake, however, to look upon Aesop as a sort of court jester, for while he came to amuse he remained to instruct, and Croesus probably learned more home truths from his fables than from all the serious disquisitions of the royal stable of philosophers.

In time, as the King acquired what amounted to practically a hegemony over the other small Greek states, Aesop began to be employed as an ambassador to the various capitals. In this capacity his shrewd use of the beast tales, or fables, stood him in good stead. At Corinth he warned his hearers against mob law in a fable, later used by Socrates. At Athens by the recital of *The Frogs Desiring a King* he warned the citizenry that the known tyranny of Pisistratus might be preferable to that of an unknown successor.

His visit to Delphi seems to have had less of a political objective. It was to cost him his life. Sent as a commissioner by Croesus to distribute some payment due the Delphians, he incurred the displeasure of the inhabitants of that important city. The story goes that as he was ready to leave on his homeward journey to Sardis, a gold cup from the temple of Apollo was found in his baggage where it had been planted. Charged with impiety and sacrilege, Aesop was brought to trial. For once his ready weapon failed to serve him. He is said to have appealed to the Delphian reverence for the laws of hospitality with the fable of *The Eagle and the Beetle*, but he appealed in vain. The enraged guardians of the temple, feeling, perhaps, that their sinecure might be in danger, condemned the ambassador of Croesus to be hurled to his death from a high cliff outside the city.

We are told that the conscience-smitten Delphians lived to regret the violent death of Aesop. After a succession of disasters the harried citizenry offered reparation for the envoy's death. It was awarded to the grandson of Iadmon, Aesop's old master. The proverb of "Aesop's blood" in aftertimes gave warning to his countrymen that a murdered man's blood will not cry to heaven in vain.

But the fame of Aesop lived on. About two hundred years after his death his statue, carved by Lysippus, was erected at Athens, and it was placed in front of the statues of the Seven Sages.

We know that Aesop never wrote down any of his fables, and we know, also, that the first recorded compilation of the tales that bear his name was not made until nearly three centuries after his death, but for generations it was deemed an indispensable accomplishment of an Athenian gentleman to be able to tell a good story of Aesop's at the club. His practical wisdom was as highly regarded as his caustic humor. The common tradition that he appeared alive again and fought at Thermopylae speaks more for the honor in which he was held as a patriot than a hundred more plausible anecdotes could do.

Did Aesop invent the fable? No. He merely used a form of the beast tale whose origin can be traced back to many Eastern nations. It was natural among primitive people to compare human motives and acts with the ways of the wily fox, the timid deer, and the noble lion. It followed that the animals of forest and barnyard should be endowed with human passions and feelings, and even with human speech. The fable in those early times was not a child's plaything. It was a nation's primer.

In Greece, during the times of the Tyrants, when free speech was dangerous, the fable began to be used for political purposes. It was in this field that Aesop developed the ancient beast tale which flourished in India long before. When neither kings nor mobs could be made to look upon the naked truth, Aesop found that this style of primitive wisdom furnished an effective garb with which to clothe it. Tyranny and rebellion alike were stayed by this offhand, readymade weapon of the man of action who united presence of mind with presence of wit. Even when free speech was established among the Hellenic democracies the custom of using fables in serious public orations as well as lighter after-dinner speeches continued.

About three centuries after Aesop's time Demetrius Phalereus of Athens, founder of the Alexandria Library, collected the fables he could find under the title *Assemblies of Aesopic Tales.* There were about two hundred fables in the compilation. Later, a Greek freedman of Augustus Caesar, named Phaedrus, in the early years of the Christian era turned them into Latin iambics. Later still, in the time of Marcus Aurelius, Valerius Babrius, a tutor to the young son of Alexander Severus, merged with the Aesopic fables a collection of Indian, or Libyan, beast tales. In the 1300's, a monk of Constantinople, named Maximus Planudes, compiled a definitive book of fables. Each collector and each translator added and changed and edited and inserted. From all these various sources the bulk of the existing fables is derived. All the anachronisms, the mixtures of pagan and Christian forms of speech and sentiment, are indications of the many hands through which the original fables, many of which had their origin in ancient India, passed.

Despite the wear and tear of twenty-five centuries, the spirit and the body of Aesop's fables are still intact, if not as they proceeded from the lips of the ex-slave in the court of Croesus, at least as they were known in the best times of Greek literature.

The Fox and the Hedgehog

A FOX in some unaccountable fashion got his tail entangled in a thicket which held him as closely as though he had been caught in a trap. In no time at all myriads of mosquitoes, seeing his plight, settled down upon him to enjoy a good meal undisturbed by his brush.

A hedgehog who chanced to be strolling by felt sorry for the fox and approached him, saying: "Friend fox, you seem to be in a most unfortunate situation. Would you like me to make you more comfortable by driving off these bloodsucking pests?"

But to the hedgehog's surprise the fox replied: "No; thank you, my good friend, but I beg you not to disturb them."

"And why not?" persisted the well-meaning hedgehog.

"Well, you see," replied the fox, "these mosquitoes which you see have already drawn their fill of blood. If you chase them away a fresh swarm of hungry ones will descend upon me and they will not leave a drop of blood in my body."

★ *Application:* A NEEDY THIEF STEALS MORE THAN ONE WHO ENJOYS PLENTY.

The Dog in the Manger

A DOG looking for a quiet and comfortable place to take a nap jumped into the manger of the ox and lay there on the hay.

Some time later the ox, returning hungry from his day's work, entered his stall and found the dog in his manger. The dog, in a rage because he had been awakened from his nap, stood up and barked and snapped whenever the ox came near his hay.

The ox is a patient beast, but finally he protested: "Dog, if you wanted to eat my dinner I would have no objection. But you will neither eat it yourself nor let me enjoy it, which strikes me as a very churlish way to act."

★ *Application:* SOME BEGRUDGE OTHERS WHAT THEY CANNOT ENJOY THEMSELVES.

The Wolf in Sheep's Clothing

A WOLF had been lurking near a flock of sheep for several days. But so vigilant had been the shepherd in guarding his animals that the wolf was becoming desperate.

Then one day the wolf found a sheepskin that had been thrown away. Quickly he slipped it on over his own hide and made his way among the flock of grazing sheep. Even the shepherd was deceived by the ruse, and when night came the wolf in his disguise was shut up with the sheep in the fold.

But that evening the shepherd, wanting something for his supper, went down to the fold, and reaching in, seized the first animal he came to. Mistaking the wolf for a sheep the shepherd killed him on the spot.

★ *Application:* APPEARANCES OFTEN ARE DECEIVING.

Mercury and the Woodman

AN HONEST, hard-working woodman was felling a tree on the bank of a deep river. In some way his hand slipped and his ax fell into the water and immediately sank to the bottom. Being a poor man who could ill afford to lose the tool by which he earned his livelihood he sat down and lamented his lost most bitterly.

But Mercury, whose river it was, suddenly appeared on the scene. When he had learned of the woodman's misfortune, he offered to do what he could to help.

Diving into the deep, swift-flowing stream, he brought up an ax made of solid gold.

"Could this be yours?" he asked.

"Alas, I wish it were," replied the woodman sadly.

Again Mercury dived into the icy-cold water and this time brought up an ax made of solid silver. But again the woodman shook his head and denied that the tool belonged to him. Mercury dived a third time and produced the identical ax which the man had lost.

Naturally the owner was delighted to see his trusty ax once more, and so was Mercury.

"You are an honest and a good man," said the messenger of the gods. "I want you to take the golden and the silver ax as a reward for telling the truth."

Thanking his benefactor, the woodman ran home to tell his wife of his good fortune. As the story spread, one of the neighbors rushed down to the same spot on the riverbank, threw his ax into the water, and began to moan and groan over his loss. Just as before, Mercury appeared, and learning what had occurred, dived into the water and fetched up a golden ax.

"Is this the ax you lost, my friend?" he asked.

"Yes, yes, that's it," lied the man, greedily reaching for the golden ax in Mercury's hand. But just as he was about to grasp the ax of gold, Mercury said: "Not so fast, sir. You are lying, and to punish you for not being truthful, I am not only denying you this, but I am leaving your own ax at the bottom of the river."

★ *Application:* HONESTY IS THE BEST POLICY.

The Fox and the Crow

A CROW who had stolen a piece of cheese was flying toward the top of a tall tree where he hoped to enjoy his prize, when a fox spied him. "If I plan this right," said the fox to himself, "I shall have cheese for supper."

So, as he sat under the tree, he began to speak in his politest tones: "Good day, mistress crow, how well you are looking today! How glossy your wings, and your breast is the breast of an eagle. And your claws—I beg pardon—your talons are as stong as steel. I have not heard your voice, but I am certain that it must surpass that of any other bird just as your beauty does."

The vain crow was pleased by all this flattery. She believed every word of it and waggled her tail and flapped her wings to show her pleasure. She liked especially what friend fox said about her voice, for she had sometimes been told that her caw was a bit rusty. So, chuckling to think how she was going to surprise the fox with her most beautiful caw, she opened wide her mouth.

Down dropped the piece of cheese! The wily fox snatched it before it touched the ground, and as he walked away, licking his chops, he offered these words of advice to the silly crow: "The next time someone praises your beauty be sure to hold your tongue."

★ *Application:* FLATTERERS ARE NOT TO BE TRUSTED.

The Gardener and His Dog

THE GARDENER was drawing water at the well to water his garden plants. His little dog was jumping and barking on the well curb until he lost his balance and fell in.

Hearing the splash, the gardener quickly drew off his clothes and descended into the well to rescue his dog. Just as he was bringing the struggling and slippery animal to the top, the ungrateful wretch bit his master's hand.

"Why, you little monster!" exclaimed the gardener. "If that is your idea of gratitude to a master who feeds you and pets you and treats you kindly, then pull yourself out of the well." With that he dropped the dog right back into the well again.

★ *Application:* DON'T BITE THE HAND THAT FEEDS YOU!

The Angler and the Little Fish

AN ANGLER after a long day's toil, had nothing to show for his pains but one small fish. As he was taking the perch off the hook the fish spoke:

"Spare me, good fisherman. I am so small that I will make you but a sorry meal. Throw me back into the river, and later when I am grown bigger and worth eating, you may come here and catch me again."

"No, no," said the wary angler, "I have you now, but if you once get back into the water, your tune will be 'catch me if you can.' "

★ *Application:* BEWARE OF THE PROMISES OF A DESPERATE MAN!

The Fawn and Her Mother

ONE DAY in the forest a fawn was browsing among some ferns with her mother. It was peaceful there in the shelter of the forest growth. Suddenly, from a distance came the sound of baying hounds. The mother deer stood stock-still and began to tremble.

"Mother," said the fawn, "you are bigger than a dog and swifter of foot and better winded, and you have horns with which to defend yourself. Why are you so afraid of the hounds?"

The mother smiled, and said: "All this, my child, I know full well. But no sooner do I hear a dog bark than, somehow or other, my heels take me off as fast as they can carry me."

★ *Application:* THERE IS NO ARGUING A COWARD INTO COURAGE.

The Milkmaid and Her Pail

A MILKMAID was on her way to market, carrying a pail of milk on the top of her head. As she walked along the road in the early morning she began to turn over in her mind what she would do with the money she would receive for the milk.

"I shall buy some hens from a neighbor," said she to herself, "and they will lay eggs every day which I shall sell to the pastor's wife. And with the egg money I'll buy myself a new frock and ribbon. Green they should be, for green becomes my complexion best. And in this lovely green gown I will go to the fair. All the young men will strive to have me for a partner. I shall pretend that I do not see them. When they become too insistent I shall disdainfully toss my head—like this."

As the milkmaid spoke she tossed her head back, and down came the pail of milk, spilling all over the ground. And so all her imaginary happiness vanished, and nothing was left but an empty pail and the promise of a scolding when she returned home.

★ *Application:* DO NOT COUNT YOUR CHICKENS BEFORE THEY ARE HATCHED.

The Ant and the Grasshopper

ONE FROSTY autumn day an ant was busily storing away some of the kernels of wheat which he had gathered during the summer to tide him over the coming winter.

A grasshopper, half perishing from hunger, came limping by. Perceiving what the industrious ant was doing, he asked for a morsel from the ant's store to save his life.

"What were you doing all during the summer while I was busy harvesting?" inquired the ant.

"Oh," replied the grasshopper, "I was not idle. I was singing and chirping all day long."

"Well," said the ant, smiling grimly as he locked his granary door, "since you sang all summer, it looks as though you would have to dance all winter."

★ *Application:* IT IS THRIFTY TO PREPARE TODAY FOR THE WANTS OF TOMORROW.

The Mice in Council

FOR MANY YEARS the mice had been living in constant dread of their enemy, the cat. It was decided to call a meeting to determine the best means of handling the situation. Many plans were discussed and rejected.

At last a young mouse got up. "I propose," said he, looking very important, "that a bell be hung around the cat's neck. Then whenever the cat approaches, we always shall have notice of her presence, and so be able to escape."

The young mouse sat down amidst tremendous applause. The suggestion was put to a motion and passed almost unanimously.

But just then an old mouse, who had sat silent all the while, rose to his feet and said: "My friends, it takes a young mouse to think of a plan so ingenious and yet so simple. With a bell about the cat's neck to warn us we shall all be safe. I have but one brief question to put to the supporters of the plan—which one of you is going to bell the cat?"

★ *Application:* IT IS ONE THING TO PROPOSE, ANOTHER TO EXECUTE.

The Fox and the Grapes

MISTER FOX was just about famished, and thirsty too, when he stole into a vineyard where the sun-ripened grapes were hanging up on a trellis in a tempting show, but too high for him to reach. He took a run and a jump, snapping at the nearest bunch, but missed. Again and again he jumped, only to miss the luscious prize. At last, worn out with his efforts, he retreated, muttering: "Well, I never really wanted those grapes anyway. I am sure they are sour, and perhaps wormy in the bargain."

★ *Application:* ANY FOOL CAN DESPISE WHAT HE CANNOT GET.

The Fox and the Goat

A FOX had the misfortune to fall into a well from which, try as he might, he could not escape. Just as he was beginning to be worried a goat came along intent on quenching his thirst.

"Why, friend fox, what are you doing down there?" he cried.

"Do you mean to say that you haven't heard about the great drought, friend goat?" the fox said. "Just as soon as I heard I jumped down here where the water is plentiful. I would advise you to come down, too. It is the best water I have ever tasted. I have drunk so much that I can scarcely move."

When the goat heard this he leaped into the well without any more ado. The fox immediately jumped to the goat's back and using her long horns was able to scramble out of the well to safety. Then he called down to the unhappy goat the following advice: "The next time, friend goat, be sure to look before you leap!"

★ *Application:* IT IS NOT SAFE TO TRUST THE ADVICE OF A MAN IN DIFFICULTIES.

The Ass Carrying Salt

THE RUMOR reached a certain huckster who owned an ass that salt was to be had cheap at the seaside. So he and the ass proceeded down to the shore to buy some. There he loaded his poor beast with as much as he could bear and started for home. As they were passing a slippery ledge of rock, the sorely laden ass fell into the stream below. The water melted the salt, thus relieving the beast of his burden. Gaining the bank with ease, he pursued his journey homeward light in body and in spirit.

The huckster, nothing daunted, set out again for the seashore for a load of salt. He piled an even heavier burden upon the ass. On their return, as they crossed the stream into which the ass previously had fallen by accident, this time he fell down on purpose. As before, the water dissolved the salt and freed him from his load.

Very much provoked by his loss, the master began to think how he could cure the animal of his tricks. So, on the next journey to the seacoast he freighted the ass with a load of sponges. When they arrived at the same stream as before, the beast was up to his old tricks once more. No sooner was he in the river than the sponges became soaked with water, and instead of lightening his burden, he found as he staggered homeward that he had more than doubled the weight of it.

★ *Application:* AN OLD TRICK MAY BE PLAYED ONCE TOO OFTEN.

The Gnat and the Bull

ONCE THERE WAS a silly gnat who kept buzzing about the head of a bull. Finally he settled himself down upon one of the bull's horns.

"Pardon me, Mr. Bull," he said, "if I am inconveniencing you. If my weight in any way is burdensome to you, pray say so, and I will be off in a moment."

"Oh, never trouble your head about that," replied the bull. "It is all the same to me whether you go or stay. To tell you the truth, I was not even aware that you were there."

★ *Application:* THE SMALLER THE MIND THE GREATER THE CONCEIT.

The Hare With Many Friends

THERE WAS ONCE a hare who had so many friends in the forest and the field that she truly felt herself to be the most popular member of the animal kingdom. One day she heard the hounds approaching.

"Why should a popular creature like me have to run for her life every time she hears a dog?" said she to herself. So she went to the horse, and asked him to carry her away from the hounds on his back.

"There is nothing I would rather do, friend hare," said the horse, "but, unfortunately, right now I have some important work to do for my master. However, a popular creature like you should have no difficulty in getting someone to help you."

Then the hare went to the bull and asked him whether he would be kind enough to ward off the hounds with his horns.

"My dear friend," replied the bull, "you know how I feel about you, and how glad I always am to be of service. But at this very moment I have an appointment with a lady. Why don't you ask our mutual friend the goat?"

But the goat was busy too, and so was the ram, and so were the calf and the pig and the ass. Each assured the hare of his undying friendship and anxiety to aid her in her trouble, but each had some excuse which prevented him from performing the service. By this time the hounds were quite near, so the hare took to her heels and luckily escaped.

★ *Application:* HE WHO HAS MANY FRIENDS HAS NO FRIENDS.

The Hare and the Hound

ONE DAY a hound, out hunting by himself, flushed a hare from a thicket and gave chase. The frightened hare gave the dog a long run and escaped. As the disappointed hound turned back toward home, a passing goatherd said jeeringly: "You are a fine hunter! Aren't you ashamed to let a little hare one-tenth your size give you the best of it?"

"You forget," replied the hound, "that I was only running for my supper, but the hare was running for his life!"

★ *Application:* NECESSITY IS OUR STRONGEST WEAPON.

The House Dog and the Wolf

THE MOON was shining very bright one night when a lean, half-starved wolf, whose ribs were almost sticking through his skin, chanced to meet a plump, well-fed house dog. After the first compliments had been passed between them, the wolf inquired:

"How is it, cousin dog, that you look so sleek and contented? Try as I may I can barely find enough food to keep me from starvation."

"Alas, cousin wolf," said the house dog, "you lead too irregular a life. Why do you not work steadily as I do?"

"I would gladly work steadily if I could only get a place," said the wolf.

"That's easy," replied the dog. "Come with me to my master's house and help me keep the thieves away at night."

"Gladly," said the wolf, "for as I am living in the woods I am having a sorry time of it. There is nothing like having a roof over one's head and a bellyful of victuals always at hand."

"Follow me," said the dog.

While they were trotting along together the wolf spied a mark on the dog's neck. Out of curiosity he could not forbear asking what had caused it.

"Oh, that's nothing much," replied the dog. "Perhaps my collar was a little tight, the collar to which my chain is fastened—"

"Chain!" cried the wolf in surprise. "You don't mean to tell me that you are not free to rove where you please?"

"Why, not exactly," said the dog, somewhat shamefacedly. "You see, my master thinks I am a bit fierce, and ties me up in the daytime. But he lets me run free at night. It really is very convenient for everybody. I get plenty of sleep during the day so that I can watch better at night. I really am a great favorite at the house. The master feeds me off his own plate, and the servants are continually offering me handouts from the kitchen. But wait, where are you going?"

As the wolf started back toward the forest he said: "Good night to you, my poor friend, you are welcome to your dainties—and your chains. As for me, I prefer my freedom to your fat."

★ *Application:* LEAN FREEDOM IS BETTER THAN FAT SLAVERY.

The Goose With the Golden Eggs

A FARMER went to the nest of his goose to see whether she had laid an egg. To his surprise he found, instead of an ordinary goose egg, an egg of solid gold. Seizing the golden egg he rushed to the house in great excitement to show it to his wife.

Every day thereafter the goose laid an egg of pure gold. But as the farmer grew rich he grew greedy. And thinking that if he killed the goose he could have all her treasure at once, he cut her open only to find—nothing at all.

★ *Application:* THE GREEDY WHO WANT MORE LOSE ALL.

The Horse and the Stag

A BITTER QUARREL arose between the horse and the stag in the days when both creatures roamed wild in the forest. The horse came to the hunter to ask him to take his side in the feud.

The hunter agreed, but added: "If I am to help you punish the stag, you must let me place this iron bit in your mouth and this saddle upon your back."

The horse was agreeable to the man's conditions and he soon was bridled and saddled. The hunter sprang into the saddle, and together they soon had put the stag to flight. When they returned, the horse said to the hunter: "Now if you will get off my back and remove the bit and the saddle, I won't require your help any longer."

"Not so fast, friend horse," replied the hunter. "I have you under bit and spur, and from now on you shall remain the slave of man."

★ *Application:* LIBERTY IS TOO HIGH A PRICE TO PAY FOR REVENGE.

The Lion and the Bulls

A LION often prowled about a pasture where three bulls grazed together. He had tried without success to lure one or the other of them to the edge of the pasture. He had even attempted a direct attack, only to see them form a ring so that from whatever direction he approached he was met by the horns of one of them.

Then a plan began to form in the lion's mind. Secretly he started spreading evil and slanderous reports of one bull against the other. The three bulls, distrustingly, began to avoid one another, and each withdrew to a different part of the pasture to graze. Of course, this was exactly what the lion wanted. One by one he fell upon the bulls, and so made easy prey of them all.

★ *Application:* UNITED WE STAND; DIVIDED WE FALL.

The Goatherd and the Goats

ONE WINTER'S DAY when the wind was blowing a gale and the snow was falling fast, a goatherd drove his goats, all white with snow, into a near-by cave for shelter. To his surprise, the goatherd found the cave already occupied by a herd of wild goats more numerous than his own.

The greedy man, thinking to secure them all, left his own goats to take care of themselves while he threw the branches which he had brought for them to the wild goats for fodder.

When the weather cleared, alas, the goatherd found that his own goats had perished from hunger, while the wild goats were off and away to the hills and woods. The foolish man returned a laughing-stock to his neighbors, for he not only had failed to gain the herd of wild goats, but he had lost his own.

★ *Application:* THEY WHO NEGLECT THEIR OLD FRIENDS FOR THE SAKE OF NEW ONES ARE RIGHTLY SERVED WHEN THEY LOSE BOTH.

Androcles and the Lion

ONCE THERE was a slave named Androcles who was cruelly treated by his master. When the opportunity came he escaped to the forest. In his wanderings he came upon a lion. His first instinct was to turn about and flee. Then he noticed that the lion seemed to be in great distress and was moaning and whimpering piteously.

As the slave came near, the lion put out his paw, which was swollen and bleeding. A large thorn had penetrated one of the lion's toes, and this was the cause of all of the animal's discomfort. Quickly Androcles pulled out the thorn and bound up the wounded paw. To show his gratitude the lion licked the man's hand like a dog, and then he led him to his cave for a shelter. Every day, after his wound had healed, he would go hunting in the forest and return with fresh meat for his master's refreshment.

But one day, when Androcles and the lion went out together, they were both captured and taken to the city to be used in the circus. The slave was to be thrown to the lion, after the animal had been kept without food for several days to make him more ferocious.

The Emperor and all his court came to the arena to view the spectacle. The despairing slave was unchained and led out into the amphitheater before the Emperor's box. Then the lion was let loose, and rushed bounding and roaring toward his victim. But as soon as he came near Androcles he recognized his friend. To the surprise of the audience, the lion seemed to fawn upon the slave whom they had expected to see torn to shreds by the savage beast. Pleased by this unusual spectacle the Emperor summoned Androcles to him, and the slave told him the whole story. Thereupon the slave was pardoned and freed, and the lion set loose to return to his native forest.

★ *Application:* GRATITUDE IS A QUALITY NOT LIMITED TO MAN.

The Hare and the Tortoise

A HARE was continually poking fun at a tortoise because of the slowness of his pace. The tortoise tried not to be annoyed by the jeers of the hare, but one day in the presence of the other animals he was goaded into challenging the hare to a foot race.

"Why, this is a joke," said the hare. "You know that I can run circles around you."

"Enough of your boasting," said the tortoise. "Let's get on with the race."

So the course was set by the animals, and the fox was chosen as judge. He gave a sharp bark and the race was on. Almost before you could say "scat" the hare was out of sight. The tortoise plodded along at his usual unhurried pace.

After a time the hare stopped to wait for the tortoise to come along. He waited for a long, long time until he began to get sleepy. "I'll just take a quick nap here in this soft grass, and then in the cool of the day I'll finish the race." So he lay down and closed his eyes.

Meanwhile, the tortoise plodded on. He passed the sleeping hare, and was approaching the finish line when the hare awoke with a start. It was too late to save the race. Much ashamed, he crept away while all the animals at the finish line acclaimed the winner.

★ *Application:* SLOW AND STEADY WINS THE RACE.

The Ass and His Masters

A DISCONTENTED ASS who felt that the gardener for whom he worked was a hard taskmaster appealed to Jupiter to give him another master. Annoyed by the ass's ingratitude, Jupiter bound him over to a potter who gave him even heavier burdens to bear.

Again the ass besought Jupiter. This time it was arranged to have him sold to a tanner. Finding that he had fallen into worse hands than ever, the ass said with a groan: "Alas, wretch that I am. Would that I had remained content with my former masters. My new owner not only works me harder while I am alive, but will not even spare my hide when I am dead!"

★ *Application:* HE THAT FINDS DISCONTENTMENT IN ONE PLACE IS NOT LIKELY TO FIND HAPPINESS IN ANOTHER.

The Lion and the Dolphin

THE KING OF BEASTS was pacing majestically along the shore of the sea one day when he spied a dolphin basking on the surface of the water.

"Hello, there, friend dolphin!" roared the lion. "This is a fortunate meeting, indeed. I long have wanted to suggest that you and I form an alliance. As I am the king of the beasts and you are the king of the fishes, what is more natural than that we should be strong friends and powerful allies?"

"There is much in what you say," replied the dolphin.

Not long afterward the lion again came to the seashore where he was challenged by a wild bull. The fight was not going too well for the lion, so he called upon the dolphin for his promised support. The latter, though ready and willing to aid his ally, found himself unable to come out of the sea to join the battle. After the wild bull had been put to flight, the lion upbraided the dolphin.

"You are a fine ally," said the lion. "I could have been killed, and you never turned a fin to help me."

"Do not blame me," said the dolphin in reply, "but blame nature, which made me powerful in the sea but altogether helpless on land."

★ *Application:* IN CHOOSING ALLIES LOOK TO THEIR POWER AS WELL AS THEIR WILL TO HELP YOU.

The Hawk and the Pigeons

A HAWK long had had his eye on a flock of pigeons, but no matter how often he had swooped down upon them from the sky they always had been able to reach their cote in safety. Thinking that it might be his shadow they had spied, he waited for a cloudy day for his next attack, but still to no avail.

At length the hungry hawk decided to use craft instead of attack. From the top of a near-by dead tree he called down to the pigeons: "Why do you prefer this life of constant fear and anxiety when, if you would make me your king, I could patrol the sky and make you safe from any attack that could be made upon you?"

The foolish pigeons, believing the hawk's interest in their welfare to be sincere, called him to the throne as their king and protector. But no sooner was he established there than he issued an order that every day one pigeon would have to be sacrificed for his dinner.

★ *Application:* THEY WHO VOLUNTARILY PUT THEMSELVES UNDER THE POWER OF A TYRANT DESERVE WHATEVER FATE THEY RECEIVE.

The Belly and the Other Members

IT IS SAID that in former times the various members of the human body did not work together as amicably as they do now. On one occasion the members began to be critical of the belly for spending an idle life of luxury while they had to spend all their time laboring for its support and ministering to its wants and pleasures.

The members went so far as to decide to cut off the belly's supplies for the future. The hands were no longer to carry food to the mouth, nor the mouth to receive, nor the teeth to chew it.

But, lo and behold, it was only a short time after they had agreed upon this course of starving the belly into subjection when they all began, one by one, to fail and flop and the whole body to waste away. In the end the members became convinced that the belly also, cumbersome and useless as it seemed, had an important function of its own, and that they could no more exist without it than it could do without them.

★ *Application:* AS IN THE BODY, SO IN THE STATE, EACH MEMBER IN HIS PROPER SPHERE MUST WORK FOR THE COMMON GOOD.

The Frogs Desiring a King

THE FROGS always had lived a happy life in the marshes. They had jumped and splashed about with never a care in the world. Yet some of them were not satisfied with their easygoing life. They thought they should have a king to rule over them and to watch over their morals. So they decided to send a petition to Jupiter asking him to appoint a king.

Jupiter was amused by the frogs' plea. Good-naturedly he threw down a log into the lake, which landed with such a splash that it sent all the frogs scampering for safety. But after a while, when one venturesome frog saw that the log lay still, he encouraged his friends to approach the fallen monster. In no time at all the frogs, growing bolder and bolder, swarmed over the log Jupiter had sent and treated it with the greatest contempt.

Dissatisfied with so tame a ruler, they petitioned Jupiter a second time, saying: "We want a real king, a king who will really rule over us." Jupiter, by this time, had lost some of his good nature and was tired of the frogs' complaining.

So he sent them a stork, who proceeded to gobble up the frogs right and left. After a few days the survivors sent Mercury with a private message to Jupiter, beseeching him to take pity on them once more.

"Tell them," said Jupiter coldly, "that this is their own doing. They wanted a king. Now they will have to make the best of what they asked for."

★ *Application:* LET WELL ENOUGH ALONE!

The Ass, the Cock, and the Lion

AN ASS AND A COCK lived at peace in a farmyard together. But one day a hungry lion chanced to pass that way. Seeing the ass so plump and well fed, he resolved to make a meal of him.

Now, they say that there is nothing that annoys a lion so much as to hear a cock crow. At that very moment the cock gave one of his proudest cock-a-doodle-doos, causing the lion to make off with all haste from the spot.

The ass, greatly amused to see the mighty lion routed by the mere crowing of a barnyard fowl, boldly galloped after the retreating king of beasts. He had, however, pursued him only a short distance, when the lion turned sharply upon the foolish ass, and with a mighty roar leaped upon him and made an end of him.

★ *Application:* FALSE CONFIDENCE IS THE FORERUNNER OF MISFORTUNE.

The Cat and the Mice

A CAT, GROWN FEEBLE with age, and no longer able to hunt for mice as she was wont to do, sat in the sun and bethought herself how she might entice them within reach of her paws.

The idea came to her that if she would suspend herself by the hind legs from a peg in the closet wall, the mice, believing her to be dead, no longer would be afraid of her. So, at great pains and with the assistance of a torn pillowcase she was able to carry out her plan.

But before the mice could approach within range of the innocent-looking paws a wise old gaffer-mouse whispered to his friends: "Keep your distance, my friends. Many a bag have I seen in my day, but never one with a cat's head at the bottom of it."

Then turning to the uncomfortable feline, he said: "Hang there, good madam, as long as you please, but I would not trust myself within reach of you though you were stuffed with straw."

★ *Application:* HE WHO IS ONCE DECEIVED IS DOUBLY CAUTIOUS.

The Miller, His Son, and Their Donkey

A MILLER AND HIS SON were driving their donkey to a neighboring fair to sell him. They had not gone far when they met a group of girls returning from town laughing and talking together.

"Look there!" cried one of them. "Did you ever see such fools, to be trudging along the road on foot, when they ought to be riding!"

So the man put the boy on the donkey, and they went on their way. Presently they came up to a group of old men in earnest debate. "There!" said one of them. "That proves exactly what I was saying. No one pays any respect to old age in these days. Look at that idle young rogue riding, while his poor old father has to walk. Get down, you lazy lout, and let the old man rest his weary limbs."

The miller made his son dismount, and got on the donkey's back in his place. And in this manner they proceeded along the way until they met a company of women and children.

"Why, shame on you, lazybones!" they cried. "How can you ride while that poor little lad can hardly keep up with you?" The good miller, wishing to please, took up his son to sit behind him.

But just as they reached the edge of the village a townsman called out to them: "I have a good mind to report you to the authorities for overloading that poor beast so shamelessly. You big hulking fellows should better be able to carry that donkey than the other way round."

So, alighting, the miller and his son tied the beast's legs together, and with a pole across their shoulders, carried the donkey over the bridge that led to the town. This was such an entertaining sight to the townsfolk that crowds came out to laugh at it. The poor animal, frightened by the uproar, began to struggle to free himself. In the midst of the turmoil the ass slipped off the pole and over the rail of the bridge into the water and was drowned.

★ *Application:* TRY TO PLEASE ALL AND YOU END BY PLEASING NONE.

The Hen and the Fox

A FOX was out looking for a late supper. He came to a henhouse, and through the open door he could see a hen far up on the highest perch, safe out of his reach.

Here, thought the fox, was a case for diplomacy. Either that or go hungry! So he gave considerable thought to just how he should approach his intended supper.

"Hello, there, friend hen," said he in an anxious voice. "I haven't seen you about of late. Somebody told me that you have had a sick spell and I was sincerely worried over you. You look pale as a ghost. If you will just step down I'll take your pulse and look at your tongue. I'm afraid you are in for quite a siege."

"You never said a truer word, cousin fox," replied the hen. "It will have to be a siege, for I am in such a state that if I were to climb down to where you are, I'm afraid it would be the death of me."

★ *Application:* BEWARE OF THE INSINCERE FRIEND!

The Lion and the Goat

ONE VERY HOT summer day, when the ground was dry and many streams were dry, a lion and a goat came at the same time to quench their thirst at the same small mountain spring.

As they looked up and saw each other they at once fell to quarreling over which was to drink first of the water. They even forgot their great thirst, so determined was each that he was to have the first drink. Just as they were about ready to fly at each other they chanced to look up. There, circling about in the blue sky over their heads they saw a flock of vultures, hovering and waiting to pounce upon whichever should fall in defeat.

Grinning foolishly at each other, the lion and

the goat said in almost the same breath: "I insist, dear friend, that *you* shall take the first drink at the spring!"

★ *Application:* IT IS BETTER TO DRINK SECOND AT THE SPRING THAN TO FURNISH FOOD FOR THE VULTURES.

The Fox and the Lion

ONE DAY a fox who had never seen a lion was walking in the wood. Suddenly the king of beasts stood in the path before him, and the fox almost died of fright. He ran away and hid himself in his den. The next time he came upon the lion he merely paused to allow the majestic beast to pass by. The third time they met, the fox boldly approached the lion and passed the time of day with him and asked after his family's health.

★ *Application:* FAMILIARITY BREEDS CONTEMPT.

The Crow and the Pitcher

A CROW, so thirsty that he could not even caw, came upon a pitcher which once had been full of water. But when he put his beak into the pitcher's mouth he found that only a little water was left in it. Strain and strive as he might he was not able to reach far enough down to get at it. He tried to break the pitcher, then to overturn it, but his strength was not equal to the task.

Just as he was about to give up in despair a thought came to him. He picked up a pebble and dropped it into the pitcher. Then he took another pebble and dropped that into the pitcher. One by one he kept dropping pebbles into the pitcher until the water mounted to the brim. Then perching himself upon the handle he drank and drank until his thirst was quenched.

★ *Application:* NECESSITY IS THE MOTHER OF INVENTION.

The Boasting Traveler

A YOUNG MAN who had been traveling in foreign parts returned to his home city where he bragged and boasted to all who would listen of the great feats he had accomplished in the places he had visited.

"Why, when I was in Rhodes," he shouted, thumping his chest, "I made the most extraordinary leap the people of that place ever had seen. I have witnesses to prove it, too."

In time his hearers became weary of the traveler's boasts, and one of them said: "These exploits of yours in Rhodes may all be true, but you can save yourself much breath by doing one of those marvelous leaps right now instead of merely talking about it."

★ *Application:* HE WHO DOES A THING WELL DOES NOT NEED TO BOAST.

The Eagle, the Wildcat, and the Sow

AN EAGLE chose the top branches of an old oak tree for her nest and hatched her young there. A wildcat had selected the hollow trunk of the same tree for her den where she would raise her little ones. And down among the roots of the old oak a sow had burrowed a hole where she planned to raise her piglets in comfort.

For some time all three families lived peaceably in the old oak, until the wildcat took the notion to start gossiping about her neighbors.

"Neighbor," she whispered to the eagle, "as you know I have the highest respect for that old sow down below. But if she keeps rooting under this tree the whole thing will come crashing down someday. That's probably what she has in mind so she can feed our babies to her litter."

Needless to say, the mother eagle was worried. She was so disturbed that she did not dare to leave her nest to go in search of food. Meanwhile, the gossiping wildcat visited the sow.

"Mrs. Sow," she whispered, "I'm no gossip, as you know, but if I were you I wouldn't leave home today. I overheard that eagle upstairs telling her children they were going to have pork for supper."

So the eagle stayed in her nest and the sow remained with her little pigs. But the wildcat sneaked off every night and got all the food for her kittens, while her neighbors lived in distrust of each other.

It is possible that both families would have starved to death had not the wildcat made the mistake of getting caught in a hunter's snare, and the sow and the eagle became reunited in caring for the abandoned kittens.

★ *Application:* GOSSIPS ARE TO BE SEEN AND NOT HEARD.

The Ass and the Grasshopper

ONE FINE SUMMER day an ass heard some grasshoppers chirping and singing merrily. Delighted with the music, and hoping to learn the secret of their musical ability, the ass approached them.

"My fine fellows," said he, "upon what do you feed that makes you sing so sweetly all day long?"

When the grasshoppers told the foolish ass that they supped upon nothing but dew, he galloped off determined to exist upon the same diet. In due time he died of hunger.

★ *Application:* EVEN A FOOL IS WISE—WHEN IT IS TOO LATE!

The Heifer and the Ox

THERE WAS ONCE a young heifer who, never having felt the yoke, gamboled about in the fields as free as the wind. With her tail in the air she frisked up to the old ox who was pulling a plow for the farmer.

"How foolish you are," she said to the toiling ox, "to work so hard all day long. Why don't you do as I do, enjoy life, go and come as you will, instead of submitting to such drudgery day in, day out?"

The old ox said nothing, but went on with his work. When evening came he was turned loose by the farmer, and he went over to the village altar where the priests were preparing to offer the heifer as a sacrifice.

The ox approached the heifer and said: "How do you feel about it now? You must know now why you were allowed to live in idleness. As for me, I had rather my neck felt the weight of the yoke than of the knife."

★ *Application:* HE LAUGHS BEST WHO LAUGHS LAST.

The Fox and the Stork

ONE DAY a fox invited a stork to have dinner with him, and the stork accepted. The fox, who enjoyed some reputation as a practical joker, provided nothing for dinner but some thin soup in a shallow dish. This the fox lapped up very readily, while the stork, unable to gain a mouthful with her long bill, was as hungry at the end of the dinner as when she began.

As they were parting the fox professed his regret that his guest had eaten so sparingly, and feared that the dish was not seasoned to her satisfaction. The stork replied: "Please do not apologize, friend fox, I have had a most interesting evening. Will you not do me the honor one week hence to return the visit and dine with me?"

True to his appointment the fox arrived, and the stork ordered the dinner to be brought in. But when it was served up, the fox found to his dismay that it was contained in a very long-necked jar with a narrow mouth. The stork readily thrust her long bill into the jar and enjoyed her dinner, while the fox was obliged to content himself with licking the neck of the jar. As the fox made his adieus with as good grace as he could muster, the stork said dryly: "I hope you do not expect an apology for the dinner."

★ *Application:* MANY GO OUT FOR WOOL AND COME HOME SHORN.

The Farmer and the Nightingale

AFTER a hard day's work a farmer went early to bed. But he could not go to sleep because of the melodious singing of a nightingale all through the summer night. So pleased was he by the bird's song that the next night he set a trap for it and captured it.

"Ah, my beauty," said he, "now that I have caught you, you shall hang in a cage and sing for me every night."

"But we nightingales never sing in a cage," replied the bird. "If you imprison me I shall sicken and die and you shall never hear my song again."

"Then I'll put you in a pie and eat you," said the farmer. "I always have heard that nightingale pie is a dainty morsel."

"Please do not kill me," begged the nightingale. "If you will set me free I'll tell you three great truths that will be worth far more to you than my poor body."

So the farmer set him loose, and he flew up to a branch of a tree.

"Hold on," said the farmer, "what are the three great truths you promised me?"

The nightingale trilled a few happy notes and said: "Never believe a captive's promise. Keep what you have. And never sorrow over what is lost forever." Then the songbird flew away.

★ *Application:* A BIRD IN THE CAGE IS WORTH TWO ON A BRANCH.

The Ass and the Lap Dog

AN ASS AND A LAP DOG belonged to the same master. Tied up in the stable the ass had plenty of corn and hay to eat, and he should have been more than contented with his lot, even though he was kept busy hauling wood all day, and on occasion had to take his turn at the mill at night.

Meanwhile the little dog was always sporting and gamboling about, caressing and fawning upon his master to such an extent that he became a great favorite, and was permitted to lie in his master's lap. Needless to say, the ass began to feel sorry for himself. It galled him to see the lap dog living in such ease and luxury, enjoying the favor of the master.

Thinking that if he behaved in the same fashion toward his master he would fare the same, one day he broke from his halter and rushed into the house where his owner was at meat. Here he pranced about, swishing his tail and imitating as best he could the frolics of the lap dog, finally upsetting the dinner table and smashing all the crockery. Nor did he stop there. He jumped upon his master and pawed him with his roughshod feet.

At length the servants, seeing their master in no little danger, released him from the ass's wild caresses. Thereupon they so belabored the silly creature with sticks and stones that he never got up again.

★ *Application:* TO BE SATISFIED WITH ONE'S LOT IS BETTER THAN TO DESIRE SOMETHING WHICH ONE IS NOT FITTED TO RECEIVE.

The Cock and the Jewel

ONE BRIGHT DAY in the spring a cock was scratching up the straw that littered the barnyard in search of food for his flock of hens. To his great surprise, his industrious claws turned up a jewel that by some chance had been lost there.

Now, the cock was a sensible cock. "Ho," said he, as his bright eyes examined the jewel, "I can see you are a very valuable thing, though how you got here I have not the least idea. I can see, too, that there are those who must prize you, but as for me, give me a kernel of corn rather than all the bright jewels in the world."

★ *Application:* THE IGNORANT DESPISE WHAT IS PRECIOUS ONLY BECAUSE THEY CANNOT UNDERSTAND IT.

Jupiter and the Bee

LONG, LONG AGO there was an industrious bee who had stored her combs with a bountiful harvest. One day she decided to fly up to heaven to present an offering of honey to Jupiter. The god was so delighted with the bee's gift that he promised her she should have whatever her heart desired.

"O great Jupiter, my creator and my master, I beg of thee, give thy servant a sting, so that when anyone approaches my hive to take the honey, I may kill him on the spot."

Jupiter was surprised to hear such a bloodthirsty request from such a humble creature. Becoming angry, he said: "Your prayer shall not be granted in exactly the way you wish. But the sting you ask for you shall have. When anyone comes to take away your honey and you attack him, the wound shall be fatal. But it shall be fatal *to you*, for your life shall go with your sting."

★ *Application:* HE WHO PRAYS HARD AGAINST HIS NEIGHBOR BRINGS A CURSE UPON HIMSELF.

The Horse and the Groom

ONCE THERE WAS a groom who was just about the meanest man in the world. He used to steal the grain intended for the horse and, without his master's knowledge, sell it in the village. But all day long he kept very busy grooming and currying the horse within an inch of its life.

"If you really are so anxious that I look well," said the horse one day to his groom, "then give me less of your brushing and more of your corn."

★ *Application:* A MAN MAY SMILE, YET BE A VILLAIN.

The Mischievous Dog

ONCE UPON A TIME there was a dog who was so wild and mischievous that his master despaired of taming him. The last straw was when he bit a servant in pretending to be playful. His master was taking him out to the forest to dispose of him when a neighbor suggested: "The way to tame that beast is to fasten a chain around his neck and attach a heavy wooden clog to the end of it. That will stop him from biting and worrying his fellows."

The master decided to try it. The next day the dog, looking upon his clog as a badge of distinction, went down to the market place, shaking and rattling the hobble to attract everyone's attention. An old dog approached him and said: "If I were in your place I would make less noise and not call people's attention to my disgrace. Wearing a hobble is anything but a mark of distinction!"

★ *Application:* MEN OFTEN MISTAKE NOTORIETY FOR FAME.

The Blind Man and the Whelp

THERE WAS ONCE a blind man who, merely by placing his hands upon an animal, could determine to what species it belonged. To test him one day they brought him a wolf's whelp. Long and carefully he felt the beast all over. Then, still being in doubt, he said: "I know not whether thy father was a dog or a wolf, but this I do know, that I would not trust thee among a flock of sheep."

★ *Application:* THE CHILD IS FATHER TO THE MAN.

The Hares and the Frogs

FOR A LONG TIME the hares had believed themselves the most persecuted of all the animals. Everyone was their enemy, they said. One day, when the prospect looked especially dark, they came to the sad resolution that there was nothing left for them but to make away with themselves, one and all. So off they ran to a lake near by, determined to throw themselves into the water to be drowned.

But at their approach a school of frogs seated on the shore took fright and dived into the water.

"Hold up!" cried the hare who was in the lead. "Let us not be too hasty. Surely our case is not so desperate yet, for here are other poor creatures even more fainthearted than ourselves."

★ *Application:* THERE IS ALWAYS SOMEONE WORSE OFF THAN YOURSELF.

The Eagle and the Fox

AN EAGLE AND A FOX long had lived together as good neighbors, the eagle at the top of a high tree and the fox in a hole at the foot of it. One day, however, while the fox was away, the eagle, seeking a tender morsel for her nestful of young ones, swooped down upon the fox's cub and carried it away to her nest.

The fox, on her return home, upbraided the eagle for this breach of friendship, and pleaded with the eagle to return the cub to her den. But the eagle, feeling sure that her own brood high up in their treetop nest were safe from any possible revenge, ignored the entreaties of the cub's mother.

Quickly running to the place where she knew an altar fire to be burning, the fox snatched a brand and hurried back to the tree. The mother eagle, who was just on the point of tearing the cub to pieces to feed to her babies, looked down and saw that the fox was going to set fire to the tree and burn it and her nest and eaglets to ashes.

"Hold on, dear neighbor!" she screamed. "Don't set fire to our tree. I'll bring back your cub to you safe and sound!"

★ *Application:* DO UNTO OTHERS AS YOU WOULD HAVE THEM DO UNTO YOU.

The Cock and the Fox

A FOX was trotting past a farmyard early one morning when he heard a cock crowing. Upon investigation he found that chanticleer was perched in a tall tree far out of reach of anyone who might be entertaining thoughts of having him for breakfast.

"Why, cousin cock," the fox called up to the bird in the tall tree, "what a pleasure it is to see you! Won't you come down and let me greet you properly?"

"I would love to," replied the cock (who was no fool), "but, as you know, there are some animals who would like nothing better than to grab me and eat me."

"Why, my dear cousin," exclaimed the fox, "do you mean to say you haven't heard the news? All the animals have agreed to live in peace with one another."

While the fox was speaking, the cock kept craning his neck as though he could see something very interesting in the distance. Naturally, the fox was consumed with curiosity.

"Cousin, what in the world do you see up there that is so interesting?"

"Oh, nothing much—just a pack of hounds headed in this direction and coming at a fast clip," said the cock.

"Please excuse me," said the fox nervously. "I just thought of something I had forgotten."

"What's the hurry?" asked the cock. "I was just coming down for a talk. You don't mean to say that you have anything to be afraid of now that you know about the wonderful peace plan?"

"Well," replied the fox, as he started to run, "maybe those hounds haven't heard about it yet!"

★ *Application:* THE BEST LIARS OFTEN GET CAUGHT IN THEIR OWN LIES.

The Horse and the Laden Ass

ONCE THERE WAS a man who kept a horse and an ass as beasts of burden. It was his custom to load the ass until he could barely stagger under the weight, while the horse was allowed to prance along in its fine trappings with a very light load.

As they were proceeding along the road one day, the ass, who had been ailing for the past several days, said to the horse: "Will you relieve me of part of my load for a few miles? I feel dreadfully unwell, but if you will carry a fair portion of the freight today I shall soon get well again. This weight is killing me."

The horse, however, merely kicked up his heels and told the ass not to trouble him with his complaints. The ass staggered along for another half mile in silence, then suddenly fell to the ground dead.

Just then the master came up, and perceiving what had happened, he removed the load from the dead ass and placed it on the horse's back. "Alas," groaned the horse, as he started off with the heavy load augmented by the carcass of the dead ass, "now am I rewarded for my ill-nature. By refusing to bear my fair share of the load, I now must carry the whole of it plus the dead weight of my poor companion."

★ *Application:* A BAD TEMPER CARRIES WITH IT ITS OWN PUNISHMENT.

The Miser

A MISER, who never stopped worrying about the safety of his many possessions, sold all his property and converted it into a huge lump of gold. This he buried in a hole in the ground near his garden wall, and every morning he went to visit it and gloat over the size of it.

The miser's strange behavior aroused the curiosity of the town thief. Spying upon the rich man from some bushes, the thief saw him place the lump of gold back in the hole and cover it up. As soon as the miser's back was turned, the thief went to the spot, dug up the gold and took it away.

The next morning when the miser came to gloat over his treasure he found nothing but an empty hole. He wept and tore his hair, and so loud were his lamentations that a neighbor came running to see what was the trouble. As soon as he had learned the cause of it, he said comfortingly: "You are foolish to distress yourself so over something that was buried in the earth. Take a stone and put it in the hole, and think that it is your lump of gold. You never meant to use it anyway. Therefore it will do you just as much good to fondle a lump of granite as a lump of gold."

★ *Application:* **THE TRUE VALUE OF MONEY IS NOT IN ITS POSSESSION BUT IN ITS USE.**

The Kid and the Wolf

THERE WAS ONCE a very active kid who would leave the other goats in the farmyard below and climb onto the steep roof of the farmhouse.

"Look at me, mother," he would call down. "You are afraid to come up here where I am." The other goats paid very little attention to the boasting kid, but one day a wolf passed by the farmhouse. He gave one look at the kid on the rooftree and would have passed by since it was easy to see that here was one dinner that was safe out of his reach. But the kid jeered and bleated: "Why don't you try to come up and catch me, coward?"

The wolf stopped, looked up again, and called back: "It is not you who call me coward, but the place on which you are standing."

★ *Application:* IF YOU MUST REVILE YOUR NEIGHBOR, MAKE CERTAIN FIRST THAT HE CANNOT REACH YOU.

The Porcupine and the Snakes

A PORCUPINE had selected a comfortable cave for his home only to find it already occupied by a family of snakes.

"Would it be agreeable if I used one corner of your cave to spend the winter?" he asked. The snakes very generously offered to share their home with the porcupine, and he moved in, curled up in a ball, stuck out all his prickly quills, and settled down for the winter.

It was not long, however, before the snakes realized that they had made a mistake, for every time one of them moved he would prick himself on one of the visitor's quills.

After bearing this discomfort for a time the snakes got up their courage to complain to the porcupine.

"That's just too bad," said their guest. "I am most comfortable here. But if you snakes aren't satisfied, why don't you move out?" And he curled up once more and resumed his nap.

★ *Application:* IT IS SAFER TO KNOW ONE'S GUEST BEFORE OFFERING HOSPITALITY.

The Falconer and the Partridge

A FALCONER discovered that he had captured a partridge in his net. The bird cried out piteously when he approached: "Please, Master Falconer, let me go. If you will set me free I promise you that I will decoy other partridges into your net."

"No," replied the falconer. "I might have set you free. But one who is ready to betray his innocent friends to save his own miserable life deserves, if possible, worse than death."

★ *Application:* TREACHERY IS THE BASEST CRIME OF ALL.

The Creaking Wheels

SLOWLY and ponderously over the dusty road a yoke of oxen were hauling a heavily laden wagon. Each time the wheels turned on their axles they set up a tremendous creaking. Driven almost frantic by the ear-piercing noise, the driver cried: "Wagon, why do you make all this clamor and complaint, when they who are drawing all the weight are silent?"

★ *Application:* HE WHO GROANS LOUDEST IS OFTEN THE LEAST HURT.

Jupiter, Neptune, Minerva, and Momus

IN ANCIENT TIMES, when the world was young, Jupiter, Neptune, and Minerva used to spend a great deal of time disputing as to which could make the most perfect thing. So it was decided that they would have a contest with Momus (at that time he had not yet been turned out of Olympus) to decide which creation had the greatest merit.

Jupiter made a man. Neptune made a bull. Minerva made a house. Then Judge Momus came to judge the contest. He began by finding fault with Neptune's bull because his horns were not below his eyes so that he could see when he gored with them. Next he found fault with the man because there was no window in his breast in order that all might see his inward thoughts and feelings. And lastly he found fault with the house because it had no wheels to enable its inhabitants to move away from bad neighbors.

Jupiter, incensed with the carping critic who could not be pleased, forthwith drove the fault-finding judge out of the home of the gods.

★ *Application:* IT IS TIME TO CRITICIZE THE WORKS OF OTHERS WHEN YOU HAVE DONE SOME GOOD THING YOURSELF.

The Lion in Love

IT HAPPENED in days of old that a lion fell in love with the beautiful daughter of a woodman, and one day he came to ask the maiden's hand in marriage. It was only natural that the woodman was not greatly pleased with the lion's offer, and he declined the honor of so dangerous an alliance.

Then the lion threatened the parents of the maiden with his royal displeasure. The poor father did not know what to do. Finally he said: "We are greatly flattered by your proposal. But, you see, our daughter is a tender child, and her mother and I fear that in expressing your affection for her you may do her an injury. Would your majesty consent to having your claws removed and your teeth extracted before becoming a bridegroom?"

So deeply was the lion in love that he permitted the operation to take place. But when he came again to the woodman's home to claim the maiden for his bride the father, no longer afraid of the tamed and disarmed king of beasts, seized a stout club and drove the unhappy suitor from his door.

★ *Application:* EVEN THE WILDEST CAT CAN BE TAMED BY LOVE.

The Arab and the Camel

THE ARAB tugged and pulled as he tightened the ropes which held the heavy bales and boxes to the kneeling camel's back. Then, as the camel arose, his master said jokingly: "What is your preference, camel, the road that goes up hill or the road that goes down?"

"Pray, master," said the camel dryly, "since you leave the choice to me, I would prefer the road that runs along the level plain."

★ *Application:* A LEVEL PATH IS PLEASING TO THE LADEN BEAST.

The Ass's Shadow

ON A HOT summer day a youth hired an ass to carry him from Athens to Megara. At mid-day the heat of the sun was so scorching that, feeling faint, he dismounted to rest himself in the shadow of the ass. Thereupon the driver disputed the place with him, declaring that he had an equal right to it with the other.

"What!" exclaimed the youth. "Did I not hire the ass for the whole journey?"

"Yes, indeed," said the driver, "you hired the ass, but you did not hire the ass's shadow."

And while they were wrangling the ass took to his heels and ran away.

★ *Application:* TOO MANY DISAGREEMENTS HAVE NAUGHT BUT A SHADOW FOR A BASIS.

The Ass Eating Thistles

IT WAS HARVEST TIME and the master and the reapers were out in the field. When the sun was high in the sky the maidservants loaded the ass with good things to eat and drink and sent him to the field. On his way he noticed a fine large thistle growing in the lane, and being hungry he began to eat it. As he chewed it slowly, he reflected: "How many greedy people would think themselves happy amidst such a variety of delicacies as I am carrying. But for my taste, this bitter, prickly thistle is more savory and appetizing than the most sumptuous banquet."

★ *Application:* ONE MAN'S MEAT MAY BE ANOTHER MAN'S POISON.

The Raven and the Swan

THE RAVEN, who earned a comfortable livelihood picking up scraps, became dissatisfied with his lot. He would be especially unhappy whenever he saw the swan floating gracefully about a near-by pool.

"What makes that swan so white and beautiful?" he would say. "Could it be that the water has magic qualities to turn one's feathers from black to white?"

So the raven left his comfortable home and betook himself to the pools and streams. There he washed and plumed his feathers, but all to no purpose. His plumage remained as black as ever, and before long he perished for want of his usual food.

★ *Application:* A CHANGE OF SCENE DOES NOT CHANGE ONE'S CHARACTER.

Hercules and the Wagoner

A LAZY FARM HAND was carelessly driving his wagon along a muddy road, when the wheels became stuck so fast in the clay that the horses could no longer pull the load.

The wagoner got down, and without making the least effort toward extricating the cart from the mire, he began to pray for Hercules, the god of strength, to come and help him out of his trouble.

But Hercules, annoyed by the man's helplessness, called down from above: "Get up from your knees, lazybones, and put your shoulder to the wheel."

★ *Application:* THE GODS HELP THEM THAT HELP THEMSELVES.

The Man and the Satyr

A MAN AND A SATYR met on a woodland path, and as they journeyed along they struck up an acquaintance. The day was wintery and cold, and while they sat resting on a log the man put his fingers to his mouth and blew on them.

"What's that for, my friend?" asked the satyr.

"Oh, I always do that," replied the man, "when my hands are cold. I blow on them to warm them."

Shortly afterward they arrived at the satyr's home, and he invited his companion in for a bowl of hot porridge. As the host placed a steaming bowl before his guest, the man raised his spoon to his lips and began blowing on it.

"And now what are you doing?" asked the satyr.

"Oh, my porridge is too hot to swallow, so I am blowing on it to cool it off," replied the man. And he went on blowing while the satyr stared in amazement.

★ *Application:* SOME MEN CAN BLOW HOT AND BLOW COLD WITH THE SAME BREATH.

The Lark and Her Young Ones

A LARK, who had her nest of young ones in a wheat field, had to leave them each day to go out and hunt food for them. As the wheat ripened, the mother, expecting the arrival of the reapers, left word that the young larks should report to her all the news they heard.

One day, while she was absent, the farmer came to view his crop. "It is high time," he called to his son, "that our grain is cut. Go, tell all our neighbors to come early in the morning to help us reap it." When the mother lark came her children told her what they had heard, and begged her to remove them to a place of safety. "There's plenty of time," said she. "If friend farmer waits for his neighbors to help him, there's no danger of the grain being harvested tomorrow."

The next day, the owner came again, and finding the day warmer and the wheat dead-ripe and nothing done, said to his son: "There is not a moment to be lost. We cannot depend upon our neighbors, we must call in all of our relatives. You run now and call all your uncles and cousins and tell them to be here tomorrow morning to begin the harvest."

In still greater fear, the young larks repeated to their mother the farmer's words when she came home to her nest. "If that is all," she said, "then do not let it frighten you, for relatives always have harvesting of their own to do. But I want you to listen very carefully to what you hear the next time, and be sure to let me know what is said."

The next day while she was away the farmer came as before, and finding the grain almost ready to fall to the ground from overripeness, and still no one at work, called to his son: "We can't wait for our neighbors and relatives any longer. You and I are going to the barn right now and sharpen our sickles. At dawn tomorrow morning we shall get to work and harvest the grain ourselves."

When the young larks told their mother what they had heard the farmer say, she cried: "Then it is time to be off, indeed. If the master has made up his mind to undertake the work himself, then the grain really will be cut." So the mother lark moved her nest, and the next day the farmer and his son came with their sickles and harvested the wheat.

★ *Application:* IF YOU WANT A TASK WELL DONE, THEN DO IT YOURSELF.

The Boy and the Filberts

A BOY put his hand into a pitcher which contained a goodly quantity of figs and filberts. Greedily he clutched as many as his fist could possibly hold. But when he tried to pull it out, the narrowness of the neck of the vessel prevented him.

Unwilling to lose any of the nuts, yet unable to draw out his hand, the lad burst into tears, bitterly bewailing his hard fortune. An honest fellow standing near by gave him this wise and reasonable advice: "Grasp only half the quantity, my boy, and you will easily succeed."

★ *Application:* HALF A LOAF IS BETTER THAN NO BREAD.

The Lion, the Ass, and the Fox

A LION, an ass, and a fox formed a hunting party, and after an exciting chase caught and killed a great stag. All three were hungry, but the lion especially so. "Here, friend ass," he roared, "divide up the spoils, and let's have our dinner. I'm just about starved."

The ass was trying his best to divide the carcass into three equal portions when the lion fell upon him with a roar and tore him to pieces.

"Now," said the lion to the fox, "let's see how good you are at dividing the stag into two parts."

Taking one look at the remains of the poor ass, the fox said never a word, but made sure that in the division of the meat he left the "lion's share" for the king of beasts and only a mouthful for himself.

The lion nodded approvingly. "A very fair division, indeed," said he. "Who could have taught you to divide so fairly?"

"If I needed any lesson," replied the fox, "I had only to look at the body of our late friend, the ass, over yonder."

★ *Application:* **WE LEARN BY THE MISFORTUNES OF OTHERS.**

The Frog and the Ox

SOME LITTLE FROGS had just had a harrowing experience down at the swampy meadow, and they came hopping home to report their adventure.

"Oh, father," said one of the little frogs, all out of breath, "we have just seen the most terrible monster in all the world. It was enormous, with horns on its head and a long tail and hoofs—"

"Why, child, that was no monster. That was only an ox. He isn't so big! If I really put my mind to it I could make myself as big as an ox. Just watch me!" So the old frog blew himself up. "Was he as big as I am now?" he asked.

"Oh, father, much bigger," cried the little frogs.

Again the father frog blew himself up, and asked his children if the ox could be as big as that.

"Bigger, father, a great deal bigger" came the chorus from the little frogs. "If you blew yourself up until you burst you could not be as big as the monster we saw in the swampy meadow."

Provoked by such disparagement of his powers, the old frog made one more attempt. He blew and blew and swelled and swelled until something went *pop*. The old frog had burst.

★ *Application:* SELF-CONCEIT LEADS TO SELF-DESTRUCTION

The Lion, the Bear, and the Fox

A LION AND A BEAR found the carcass of a fawn. Both were hungry. Both wanted it. So they started to fight for it. The contest was long and hard and savage. At last, when both of them, half blinded and half dead, lay panting on the ground without the strength to touch the prize before them, a fox came by.

Noting the helpless condition of the two beasts, the impudent fox stepped nimbly between them, seized the fawn over which they had battled, and with never a "thank you" dragged it away to his den.

★ *Application:* ONLY FOOLS FIGHT TO EXHAUSTION WHILE A ROGUE RUNS OFF WITH THE DINNER.

The Cat and the Fox

A FOX was boasting to a cat one day about how clever he was. "Why, I have a whole bag of tricks," he bragged. "For instance, I know of at least a hundred different ways of escaping my enemies, the dogs."

"How remarkable," said the cat. "As for me, I have only one trick, though I usually make it work. I wish you could teach me some of yours."

"Well, sometime when I have nothing else to do," said the fox, "I might teach you one or two of my easier ones."

Just at that moment they heard the yelping of a pack of hounds. They were coming straight toward the spot where the cat and the fox stood. Like a flash the cat scampered up a tree and disappeared in the foliage. "This is the trick I told you about," she called down to the fox. "It's my only one. Which trick are you going to use?"

The fox sat there trying to decide which of his many tricks he was going to employ. Nearer and nearer came the hounds. When it was quite too late, the fox decided to run for it. But even before he started, the dogs were upon him, and that was the end of the fox, bagful of tricks and all!

★ *Application:* ONE GOOD PLAN THAT WORKS IS BETTER THAN A HUNDRED DOUBTFUL ONES.

The Ass in the Lion's Skin

ONCE UPON A TIME an ass found a lion's skin and put it on. In this disguise he roamed about, frightening all the silly animals he met. When a fox came along, the ass in the lion's skin tried to frighten him too. But the fox, having heard his voice, said: "If you really want to frighten me you will have to disguise your bray."

★ *Application:* CLOTHES MAY DISGUISE A FOOL, BUT HIS WORDS WILL GIVE HIM AWAY.

The Monkey and the Camel

AT A GREAT GATHERING of all the beasts the monkey got up to entertain his friends by doing a dance. So nimble were his feet and so amusing his gestures and grimaces that all the animals roared with laughter. Even the lion, the king of beasts, forgot his royal dignity and rolled on the ground with glee.

Only the camel seemed to be bored by the monkey's performance. "I don't see anything so funny in that exhibition," she sniffed. "As a matter of fact, it seems very crude and amateurish to me."

"All right, then," cried all the animals, "suppose you show us what you can do!"

Realizing what she had let herself in for, the camel shambled into the circle, and in no time at all had made herself utterly ridiculous by her awkward and stumbling performance. All the beasts booed her and set upon her with clubs and claws and drove her out into the desert.

★ *Application:* STRETCH YOUR ARM NO FARTHER THAN YOUR SLEEVE WILL REACH.

The Hawk and the Farmer

A PRUDENT FARMER had spread a net over his cornfield to catch the crows who liked to dig up his newly planted seeds. One day a hawk, pursuing a pigeon, flew so swiftly over the farmer's cornfield that before he knew it he found himself caught in the snare.

The farmer, observing the hawk struggling in the net, went over to the captured bird of prey.

"This is all a mistake," said the hawk as the farmer approached. "I was just chasing a pigeon, and the wretched bird flew right over your field. I was not going to do a bit of harm to you. Believe me, sir!"

"That may be," replied the farmer. "But unless you can tell me just what harm the pigeon had done to you, I'm afraid I'm going to have to wring your neck."

★ *Application:* HYPOCRISY IS THE CLOAK OF VILLAINY.

The Lioness

A GREAT RIVALRY existed among the beasts of the forest over which could produce the largest litter. Some shamefacedly admitted having only two, while others boasted proudly of having a dozen.

At last the committee called upon the lioness.

"And to how many cubs do you give birth?" they asked the proud lioness.

"One," she replied sternly, "but that one is a lion!"

★ *Application:* QUALITY IS MORE IMPORTANT THAN QUANTITY.

Mercury and the Sculptor

THERE WERE TIMES when Mercury, between errands on Olympus, yearned to know whether he still was held in high esteem by mankind.

So one day, disguising himself as a traveler, he visited a sculptor's studio. Walking about among the many statues displayed there, he pointed to an image of Jupiter.

"How much are you asking for this odd piece?" he asked.

"I'll let you have that one cheap," replied the sculptor. "It is one of our less popular numbers. One drachma."

Mercury laughed in his sleeve. Then he asked: "How much for this stout lady here?"

The sculptor said: "Oh, that one is Juno. I have to get a little more for females."

Mercury's eye now caught sight of an image of himself. Thinking that as messenger of the gods and source of all commercial gain his image would command a gratifyingly high price, he said: "I see you have a very handsome statue there of Mercury. How high do you value that excellent likeness?"

"Well," replied the sculptor, "I am willing to make you a bargain. If you will pay me the price I quoted to you on the other two statues, I will throw this one in free."

★ *Application:* HE WHO SEEKS A COMPLIMENT SOMETIMES DISCOVERS THE TRUTH.

The Farmer and His Sons

A FARMER, being on the point of death, called his two sons to him and said: "My sons, I am now departing from this life, but all that I have to leave you is to be found in the vineyard."

As soon as the old man was dead, the two sons, believing that their father had meant to tell them of some hidden treasure, set to work with their spades and plows and turned over the soil of the vineyard again and again. They found no treasure, it is true, but the vines, strengthened and improved by this thorough tillage, yielded a finer vintage than they ever had yielded before, and more than repaid the farmer's sons for their efforts.

★ *Application:* INDUSTRY SOMETIMES PAYS UNEXPECTED DIVIDENDS.

The Bundle of Sticks

ONCE THERE WAS a wise farmer whose quarrelsome family drove him almost to distraction. He strove in vain to reconcile his bickering sons with words of good counsel. Then one day he called his sons to his room. Before him lay a bundle of sticks which he had tied together to form a fagot.

Each one of his sons in turn was commanded by the farmer to take up the fagot and break it in two. They all tried, but tried in vain. Then, untying the bundle, the father gave them the sticks to break one by one. This, of course, they did with the greatest ease.

Then said the father: "My sons, by this example you all can see that as long as you remain united, you are a match for all your enemies. But once you quarrel and become separated, then you are destroyed."

★ *Application:* IN UNION THERE IS STRENGTH.

The Eagle and the Crow

AN EAGLE swooped down from a high rock and pounced upon a lamb, grazing near her mother in the field. With a great beating of powerful wings he seized the lamb and flew away to his nest.

A crow sat in an oak tree watching the eagle's exploit. Said he to himself: "Surely that is an easy way to find oneself a dinner." So, spying a sturdy old ram below him, he bore down with all the force he could muster, intending to carry the ram off as a prize. He fastened his claws in the wool and tugged with all his might. But nothing happened. As a matter of fact, the ram wouldn't have known he was there if it had not been for the crow's frantic efforts to disentangle his claws from the wool.

The crow's squawking attracted the attention of the shepherd, who came up and caught him and clipped his wings and took him home to the children for a pet.

★ *Application:* IT REQUIRES MORE THAN WINGS TO BE AN EAGLE.

The Mule

A MULE had been having an easy time of it with nothing to do but eat. One day as he was frisking about the pasture he began to fancy himself a runner.

"My mother was a famous race horse. I'll bet I can run as fast as ever she could," he said to himself. And to prove it he set off at what he thought was a fast pace toward the barn.

Not so long afterward the mule's master found it necessary to get to the village in a great hurry. Jumping upon the animal's back the farmer began to flog him and urge him to greater speed, until the mule, gasping for breath, said: "My mother may have been a race horse, but my father was only a jackass."

★ *Application:* EVERY TRUTH HAS TWO SIDES.

The Nurse and the Wolf

"IF YOU DON'T stop crying this instant," said an old nurse to the child who sat screaming on her lap, "I will throw you out the window to the wolf."

At that very moment a wolf happened to be passing under the window and heard what the nurse had said. So he sat down to wait, saying to himself: "This must be my lucky day. From the way that baby is crying, my dinner ought to be coming out that window any minute now."

He waited and he waited. The baby stopped crying and went to sleep, and nothing happened. All through the cold night the wolf sat there, his mouth watering whenever he thought of the dainty morsel. He was tired and stiff from sitting in one position. Then, toward morning, the glad sound of a baby crying came from the window again.

Rushing to the window he looked up at the nurse and wagged his tail. But all the old nurse did was to shut the window with a bang and set the dogs upon the hungry wolf.

As he trotted away the wolf said to himself: "Next time I won't believe all I hear."

★ *Application:* ENEMIES' PROMISES ARE MADE TO BE BROKEN.

The Wolf and the Lamb

AS A WOLF was lapping at the head of a running brook he spied a lamb daintily paddling his feet some distance down the stream.

"There's my supper," thought the wolf. "But I'll have to find some excuse for attacking such a harmless creature."

So he shouted down at the lamb: "How dare you stir up the water I am drinking and make it muddy?"

"But you must be mistaken," bleated the lamb. "How can I be spoiling your water, since it runs from you to me and not from me to you?"

"Don't argue," snapped the wolf. "I know you. You are the one who was saying those ugly things about me behind my back a year ago."

"Oh, sir," replied the lamb, trembling, "a year ago I was not even born."

"Well," snarled the wolf, "if it was not you, then it was your father, and that amounts to the same thing. Besides, I'm not going to have you argue me out of my supper."

Without another word he fell upon the helpless lamb and tore her to pieces.

★ *Application:* ANY EXCUSE WILL SERVE A TYRANT.

The Bull and the Goat

A BULL, pursued by a lion, took shelter in a cave which was the home of a wild goat. Greatly annoyed with the intruder, the goat began to butt the tired bull with his horns. He bore the ill-treatment of the goat with patience, saying: "Because I permit you to vent your displeasure on me now does not mean that I am afraid of you. As soon as the lion is out of sight and the danger is past, then I will show you the difference between a lion and a goat."

★ *Application:* THOSE WHO TAKE TEMPORARY ADVANTAGE OF THEIR NEIGHBORS' DIFFICULTIES MAY LIVE TO REPENT OF THEIR INSOLENCE.

The Ant and the Dove

A THIRSTY ANT went to a spring for a drink of water. While climbing down a blade of grass to reach the spring he fell in. The ant might very well have drowned had it not been for a dove who happened to be perched in a near-by tree. Seeing the ant's danger the dove quickly plucked off a leaf and let it drop into the water near the struggling insect. The ant climbed upon the leaf and presently was wafted safely ashore.

Just at that time a hunter was spreading his net in the hope of snaring the dove. The gratified ant, perceiving the hunter's plan, bit him in the heel. Startled, the huntsman dropped his net, and the dove flew away to safety.

★ *Application:* ONE GOOD TURN DESERVES ANOTHER.

The Fox Without a Tail

A FOX had the misfortune to have his bushy tail caught in a trap. When he saw that it was a question of his life or his tail he left his tail behind him. He felt himself disgraced, however, and for a time did not go near his friends for fear of ridicule.

But one day the idea came to him how he could make the best of a bad bargain. He called a meeting of all the rest of the foxes and proposed to them that they should follow his example.

"You have no idea," said he, "of the ease and comfort I am enjoying. I don't know why I didn't cut off my tail long ago. I could never have believed it if I had not tried it myself. When you come to think about it, friends, a tail is such an inconvenient and unnecessary appendage that it is strange we have put up with it so long. My sincere advice to you all is to share this new freedom and part with your tails at once."

As he concluded, one of the older and wiser foxes stepped forward and said: "There is not one of us who does not believe that you found it convenient to cut off your tail. However, we are not so convinced that you would advise us to part with our tails if there were any chance of recovering your own."

★ *Application:* MISERY LOVES COMPANY.

The Shepherd Boy and the Wolf

EVERY DAY the shepherd boy was sent with his father's sheep into the mountain pasture to guard the flock. It was, indeed, a lonely spot at the edge of a dark forest, and there were no companions with whom he could pass the long, weary hours of the day.

One day, just to stir up some excitement, he rushed down from the pasture, crying "Wolf! Wolf!" The villagers heard the alarm and came running with clubs and guns to help chase the marauder away, only to find the sheep grazing peacefully and no wolf in sight.

So well had the trick worked that the foolish boy tried it again and again, and each time the villagers came running, only to be laughed at for their pains.

But there came a day when a wolf really came. The boy screamed and called for help. But all in vain! The neighbors, supposing him to be up to his old tricks, paid no heed to his cries, and the wolf devoured the sheep.

★ *Application:* LIARS ARE NOT BELIEVED EVEN WHEN THEY TELL THE TRUTH.

The Hen and the Cat

ALL THE BARNYARD knew that the hen was indisposed. So one day the cat decided to pay her a visit of condolence. Creeping up to her nest the cat in his most sympathetic voice said: "How are you, my dear friend? I was so sorry to hear of your illness. Isn't there something that I can bring you to cheer you up and to help you feel like yourself again?"

"Thank you," said the hen. "Please be good enough to leave me in peace, and I have no fear but I shall soon be well."

★ *Application:* UNINVITED GUESTS ARE OFTEN MOST WELCOME WHEN THEY ARE GONE.

The Wolf and the Goat

A WOLF saw a goat browsing near the edge of a high cliff. "My dear friend," he cried in his most sympathetic voice, "aren't you afraid you will get dizzy and fall and hurt yourself?" But the goat went on feeding.

The wolf tried again. "Isn't it terribly windy up there so high with no shelter at all?" But the goat went on plucking grass.

"Besides," shouted the wolf, "I am sure that you will find the grass far sweeter and more abundant down here."

Then the goat replied: "Are you quite sure, friend wolf, that it is my dinner you are so solicitous about, and not your own?"

★ *Application:* BEWARE OF A FRIEND WITH AN ULTERIOR MOTIVE.

The Farthing Rushlight

IN OLDEN TIMES people lighted their homes with lamps in which the pith of rushes served as wicks. There was one particular rushlight which had soaked up considerable grease and was feeling more than a little boastful.

One evening it announced before a large company that it could outshine the sun, the moon, and the stars. At that very moment a puff of wind came and blew it out. The servant who relighted it said: "Shine on, friend rushlight, and hold your tongue, there is no wind strong enough to blow out the lights of heaven."

★ *Application:* KNOW THY PLACE AND KEEP IT.

The Lion and the Mouse

A LION was asleep in his den one day, when a mischievous mouse for no reason at all ran across the outstretched paw and up the royal nose of the king of beasts, awakening him from his nap. The mighty beast clapped his paw upon the now thoroughly frightened little creature and would have made an end of him.

"Please," squealed the mouse, "don't kill me. Forgive me this time, O King, and I shall never forget it. A day may come, who knows, when I may do you a good turn to repay your kindness." The lion, smiling at his little prisoner's fright and amused by the thought that so small a creature ever could be of assistance to the king of beasts, let him go.

Not long afterward the lion, while ranging the forest for his prey, was caught in the net which the hunters had set to catch him. He let out a roar that echoed through the forest. Even the mouse heard it, and recognizing the voice of his former preserver and friend, ran to the spot where he lay tangled in the net of ropes.

"Well, your majesty," said the mouse, "I know you did not believe me once when I said I would return a kindness, but here is my chance." And without further ado he set to work to nibble with his sharp little teeth at the ropes that bound the lion. Soon the lion was able to crawl out of the hunter's snare and be free.

★ *Application:* NO ACT OF KINDNESS, NO MATTER HOW SMALL, IS EVER WASTED.

The Boy and the Nettle

A BOY playing in the fields one day was stung in the hand by a nettle. Running home to his mother he cried: "See what the nasty weed did to me. I barely touched it when it buried its prickers in my hand."

"It was because you touched it lightly," replied the boy's mother, "that it stung you. The next time, dear son, that you play with a nettle, grasp it tightly, and it will do you no harm."

★ *Application:* DO BOLDLY WHAT YOU DO AT ALL.

The Thief and His Mother

A SCHOOLBOY stole a hornbook from one of his fellows and brought it home to his mother. Instead of chastising him, she said: "That was very clever of you, my son." As the boy grew older he began to steal things of greater value, until at length, being caught in the very act, he was arrested, tried, found guilty, and sentenced to be hanged.

The day of his execution arrived, and he was taken from his cell and led to the gallows. In the crowd that followed the cart the thief saw his mother, weeping and beating her breast. He begged the officers to be allowed to speak one word in his sorrowing mother's ear.

When she came near and inclined her head to hear his last words he suddenly bared his teeth and bit her savagely in the lobe of her ear. All the bystanders were horrified and pushed forward with threatening gestures toward the thief. They could not understand such inhuman conduct of a son toward his mother.

Then he cried out: "You think me a brute, and I am. But I have this woman to thank for the fact that I shall soon be swinging on the gallows. She is my mother. But when I was small and did mischief, instead of punishing me, she encouraged me to my ruin. Behold an unnatural son, because when I was small I had an unnatural mother."

★ *Application:* SPARE THE ROD AND SPOIL THE CHILD.

The Eagle and the Beetle

A HARE, pursued by an eagle, sought refuge in the nest of a beetle whom he entreated to save him. The beetle interceded with the eagle and begged him not to break the law of sanctuary. But the eagle in his wrath gave the beetle a flop with his wing and straightway seized upon the hare and devoured him.

When the eagle flew away, the beetle flew after him in order to learn where his nest was hidden. Then one day when the eagle was away the beetle returned and rolled the eagle's eggs out of the nest, one by one, and broke them. Grieved and enraged that anyone should attempt so audacious a thing, the eagle built his nest in a higher place. But again his eggs suffered a similar fate.

In desperation the eagle flew up to Jupiter, his lord and king, and placed the third brood of eggs, as a sacred deposit, in his lap, begging him to guard them from harm. But the beetle, having made a little ball of dirt, flew up with it and dropped it in Jupiter's lap. The god, rising quickly to shake it off, and forgetting the eggs, dropped them and they were broken.

Jupiter, knowing that the beetle was in the right, but loath to see the race of eagles diminished, used his good offices to persuade the beetle to call a truce with the eagle. This the beetle would not agree to do, and Jupiter was forced to transfer the eagle's breeding to another season, when there were no beetles to be seen.

★ *Application:* THE LAWS OF HOSPITALITY ARE NOT TO BE BROKEN WITH IMPUNITY.

The Wolf and the Crane

A WOLF, in gorging himself upon some poor animal he had killed, had got a small bone stuck in his throat. The pain was terrible, and he ran up and down beseeching every animal he met to relieve him. None of the animals, however, felt very sorry for the wolf, for, as one of them put it, "That bone which is stuck in the wolf's throat might just as well be one of mine."

Finally the suffering wolf met the crane. "I'll give you anything," he whined, "if you will help take this bone out of my throat."

The crane, moved by his entreaties and promises of reward, ventured her long neck down the wolf's throat and drew out the bone. She then modestly asked for the promised reward.

"Reward?" barked the wolf, showing his teeth. "Of all the ungrateful creatures! I have permitted you to live to tell your grandchildren that you put your head in a wolf's mouth without having it bitten off, and then you ask for a reward! Get out of here before I change my mind!"

★ *Application:* **THOSE WHO LIVE ON EXPECTATION ARE SURE TO BE DISAPPOINTED.**

The Country Mouse and the Town Mouse

ONCE UPON A TIME a country mouse who had a friend in town invited him, for old acquaintance's sake, to pay him a visit in the country. Though plain and rough and somewhat frugal in his nature, the country mouse opened his heart and store in honor of an old friend. There was not a carefully stored-up morsel that he did not produce from his larder—peas and barley, cheese parings and nuts—to please the palate of his city-bred guest.

The town mouse, however, turned up his long nose at the rough country fare. "How is it, my friend," he exclaimed, "that you can endure the boredom of living like a toad in a hole? You can't really prefer these solitary rocks and woods to the excitement of the city. You are wasting your time out here in the wilderness. A mouse, you know, does not live forever, one must make the most of life while it lasts. So come with me and I'll show you life and the town."

In the end, the country mouse allowed himself to be persuaded, and the two friends set out together on their journey to town. It was late in the evening when they crept stealthily into the city, and midnight before they reached the great house where the town mouse lived.

On the table of the splendid banquet room were the remains of a lavish feast. It was now the turn of the city mouse to play host. He ran to and fro to supply all the guest's wants. He pressed dish upon dish and dainty upon dainty upon him as though he were waiting on a king. The country mouse, for his part, pretended to feel quite at home, and blessed the good fortune that had wrought such a change in his way of life.

But in the midst of his enjoyment, just as he was beginning to feel contempt for his frugal life in the country, the sound of barking and growling could be heard outside the door.

"What is that?" said the country mouse.

"Oh, that is only the master's dogs," replied the town mouse.

"Only!" replied the visitor in dismay. "I can't say that I like music with my dinner."

At that moment the door flew open and a party of revelers, together with two huge dogs, burst into the room. The affrighted friends jumped from the table and concealed themselves in a far corner of the chamber. At length, when things seemed quiet, the country mouse stole out from his hiding place, and bidding his friend good-bye, whispered in his ear: "This fine way of living may do for those who like it. But give me my barley bread in peace and in security in preference to your dainty fare partaken with fear and trembling."

★ *Application:* A CRUST EATEN IN PEACE IS BETTER THAN A BANQUET PARTAKEN IN ANXIETY.

The Two Pots

TWO POTS, one of earthenware and the other of brass, were carried downstream by a river in flood. The brass pot begged his companion to remain as close by his side as possible, and he would protect him.

"You are very kind," replied the earthen pot, "but that is just what I am afraid of. If you will only keep your distance, I shall be able to float down in safety. But should we come too close, whether I strike you or you strike me, I am sure to be the one who will get the worst of it."

★ *Application:* AVOID TOO POWERFUL NEIGHBORS.

The Young Man and the Swallow

A FOOLISH MAN received his inheritance from his father, and lost no time in spending it in gambling and riotous living.

The day the last of his substance was lost he was walking along the road. It was wintertime, but the sun was shining and it was unseasonably warm. A foolish swallow, pretending that it was spring, flew gaily around in the sky.

"It looks as though spring was here," said the foolish man. "I won't be needing all these clothes." So he pawned them, gambled with the proceeds, and lost.

But now, when he left the town, the sun was gone. Snow lay on the ground, and everything was frozen hard. The foolish swallow, frozen stiff, lay dead in the snow. Looking at the dead bird, the shivering man said with chattering teeth: "It is all your fault that I am in this unhappy fix!"

★ *Application:* THERE IS NO PROFIT IN BLAMING YOUR FOOLISH MISTAKES ON FOOLISH ADVISERS.

The Farmer and the Stork

A FARMER, who was tired of having his newly planted corn stolen by the cranes, set a net in his field. When he went to examine his snare he found that he had caught several of them, and included in their number was a stork.

"Please, sir," begged the stork, "don't kill me. I am not one of these greedy cranes who eat all your corn. I am a good and pious bird. I take care of my aged parents. I—"

But the farmer cut him short. "All that you say about yourself may be true. All I know, however, is that I have caught you with those who were destroying my crops, and I'm afraid that you will have to suffer the same fate as those in whose company you were captured."

★ *Application:* YOU ARE JUDGED BY THE COMPANY YOU KEEP.

The Man and the Lion

ONCE UPON A TIME a man and a lion met on the highway, and for some distance journeyed along together quite agreeably. But when the conversation began to concern which creature was superior, a man or a lion, the dispute waxed warmer and warmer.

They were passing a statue which depicted Hercules strangling a lion. "See there!" said the man. "That statue proves that I am right. What stronger proof of man's superiority over a lion could you ask?"

"That doesn't prove a thing," retorted the lion. "Just let us lions be the sculptors and every statue will show a lion standing over a man!"

★ *Application:* WE ARE BUT SORRY WITNESSES IN OUR OWN CAUSE.

The Lion and His Three Counselors

THE KING OF BEASTS was in an irritable mood. That morning his mate had told him that his breath was most unpleasant. After doing considerable roaring to prove that he was king he summoned his counselors.

First he called the sheep.

"Friend sheep," he roared, opening wide his great mouth, "would you say that my breath smells unpleasant?"

Believing that the lion wanted an honest answer, the sheep gave it, and the king of beasts bit off her head for a fool.

Then he called the wolf and asked him the same question. The wolf, catching sight of the carcass of the sheep, said: "Why, your majesty, you have a breath as sweet as blossoms in the spring—"

Before he could finish he had been torn to pieces for a flatterer.

At last the lion called the fox and put the question to him. The fox gave a hollow cough, then cleared his throat. "Your majesty," he whispered, "truly, I have such a cold in the head that I cannot smell at all."

★ *Application:* IN DANGEROUS TIMES WISE MEN SAY NOTHING.

The Stag in the Ox Stall

A STAG closely pursued by a pack of hounds sought refuge in the stable of a farmer. Trembling with fear he entered an empty ox stall where he tried to conceal himself under the straw. Only the stag's horns remained in sight. But the stable was dark, and when the hunters came along and asked whether anyone had seen the stag the stableboys looked, but could see nothing.

The stag began to take courage because he had not been discovered and thought that with the coming of darkness he would be able to make his escape.

"Don't be too sure," said one of the oxen in an adjoining stall. "When the master has finished his supper he will come to see that all is safe for the night. And then I fear that your life will be in jeopardy, for the master has eyes in the back of his head."

Even as he spoke, the farmer entered the stable. Pointing to the mount of straw, he called to the stableboys: "What are these two curious things sticking up out of the straw?" And when the stableboys came the stag was discovered and captured.

★ *Application:* THERE IS NO EYE LIKE THE MASTER'S.

The Fox and the Woodman

A FOX, hard pressed by a pack of hounds who had been chasing him over hill and dale, came up to a man who was cutting wood outside his cottage.

"Please, kind sir," panted the weary fox, "will you hide me in a corner where I will be safe from the hunters' hounds who wish to kill me?"

The man showed him his own hut, and the fox, creeping in, hid himself in a corner. Presently the hunters came up.

"Have you seen a fox hereabouts?" they asked.

"Why, no," replied the woodman. "I have been chopping wood here all morning." As he spoke he pointed with his finger to the very corner of the cottage where the fox was hiding. The hunters, not knowing what he meant, called their dogs and rode away.

As soon as the danger was past, the fox sneaked out of his hiding place and would have departed without a word of thanks.

"Just a moment, there, friend fox," the woodman said. "Is this the way you take leave of your host, without even a thank you for saving your life?"

"A pretty host!" snapped the fox. "If you had been as honest with your finger as you were with your tongue, then I should not have left your roof without bidding you farewell."

★ *Application:* THERE IS AS MUCH MALICE IN A WINK AS IN A WORD.

The Lion and Other Beasts Go Hunting

THE LION preferred to hunt alone, but now and then he would invite other beasts to accompany him. Upon one such occasion, the hunters cornered and killed a fat stag.

Taking a commanding position before the dead stag, the lion roared: "Beasts, it is time to divide the spoils. I demand that it be quartered. The first quarter shall fall to me as king of the beasts. The second is mine as arbiter. A third quarter is due me for my part in the chase. Now, as for the fourth part—" and here the lion gave an ominous growl —"let him take it who dares!"

★ *Application:* MANY MAY SHARE IN THE LABORS BUT NOT IN THE SPOILS.

The Sick Lion

THE LION allowed word to get around that he was on his deathbed and wished all the animals of his kingdom to come to his cave to hear his last will and testament.

The fox, who lived by his wits, did not wish to be the first to enter the cave. So he lingered near the entrance while the goat and the sheep and the calf went in to receive the last wishes of the king of beasts.

After a time, the lion seemed to make a remarkable recovery, and came to the mouth of the cave. Seeing the fox a safe distance away, he bellowed: "Why do you not come in to pay your respects to me, friend fox?"

"Please pardon me, your majesty," replied the fox, "but I did not wish to crowd you. I noticed the tracks of many of your subjects going into your cave, but so far I have seen none coming out. Until some of them come out, and there is more room in the cave, I think I'll stay out here in the open air."

★ *Application:* DON'T BELIEVE ALL YOU HEAR.

The Stag at the Pool

A STAG, one summer day, came to a pool of clear, still water to quench his thirst. As he drank he noticed his reflection in the pool and could not help admiring the image he saw there.

"I am really very handsome," said he to himself. "I should be proud of those beautiful, stately antlers. But those spindling legs and tiny feet are another matter. I wish that nature might have been more kind to me and had given me legs more worthy to bear such a noble crown."

Just at that moment the stag's sensitive nostrils scented the approach of a hunter, and even as he lingered an arrow whizzed past him. With a bound he was away, and the legs and feet of which he had just been so critical carried him speedily to a place of safety.

But once out of harm's way, the stag again fell to musing over his appearance, and before he knew it he had wandered into a thicket. The noble antlers which he had so greatly admired now held him fast, and the more he struggled the more firmly entangled he became. Then the hunters came, and as the arrow found its mark, he gasped: "Now that it is too late I realize that my own vanity led to my undoing."

★ *Application:* TOO OFTEN WE DESPISE THE VERY THINGS THAT ARE MOST USEFUL TO US.

The Travelers and the Bear

TWO MEN were traveling together in a wild and lonely part of the country. Before they had set out on their journey they had promised that if any danger should overtake them they would stand by each other to the death.

They had gone only a short way when a bear rushed out of the bushes and made straight for them. One of the men, quick as a flash, took to a tree and scrambled up into its branches. The other, seeing he had no time to escape, threw himself flat upon the ground, pretending to be dead.

As he lay there in the dust holding his breath the bear came near, sniffing and smelling, and putting his muzzle close to the man's ear. Then, at last, with a growl he shook his head and lumbered away, for bears will not touch a dead body.

When the animal was completely out of sight the man in the tree slid down to the ground, and somewhat shamefacedly approached his companion, who now was sitting on a stone.

"Well, old fellow," he said, "that was a close one, wasn't it? By the way, didn't I see that bear whispering to you? What did he say when he put his mouth to your ear?"

"Why," replied the other, looking his companion straight in the eye, "it was no great secret. He just told me that the next time I should not place any faith in the word of a cowardly knave like you."

★ *Application:* DON'T TRUST A FRIEND WHO IS LIABLE TO DESERT YOU WHEN TROUBLE COMES.

The Father and His Two Daughters

A MAN WHO had two daughters gave one in marriage to a gardener and the other to a potter. After the weddings the daughters departed with their husbands to their new homes, and the father was left alone.

The following spring the father went to visit the daughter who married the gardener. "How fares it with you, daughter?" he asked.

"Very well, indeed," she replied. "We have everything we want. I have but one wish. And that is that we have a heavy shower to water all our growing plants."

Later the father visited the daughter who had married the potter. "And how is everything with you, daughter?" he inquired.

"There is not a thing we lack," said she. "My only hope is that this fine weather and hot sun may continue so that all our tiles may be baked."

"Alas," said the father, "if you must have fine weather and your sister must have rain, what am I to pray for myself?"

★ *Application:* YOU CAN'T PLEASE EVERYBODY.

The Tortoise and the Eagle

THE TORTOISE once upon a time was not the contented fellow that he is today. There was a time when he wished with all his heart that he could fly. As he watched the birds disporting themselves in the clouds he felt sure that if he could get up into the air he could soar with the best of them.

One day he called to an eagle who was hovering overhead: "Friend eagle, you are the best flier among all the birds. If you will teach me to fly I will bring you all the treasures of the sea."

The eagle replied: "But you are asking the impossible, friend tortoise. In the first place, you have no wings and, in the second, nature never intended you to fly."

But the tortoise kept pleading and promising greater and greater rewards. So finally the eagle said that he would do the best he could. Telling the tortoise to hang on, he bore him high into the sky. Then he loosed his hold upon the now thoroughly frightened tortoise and cried: "All right, start flying."

The poor tortoise, however, dropped like a plummet and was dashed to pieces on the rocks below.

★ *Application:* VANITY CARRIES ITS OWN PUNISHMENT.

The Dog Invited to Supper

A GENTLEMAN, having prepared a great feast, invited his good friend to supper. It chanced that on that same day the gentleman's dog met the friend's dog. "Come," said he, "my good fellow, and sup with us tonight."

The dog was delighted with the invitation, and as he stood watching the dinner being brought from the kitchen, he licked his chops and said: "My, but that smells good. This is luck, indeed! I shall make the most of my opportunity and eat my fill tonight, for I may have nothing to eat tomorrow."

As he spoke thus to himself he wagged his tail and gave a sly look at his friend who had invited him. But his tail wagging to and fro caught the attention of the cook, who, seeing a stranger, straightway seized him by the legs and threw him out the window.

When he reached the ground he set off yelping down the street. Thereupon the neighbors' dogs ran up to him and asked him how he had enjoyed his supper. "To tell you the truth," said he with a sorry smile, "we drank so deep that I can't even tell you which way I got out of the house."

★*Application:* THEY WHO ENTER BY THE BACK STAIRS MAY EXPECT TO BE SHOWN OUT AT THE WINDOW.

The Mountebank and the Farmer

A HUGE CROWD had gathered to watch the performance of the famous mountebank. According to rumor, he had come with an act so new and so miraculous that its like had never before been seen on any stage.

The curtains parted, and there stood the artist alone upon the stage without any assistants or apparatus of any kind. Curiosity and suspense kept the audience in complete silence. You could have heard a pin drop. Suddenly the mountebank thrust his head into his cloak, and so cleverly mimicked the squeaking of a young pig that the audience insisted he had one concealed somewhere about him. But when he was searched no pig could be found.

Just then a farmer stood up and bellowed: "Do you call that a pig's squeak? If you folks want to hear what a pig's squeak is really like, then come around here tomorrow!"

The next day found a great crowd assembled. They had come to see the clever mountebank put the boasting farmer to shame. Both men appeared on the stage. First the clown gave some most realistic grunts and squeals while the crowd roared and applauded.

Then the farmer put his head down into his cloak, and immediately hideous squeals came forth.

"Booh, booh!" yelled the crowd. "That sounds no more like a pig than a cow! We want the mountebank! Get off the stage, you country lout! Who taught you to squeal? Get back to your barnyard!"

But the farmer stood his ground. "You fools," he cried, "this is what you ignoramuses have been hissing!" And he drew from his cloak a real live little pig whose ear he had been pinching to make him squeal. "The next time, my smart city friends, let your own senses help you to judge instead of your pretty prejudices!"

★ *Application:* DO NOT DENOUNCE THE GENUINE, ONLY TO APPLAUD AN IMITATION.

The Dog and the Shadow

ONE DAY a dog stole a piece of meat out of a butcher shop, and on his way to a safe place where he could eat it without interruption he had to cross a footbridge over a clear stream. Looking down he saw his own reflection in the water.

Thinking that the reflection was another dog with another piece of meat, and being a greedy dog, he made up his mind to have that also. So he snarled and made a grab for the other dog's meat.

As his greedy mouth opened, out dropped the piece of meat and fell into the stream and was lost.

★ *Application:* GRASP AT THE SHADOW AND LOSE THE SUBSTANCE.

The Mouse and the Frog

IT WAS an evil day for the mouse when he made the acquaintance of a frog on the eve of a journey into the country. Protesting his great affection, the frog persuaded the mouse to allow him to go along. But we shall never know what possessed the mouse when he let the frog tie one of his own forefeet to one of the frog's hindfeet, for surely it made traveling most uncomfortable indeed.

However, they limped and hopped along the path until they came to a stream of water. The frog immediately jumped in, saying: "Follow me, friend mouse, and have no fear. You may find the harness a bit awkward, but remember that I'll be right by your side as we swim across."

So they began to swim. Scarcely had they reached midstream, however, when the frog took a sudden plunge to the bottom, dragging the unfortunate mouse after him. The struggling and threshing of the mouse caused such a great commotion in the water that it attracted the attention of a hawk sailing in the sky overhead. Swift as lightning he pounced down upon the drowning mouse and carried him away. And with them, of course, went the frog as well.

★ *Application:* HE WHO COMPASSES THE DESTRUCTION OF HIS NEIGHBOR OFTEN IS CAUGHT IN HIS OWN SNARE.

The Oak and the Reed

A PROUD OAK grew upon the bank of a stream. For a full hundred years it had withstood the buffeting of the winds, but one day there came a violent storm. The great oak fell with a mighty crash into the swollen river and was carried down toward the sea.

Later the oak tree came to rest on the shore where some reeds were growing. The tree was amazed to see the reeds standing upright.

"How ever did you manage to weather that terrible storm?" he asked. "I have stood up against many a storm, but this one was too strong for me."

"That's just it," replied the reed. "All these years you have stubbornly pitted your great strength against the wind. You were too proud to yield a little. I, on the other hand, knowing my weakness, just bend and let the wind blow over me without trying to resist it. The harder the wind blows the more I humble myself, so here I am!"

★ *Application:* IT IS BETTER TO BEND THAN TO BREAK.

The Old Man and Death

AN OLD MAN, stooped by age and hard work, was gathering sticks in the forest. As he hobbled painfully along he thought of his troubles and began to feel very sorry for himself.

With a hopeless gesture he threw his bundle of sticks upon the ground and groaned: "Life is too hard. I cannot bear it any longer. If only Death would come and take me!"

Even as the words were out of his mouth Death, in the form of a skeleton in a black robe, stood before him. "I heard you call me, sir," he said. "What can I do for you?"

"Please, sir," replied the old man, "could you please help me put this bundle of sticks back on my shoulder again?"

★ *Application:* HOW SORRY WE WOULD BE IF MANY OF OUR WISHES WERE GRANTED.

The Swallow's Advice

A FARMER was sowing his field with hemp seeds while a swallow and some other birds sat on the fence watching him.

"Beware of that man," said the swallow solemnly.

"Why should we be afraid of him?" asked the other birds.

"That farmer is sowing hemp seed," replied the swallow. "It is most important that you pick up every seed that he drops. You will live to regret it if you don't."

But, of course, the silly birds paid no heed to the swallow's advice. So, with the coming of the spring rains, the hemp grew up. And one day the hemp was made into cord, and of the cord nets were made. And many of the birds that had despised the swallow's advice were caught in the nets made of the very hemp that was grown from the seeds they had failed to pick up.

★ *Application:* UNLESS THE SEED OF EVIL IS DESTROYED IT WILL GROW UP TO DESTROY US.

The Old Woman and the Physician

AN OLD WOMAN, who had become blind, summoned a physician.

"Since you are a healer of such great renown," said she, "I would like to strike a bargain with you. If you will restore my eyesight I will give you a most handsome reward. But if, within a reasonable time, you fail and my malady still remains, then you shall receive nothing."

The physician, observing that the old woman was comfortably off and had many possessions, concluded the agreement. So he called regularly and pretended to treat the woman's eyes, meanwhile, bit by bit, carrying off all her goods.

After a time, whatever had been causing the old lady's blindness disappeared, and she found her sight again. Thereupon the physician demanded the stipulated fee. But discovering that nearly all of her possessions had disappeared since the coming of the physician, she kept putting him off with excuses. At length he grew impatient and had his patient summoned before a judge.

When called upon for her defense, the old woman said: "What this man says is true enough. I promised to give him his fee if my sight were restored, but nothing if my eyes remained blind. Now, then, he says that I am cured, but it cannot be true. For before my malady came upon me I could see all sorts of furniture and goods in my house. But now I cannot see a single stick, yet he tells me that he has restored my sight!"

★ *Application:* HE WHO PLAYS A TRICK MUST BE PREPARED TO TAKE A JOKE.

The Eagle and the Arrow

ONE DAY a bowman saw an eagle soaring lazily in the sky. Quickly he notched an arrow and sent it whizzing after the bird. It found its mark, and the eagle felt itself wounded to death. As it slowly fluttered down to earth it saw that the haft of the arrow which had pierced its breast was fitted with one of its own feathers.

★ *Application:* HOW OFTEN DO WE SUPPLY OUR ENEMIES WITH THE MEANS OF OUR OWN DESTRUCTION!

The Thief and the Boy

A BOY WAS PLAYING by the well curb when a thief came walking by. Suddenly the boy began to cry. His little shoulders heaved with his sobbing. His wailing could be heard for a mile or more. When his grief had abated somewhat the thief said: "Why all the tears, my little friend?"

"Oh, dear, oh, dear," whimpered the boy. "I was playing with my beautiful silver mug. B-b-but the string broke and it fell down into the well."

"That's easy," replied the thief. Tossing off his clothes he let himself down into the well. It was his intention to recover the valuable mug and keep it for himself.

Down, down, down he went. Colder and colder grew the water, but he couldn't find the mug—for the simple reason that there wasn't any! After a while the thief began to realize that the boy, having recognized him for a thief, had sent him down into the well to get him out of the way.

Painfully he climbed out of the well, shivering with the cold. When he reached the top again both the boy and the thief's clothes were gone.

★ *Application:* HE WHO TRIES TO OUTSMART HIS NEIGHBOR WINDS UP BY OUTSMARTING HIMSELF.

The Fir Tree and the Bramble

A FIR TREE which grew tall and straight over most of the forest trees was boasting one day to a humble bramblebush beneath him. His haughtiness and boasting made the bramblebush annoyed, and he said: "If I were as tall as you I would not need to put on such airs."

"How can a wretched bramblebush understand the feelings of a tree whose top brushes the clouds," was the haughty reply.

"Just wait," said the bramble. "I hope I am here the day the woodmen come with their sharp axes and saws looking for a tall fir tree. Then, I wager, you will wish you were nothing but a humble, useless bramblebush."

★ *Application:* THE HUMBLE ARE SECURE FROM MANY DANGERS TO WHICH THE PROUD ARE SUBJECT.

The Vain Crow

ONE DAY a vain crow found some feathers which a peacock had shed. Sticking them among his own rusty black ones, he began to strut about ignoring and despising his old friends and companions.

Dressed in his borrowed plumage, he very cockily sought out a flock of peacocks who were walking with stately steps on the park lawn. Instantly detecting the true nature of the intruder, they stripped him of his finery and falling upon him with their sharp beaks, they sent him packing.

The bedraggled crow, sadder but wiser, betook himself to his former companions, and would have been satisfied to associate with them again. But the crows, remembering how obnoxious he had been with his airs and his vanity, drummed him out of their society. One of those whom he had so lately despised offered him the following advice: "Be contented with what nature made you and you will avoid the contempt of your peers and the punishment of your betters."

★ *Application:* HAPPINESS IS NOT TO BE FOUND IN BORROWED FINERY.

The Two Crabs

A MOTHER CRAB and her child were strolling along the beach one day. It was a fine morning, but the mother crab was too busy scolding her offspring to pay any attention to the weather.

"Why in the world, child, do you not walk as the other creatures do—forward instead of backward?" she complained.

"Mother, dear," replied the little crab, "do but set the example, yourself, and I will follow you."

★ *Application:* EXAMPLE IS THE BEST PRECEPT.

The Mountain in Labor

ONE DAY the people of a certain country heard a mighty rumbling in the near-by mountain. Smoke was pouring from the summit. The earth was trembling, and great rocks came hurtling down into the valley. The mountain seemed to be in labor, and all the people rushed to a vantage point where they could see what terrible thing was about to happen.

They waited and waited, while the sky grew dark and the rumblings and thunderings increased. Finally, as the people watched, there was one earthquake more violent than all the others. Suddenly, a huge fissure appeared in the side of the mountain. The people threw themselves down upon their knees. Some of them fainted. All the rest waited with bated breath to see what would happen next.

The thundering stopped. A deep silence fell. And out of the gap in the side of the mountain popped a mouse!

★ *Application:* MAGNIFICENT PROMISES OFTEN END IN PALTRY PERFORMANCES.

The Fisherman Piping

THERE WAS ONCE a fisherman who enjoyed playing on the bagpipes as much as he did fishing. He sat down on the riverbank and played a gay tune, hoping that the fish would be attracted and jump ashore.

When nothing happened, he took a casting net, threw it into the water, and soon drew it forth filled with fish. Then, as the fish danced and flopped about in the net on shore, the fisherman shook his head and said: "Since you would not dance when I piped, I will have none of your dancing now."

★ *Application:* TO DO THE RIGHT THING AT THE RIGHT SEASON IS A GREAT ART.

The Man and His Two Wives

BACK IN THE DAYS when a man was allowed more wives than one, a middle-aged bachelor whose hair was only just beginning to turn gray fell in love with two women at one time, and married both of them.

One was young and blooming, and wished her husband to appear as youthful as herself. So every night she would comb his hair, and as she did so she would pull out all the gray hairs.

The other wife, who was older, saw her husband growing gray with pleasure, for she did not like to be mistaken for his mother. So each morning when she brushed his hair she would industriously pluck out every black hair she could find.

For a time the man enjoyed the attention and devotion of his wives, until one morning when he looked into the mirror and found that he was completely bald.

★ *Application:* YIELD TO THE CAPRICES OF ALL AND YOU SOON WILL HAVE NOTHING TO YIELD AT ALL.

The Old Woman and Her Maids

A THRIFTY OLD WOMAN kept two serving maids to help her with the housework. The two maids slept together in the loft, and it was their old mistress's custom to rouse them up at cock-crow.

Naturally, the maidservants disliked very much being awakened before daylight every morning. They decided that if they could prevent the cock from giving his alarm each morning they would be able to lie longer in bed. The opportunity came, and the cock's neck was wrung. But, lo and behold, the next night, the old woman, missing her usual alarm, and being afraid of oversleeping, climbed up into the loft with her candle and awakened the sleeping maids at midnight.

★ *Application:* TOO MUCH CUNNING OVERREACHES ITSELF.

The Monkey and the Dolphin

IT WAS an old custom among sailors to take with them on their voyages monkeys and other pets to amuse them while they were at sea. So it happened that on a certain voyage a sailor took with him a monkey as a companion on board ship.

Off the coast of Sunium, the famous promontory of Attica, the ship was caught in a violent storm and was wrecked. All on board were thrown into the water and had to swim for land as best they could. And among them was the monkey.

A dolphin saw him struggling in the waves, and taking him for a man, went to his assistance. As they were nearing the shore just opposite Piraeus, the harbor of Athens, the dolphin spoke. "Are you an Athenian?" he asked.

"Yes, indeed," replied the monkey, as he spat out a mouthful of sea water. "I belong to one of the first families of the city."

"Then, of course, you know Piraeus," said the dolphin.

"Oh, yes," said the monkey, who thought Piraeus must be the name of some distinguished citizen, "he is one of my very dearest friends."

Disgusted by so obvious a falsehood, the dolphin dived to the bottom of the sea and left the monkey to his fate.

★ *Application:* THOSE WHO PRETEND TO BE WHAT THEY ARE NOT, SOONER OR LATER, FIND THEMSELVES IN DEEP WATER.

The Wild Boar and the Fox

A WILD BOAR was busily whetting his tusks against a tree in the forest when a fox came by.

"Why are you wasting your time in this manner?" asked the fox. "Neither a hunter nor a hound is in sight, and no danger is at hand."

"True enough," replied the boar; "but when the danger does arise, I shall have something else to do than to sharpen my weapons."

★ *Application:* IT IS TOO LATE TO WHET THE SWORD WHEN THE TRUMPET SOUNDS.

The Trees and the Ax

A WOODMAN came into the forest one day carrying an ax without any handle. He sat down upon the mossy ground and looked about him rather helplessly.

"What's the trouble, friend woodman?" inquired a friendly old oak.

"I need a handle for my ax," replied the man. "Most any piece of wood will do."

After a whispered consultation, the trees good-naturedly offered the woodman a fine piece of tough ashwood for a handle.

But no sooner had the woodchopper fitted the helve with his ax when he set to work on all sides, felling the noblest trees in the wood.

The old oak, witnessing the destruction all about him, whispered to the cedar tree: "If we had not sacrificed our humble neighbor, the ash tree, to please the woodchopper, we might all of us remain standing for ages."

★ *Application:* THEY ARE FOOLISH WHO GIVE THEIR ENEMY THE MEANS OF DESTROYING THEM.

The Mouse and the Weasel

A LITTLE MOUSE, who had gone without food for days and was almost starved, had the good fortune to come upon a basket of corn. Weak as he was, he was able to make his way into the basket, where he stuffed and gorged himself to his heart's content. His hunger appeased, the mouse decided to go home, only to find to his dismay that his enlarged belly would not go through the hole in the basket.

So there he sat bewailing his fate, until a weasel, brought to the spot by the mouse's squeaks, said to him: "Stop your weeping and wailing, friend mouse. The thing for you to do is to fast where you are until you are thin again. When you reduce yourself to the same condition you were in when you entered, then you can get out the same way."

★ *Application:* DON'T COVET MORE THAN YOU CAN CARRY.

The Lion and the Ass Go Hunting

AS EVERYONE KNOWS, the lion is a mighty hunter. But even the king of beasts at times grows tired of hunting for his food. So once a lion made an agreement with an ass to go hunting together.

The plan was that they were to proceed to a certain cave where a herd of wild goats were accustomed to take shelter. The lion was to take a position near the mouth of the cave while the ass went inside and made such a hideous noise by braying and kicking and stamping that the terrified animals would run right into the lion's trap.

The plan worked beautifully. The lion caught and killed and devoured several goats, and after his hearty meal he stretched out to take his ease.

Just then the ass, anxious to claim his share of

the noble victory, came up to the reclining lion and said: "How was that for a job? Didn't I give those goats the worst of it? And what do you think of the noise I made? Wasn't it wonderful?"

"Yes, indeed," replied the lion sleepily. "As a matter of fact if I hadn't known you to be only an ass I think I would have been scared myself."

★ *Application:* BRAGGARTS USUALLY GET THEMSELVES LAUGHED AT IN THE END.

The Fox and the Bramble

THE HOUNDS were in full cry in pursuit of the wily fox and were gaining on him rapidly. Turning suddenly from his course, the fox dived through a hedge that was full of sharp thorns.

"Those dogs will never follow me through these brambles," said the fox to himself.

Just then he stepped on one of the thorns.

"That was a dirty trick," he snarled. "What kind of bramble are you? Here I come to you for help, but you only stab me for my pains."

"Wait a minute, friend fox," replied the bramble. "I'm the one who should be angry. You came running to me for help with your tail between your legs. I didn't ask you to come this way, did I? You knew I had thorns, and you were perfectly willing to have the dogs wounded by them. Now that you, yourself, got caught on one of them you complain. Next time I hope the hounds catch you!"

All that the fox could do was lick his smarting paw.

★ *Application:* TO THE SELFISH ALL ARE SELFISH.

The Horse and the Lion

THE LION was hungry. Hunting had not been too good during the past week. He was sitting by the roadside feeling sorry for himself when a handsome horse came trotting past. The lion's mouth watered as he thought what a wonderful dinner that horse would make if only he could catch him.

The lion just couldn't get his mind off that horse. So he let it be noised about that he had become a wonderful doctor who could heal any animal's complaint.

A day or two later the horse, pretending that he had a thorn in one hoof, came to the lion's den for help. The lion licked his chops. This was the chance he had been looking for. He asked the horse to raise one of his hind feet so he could make an examination. Solicitously, in his best bedside manner, he bent his head as though to examine the ailing hoof.

Just as he was ready to spring, the horse let go with his upraised hoof. There was a sickening thud as hoof met nose. And the last thing the lion remembered was a whinny of laughter as the horse galloped away toward the forest.

★ *Application:* THE BEST LAID-OUT SCHEME OFTEN HAS A KICKBACK.

The Two Frogs

ALL SUMMER LONG there had been no rain, and all the lakes and streams had dried up. Two frogs, looking for water, came upon a deep well. They sat down and argued as to whether they should dive in or not.

Said one frog: "My, but that water looks good down there! I think we should hop in without delay. Not only will we have plenty of good fresh water, but we'll have it all to ourselves."

"What you say may be true," said the second frog, "but suppose this well dries up too? Then where will we be—no water and no way of getting out either!"

★ *Application:* THINK TWICE BEFORE YOU LEAP!

The Travelers and the Hatchet

TWO MEN were traveling along the highroad toward the town. Suddenly one of them spied a hatchet half hidden in the fallen leaves.

"Look what I have found!" he cried, picking up the tool.

"Do not say '*I*,' " replied his companion. "It is more proper to say, 'Look what *we* have found!' "

The finder of the hatchet shrugged his shoulders, and they continued on their way. Presently they came upon a group of men whose eyes were on the roadway as though they were looking for something. Suddenly one of the strangers pointed to the approaching twain, and they rushed up to them, pointing to the hatchet.

"Alas," said the traveler who had found the hatchet, "it looks as though we are in trouble."

"What do you mean '*we* are in trouble'? What you really mean to say is that '*I* am in trouble!' "

★ *Application:* HE WHO WILL NOT ALLOW HIS FRIEND TO SHARE THE PRIZE MUST NOT EXPECT HIM TO SHARE THE DANGER.

The Fighting Cocks and the Eagle

TWO YOUNG fighting cocks were battling fiercely to see which of them would be the barnyard champion. At last the one that was beaten crept into a corner to hide his wounds and his shame.

But the conqueror flapped his wings and crowed lustily. Then he flew up to the top of the house where he continued to flap his wings and crow so that everyone would be sure to know who was victor. Just then an eagle, sailing by overhead, spied the crowing cock. Swooping down he seized him in his talons and carried him off for dinner. Meanwhile the defeated rival came out from his hiding place and took possession of the barnyard over which they had contended.

★ *Application:* PRIDE GOETH BEFORE A FALL.

The Birds, the Beasts, and the Bat

ONCE UPON A TIME war broke out between the birds and the beasts of the earth. For a long while the issue of the battle was uncertain. The bat, taking advantage of the fact that he had certain characteristics of both, kept aloof and remained neutral.

The birds said, "Come with us." But he shook his head and said, "I am a beast." Later some of the animals approached him and asked him to join their side. "I am a bird," said he.

In due course, a peace was concluded between the embattled birds and beasts. So the bat flew blithely up to the birds to join them in their rejoicings. But the birds gave him the cold shoulder and flew away. And the beasts gave him exactly the same treatment. Condemned by both sides and acknowledged by neither, the unhappy bat was obliged to skulk away and live in holes and corners, never caring to show his face except in the dusk of twilight.

★ *Application:* HE WINDS UP FRIENDLESS WHO PLAYS BOTH SIDES AGAINST THE MIDDLE.

The Farmer and the Snake

ONE WINTER'S DAY as a farmer was homeward bound from market he found a snake lying half dead with cold by the roadside. Taking compassion on the frozen creature, he placed it under his coat to warm it. Then he hastened home and put the serpent down on the hearth where a cheery fire was blazing.

The children watched it with great interest and rejoiced to see it slowly come to life again. But as one of them knelt down to stroke the reviving snake it raised its head and darted out its fangs and would have stung the child to death. Quickly the farmer seized his matlock and with one stroke cut the serpent in two.

★ *Application:* NO GRATITUDE IS TO BE EXPECTED FROM THE WICKED.

The Thief and the Dog

A THIEF was clambering over the wall when the watchdog began barking.

"Be still," hissed the thief, "I am one of your master's friends."

But the dog kept on growling and barking. Hoping to silence him, the thief reached into a bag and tossed some scraps of food down to the dog.

"No, you don't," snapped the watchdog. "I had my suspicions of you before, but now that you are so free with your gifts I am sure your intentions are evil."

★ *Application:* A BRIBE IN HAND BETRAYS MISCHIEF AT HEART.

The Trumpeter Taken Prisoner

DURING A BATTLE, a trumpeter very rashly ventured too near the enemy and was taken prisoner.

"Spare me, good sirs, I beseech you," he begged of his captors. "Do not put me to death. I do not fight. I have never taken a life. I do not even carry any weapon, except this harmless trumpet, which I blow now and then."

"All the more reason why you should die," replied the captors. "While you, yourself, have not the spirit to fight, you stir up the others to do battle and to take the lives of our comrades."

★ *Application:* HE WHO INCITES TO STRIFE IS WORSE THAN HE WHO TAKES PART IN IT.

The Three Tradesmen

THE ENEMY stood outside the walls of a certain city. As they brought up their siege weapons and arranged their forces for the attack, the desperate defenders within held a council of war to determine the best means of holding their city.

A bricklayer arose. "Sirs," said he, "it is my opinion that the best material for this purpose is brick." Then he sat down.

A carpenter asked to be recognized. "I beg to differ with the bricklayer. The material that will best serve our desperate needs is wood. Let timber be our defense!"

Then a tanner jumped to his feet. "Citizens," he cried, "when you all have had your say, I wish to remind you that there is nothing in the world like leather!"

★ *Application:* IT IS DIFFICULT TO SEE BEYOND ONE'S OWN NOSE.

The Shepherd and the Sea

THE GRAZING being poor in the hills, a shepherd moved his flock down near the shore where the sea mists kept the grass fresh and green. As he guarded his sheep he delighted in gazing out over the tranquil sea, so smooth and calm and limitless. One day he was seized with a strong desire to sail over that peaceful expanse of blue water.

So the shepherd sold his flock and received a good price because of the fatness of the sheep. With the money he bought a cargo of dates which he loaded on a vessel and set sail for another port. He had not gone far, however, when the sky became dark and a storm arose. The boat was driven upon the rocks and wrecked, and his cargo of dates and everything he owned was swallowed up by the sea. Indeed, it was only by good fortune that the one-time shepherd was rescued and able to get to land.

Not long after this unhappy experience, the shepherd was sitting sorrowfully on the shore looking out to sea (which now was calm and serene once more) when one of his friends came up to him and said: "I see you are admiring the ocean. How beautiful and tranquil is the sea. Could any vista be more inviting!"

"Have a care, my good fellow," replied the shepherd sourly, "of that smooth surface; it is only looking out for your dates."

★ *Application:* TRUST NOT IN HIM THAT SEEMS A SAINT.

The Farmer and His Dogs

IT WAS the coldest winter within the memory of the oldest living inhabitant. The roads were blocked by snowdrifts so deep that people could not struggle through them. A farmer found himself completely isolated with the drifts piled up to the eaves of his house. When his provisions ran out he was forced to slaughter one of his own sheep for food. Still the bitter weather continued. When all his sheep had been consumed he was forced to eat up his goats. And at last—for there still was no break in that terrible winter—the farmer had to sacrifice his valuable plow oxen to keep his family from starving.

When the dogs observed that the cattle had gone the same way as the sheep and goats they said to one another: "Let us be off, no matter how deep the snow. For if our master has had no pity on the working oxen, how is it likely then that he will spare us?"

★ *Application:* WHEN OUR NEIGHBOR'S HOUSE IS ON FIRE, IT IS TIME TO LOOK TO OUR OWN.

The Bald Knight

A CERTAIN knight observing himself in the mirror one day noted that he was growing old. His hair no longer grew as luxuriantly upon his head as once it had. Indeed, he had become quite bald. To conceal such a noticeable imperfection he ordered a very handsome periwig.

One day with a group of his friends he went riding to the hounds. He was dressed in his gayest apparel and on his naked pate he wore his brand-new wig. A sudden gust of wind snatched off the knight's toupee, exposing his bald noggin much to the amusement of his companions. He himself laughed as loud as anybody, saying: "How was it to be expected that I should keep someone's else hair upon my head, when my own would not stay there?"

★ *Application:* THY PRIDE IS BUT THE PROLOGUE OF THY SHAME.

The Wind and the Sun

A DISPUTE once arose between the wind and the sun over which was the stronger of the two. There seemed to be no way of settling the issue. But suddenly they saw a traveler coming down the road.

"This is our chance," said the sun, "to prove who is right. Whichever of us can make that man take off his coat shall be the stronger. And just to show you how sure I am, I'll let you have the first chance."

So the sun hid behind a cloud, and the wind blew an icy blast. But the harder he blew the more closely did the traveler wrap his coat around him. At last the wind had to give up in disgust. Then the sun came out from behind the cloud and began to shine down upon the traveler with all his power.

The traveler felt the sun's genial warmth, and as he grew warmer and warmer he began to loosen his coat. Finally he was forced to take it off altogether and to sit down in the shade of a tree and fan himself. So the sun was right, after all!

★ *Application:* **PERSUASION IS BETTER THAN FORCE.**

The Quack Frog

A FROG, emerging from the mud of the swamp, announced to all the animal world that he could cure every manner of disease. Interested to see what all the croaking was about, the animals gathered around, and the frog, more puffed up than ever by the attention he was receiving, bellowed:

"Here, come and see! You are looking upon the greatest physician in all the world. Not even Aesculapius, Jove's court doctor—"

He was interrupted by a loud bray from the jackass. A goat, also, seemed to be somewhat skeptical of the frog's boastings and said so. Then up spoke the fox: "How dare you set up to heal others? Why do you not try first to cure your own limping gait?"

"And your own blotched and wrinkled skin," added the hare.

"And your own bulging and ugly eyes," said the sheep.

At this the quack frog drew in his head and hopped away in the direction of the bog whence he had come while the animals laughed him to scorn.

★ *Application:* PHYSICIAN, HEAL THYSELF!

The Ass and His Driver

A FARMER was driving an ass along a country lane on the way to town. The beast bore no burden and was being allowed to amble along at his own gait. Suddenly the idea came to him to leave the beaten track and make for the edge of a precipice which bordered the roadway.

When he was just on the point of falling over, his master ran up and, seizing him by the tail, tried with might and main to pull him back. Willfully the ass resisted, pulling the contrary way. The farmer, seeing that he was about to be pulled over the precipice along with the stubborn beast, let go his hold. As the ass went hurtling over the brink his master cried after him: "Well, Jack, if you will be master, you will have to continue on alone."

★ *Application:* A WILLFUL BEAST MUST GO HIS OWN WAY.

Venus and the Cat

IN ANCIENT TIMES there lived a beautiful cat who fell in love with a young man. Naturally, the young man did not return the cat's affections, so she besought Venus, the goddess of love and beauty, for help. The goddess, taking compassion on her plight, changed her into a fair damsel.

No sooner had the young man set eyes on the maiden than he became enamored of her beauty and in due time led her home as his bride. One evening a short time later, as the young couple were sitting in their chamber, the notion came to Venus to discover whether in changing the cat's form she had also changed her nature. So she set down a mouse before the beautiful damsel. The girl, reverting completely to her former character, started from her seat and pounced upon the mouse as if she would eat it on the spot, while her husband watched her in dismay.

The goddess, provoked by such clear evidence that the girl had revealed her true nature, turned her into a cat again.

★ *Application:* WHAT IS BRED IN THE BONE WILL NEVER BE ABSENT IN THE FLESH.

The Wolf and the Shepherds

A WOLF chanced to be looking through the doorway of a hut where some shepherds were comfortably regaling themselves upon a joint of mutton. As he heard them smack their lips over the juicy morsels and watched them carving the roasted carcass with their knives, his lips curled with scorn.

Said he to himself: "These shepherds seem mightily pleased with themselves. But what would they do were they to observe me partaking of a similar supper?"

★ *Application:* MEN ARE TOO APT TO CONDEMN IN OTHERS THE VERY THINGS THEY DO THEMSELVES.

The Hedge and the Vineyard

A FOOLISH young heir came into the possession of his wise father's estate. After the funeral, and when his patrimony was securely in his hands, the young man ordered his servants to cut down all of the hedges that surrounded his vineyard. When the servants sought to dissuade their new master from his purpose he shouted: "Why should they not be grubbed up? They bear no grapes; they yield no harvest; they occupy good land that should be planted to vines. Grub them up and burn them."

So the fences were torn down and the vineyard was open to the ravages of man and beast, and it was not long before the vines were all destroyed. And thus the simple fellow learned, when it was too late, that while it is true that one ought not to expect to gather grapes from brambles, yet it is quite as important to protect one's vineyard as to possess it.

★ *Application:* **THEY ALSO SERVE WHO ONLY STAND AND WAIT.**

The Widow and the Hen

A POOR WIDOW living alone in the country kept a faithful hen. Each morning the hen laid a big brown egg for the woman's breakfast.

One day the widow thought to herself: "Now if I were to double my hen's allowance of barley, she would lay me two eggs a day instead of one." So she started feeding her biddy a double measure of grain, and soon the hen began to grow fat and sleek and lazy. It wasn't long before she stopped laying altogether.

★ *Application:* FIGURES DON'T LIE, BUT THEY WON'T MAKE A HEN LAY.

The Stag and the Vine

A STAG, pursued by hunters and weary from the long chase, took refuge among the branches of a vine where he concealed himself amidst the foliage. The hunters passed within a few yards of him without discovering his hiding place. As the sound of their voices died away and the stag thought that all was safe, he began nibbling at the tender green leaves that had sheltered him.

As he tugged at the leaves the movement of the branches caught the attention of one of the hunters. Guessing at once that his prey was there, the hunter drew his bow and shot an arrow into the rustling vine and killed the stag. As the animal lay dying he groaned: "I am being justly punished for my ingratitude toward the vine that had protected me in time of danger."

★ *Application:* THROW NO STONES INTO THE WELL THAT QUENCHED YOUR THIRST.

The Arabian Nights

HUNDREDS OF YEARS ago, a powerful Sultan of Persia cruelly decided to marry a new wife every day and have her executed the next morning. But when Shahriar, the Sultan, married Scheherazade, he did not know that she was as clever as she was beautiful. She decided to stop his reign of terror by telling him such wonderful stories that he would want to have her near him always. Shahriar was so enchanted with Scheherazade's first tale that he begged her to continue and delayed her death.

For a thousand and one nights, the beautiful Sultana entertained her husband with the thrilling stories of Sinbad, Ali Baba, Aladdin, and other tales of romance and magic which form this book.

And what happened to Scheherazade when her tales were ended? The Sultan was so delighted with her that he decided to mend his ways, and together they lived happily ever after.

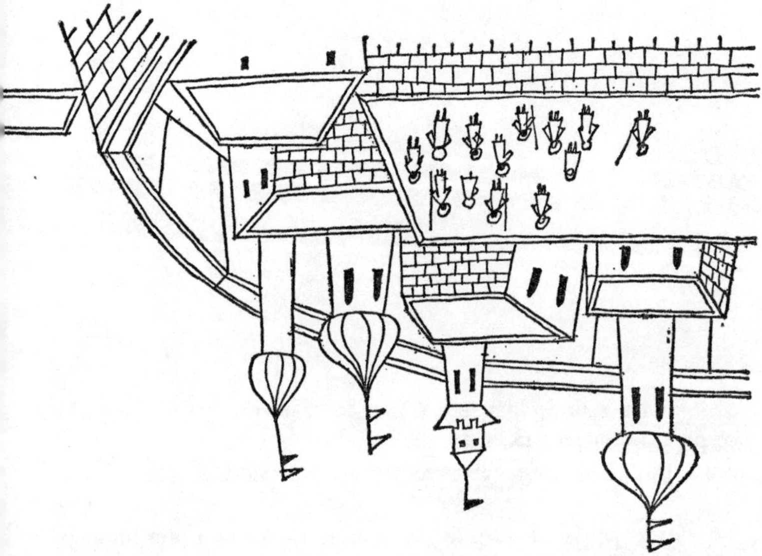

Arabian Nights

ILLUSTRATED BY MAMORU FUNAI

COMPANION LIBRARY

PUBLISHERS GROSSET & DUNLAP NEW YORK

PRINTED IN THE UNITED STATES OF AMERICA

CONTENTS

CONTENTS

The Arabian Nights

Scheherazade

THE CHRONICLES of the Sassanians, ancient Kings of Persia, tell us that there was formerly a King of that powerful family who was regarded as the most excellent prince of his time. He was as much beloved by his subjects for his wisdom and prudence as he was dreaded by his neighbors on account of his valor and well-disciplined troops. He had two sons: the elder, Shahriar, the worthy heir of his father, and endowed with all his virtues; the younger, Shahzenan, a prince of equal merit.

After a long and glorious reign, this King died; and Shahriar mounted the throne. Shahzenan, being excluded from all share in the government by the laws of the empire, was so far from envying the happiness of his brother that he made it his whole business to please him, and in this succeeded without much difficulty. Shahriar, who had naturally a great affection for the prince his brother, gave him the Kingdom of Great Tartary. Shahzenan went immediately and took possession of it, and fixed the seat of his government at Samarcand, the metropolis of the country. After they had been separated ten years, Shahriar, being very desirous of seeing his

brother, resolved to send his Vizier to invite him to his court. When he came near the city, Shahzenan was informed of his approach, and went to meet him, attended by the principal lords of his court, who, to show the greater honor to the Sultan's minister, appeared in magnificent apparel.

The King of Tartary received the ambassador with the greatest demonstrations of joy, and immediately asked him concerning the welfare of the Sultan his brother. The Vizier, having acquainted him that he was in health, informed him of the purpose of his embassy. Shahzenan was much affected, and answered, "Sage Vizier, the Sultan my brother does me too much honor; nothing could be more agreeable to me, for I as ardently long to see him as he does to see me. My kingdom is at peace, and I want no more than ten days to get myself ready to return with you. There is, therefore, no necessity for your entering the city for so short a period. I pray you to pitch your tents here, and I will order everything necessary to be provided for yourself and your attendants."

The Vizier readily complied; and Shahzenan, having made his preparations, at the end of ten days took leave of the Queen his wife, and went out of town in the evening with his retinue. He pitched his royal pavilion near the Vizier's tent and conversed with him till midnight. Wishing once more to see the Queen, whom he ardently loved, he returned alone to his palace, when, to his inexpressible grief, he found her trafficking with his enemies for his betrayal. Before the conspirators were aware of his presence, the King, urged by his just resentment, drew his scimitar and slew them, and then pitched their bodies into the fosse which surrounded the palace.

Having thus avenged himself, he returned to his pavilion without saying one word of what had happened, gave orders that the tents should be struck, and before day began his march, with kettledrums and other instruments of music, that filled everyone with joy, excepting the King. He was so much afflicted by the disloyalty of his wife that he was seized with

extreme melancholy, which preyed upon his spirits during the whole of his journey.

When he drew near the capital of Persia, the Sultan Shahriar and all his court came out to meet him. The princes were overjoyed to see one another, and having alighted, after mutual embraces and other marks of affection and respect, remounted, and entered the city, amidst the acclamations of the people. The Sultan conducted his brother to the palace provided for him, which had a communication with his own by a garden. It was so much the more magnificent because it was set apart as a banqueting house for public entertainments, and other diversions of the court.

Shahriar immediately left the King of Tartary, that he might give him time to bathe, and to change his apparel. As soon as his guest had completed his toilet, he returned to him again, and they sat down together on a sofa or alcove, and the two princes entertained one another suitably to their friendship and their long separation. The time of supper being come, they ate together, after which they renewed their conversation, till Shahriar, perceiving that it was very late, left his brother to repose.

The unfortunate Shahzenan retired to bed. Although the conversation of his brother had suspended his grief for some time, it now returned again with increased violence. Far into the night, instead of taking his necessary rest, he tormented himself with the bitterest reflections. All the circumstances of his wife's treachery presented themselves afresh to his imagination, in so lively a manner that he was like one distracted. Not being able to sleep, he arose, and abandoned himself to the afflicting thoughts, which made such an impression upon his countenance it was impossible for the Sultan not to observe. Shahriar, distressed by the melancholy of his brother, endeavored to divert him every day by new objects of pleasure, and the most splendid entertainments. But these, instead of affording him ease, only increased his sorrow.

One day, Shahriar having appointed a great hunting

match, about two days' journey from his capital, in a place that abounded with deer, Shahzenan besought him to excuse his attendance, for his health would not allow him to bear him company. The Sultan, unwilling to put any constraint upon him, left him at his liberty, and went a-hunting with his nobles. The King of Tartary, being thus left alone, shut himself up in his apartment, and sat down at a window that looked into the garden. In this place, where he could see and not be seen, he soon became a witness of a circumstance which attracted the whole of his attention. A secret gate of the Sultan's palace suddenly opened, and there came out of it several persons, in the midst of whom walked the Sultana, who was easily distinguished from the rest by her majestic air. This princess, thinking that the King of Tartary was gone a-hunting with his brother the Sultan, came with her retinue near the windows of his apartment, and the prince heard her hold treasonable conversation with some of her companions.

The baseness of his brother's wife filled the King of Tartary with a multitude of reflections. "How little reason had I," said he, "to think that none was so unfortunate as myself? It is surely the unavoidable fate of all in power and high position to have their honor and estate conspired against. Such being the case, what a fool am I to kill myself with grief! I am resolved that the remembrance of a misfortune so common shall never more disturb my peace."

From that moment he forbore afflicting himself. He called for his supper, ate with a better appetite than he had done since his leaving Samarcand, and listened with some degree of pleasure to the concert of vocal and instrumental music that was appointed to entertain him while at table.

He continued after this to be very cheerful. And when he was informed that the Sultan was returning, went to meet him, and paid him his compliments with great gaiety.

Shahriar, who expected to have found his brother in the same state as he had left him, was overjoyed to see him so cheerful.

"Dear brother," said he, "I return thanks to Heaven for the happy change it has wrought in you during my absence. Pray do me the favor to tell me why you were so melancholy, and wherefore you are no longer so."

The King of Tartary continued for some time as if he had been meditating and contriving what he should answer, but at last replied, "You are my Sultan and master. But excuse me, I beseech you, from answering your question."

"No, dear brother," said the Sultan, "you must answer me; I will take no denial."

Shahzenan, not being able to withstand these pressing entreaties, replied, "Well then, brother, I will satisfy you, since you command me." And having told him the story of the Queen of Samarcand's treachery, "This," said he, "was the cause of my grief. Judge whether I had not sufficient reason for my depression."

"Oh! my brother," said the Sultan, "what a horrible event do you tell me! I commend you for punishing the traitors to your state and person. None can blame you for what you have done. It was just; and, for my part, had the case been mine, I should scarcely have been so moderate. I now cease to wonder at your melancholy. The cause was too afflicting and too mortifying not to overwhelm you. O Heaven! what a strange adventure! But I must bless God, who has comforted you. And since I doubt not but your consolation is well grounded, be so good as to inform me what it is, and conceal nothing from me."

Shahzenan was not so easily prevailed upon in this point as he had been in the other, on his brother's account. But being obliged to yield to his pressing insistence he related to his brother the conversation he had overheard. After having heard these things, he continued, "I believed all women to be naturally treacherous. Being of this opinion, it seemed to me to be in men an unaccountable weakness to place any confidence in their fidelity. This reflection brought on many others; and, in short, I thought the best thing I could do was to

make myself easy on my own account, and warn you to anticipate the Sultana in her designs upon you."

On hearing the dreadful tidings which his brother imparted to him, the Sultan fell into an incontrollable rage, and instantly gave instructions for the execution of the Sultana and her fellow conspirators.

After this rigorous measure, being persuaded that no woman was to be trusted, he resolved, in order to prevent the disloyalty of such as he should afterward marry, to wed one every day, and have her strangled next morning. Having imposed this cruel law upon himself, he swore that he would put it in force immediately after the departure of the King of Tartary, who shortly took leave of him, and, being laden with magnificent presents, set forward on his journey.

Shahzenan having departed, Shahriar informed his Grand Vizier of his vow, and ordered him to provide him with a new wife every day. Whatever reluctance the Vizier might feel to put such orders in execution, as he owed blind obedience to the Sultan his master, he was forced to submit. And thus, every day, was a maid married and a wife murdered.

The rumor of this unparalleled barbarity occasioned a general consternation in the city, where there was nothing but crying and lamentation. Here, a father in tears, and inconsolable for the loss of his daughter; and there, tender mothers dreading lest their daughters should share the same fate, filled the air with cries of distress and apprehension. So that, instead of the commendations and blessing which the Sultan had hitherto received from his subjects, their mouths were now filled with imprecations.

The Grand Vizier, who, as has already been observed, was the unwilling executioner of this horrid course of injustice, had two daughters, the elder called Scheherazade, and the younger Dinarzade. The latter was highly accomplished; but the former possessed courage, wit, and penetration infinitely above her sex. She had read much, and had so admirable a memory that she never forgot anything she had read. She

had successfully applied herself to philosophy, medicine, history, and the liberal arts; and her poetry excelled the compositions of the best writers of her time. Besides this, she was of perfect beauty, and all her accomplishments were crowned by surpassing virtue.

The Vizier passionately loved this daughter, so worthy of his affection. One day, as they were conversing together, she said to him, "Father, I have one favor to beg of you, and most humbly pray you to grant it."

"I will not refuse," answered he, "provided it be just and reasonable."

"For the justice of it," resumed she, "there can be no question, and you may judge of this by the motive which obliges me to make the request. I wish to stop that barbarity which the Sultan exercises upon the families of this city. I would dispel those painful apprehensions which so many mothers feel of losing their daughters in such a fatal manner."

"Your design, daughter," replied the Vizier, "is very commendable; but the evil you would remedy seems to me incurable. How do you propose to effect your purpose?"

"Father," said Scheherazade, "since by your means the Sultan makes every day a new marriage, I conjure you, by the tender affection you bear me, to procure me the honor of his hand." The Vizier could not hear this without horror.

"O Heaven!" he replied in a passion, "have you lost your senses, daughter, that you make such a dangerous request? You know the Sultan's vow; would you, then, have me propose you to him? Consider well to what your indiscreet zeal will expose you."

"Yes, dear father," replied the virtuous daughter, "I know the risk I run; but that does not alarm me. If I perish, my death will be glorious. And if I succeed, I shall do my country an important service."

"No, no," said the Vizier, "whatever you may offer to induce me to let you throw yourself into such imminent danger, do not imagine that I will ever consent. When the Sultan

shall command me to strike my poniard into your heart, alas! I must obey. And what an employment will that be for a father! Ah! if you do not dread death, at least cherish some fears of afflicting me with the mortal grief of imbruing my hands in your blood."

"Once more, father," replied Scheherazade, "grant me the favor I solicit."

"Your stubbornness," resumed the Vizier, "will rouse my anger. Why will you run headlong to your ruin? They who do not foresee the end of a dangerous enterprise can never conduct it to a happy issue."

"Father," replied Scheherazade, "I wish you would not take it so ill that I persist in my opinion. Besides, pardon me for declaring that your opposition is vain; for if your paternal affection should hinder you from granting my request, I will go and offer myself to the Sultan."

In short, the father, being overcome by the resolution of his daughter, yielded to her importunity, and though he was much grieved that he could not divert her from so fatal a

resolution, he went instantly to acquaint the Sultan that next night he would bring him Scheherazade.

The Sultan was much surprised at the sacrifice which the Grand Vizier proposed to make. "How could you," said he, "resolve to bring me your own daughter?"

"Sire," answered the Vizier, "it is her own offer. The sad destiny that awaits her could not intimidate her. She prefers the honor of being your Majesty's wife for one night, to her life."

"But do not act under a mistake, Vizier," said the Sultan. "Tomorrow, when I place Scheherazade in your hands, I ex-

pect you will put her to death. And if you fail, I swear that your own life shall answer."

"Sire," rejoined the Vizier, "though I am her father, I will answer for the fidelity of my hand to obey your order."

When the Grand Vizier returned to Scheherazade, she

thanked her father for having obliged her. And perceiving that he was overwhelmed with grief, told him that she hoped he would never repent of having married her to the Sultan; and that, on the contrary, he should have reason to rejoice at his compliance all his days.

Her business now was to adorn herself to appear before the Sultan. But before she went, she took her sister Dinarzade apart, and said to her, "My dear sister, I have need of your assistance in a matter of great importance, and must pray you not to deny it me. My father is going to conduct me to the Sultan. Do not let this alarm you, but hear me with patience. As soon as I am in his presence, I will pray him to allow you to come early on the morrow, that I may enjoy your company for an hour or two ere I bid you farewell and go to my death. If I obtain that favor, as I hope to do, remember, shortly after your arrival, to address me in these or some such words: 'My sister, I pray you that, ere I leave you, which must be very shortly, you will relate to me one of the entertaining stories of which you have recounted so many.' I will immediately tell you one; and I hope by this means to deliver the city from the consternation it is under at present." Dinarzade answered that she would with pleasure act as she required her.

The Grand Vizier conducted Scheherazade to the palace, and retired, after having introduced her into the Sultan's apartment. As soon as the Sultan was left alone with her, he ordered her to uncover her face. He found her so beautiful that he was perfectly charmed; but, perceiving her to be in tears, demanded the reason.

"Sire," answered Scheherazade, "I have a sister who loves me tenderly, and I could wish that she might be allowed to come early on the morrow to this chamber, that I might see her, and once more bid her adieu. Will you be pleased to allow me the consolation of giving her this last testimony of my affection?"

Shahriar having consented, Dinarzade came an hour before dawn on the next day, and failed not to do as her sister had

ordered. "My dear sister," cried she, "ere I leave you, which will be very shortly, I pray you to tell me one of those pleasant stories you have read. Alas! this will be the last time that I shall enjoy that pleasure."

Scheherazade, instead of answering her sister, addressed herself to the Sultan: "Sire, will your Majesty be pleased to allow me to afford my sister this satisfaction?"

"With all my heart," replied the Sultan. Scheherazade then bade her sister attend, and afterward addressing herself to Shahriar, proceeded as follows:

The Merchant and the Genie

THERE was formerly a merchant who possessed much property in lands, goods, and money. One day, being under the necessity of going a long journey on an affair of importance, he took horse, and carried with him a wallet containing biscuits and dates, because he had a great desert to pass over, where he could procure no sort of provisions. He arrived without any accident at the end of his journey; and having dispatched his affairs, took horse again, in order to return home.

The fourth day of his journey, he was so much incommoded by the heat of the sun that he turned out of the road to refresh himself under some trees, where he found a fountain of clear water. Having alighted, he tied his horse to a branch, and, sitting down by the fountain, took some biscuits and dates out of his wallet. As he ate his dates, he threw the stones carelessly in different directions. When he had finished his repast, being a good Mussulman, he washed his hands, face, and feet, and said his prayers.

Before he had finished, and while he was yet on his knees, he saw a genie of monstrous bulk advancing toward him with great fury, whirling a scimitar in his hand.

The genie spoke to him in a terrible voice: "Rise, that I

may kill thee with this scimitar, as thou hast killed my son"; and accompanied these words with a frightful roar.

The merchant, being as much alarmed by the hideous shape of the monster as by his threats, answered him, trembling, "Alas! how could I kill your son? I never knew, never saw him."

"Did not you, when you came hither," demanded the genie, "take dates out of your wallet, and as you ate them, throw the stones about in different directions?"

"I did all that you say," answered the merchant. "I cannot deny it."

"When thou wert throwing the stones about," resumed the genie, "my son was passing by, and thou didst throw one into his eye, which killed him. Therefore I must kill thee."

"Ah! my lord! pardon me," cried the merchant.

"No pardon," exclaimed the genie, "no mercy. Is it not just to kill him that has killed another?"

"I agree it is," replied the merchant, "but certainly I never killed your son. And if I have, it was unknown to me, and I did it innocently. I beg you therefore to pardon me, and suffer me to live."

"No, no," returned the genie, persisting in his resolution, "I must kill thee, since thou hast killed my son." Then, taking the merchant by the arm, he threw him with his face on the ground, and lifted up his scimitar to cut off his head.

As soon as she had spoken these words, perceiving it was day, and knowing that the Sultan rose early in the morning to say his prayers, and hold his council, Scheherazade discontinued her story.

"Dear sister," said Dinarzade, "what a wonderful story is this!"

"The remainder of it," replied Scheherazade, "is more surprising, as you will allow, if the Sultan will but permit me to live this day, and allow me to proceed with the relation on the morrow."

Shahriar, who had listened to Scheherazade with much in-

terest, resolved not to put her to death that day, but decided to execute her when she had finished the story. He arose, went to his prayers, and then attended his council.

During this time the Grand Vizier was in the utmost distress. Instead of sleeping, he spent the night bewailing the lot of his daughter, of whom he believed he should himself shortly be the executioner. As, with this melancholy prospect before him, he dreaded to meet the Sultan, he was agreeably surprised when he found the prince entered the council chamber without giving him the fatal orders he expected.

The Sultan, according to his custom, spent the day in regulating his affairs; and, when the night had closed in, retired with Scheherazade. The next morning before day, the Sultan, without waiting for Scheherazade to ask his permission, bade her proceed with the story of the genie and the merchant; upon which Scheherazade continued her relation as follows:

When the merchant saw that the genie was going to cut off his head, he cried to him, "For Heaven's sake hold your hand! Allow me one word. Have the goodness to grant me a respite of one year, to bid my wife and children adieu, and to divide my estate among them. But I promise you that this day twelve months I will return under these trees, to put myself into your hands."

"Do you take Heaven to be witness to this promise?" said the genie.

"I do," answered the merchant, "and you may rely on my oath." Thereupon the genie left him near the fountain, and disappeared.

When the merchant, on reaching home, related what had passed between him and the genie, his wife uttered the most piteous cries, beat her face, and tore her hair. The children, all in tears, made the house resound with their groans. And the father, not being able to resist the impulse of nature, mingled his tears with theirs.

At last the year expired, and he was obliged to depart. He put his burial clothes in his wallet. But when he came to bid his wife and children adieu, their grief surpassed description. Affected beyond measure by the parting with his dear ones, the merchant journeyed to the place where he had promised to meet the genie. Seating himself down by the fountain, he awaited the coming of the genie, with all the sorrow imaginable. While he languished under this painful expectation, an old man leading a hind appeared and drew near him. After they had saluted one another, the old man inquired of him why he was in that desert place.

The merchant related his adventures, to the old man's astonishment. When he had done the old man exclaimed, "This is the most surprising thing in the world! And you are bound by the most inviolable oath. However, I will be witness of your interview with the genie." He then seated himself by the merchant, and they entered into conversation.

While the merchant and the old man who led the hind were talking, they saw another old man coming toward them, followed by two black dogs. When the newcomer was informed of the merchant's adventure, he declared his resolve to stay and see the issue.

In a short time they perceived a thick vapor, like a cloud of dust raised by a whirlwind, advancing toward them. When it had come up to them, it suddenly vanished, and the genie appeared. The genie, without saluting them, went to the merchant with a drawn scimitar, and, taking him by the arm, said, "Get thee up, that I may kill thee, as thou didst my son." The merchant and the two old men began to lament and fill the air with their cries.

When the old man who led the hind saw the genie lay hold of the merchant, and about to kill him, he threw himself at the feet of the monster, and kissing them, said to him, "Prince of genii, I most humbly request you to suspend your anger, and do me the favor to listen to the history of my life, and of the hind you see. And if you think it more wonderful

and surprising than the adventure of the merchant, I hope you will pardon the unfortunate man one half of his offense."

The genie took some time to deliberate on this proposal, but answered at last, "Well, then, I agree."

Whereupon the old man with the hind told his story.

"This hind you see is my wife, whom I married when she was twelve years old, and we lived together for twenty years without having any children.

"My desire of having children induced me to adopt the son of a slave. My wife, being jealous, cherished a hatred for both the child and his mother, but concealed her aversion so well that I knew nothing of it till it was too late.

"While I was away on a long journey, she applied herself to magic, and by her enchantments she changed the child into a calf, and the mother into a cow, and gave them both into the charge of my farmer.

"On my return, I inquired for the mother and child. She informed me that the slave was dead, and that as for my adopted son she had not seen him in months. I regretted the death of the slave; but as my son had only disappeared, I was in hopes he would shortly return. However, eight months passed, and I heard nothing of him. When the festival of the great Bairam was to be celebrated, I sent to my farmer for one of the fattest cows to sacrifice. He accordingly sent me one, and I bound her. But as I was going to sacrifice her, she bellowed piteously, and I could perceive tears streaming from her eyes. This seemed to me very extraordinary, and finding myself moved with compassion, I could not find it in my heart to give her a blow, but ordered my farmer to get me another.

"My wife, who was present, was enraged at my tenderness and resistance to an order which disappointed her malice. She upbraided me for not sacrificing the cow for the festival. Out of deference to my wife, I ordered the farmer, less compassionate than myself, to sacrifice her. But when he flayed her, he found her to be nothing except bones, though to us she seemed very fat. I ordered him to take her away, and dispose of her in alms, or any way he pleased; but if he had a very

fat calf, to bring it me in her stead. He returned with a fat calf, which, as soon as it beheld me, made so great an effort to come near me that he broke his cord, threw himself at my feet, with his head against the ground, as if he meant to excite my compassion, and implore me not to be so cruel as to take his life.

"I was more surprised and affected with this action than with the tears of the cow, and told my wife that I would not sacrifice this calf, no matter what she said. The wicked woman had no regard for my wishes, but urged me until I yielded. I tied the poor creature, and, taking up the fatal knife, was going to plunge it into the calf's throat, when turning his eyes, bathed with tears, in a languishing manner, toward me, he affected me so much that I had not the strength to kill him. I let the knife fall, and told my wife positively that I would have another calf to sacrifice, and pacified her a little by promising that I would sacrifice him against the Bairam of the following year.

"The next morning my farmer desired to speak with me alone. He told me that his daughter, who had some skill in magic, desired to see me. When she was admitted, she informed me that while I was on my journey my wife had changed the slave into a cow, and the child into a calf. She could not restore the slave, who, in the shape of a cow, had been sacrificed, but she could give me my adopted son again, and would do so if she might have him for a husband, and also punish my wife as she deserved.

"When I had given my consent to these proposals, the damsel then took a vessel full of water, pronounced over it words that I did not understand, and throwing the water over the calf, he in an instant recovered his natural form.

"I immediately embraced him, and told him how the damsel had freed him from his enchantment, and how I had promised her that he would be her husband. He joyfully consented; but, before they married, she changed my wife into a hind. And this is she whom you see here.

"Since that time, my son is become a widower, and gone to

travel. It being now several years since I heard of him, I am come abroad to inquire after him. And not being willing to trust anybody with my wife, till I should return home, I thought fit to take her everywhere with me. This is the history of myself and this hind. Is it not one of the most wonderful and surprising?"

"I admit it is," said the genie, "and on that account I forgive the merchant one half of his crime."

When the first old man had finished his story, the second, who led the two black dogs, addressed the genie, and said, "I am going to tell you what happened to me, and these two black dogs you see by me. But when I have done this, I hope you will pardon the merchant the other half of his offense."

"I will," replied the genie, "provided your story surpass that of the hind."

Then the second old man began in this manner:

"Great prince of genii, you must know that we are three brothers, the two black dogs and myself. Our father, when he died, left each of us one thousand sequins. With that sum, we all became merchants. My brothers resolved to travel, and trade in foreign countries.

"At the end of a year they returned in abject poverty, having, in unfortunate enterprises, lost all. I welcomed them home, and having prospered, gave each of them a thousand sequins to start them again as merchants. After a while they came to me to propose that I should join them in a trading voyage. I immediately declined. But after having resisted their solicitation five whole years, they importuned me so much that at last they overcame my resolution.

"When, however, the time arrived that we were to buy the goods necessary to the undertaking, I found they had spent all, and had nothing left of the thousand sequins I had given to each of them. I did not, on this account, upbraid them. On the contrary, my stock being now six thousand sequins, I gave each of them a thousand, and keeping as much for myself, I buried the other three thousand in a corner of my house.

We purchased goods, and having embarked them on board a vessel, which we freighted betwixt us, we put to sea with a favorable wind. After two months' sail, we arrived happily at port, where we landed, and had a very good market for our goods. I, especially, sold mine so well that I gained ten to one.

"When we were ready to embark on our return, I met on the seashore a lady, very handsome but poorly clad. She walked up to me gracefully, kissed my hand, and besought me with the greatest earnestness imaginable to marry her. I made some difficulty before agreeing to this proposal. But she urged so many things to persuade me that I ought not to object to her on account of her poverty, and that I should have all the reason in the world to be satisfied with her conduct, that at last I yielded.

"I ordered proper apparel to be made for her. And after having married her, according to form, I took her on board, and we set sail. I found that my wife possessed so many good qualities that my love for her every day increased. In the meantime my two brothers, who had not managed their affairs as successfully as I had mine, envied my prosperity. They suffered their feelings to carry them so far that they conspired against my life. One night, when my wife and I were asleep, they threw us both into the sea.

"I had scarcely fallen into the water, when she took me up, and carried me to an island. When daylight appeared, my wife informed me that she was in reality a fairy who had presented herself to me in disguise to test my goodness. As I had dealt generously with her, said she, now she would deal generously with me, but that my brothers would have to pay for their treachery with their lives.

"I listened to this discourse with admiration. I thanked the fairy, the best way I could, for the great kindness she had done me; but, as for my brothers, I begged her to pardon them. Whatever cause of resentment they might have given me, I was not cruel enough to desire their death. I then informed her what I had done for them, but this only increased

her indignation; and she exclaimed that she must immediately pursue those ungrateful traitors, and take speedy vengeance on them.

"I pacified her as best I could. And as soon as I had concluded, she transported me in a moment from the island to the roof of my own house. I descended, opened the doors, and dug up the three thousand sequins I had previously secreted. I went afterward to my shop, which I also opened; and was complimented by the merchants, my neighbors, upon my return. When I went back to my house, I perceived there two black dogs, which came up to me in a very submissive manner. I could not divine the meaning of this circumstance, which greatly astonished me. But the fairy, who immediately appeared, told me not to be surprised to see these dogs, that they were my brothers. I was troubled at this declaration, and asked her by what power they were so transformed. Then she told me that she had done it at the same time that she had sunk their ship. They were to remain in their present form for five years. Then, telling me where I might find her after the five years had passed, she disappeared.

"The five years being now nearly expired, I am traveling in quest of her. This is my history, O prince of genii! Do not you think it very extraordinary?"

"I own it is," replied the genie, "and on that account I remit the merchant the other half of the crime which he has committed against me." With these words the genie rose, and disappeared in a cloud of smoke, to the great delight of the merchant and the two old men.

The merchant failed not to make due acknowledgment to his deliverers. They rejoiced to see him out of danger; and bidding him adieu, each of them proceeded on his way. The merchant returned to his wife and children, and passed the rest of his days with them in peace.

The Story of the Fisherman and the Genie

THERE ONCE was an aged fisherman, who was so poor that he could scarcely earn as much as would maintain himself, his wife, and three children. He went early every day to fish in the morning, and imposed it as a law upon himself not to cast his nets above four times a day. He went one morning before the moon had set, and, coming to the seaside, undressed himself. Three times did he cast his net, and each time he made a heavy haul. Yet, to his indescribable disappointment and despair, the first proved to be an ass, the second a basket full of stones, and the third a mass of mud and shells.

As daylight now began to appear he said his prayers, for he was a good Mussulman, and commended himself and his needs to his Creator. Having done this, he cast his nets the fourth time, and drew them as formerly, with great difficulty. But, instead of fish, he found nothing in them but a vessel of yellow copper, having the impression of a seal upon its leaden cover.

This turn of fortune rejoiced him. "I will sell it," said he, "to the smelter, and with the money buy a measure of corn."

He examined the vessel on all sides, and shook it, to see if its contents made any noise, but heard nothing. This circumstance, together with the impression of the seal upon the

leaden cover, made him think it enclosed something precious. To satisfy himself, he took his knife and pried open the lid. He turned the mouth downward, but to his surprise, nothing came out. He placed it before him, and while he sat gazing at it attentively, there came forth a very thick smoke, which obliged him to retire two or three paces.

The smoke ascended to the clouds, and, extending itself along the sea and upon the shore, formed a great mist which we may well imagine filled the fisherman with astonishment. When the smoke was all out of the vessel, it re-formed, and became a solid mass, which changed before his eyes into a genie twice as high as the greatest of giants. At the sight of such a monster, the fisherman would fain have fled, but was so frightened that he could not move.

The genie regarded the fisherman with a fierce look, and exclaimed in a terrible voice, "Prepare to die, for I will surely kill thee."

"Ah!" replied the fisherman, "why would you kill me? Did I not just now set you at liberty, and have you already forgotten my kindness?"

"Yes, I remember it," said the genie, "but that shall not save thy life. I have only one favor to grant thee."

"And what is that?" asked the fisherman.

"It is," answered the genie, "to give thee thy choice, in what manner thou wouldst have me put thee to death."

"But wherein have I offended you?" demanded the fisherman. "Is that your reward for the service I have rendered you?"

"I cannot treat thee otherwise," said the genie. "And that thou mayest know the reason, hearken to my story.

"I am one of those rebellious spirits that opposed the will of Heaven.

"Solomon, the son of David, commanded me to acknowledge his power, and to submit to his commands. I refused, and told him I would rather expose myself to his resentment than swear fealty as he required. To punish me, he shut me up in this copper vessel. And that I might not break my prison, he himself stamped upon this leaden cover his seal with the great name of God engraved upon it. He then gave the vessel to a genie, with orders to throw me into the sea.

"During the first hundred years of my imprisonment, I swore that if anyone should deliver me before the expiration of that period I would make him rich. During the second, I made an oath that I would open all the treasures of the earth to anyone that might set me at liberty. In the third, I promised to make my deliverer a potent monarch, to be always near him in spirit and to grant him every day three requests, of whatsoever nature they might be. At last, being angry to find myself a prisoner so long, I swore that if anyone should deliver me I would kill him without mercy, and grant him no other favor than to choose the manner of his death. And therefore, since thou hast delivered me today, I give thee that choice."

The fisherman was extremely grieved, not so much for himself, as on account of his three children; and bewailed the misery to which they must be reduced by his death. He endeavored to appease the genie, and said, "Alas! be pleased to take pity on me in consideration of the service I have done you."

"I have told thee already," replied the genie, "it is for that very reason I must kill thee. Do not lose time. All thy reasonings shall not divert me from my purpose. Make haste, and tell me what manner of death thou preferrest?"

Necessity is the mother of invention. The fisherman bethought himself of a stratagem. "Since I must die then," said he to the genie, "I submit to the will of Heaven. But before I choose the manner of my death, I conjure you by the great name which was engraved upon the seal of the prophet Solomon, the son of David, to answer me truly the question I am going to ask you."

The genie, finding himself obliged to make a positive answer by this adjuration, trembled. Then he replied to the fisherman, "Ask what thou wilt, but make haste."

"I wish to know," asked the fisherman, "if you were actually in this vessel. Dare you swear it by the name of the great God?"

"Yes," replied the genie, "I do swear, by that great name, that I was."

"In good faith," answered the fisherman, "I cannot believe you. The vessel is not capable of holding one of your stature, and how is it possible that your whole body could lie in it?"

"Is it possible," replied the genie, "that thou dost not believe me after the solemn oath I have taken?"

"Truly not I," said the fisherman. "Nor will I believe you, unless you go into the vessel again."

Thereupon the body of the genie dissolved and changed itself into smoke, extending as before upon the seashore. And at last, being collected, it began to re-enter the vessel, which it continued to do till no part remained outside. Immediately the fisherman took the cover of lead, and speedily replaced it on the vessel.

"Genie," cried he, "now it is your turn to beg my favor. But I shall throw you into the sea, whence I took you. Then I will build a house upon the shore, where I will reside and give

notice to all fishermen who come to throw in their nets, to beware of such a wicked genie as you are, who has made an oath to kill the person who sets you at liberty."

The genie began to plead with the fisherman. "Open the vessel," said he, "give me my liberty, and I promise to satisfy thee to thy own content."

"You are a traitor," replied the fisherman. "I should deserve to lose my life if I were such a fool as to trust you. You would not fail to treat me in the same manner as a certain Grecian King treated the physician Douban. It is a story I have a mind to tell you. Therefore listen to it."

The Story of the King and the Physician

THERE WAS once a King who suffered from leprosy, and his physicians had in vain endeavored his cure; when a very able physician, named Douban, arrived at his court.

He was an experienced natural philosopher, and fully understood the good and bad qualities of plants and drugs. As soon as he was informed of the King's distemper, and understood that his physicians had given him up, he found means to present himself before the throne. "I know," said he, after the usual ceremonials, "that your Majesty's physicians have not been able to heal you of the leprosy. But if you will accept my service, I will engage to cure you without potions, or external applications."

The King answered, "If you are able to perform what you promise, I will enrich you and your posterity. You may make the trial."

The physician returned to his quarters, made a hollow mace, and in the handle he put drugs. He made also a ball

in such a manner as suited his purpose, with which next morning he presented himself before the King, and said to him, "Let your Majesty take horse, and exercise yourself with this mace, and strike the ball until you find your hands and body perspire. When the medicine I have put up in the handle of the mace is heated by your hand, it will penetrate your whole body. And as soon as you perspire, you may leave off the exercise, for then the medicine will have had its effect. Immediately on your return to your palace, go into the bath, and cause yourself to be well washed and rubbed. Then retire to bed, and when you rise tomorrow you will find yourself cured."

The King took the mace, and struck the ball, which was returned by his officers who played with him. He played so long, that his hands and his whole body were in a sweat, and then the medicine shut up in the handle of the mace operated as the physician had said. Thereupon the King left off play, returned to his palace, entered the bath, and observed very exactly what his physician had prescribed to him.

The next morning when he arose, he perceived with equal wonder and joy that his leprosy was cured, and his body as clean as if it had never been affected. As soon as he was dressed, he came into the hall of audience, where he ascended his throne, and showed himself to his courtiers. They, eager to know the success of the new medicine, gathered round the throne, and, when they saw the King perfectly cured, expressed great joy. The physician Douban, entering the hall, bowed himself before the throne, with his face to the ground. The King, perceiving him, made him sit down by his side, presented him to the assembly, and gave him all the commendation he deserved. His Majesty did not stop here, but daily showered upon him marks of his esteem.

Now this King had a Vizier, who was avaricious, envious, and naturally capable of every kind of mischief. He could not behold without envy the presents that were given to the

physician, and he therefore resolved to lessen him in the King's esteem. "Sire," said he to the King, "are you wise in allowing about your person a man who, for aught you know, may have been sent here by your enemies to attempt your life?"

"No, no, Vizier," interrupted the King, "I am certain that this physician, whom you suspect of being a villain and a traitor, is one of the best and most virtuous of men. You know he cured me of my leprosy. If he had had a design upon my life, why did he save me then? He needed only to have left me to my disease. I perceive it to be his virtue that raises your envy. But do not think I will be prejudiced against him."

"He has cured you, you say. But, alas! who can assure you of that? Who knows but the medicine he has given you may in time have pernicious effects?"

The King was not able to discover the wicked design of his Vizier, nor had he firmness enough to persist in his first opinion. This discourse staggered him. "Vizier," said he, "thou art in the right. The stranger may be come on purpose to take away my life, which he may easily do by his drugs."

When he had spoken thus, he called for one of his officers, and ordered him to go for the physician; who, knowing nothing of the King's purpose, came to the palace in haste.

"Knowest thou," said the King, when he saw him, "why I sent for thee?"

"No, sire," answered he; "I wait till your Majesty be pleased to inform me."

"I sent for thee," replied the King, "to rid myself of thee by taking away thy life."

No man can express the surprise of the physician, when he heard these words. "Sire," said he, "why would your Majesty take my life? What crime have I committed?"

"I am informed," replied the King, "that you came to my court only to attempt my life. But to prevent you, I will be sure of yours. Give the blow," said he to the executioner, who

was present, "and deliver me from a perfidious wretch, who came hither on purpose to assassinate me."

When the physician heard this cruel order, he readily judged that the honors and presents he had received from the King had procured him enemies, and that the weak prince had been imposed on. He repented that he had cured the leper of his leprosy; but it was now too late. "Is it thus," asked the physician, "that you reward me for curing you? Alas, sire," cried he, "prolong my days, and God will prolong yours. Do not put me to death, lest God treat you in the same manner."

The King cruelly replied, "No, no; I must of necessity cut you off, otherwise you may assassinate with as much art as you cured me."

The physician, without bewailing his fate for being so ill rewarded by the King, prepared for death. The executioner tied his hands, and was going to draw his scimitar when the physician addressed himself once more to the King. "Sire," said he, "since your Majesty will not revoke the sentence of death, I beg, at least, that you would give me leave to return to my house, to give orders about my burial, to bid farewell to my family, to give alms, and to bequeath my books to those who are capable of making good use of them. I have one particularly I would present to your Majesty. It is a very precious book, and worthy of being laid up carefully in your treasury."

"What is it," demanded the King, "that makes it so valuable?"

"Sire," replied the physician, "it possesses many singular and curious properties, of which the chief is, that if your Majesty will give yourself the trouble to open it at the sixth leaf, and read the third line of the left page, my head, after being cut off, will answer all the questions you ask of it."

The King, being curious, deferred his death till the next day, and sent him home under a strong guard.

The physician, during that time, put his affairs in order. Meanwhile, a report being spread that an unheard-of miracle was to happen after his death, the Viziers, Emirs, officers of

the guard, and, in a word, the whole court, repaired next day to the hall of audience, that they might be witnesses of it.

The physician Douban, was brought in, and advancing to the foot of the throne, with a book in his hand, he called for a basin, and laid upon it the cover in which the book was wrapped. Then presenting the book to the King, he said, "Take this, and after my head is cut off, order that it be put into the basin upon that cover. As soon as it is placed there, the blood will stop flowing. Then open the book, and my head will answer your questions. But permit me once more to implore your Majesty's clemency. I protest to you that I am innocent."

"Your prayers," answered the King, "are in vain. And were it for nothing but to hear your head speak after your death, it is my will you should die." As he said this, he took the book out of the physician's hand, and ordered the executioner to do his duty.

The head was so dexterously cut off that it fell into the basin, and was no sooner laid upon the cover of the book than the blood stopped flowing. Then, to the great surprise of the King, and all the spectators, it opened its eyes, and said, "Sire, will your Majesty be pleased to open the book?" The King proceeded to do so. But finding that the leaves adhered to each other, in order that he might turn them with more ease, he put his finger to his mouth and wetted it. He did this till he came to the sixth leaf, and finding no writing on the place where he desired to look for it, he said, "Physician, there is nothing written here."

"Turn over some more leaves," replied the head.

The King went on, putting always his finger to his mouth, until he found himself suddenly taken with an extraordinary fit. His eyesight failed, and he fell down at the foot of the throne in violent convulsions.

When the physician Douban, or rather his head, saw that the poison had taken effect and that the King had but a few moments to live, it cried, "Tyrant, now you see how princes

are treated, who, abusing their authority, cut off the heads of innocent men. God punishes soon or late their injustice and cruelty." Scarcely had the head spoken these words, when the King fell down dead, and the head itself lost what life it had.

As soon as the fisherman had concluded the history of the Greek King and his physician Douban, he applied it to the genie, whom he still kept shut up in the vessel. "If the King," said he, "had suffered the physician to live, God would have continued his life also. The case is the same with you, O genie. But I am obliged, in my turn, to be equally hardhearted with you."

"Hear me one word more," cried the genie. "I promise to do thee no hurt. Nay, far from that, I will show thee a way to become exceedingly rich."

The hope of delivering himself from poverty prevailed with the fisherman. "I could listen to you," said he, "were there any credit to be given to your word. Swear to me by the great name of God that you will faithfully perform what you promise, and I will open the vessel. I do not believe you will dare to break such an oath."

The genie gave the fisherman his oath, upon which the fisherman immediately took off the covering of the vessel, and at once the smoke ascended, and the genie having resumed his form, kicked the vessel into the sea.

"Be not afraid, fisherman," said the genie. "I only did it to see if thou wouldst be alarmed. But to convince thee that I am in earnest, take thy nets and follow me."

They passed by the town, and came to the top of a mountain, from whence they descended into a vast plain, which brought them to a lake, that lay betwixt four hills.

When they reached the side of the lake, the genie said to the fisherman, "Cast in thy nets, and catch fish."

The fisherman did not doubt of taking some, because he saw a great number in the water. But he was extremely surprised when he found they were of four colors, that is to say,

white, red, blue, and yellow. He threw in his nets, and brought out one of each color. Having never seen the like before, he could not but admire them, and, judging that he might get a considerable sum for them, he was very joyful.

"Carry those fish," said the genie to him, "and present them to thy Sultan. He will give thee much money for them. Thou mayest come every day to fish in this lake. But I give thee warning not to throw in thy nets more than once a day, otherwise thou wilt repent."

Having thus spoken, he struck his foot upon the ground, which opened, and after it had swallowed him up, closed again.

Further Adventures of the Fisherman and the Genie

THE FISHERMAN being resolved to follow the genie's advice, forbore casting in his nets a second time, and returned to the town very well satisfied. He went immediately to the Sultan's palace, to offer his fish.

The Sultan was much surprised when he saw the four fish which the fisherman presented. He took them up one after another, and viewed them with attention. After having admired them a long time, he said to his Vizier, "Take these fish and carry them to the cook; I am sure that they must be as good as they are beautiful. And give the fisherman four hundred pieces of gold."

The fisherman, who had never seen so much money, could scarcely believe his good fortune, but thought the whole must be a dream, until he found it otherwise, by being able to provide necessities for his family.

As soon as the cook had cleaned the fish, she put them upon the fire in a frying pan, with oil, and when she thought

them fried enough on one side, she turned them upon the other. But, miracle of miracles, scarcely were they turned, when the wall of the kitchen divided, and a young lady of wondrous beauty entered through the opening. She was clad in flowered satin, with pendants in her ears, a necklace of large pearls about her throat, and bracelets of gold set with rubies about her wrists, and with a rod in her hand. She moved toward the frying pan, to the great amazement of the cook, who continued to be transfixed by the sight. And striking one of the fish with the end of the rod, she said, "Fish, fish, are you in duty?" The fish having answered nothing, she repeated these words, and then the four fish lifted up their heads, and replied, "Yes, yes, if you reckon, we reckon; if you pay your debts, we pay ours; if you fly, we overcome, and are content." As soon as they had finished these words, the lady overturned the frying pan, and returned into the open part of the wall which closed immediatly, and became as it was before.

The cook was greatly frightened at what had happened. But recovering somewhat she stooped to take up the fish that had fallen on the hearth, only to find them blacker than coal, and not fit to be carried to the Sultan. "Alas!" said she, "what will become of me? If I tell the Sultan what I have seen, I am sure he will not believe me, but will be greatly angered with me."

While she was thus bewailing herself, the Grand Vizier entered, and asked her if the fish were ready. She told him all that had occurred, which we may easily imagine caused him to be astonished. But without speaking a word of it to the Sultan, he invented an excuse that satisfied him, and sending immediately for the fisherman, bade him bring four more such fish, which the fisherman promised to do on the morrow.

Accordingly the fisherman threw in his nets early the next morning, took four fish like the former, and brought them to the Vizier at the hour appointed. The minister took them

himself, carried them to the kitchen, and shut himself up with the cook. She cleaned them, and put them on the fire, as she had done with the four others the day before. And when they were fried on one side, and she had turned them upon the other, the Vizier became a witness to the same events as the cook had narrated to him.

"This is too wonderful and extraordinary," said he, "to be concealed from the Sultan. I will inform him of this miracle."

The Sultan, being much surprised, sent immediately for the fisherman, and said to him, "Friend, cannot you bring me four more such fish?"

The fisherman replied, "If your Majesty will be pleased to allow me until tomorrow, I will do it." On the morrow he caught four fish, and brought them to the Sultan, who was so much rejoiced that he ordered the fisherman four hundred pieces of gold. The Sultan had the fish carried into his closet, with all that was necessary for frying them. And having shut himself up with the Vizier, the minister put them into the pan, and when they were fried on one side, turned them upon the other. Then the wall of the closet opened, but instead of the young lady, there came out a black, in the habit of a slave, and of gigantic stature, with a great green staff in his hand. He advanced toward the pan, and touching one of the fish with his staff, said in a terrible voice, "Fish, are you in your duty?" At these words, the fish raised up their heads, and answered, "Yes, yes, we are. If you reckon, we reckon; if you pay your debts, we pay ours; if you fly, we overcome, and are content."

The fish had no sooner finished these words, than the black threw the pan into the middle of the closet, and reduced the fish to a coal. Having done this, he retired fiercely, and entering again into the aperture, it closed, and the wall appeared just as it did before.

"After what I have seen," said the Sultan to the Vizier, "it will not be possible for me to be easy. These fish, without

doubt, signify something extraordinary." He sent for the fisherman, and on hearing where the fish had been caught, he commanded all his court to take horse, and the fisherman served them for a guide. They all ascended the mountain, and at the foot of it they saw, to their great surprise, a vast plain, that nobody had observed till then, and at last they came to the lake, which they found to be situated betwixt four hills as the fisherman had described. The water was so transparent that they observed all the fish to be exactly like those which the fisherman had brought to the palace.

The Sultan stood upon the bank of the lake, beholding the fish with admiration. On his demanding of his courtiers, if it were possible they had never seen this lake, which was within so short a distance of the town, they all answered, that they had never so much as heard of it.

"Since you all agree that you never heard of it, and as I am no less astonished than you are at this novelty, I am resolved not to return to my palace till I learn how this lake came here, and why all the fish in it are of four colors." Having spoken thus, he ordered his court to encamp; and immediately his pavilion and the tents of his household were planted upon the banks of the lake.

Resolved to withdraw alone from the camp to discover the secret of the portents that so disturbed his mind, the Sultan bade his Grand Vizier inform the court that illness accounted for his absence until such time as he should return.

The Grand Vizier endeavored to divert the Sultan from his design. But all to no purpose; the Sultan was resolved. He put on a suit fit for walking, and took his scimitar. And as soon as he found that all was quiet in the camp, he went out alone. As the sun arose, he saw before him, at a considerable distance, a vast building of black polished marble, covered with fine steel, as smooth as glass. Being highly pleased that he had so speedily met with something worthy of his curiosity, he advanced toward the gate, which was partially open.

Though he might immediately have entered, yet he thought it best to knock. This he did again and again, but no one appearing, he was exceedingly surprised.

At last he entered, and when he came within the porch, he cried, "Is there no one here to receive a stranger, who comes in for some refreshment as he passes by?" But though he spoke very loud, he was not answered. The silence increased his astonishment. Soon he came into a spacious court, and looked on every side for inhabitants, but discovered none.

He then entered several grand halls, which were hung with silk tapestry, the alcoves and sofas being covered with stuffs of Mecca, and the porches with the richest stuffs of India, mixed with gold and silver. He came next into a superb saloon, in the middle of which was a fountain, with a lion of solid gold at each angle.

The castle, on three sides, was encompassed by a garden, with parterres of flowers and shrubberies. And to complete the beauty of the place, an infinite number of birds filled the air with their harmonious notes. The Sultan walked from apartment to apartment, where he found everything rich and magnificent. Being tired with walking, he sat down in a veranda, which had a view over the garden. Suddenly he heard the voice of one complaining, in lamentable tones. He listened with attention, and heard these words: "O fortune! thou who wouldst not suffer me long to enjoy a happy lot, forbear to persecute me, and by a speedy death put an end to my sorrows."

The Sultan rose up, advanced toward the place whence came the voice, and opening the door of a great hall, pushed aside a curtain. A handsome young man, richly habited, was seated upon a throne. Melancholy was depicted on his countenance. The Sultan drew near, and saluted him. The young man returned his salutation, by an inclination of his head, at the same time saying, "My lord, I should rise to receive you; but I am hindered by sad necessity, and therefore hope you will not be offended."

"My lord," replied the Sultan, "I am much obliged to you for having so good an opinion of me. As to the reason for your not rising, whatever your apology be, I heartily accept it. Being drawn hither by your complaints, I come to offer you my help. Would to God that it lay in my power to ease you of your trouble! Relate to me the history of your misfortunes. But inform me first of the meaning of the lake near the palace, where the fish are of four colors. To whom belongs this castle? How came you to be here? Why you are alone?"

Instead of answering these questions, the young man began to weep bitterly. "How inconstant is fortune!" cried he; "she takes pleasure to pull down those she has raised. How is it possible that I should grieve, and my eyes be inexhaustible fountains of tears?" At these words, lifting up his robe, he showed the Sultan that he was a man only from the head to the girdle, and that the other half of his body was black marble.

You may easily imagine that the Sultan was much surprised when he saw the deplorable condition of the young man. "That which you show me," said he, "while it fills me with horror, excites my curiosity, so that I am impatient to hear your history. And I am persuaded that the lake and the fish make some part in it. Therefore I conjure you to relate it."

"I will not refuse your request," replied the young man, "though I cannot comply without renewing my grief." Thereupon he narrated:

The Story of the Young King of the Black Isles

YOU MUST know, my lord, that my father, named Mahmoud, was King of this country. This is the kingdom of the Black Isles, which takes its name from the four small neighboring mountains. For those mountains were formerly isles. The capital was on the spot now occupied by the lake you have seen.

The King my father died when he was seventy years of age. I had no sooner succeeded him than I married my cousin. At first nothing could surpass the harmony and pleasure of our union. This lasted five years, at the end of which time I perceived she ceased to delight in my attentions.

One day, after dinner, while she was at the bath, I lay down upon a sofa. Two of her ladies came and sat down, one at my head, and the other at my feet, with fans in their hands to moderate the heat, and to prevent the flies from disturbing me. They thought I was asleep, and spoke in whispers. But as I only closed my eyes, I heard all their conversation.

One of them said to the other, "Is not the Queen wrong, not to love so amiable a prince?" "Certainly," replied the other; "I do not understand the reason, neither can I perceive why she goes out every night, and leaves him alone. Is it possible that he does not perceive it?" "Alas," said the first, "how should he? She mixes every evening in his liquor the juice of a certain herb, which makes him sleep so sound all night that she has time to go where she pleases, and as day begins to appear she comes and lies down by him again, and wakes him by the smell of something she puts under his nostrils."

You may guess, my lord, how much I was surprised at this conversation. I had, however, self-control enough to dissemble and feign to awake without having heard a word.

The Queen returned from the bath. We supped together, and she presented me with a cup full of such water as I was accustomed to drink. But instead of putting it to my mouth, I went to a window that was open, and threw out the water so quickly that she did not perceive it, and returned.

Soon after, believing that I was asleep, she said, loud enough fo me to hear her distinctly, "Sleep on, and may you never wake again!" So saying, she dressed herself, and went out of the chamber.

No sooner was she gone than I dressed myself in haste, took my scimitar, and followed her so quickly that I soon heard the sound of her feet before me, and then walked softly after her, for fear of being heard. She passed through several gates, which opened upon her pronouncing some magical words, and the last she opened was that of the garden, which she entered. I stopped at this gate, that she might not perceive me, as she passed along a parterre. Then looking after her as far as the darkness of the night permitted, I saw her enter a little wood. I went thither by another way, and concealing myself, saw her walking there with a man.

I did not fail to lend the most attentive ear to their discourse, and heard her address herself thus to her gallant: "What proof of my devotion is lacking, that you doubt my

constancy? Bid me but do so, and before sunrise I will convert this great city, and this superb palace, into frightful ruins, inhabited only by wolves, owls, and ravens. Or would you have me transport all the stones of these walls, so solidly built, beyond Mount Caucasus, or the bounds of the habitable world? Speak but the word, and all shall be changed."

As the Queen finished these words, she and her lover turned and passed before me. I had already drawn my scimitar, and her lover being next me, I struck him to the ground. I concluded I had killed him, and therefore retired speedily without making myself known to the Queen.

The wound I had given her lover was mortal. But by her enchantments she preserved him in an existence in which he could not be said to be either dead or alive. As I crossed the garden to return to the palace, I heard the Queen loudly lamenting, and judging by her cries how much she was grieved, I was pleased that I had spared her life.

As soon as I had reached my apartment, I went to bed, and being satisfied with having punished the villain who had injured me, fell asleep; and when I awoke next morning, found the Queen lying by me.

I cannot tell you whether she slept or not. But I arose, went to my closet, and dressed myself. I afterward held my council. At my return the Queen, clad in mourning, her hair disheveled, and part of it torn off, presented herself before me, and said, "I come to beg your Majesty not to be surprised to see me in this condition. My heavy affliction is occasioned by intelligence of three distressing events—the death of the Queen my dear mother, that of the King my father killed in battle, and of one of my brothers, who has fallen down a precipice."

I was not displeased that she used this pretext to conceal the true cause of her grief, and I concluded she had not suspected me of being the author of her lover's death. "Madam," said I, "so far from blaming, I assure you I heartily com-

miserate with you in your sorrow." I merely therefore expressed the hope that time and reflection would moderate her grief.

After a whole year's mourning, she begged permission to erect a burying place for herself, within the bounds of the palace, where she would continue, she told me, to the end of her days. I consented, and she built a stately edifice, and called it the Palace of Tears. When it was finished, she caused her lover to be conveyed thither. She had hitherto prevented his dying, by potions which she had administered to him; and she continued to convey them to him herself every day after he came to the Palace of Tears.

Yet, with all her enchantments, she could not cure him. He was not only unable to walk or support himself, but had also lost the use of his speech, and exhibited no sign of life except in his looks. Every day the Queen made him two long visits, a fact of which I was well apprised, but pretended ignorance.

One day, my curiosity inducing me to go to the Palace of Tears, I heard her thus address her lover: "I am afflicted to the highest degree to behold you in this condition; I am as sensible as yourself of the tormenting pain you endure; but, dear soul, I am continually speaking to you, and you do not answer me. How long will you remain silent? O tomb! hast thou destroyed that excess of affection which he bore me? Hast thou closed those eyes that evinced so much love, and were all my delight? No, no, this I cannot think. Tell me rather, by what miracle thou becamest the depository of the rarest treasure the world ever contained."

I must confess, my lord, I was enraged at these expressions, and apostrophizing the tomb in my turn, I cried, "O tomb! why dost not thou swallow up that monster so revolting to human nature, or rather why dost not thou swallow up both the lover and his mistress?"

I heard scarcely uttered these words, when the Queen rose up like a fury. "Miscreant!" said she, "thou art the cause of

my grief; do not think I am ignorant of this. I have dissembled too long." At the same time, she pronounced words I did not understand; and afterward added, "By virtue of my enchantments, I command thee to become half marble and half man."

Immediately, my lord, I became what you see, a dead man among the living, and a living man among the dead.

After this cruel sorceress unworthy of the name of Queen had metamorphosed me thus, and brought me into this hall, by another enchantment she destroyed my capital, which was very flourishing and populous. She annihilated the houses, the public places and markets, and reduced the site of the whole to the lake and desert plain you have seen. The fishes of four colors in the lake are the four kinds of inhabitants of different religions, which the city contained. The white are the Mussulmans; the red, the Persians, who worship fire; the blue, the Christians; and the yellow, the Jews. The four little hills were the four islands that gave name to this kingdom. But her revenge not being satisfied with the destruction of my dominions, and the metamorphosis of my person, she comes every day, and gives me over my naked shoulders a hundred lashes with a whip until I am covered with blood. When she has finished this part of my punishment, she throws over me a coarse stuff of goat's hair, and over that this robe of brocade, not to honor, but to mock me.

When he came to this part of his narrative, the Sultan, filled with righteous anger and anxious to revenge the sufferings of the unfortunate Prince, said to him, "Inform me whither this perfidious sorceress retires, and where may be found her vile paramour, who is entombed before his death."

"My lord," replied the Prince, "her lover, as I have already told you, is lodged in the Palace of Tears, in a superb tomb constructed in the form of a dome. This palace joins the castle on the side in which the gate is placed. Every day at sunrise the Queen goes to visit her paramour, after having exe-

cuted her bloody vengeance upon me. And you see I am not in a condition to defend myself."

"Prince," said the Sultan, "your condition can never be sufficiently deplored. It surpasses all that has hitherto been recorded. One thing only is wanting: the revenge to which you are entitled, and I will omit nothing in my power to effect it."

In subsequent conversation they agreed upon the measures they were to take for accomplishing their design for revenge, but deferred the execution of it till the following day.

The young Prince, as was his wont, passed the time in continual watchfulness, never having slept since he was enchanted.

The Sultan arose with the dawn, and proceeded to the Palace of Tears. He found it lighted up with an infinite number of flambeaux of white wax, and perfumed by a delicious scent issuing from several censers of fine gold of admirable workmanship. As soon as he perceived the bed where the black lay, he drew his scimitar, and without resistance deprived him of his wretched life, dragged his corpse into the court of the castle, and threw it into a well. After this, he went and lay down in the black's bed, placed his scimitar under the covering, and waited to complete his design.

The Queen arrived shortly after. She first went into the chamber of her husband, the King of the Black Isles, stripped him, and with unexampled barbarity gave him a hundred stripes.

She then put on again his covering of goat's hair, and his brocade gown over all. She went afterward to the Palace of Tears, and thus addressed herself to the person whom she conceived to be the black: "My sun, my life, will you always be silent? Are you resolved to let me die, without affording me the comfort of hearing again from your own lips that you love me? My soul, speak one word to me at least, I conjure you."

The Sultan, as if he had awaked out of a deep sleep, and

counterfeiting the pronunciation of the blacks, answered the Queen with a grave tone, "There is no strength or power but in God alone, who is almighty."

At these words the enchantress uttered a loud exclamation of joy. "My dear lord," cried she, "do not I deceive myself; is it certain that I hear you, and that you speak to me?"

"Unhappy woman," said the Sultan, "art thou worthy that I should answer thee?"

"Alas!" replied the Queen, "why do you reproach me thus?"

"The cries," returned the Sultan, "the groans and tears of thy husband, whom thou treatest every day with so much indignity and barbarity, prevent my sleeping night or day. Make haste to set him at liberty, that I be no longer disturbed by his lamentations."

The enchantress went immediately out of the Palace of Tears to fulfill these commands, and by the exercise of her spells soon restored to the young King his natural shape, bidding him, however, on pain of death, to be gone from her presence instantly. The young King, yielding to necessity, retired to a remote place, where he patiently awaited the fulfillment of the plan which the Sultan had so happily begun. Meanwhile, the enchantress returned to the Palace of Tears, and supposing that she still spoke to the black, assured him his behest had been obeyed.

The Sultan, still counterfeiting the pronunciation of the blacks, said, "What you have now done is by no means sufficient for my cure. Bethink thee of the town, the islands, and the inhabitants destroyed by thy fatal enchantments. The fish every night at midnight raise their heads out of the lake and cry for vengeance against thee and me. This is the true cause of the delay of my cure. Go speedily, restore things to their former state, and at thy return I will give thee my hand, and thou shalt help me to arise."

The enchantress, inspired with hope, lost no time, but betook herself in all haste to the brink of the lake, where she

took a little water in her hand, and sprinkling it, pronounced some word over the fish, whereupon the city was immediately restored. The fish became men, women, and children; Mohammedans, Christians, Persians, or Jews; freemen or slaves, as they were before: every one having recovered his natural form. The houses and shops were immediately filled with their inhabitants, who found all things as they were before the enchantment. The Sultan's numerous retinue, who found themselves encamped in the largest square, were astonished to see themselves in an instant in the middle of a large, handsome, well-peopled city.

As soon as the enchantress had effected this wonderful change, she returned with all expedition to the Palace of Tears, in order that she might receive her reward. "Come near," said the Sultan, still counterfeiting the pronunciation of the blacks. She did so. "You are not near enough," he continued; "approach nearer." She obeyed. He then rose up, and seizing her by the arm so suddenly that she had not time to discover him, he, with a blow of his scimitar, cut her in two, so that one half fell one way and the other another.

This done, he left the body on the spot, and going out of the Palace of Tears, went to seek the young King of the Black Isles. "Prince," said he, embracing him, "rejoice; you have now nothing to fear. Your cruel enemy is dead."

The young man returned thanks to the Sultan, and wished him long life and happiness. "You may henceforward," said the Sultan, "dwell peaceably in your capital, unless you will accompany me to mine, which is not above four or five hours' journey distant."

"Potent monarch," replied the Prince, "I do indeed believe that you came hither from your capital in the time you mention, because mine was enchanted. But since the enchantment is taken off, things are changed. It will take you no less than a year to return. However, this shall not prevent my following you, were it to the utmost corners of the earth."

The Sultan was extremely surprised to understand that he

was so far from his dominions, and could not imagine how it could be. "But," said he, "it is no matter. The trouble of returning to my own country is sufficiently recompensed by the satisfaction of having obliged you, and by acquiring you for a son. For since you will do me the honor to accompany me, as I have no child, I look upon you as such, and from this moment appoint you my heir and successor."

At length, the Sultan and the young Prince began their journey, with a hundred camels laden with inestimable riches from the treasury of the young King, followed by fifty handsome gentlemen on horseback, perfectly well mounted and dressed. The inhabitants came out in great crowds, received him with acclamations, and made public rejoicings for several days.

The day after his arrival the Sultan gave all his courtiers a complete account of the circumstances which, contrary to his expectations, had detained him so long. He informed them that he had adopted the King of the Four Black Isles, who was willing to leave a great kingdom, to accompany and live with him; and, in reward for their loyalty, he made each of them presents according to their rank.

As for the fisherman, as he was the first cause of the deliverance of the young Prince, the Sultan gave him a plentiful fortune, which made him and his family happy the rest of his days.

The Story of the Enchanted Horse

ON THE FESTIVAL of the Nooroze, which is the first day of the year and of spring, the Sultan of Shiraz was just concluding his public audience, when a Hindu appeared at the foot of the throne with an artificial horse, so spiritedly modeled that at first sight he was taken for a living animal.

The Hindu prostrated himself before the throne, and pointing to the horse, said to the Sultan, "This horse is a great wonder; if I wish to be transported to the most distant parts of the earth, I have only to mount him. I offer to show your Majesty this wonder if you command me."

The Sultan, who was very fond of everything that was curious, and who had never beheld or heard anything quite so strange as this, told the Hindu that he would like to see him perform what he had promised.

The Hindu at once put his foot into the stirrup, swung himself into the saddle, and asked the Sultan whither he wished him to go.

"Do you see yonder mountain?" said the Sultan, pointing to it. "Ride your horse there, and bring me a branch from the palm tree that grows at the foot of the hill."

No sooner had the Sultan spoken than the Hindu turned a peg, which was in the hollow of the horse's neck, just by the pommel of the saddle. Instantly the horse rose from the ground, and bore his rider into the air with the speed of lightning, to the amazement of the Sultan and all the spectators. Within less than a quarter of an hour they saw him returning with the palm branch in his hand. Alighting amidst the acclamations of the people, he dismounted and, approaching the throne, laid the palm branch at the Sultan's feet.

The Sultan, still marveling at this unheard-of sight, was filled with a great desire to possess the horse, and said to the Hindu, "I will buy him of you, if he is for sale."

"Sire," replied the Hindu, "there is only one condition on which I will part with my horse, namely, the hand of the Princess, your daughter, as my wife."

The courtiers surrounding the Sultan's throne could not restrain their laughter at the Hindu's extravagant proposal. But Prince Feroze Shah, the Sultan's eldest son, was very indignant. "Sire," said he, "I hope that you will at once refuse this impudent demand, and not allow this miserable juggler to flatter himself for a moment with the hope of a marriage with one of the most powerful houses in the world. Think what you owe to yourself and to your noble blood!"

"My son," replied the Sultan, "I will not grant him what he asks. But putting my daughter the Princess out of the question, I may make a different bargain with him. First, however, I wish you to examine the horse; try him yourself, and tell me what you think of him."

On hearing this the Hindu eagerly ran forward to help the Prince mount, and show him how to guide and manage the horse. But without waiting for the Hindu's assistance, the Prince mounted and turned the peg as he had seen the other do. Instantly the horse darted into the air, swift as an arrow shot from a bow; and in a few moments neither horse nor Prince could be seen. The Hindu, alarmed at what had happened, threw himself before the throne and begged the Sultan not to be angry.

"Your Majesty," he said, "saw as well as I with what speed the horse flew away. The surprise took away my power of speech. But even if I could have spoken to advise him, he was already too far away to hear me. There is still room to hope, however, that the Prince will discover that there is another peg, and as soon as he turns that, the horse will cease to rise, and will descend gently to the ground."

Notwithstanding these arguments the Sultan was much alarmed at his son's evident danger, and said to the Hindu, "Your head shall answer for my son's life, unless he returns safe in three months' time, or unless I hear that he is alive." He then ordered his officers to secure the Hindu and keep him a close prisoner; after which he retired to his palace, sorrowing that the Festival of Nooroze had ended so unluckily.

Meanwhile, the Prince was carried through the air with fearful rapidity. In less than an hour he had mounted so high that the mountains and plains below him all seemed to melt together. Then for the first time he began to think of returning, and to this end he began turning the peg, first one way and then the other, at the same time pulling upon the bridle. But when he found that the horse continued to ascend he was greatly alarmed, and deeply repented of his folly in not learning to guide the horse before he mounted. He now began to examine the horse's head and neck very carefully, and discovered behind the right ear a second peg, smaller than the first. He turned this peg and presently felt that he was descending in the same oblique manner as he had mounted, but not so swiftly.

Night was already approaching when the Prince discovered and turned the small peg; and as the horse descended he gradually lost sight of the sun's last setting rays, until presently it was quite dark. He was obliged to let the bridle hang loose, and wait patiently for the horse to choose his own landing place, whether it might be in the desert, in the river or in the sea.

At last, about midnight, the horse stopped upon solid ground, and the Prince dismounted, faint with hunger, for he

had eaten nothing since the morning. He found himself on the terrace of a magnificent palace; and groping about, he presently reached a staircase which led down into an apartment, the door of which was half open.

The Prince stopped and listened at the door, then advanced cautiously into the room, and by the light of a lamp saw a number of black slaves, sleeping with their naked swords beside them. This was evidently the guard chamber of some Sultan or Princess. Advancing on tiptoe, he drew aside the curtain and saw a magnificent chamber, containing many beds, one of which was placed higher than the others on a raised dais—evidently the beds of the Princess and her women. He crept softly toward the dais, and beheld a beauty so extraordinary that he was charmed at the first sight. He fell on his knees and gently twitched the sleeve of the Princess, who opened her eyes and was greatly surprised to see a handsome young man bending over her, yet showed no sign of fear. The Prince rose to his feet, and, bowing to the ground, said:

"Beautiful Princess, through a most extraordinary adventure you see at your feet a suppliant Prince, son of the Sultan of Persia, who prays for your assistance and protection."

In answer to this appeal of Prince Feroze Shah, the beautiful Princess said:

"Prince, you are not in a barbarous country, but in the kingdom of the Rajah of Bengal. This is his country estate, and I am his eldest daughter. I grant you the protection that you ask, and you may depend upon my word."

The Prince of Persia would have thanked the Princess, but she would not let him speak. "Impatient though I am," said she, "to know by what miracle you have come here from the capital of Persia, and by what enchantment you escaped the watchfulness of my guards, yet I will restrain my curiosity until later, after you have rested from your fatigue."

The Princess' women were much surprised to see a Prince in her bedchamber, but they at once prepared to obey her command, and conducted him into a handsome apartment.

Here, while some prepared the bed, others brought and served a welcome and bountiful supper.

The next day the Princess prepared to receive the Prince, and took more pains in dressing and adorning herself than she ever had done before. She decked her neck, head and arms with the finest diamonds she possessed, and clothed herself in the richest fabric of the Indies, of a most beautiful color, and made only for Kings, Princes and Princesses. After once more consulting her glass, she sent word to the Prince of Persia that she would receive him.

The Prince, who had just finished dressing when he received the Princess' message, hastened to avail himself of the honor conferred on him. He told her of the wonders of the Enchanted Horse, of his wonderful journey through the air, and of the means by which he had gained entrance to her chamber. Then, after thanking her for her kind reception, he expressed a wish to return home and relieve the anxiety of the Sultan his father. The Princess replied:

"I cannot approve, Prince, of your leaving so soon. Grant me the favor of a somewhat longer visit, so that you may take back to the court of Persia a better account of what you have seen in the Kingdom of Bengal."

The Prince could not well refuse the Princess this favor, after the kindness she had shown him; and she busied herself with plans for hunting parties, concerts and magnificent feasts to render his stay agreeable.

For two whole months the Prince of Persia abandoned himself entirely to the will of the Princess, who seemed to think that he had nothing to do but pass his whole life with her. But at last he declared that he could stay no longer, and begged leave to return to his father.

"And, Princess," he added, "if I were not afraid of giving offense, I would ask the favor of taking you along with me."

The Princess made no answer to this address of the Prince of Persia; but her silence and downcast eyes told him plainly that she had no reluctance to accompany him. Her only fear,

she confessed, was that the Prince might not know well enough how to govern the horse. But the Prince soon removed her fear by assuring her that after the experience he had had, he defied the Hindu himself to manage the horse better. Accordingly they gave all their thoughts to planning how to get away secretly from the palace, without anyone having a suspicion of their design.

The next morning, a little before daybreak, when all the attendants were still asleep, they made their way to the terrace of the palace. The Prince turned the horse toward Persia, and as soon as the Princess had mounted behind him and was well settled with her arms about his waist, he turned the peg, whereupon the horse mounted into the air with his accustomed speed, and in two hours' time they came in sight of the Persian capital.

Instead of alighting at the palace, the Prince directed his course to a kiosk a little distance outside the city. He led the Princess into a handsome apartment, ordered the attendants to provide her with whatever she needed, and told her that he would return immediately after informing his father of their arrival. Thereupon he ordered a horse to be brought and set out for the palace.

The Sultan received his son with tears of joy, and listened eagerly while the Prince related his adventures during his flight through the air, his kind reception at the palace of the Princess of Bengal, and his long stay there due to their mutual affection. He added that, having promised to marry her, he had persuaded her to accompany him to Persia. "I brought her with me on the Enchanted Horse," he concluded, "and left her in your summer palace till I could return and assure her of your consent."

Upon on hearing these words, the Sultan embraced his son a second time, and said to him, "My son, I not only consent to your marriage with the Princess of Bengal, but will myself go and bring her to the palace, and your wedding shall be celebrated this very day."

The Sultan now ordered that the Hindu should be released from prison and brought before him. When this was done, the Sultan said, "I held you prisoner that your life might answer for that of the Prince, my son. Thanks be to God, he has returned in safety. Go, take your horse, and never let me see your face again."

The Hindu had learned of those who brought him from prison, all about the Princess whom Prince Feroze Shah had brought with him and left at the kiosk, and at once he began to think of revenge. He mounted his horse and flew directly to the kiosk, where he told the Captain of the Guard that he came with orders to conduct the Princess of Bengal through the air to the Sultan, who awaited her in the great square of his palace.

The Captain of the Guard, seeing that the Hindu had been released from prison, believed his story. And the Princess at once consented to do what the Prince, as she thought, desired of her.

The Hindu, overjoyed at the ease with which his wicked plan was succeeding, mounted his horse, took the Princess up behind him, turned the peg, and instantly the horse mounted up into the air.

Meanwhile, the Sultan of Persia, attended by his court, was on the road to the kiosk where the Princess of Bengal had been left, while the Prince himself had hurried on ahead to prepare the Princess to receive his father. Suddenly the Hindu, to brave them both, and avenge himself for the ill-treatment he had received, appeared over their heads with his prize.

When the Sultan saw the Hindu, his surprise and anger were all the more keen because it was out of his power to punish his outrageous act. He could only stand and hurl a thousand maledictions at him, as did also the courtiers who had witnessed this unequaled piece of insolence. But the grief of Prince Feroze Shah was indescribable, when he beheld the Hindu bearing away the Princess whom he loved so passion-

ately. He made his way, melancholy and brokenhearted, to the kiosk where he had last taken leave of the Princess. Here, the Captain of the Guard, who had already learned of the Hindu's treachery, threw himself at the Prince's feet, and condemned himself to die by his own hand, because of his fatal credulity.

"Rise," said the Prince, "I blame, not you, but my own want of precaution, for the loss of my Princess. But lose no time, bring me a dervish's robe, and take care that you give no hint that it is for me."

When the Captain of the Guard had procured the dervish's robe, the Prince at once disguised himself in it, and taking with him a box of jewels, left the palace, resolved not to return until he had found his Princess or perish in the attempt.

Meanwhile, the Hindu, mounted on his Enchanted Horse, with the Princess behind him, arrived at the capital of the Kingdom of Cashmere. He did not enter the city, but alighted in a wood, and left the Princess on a grassy spot close to a rivulet of fresh water, while he went to seek food. On his return, and after he and the Princess had partaken of refreshment, he began to maltreat the Princess, because she refused to become his wife.

Now it happened that the Sultan of Cashmere and his court were passing through the wood on their return from hunting, and hearing a woman's voice calling for help, went to her rescue. The Hindu with great impudence asked what business anyone had to interfere, since the lady was his wife! Whereupon the Princess cried out:

"My Lord, whoever you are whom Heaven has sent to my assistance, have compassion on me! I am a Princess. This Hindu is a wicked magician who has forced me away from the Prince of Persia, whom I was to marry, and has brought me hither on the Enchanted Horse that you see there."

The Princess' beauty, majestic air, and tears all declared that she spoke the truth. Justly enraged at the Hindu's insolence, the Sultan of Cashmere ordered his guards to seize him

and strike off his head, which sentence was immediately carried out.

The Princess' joy was unbounded at finding herself rescued from the wicked Hindu. She supposed that the Sultan of Cashmere would at once restore her to the Prince of Persia, but she was much deceived in these hopes. For her rescuer had resolved to marry her himself the next day, and issued a proclamation commanding the general rejoicing of the inhabitants.

The Princess of Bengal was awakened at break of day by drums and trumpets and sounds of joy throughout the palace, but was far from guessing the true cause. When the Sultan came to wait upon her, he explained that these rejoicings were in honor of their marriage, and begged her to consent to the union. On hearing this the Princess fainted away.

The serving-women who were present ran to her assistance, but it was long before they could bring her back to consciousness. When at last she recovered, she resolved that sooner than be forced to marry the Sultan of Cashmere she would pretend that she had gone mad. Accordingly she began to talk wildly, and show other signs of a disordered mind, even springing from her seat as if to attack the Sultan, so that he became greatly alarmed and sent for all the court physicians to ask if they could cure her of her disease.

When he found that his court physicians could not cure her, he sent for the most famous doctors in his kingdom, who had no better success. Next, he sent word to the courts of neighboring Sultans with promises of generous reward to anyone who could cure her malady. Physicians arrived from all parts, and tried their skill, but none could boast of success.

Meanwhile, Prince Feroze Shah, disguised as a dervish, traveled through many provinces and towns, everywhere inquiring about his lost Princess. At last in a certain city of Hindustan he learned of a Princess of Bengal who had gone mad on the day of her intended marriage with the Sultan of Cashmere. Convinced that there could be but one Princess of Ben-

gal, he hastened to the capital of Cashmere and upon arriving was told the story of the Princess, and the fate of the Hindu magician. The Prince was now convinced that he had at last found the beloved object of his long search.

Providing himself with the distinctive dress of a physician, he went boldly to the palace and announced his wish to be allowed to attempt the cure of the Princess. Since it was now some time since any physician had offered himself, the Sultan had begun to lose hope of ever seeing the Princess cured, though he still wished to marry her. So he at once ordered the new physician to be brought before him; and upon the Prince being admitted, told him that the Princess could not bear the sight of a physician without falling into the most violent paroxysms. Accordingly he conducted the Prince to a closet from which he might see her through a lattice without himself being seen. There Feroze Shah beheld his lovely Princess sitting in hopeless sorrow, the tears flowing from her beautiful eyes, while she sang a plaintive air deploring her unhappy fate. Upon leaving the closet, the Prince told the Sultan that he had assured himself that the Princess' complaint was not incurable, but that if he was to aid her he must speak with her in private and alone.

The Sultan ordered the Princess' chamber door to be opened, and Feroze Shah went in. Immediately the Princess resorted to her old practice of meeting physicians with threats, and indications of attacking them. But Feroze Shah came close to her and said in so low a voice that only she could hear, "Princess, I am not a physician, but Feroze Shah, and have come to obtain your liberty."

The Princess, who knew the sound of his voice, and recognized him, notwithstanding he had let his beard grow so long, grew calm at once, and was filled with secret joy at the unexpected sight of the Prince she loved. After they had briefly informed each other of all that had happened since their separation, the Prince asked if she knew what had become of the horse after the death of the Hindu magician. She replied that

she did not know, but suppposed that he was carefully guarded as a curiosity. Feroze Shah then told the Princess that he intended to obtain and use the horse to convey them both back to Persia; and they planned together, as the first step to this end, that the Princess the next day should receive the Sultan.

On the following day the Sultan was overjoyed to find that the Princess' cure was apparently far advanced, and regarded the Prince as the greatest physician in the world. The Prince of Persia, who accompanied the Sultan on his visit to the Princess, inquired of him how she had come into the Kingdom of Cashmere from her far-distant country.

The Sultan then repeated the story of the Hindu magician, adding that the Enchanted Horse was kept safely in his treasury as a great curiosity, though he knew not how to use it.

"Sire," replied the pretended physician, "this information affords me a means of curing the Princess. When she was brought hither on the Enchanted Horse, she contracted part of the enchantment, which can be dispelled only by a certain incense of which I have knowledge. Let the horse be brought tomorrow into the great square before the palace, and leave the rest to me. I promise to show you and all your assembled people, in a few moments' time, the Princess of Bengal completely restored in body and mind. But to assure the success of what I propose, the Princess must be dressed as magnificently as possible and adorned with the most valuable jewels in your treasury."

All this the Sultan eagerly promised, for he would have undertaken far more difficult things to assure his marriage with the Princess.

The next day the Enchanted Horse was taken from the treasury and brought to the great square before the palace. The rumor of something extraordinary having spread through the town, crowds of people flocked thither from all sides. The Sultan of Cashmere, surrounded by his nobles and ministers of state, occupied a gallery erected for the purpose. The Princess of Bengal, attended by her ladies in waiting, went up to

the Enchanted Horse, and the women helped her to mount. The pretended physician then placed around the horse many vessels full of burning charcoal, into which he cast handfuls of incense. After which, he ran three times about the horse, pretending to utter certain magic words. The pots sent forth a dark cloud of smoke that surrounded the Princess, so that neither she nor the horse could be seen. The Prince mounted nimbly behind her and turned the peg; and as the horse rose with them into the air, the Sultan distinctly heard these words, "Sultan of Cashmere, when you would marry Princesses who implore your protection, learn first to obtain their consent!"

Thus the Prince delivered the Princess of Bengal, and carried her that same day to the capital of Persia where the Sultan his father made immediate preparation for the solemnization of their marriage with all fitting pomp and magnificence. After the days appointed for rejoicing were over, the Sultan named and appointed an ambassador to go to the Rajah of Bengal, to ask his approval of the alliance contracted by this marriage; which the Rajah of Bengal took as an honor, and granted with great pleasure and satisfaction.

The Story of Sinbad the Sailor

IN THE REIGN of the Caliph Haroun al-Raschid there dwelt, in Bagdad, a poor porter named Hindbad, who often had to carry heavy burdens, which he could scarcely support. One very hot day he was laboring along a strange street, and overcome by fatigue he sat down near a great house to rest. The porter complimented himself upon his good fortune in finding such a pleasant place, for while he sat there reached his ear sweet sounds of music, and his senses were also soothed by sweet smells. Wondering who lived in so fine a house, he inquired of one of the servants.

"What," said the man, "do you not know that Sinbad the Sailor, the famous circumnavigator of the world, lives here?"

"Alas," replied Hindbad, "what a difference there is between Sinbad's lot and mine. Yet what greater merits does he possess that he should prosper and I starve?"

Now Sinbad happened to overhear this remark, and anxious to see a man who expressed such strange views he sent for Hindbad. Accordingly Hindbad was led into the great hall, where there was a sumptuous repast spread, and a goodly company assembled. The poor porter felt very uncomfortable, un-

til Sinbad bade him draw near, and seating him at his right hand, served him himself, and gave him excellent wine, of which there was abundance upon the sideboard.

When the repast was over, Sinbad asked him why he complained of his condition.

"My lord," replied Hindbad, "I confess that my fatigue put me out of humor, and occasioned me to utter some indiscreet words, which I beg you to pardon."

"Do not think I am so unjust," resumed Sinbad, "as to resent such a complaint. But that you may know that my wealth has not been acquired without labor, I recite the history of my travels for your benefit; and I think that, when you have heard it, you will acknowledge how wonderful have been my adventures." Sinbad then related the story of his first voyage as follows:

THE FIRST VOYAGE

When still a very young man I inherited a large fortune from my father, and at once set about amusing myself. I lived luxuriously, and soon found that money was decreasing, while nothing was added to replace expenditure. Quickly seeing the folly of my ways, I invested the remainder of my fortune with some merchants of Bussorah, and joined them in their voyage, which was toward the Indies by way of the Persian Gulf.

In our voyage we touched at several islands, where we sold or exchanged our goods. One day, while under sail, we were becalmed near a small island, but little elevated above the level of the water, and resembling a green meadow. The captain ordered his sails to be furled, and permitted such persons as were so inclined to land; of this number I was one.

But while we were enjoying ourselves in eating and drinking, and recovering ourselves from the fatigue of the sea, the island on a sudden trembled, and shook us terribly.

The trembling of the island was perceived on board the ship, and we were called upon to re-embark speedily, or we

should all be lost; for what we took for an island proved to be the back of a sea monster. The nimblest got into the sloop, others betook themselves to swimming; but for myself I was still upon the back of the creature, when he dived into the sea, and I had time only to catch hold of a piece of wood that we had brought out of the ship to make a fire. Meanwhile, the captain, having received those on board who were in the sloop, and taken up some of those that swam, resolved to improve the favorable gale that had just risen, and hoisting his sails pursued his voyage, so that it was impossible for me to recover the ship.

Thus was I exposed to the mercy of the waves. I struggled for my life all the rest of the day and the following night. By this time I found my strength gone, and despaired of saving my life, when happily a wave threw me against an island. I struggled up the steep bank by aid of some roots, and lay down upon the ground half dead, until the sun appeared. Then, though I was very feeble, both from hard labor and want of food, I crept along to find some herbs fit to eat, and had the good luck not only to procure some, but likewise to discover a spring of excellent water, which contributed much to recover me. As I advanced farther into the island, I was not a little surprised and startled to hear a voice and see a man, who asked me who I was. I related to him my adventure, after which, taking me by the hand, he led me into a cave, where there were several other people, no less amazed to see me than I was to see them.

I partook of some provisions which they offered me. I then asked them what they did in such a desert place, to which they answered that they were grooms belonging to a Maharajah, sovereign of the island, and that they were about to lead the King's horses back to the palace. They added that they were to return home on the morrow, and, had I been one day later, I must have perished, because the inhabited part of the island was at a great distance, and it would have been impossible for me to have got thither without a guide.

When the grooms set out I accompanied them, and was duly presented to the Maharajah, who was much interested in my adventure, and bade me stay with him as long as I desired.

Being a merchant, I met with men of my own profession, and particularly inquired for those who were strangers, that perchance I might hear news from Bagdad, or find an opportunity to return. For the Maharajah's capital is situated on the seacoast, and has a fine harbor, where ships arrive daily from the different quarters of the world. I frequented also the society of the learned Indians, and took delight to hear them converse; but withal, I took care to make my court regularly to the Maharajah, and conversed with the governors and petty kings, his tributaries, that were about him. They put a thousand questions respecting my country; and I, being willing to inform myself as to their laws and customs, asked them concerning everything which I thought worth knowing.

There belongs to this King an island named Cassel. They assured me that every night a noise of drums was heard there, whence the mariners fancied that it was the residence of Degial. I determined to visit this wonderful place, and in my way thither saw fishes of one hundred and two hundred cubits long, that occasion more fear than hurt; for they are so timorous that they will fly upon the rattling of two sticks or boards. I saw likewise other fish, which had heads like owls.

As I was one day at the port after my return, the ship in which I had set sail arrived, and the crew began to unload the goods. I saw my own bales with my name upon them, and going up to the captain said, "I am that Sinbad whom you thought to be dead, and those bales are mine."

When the captain heard me speak thus, he exclaimed, "Heavens! whom can we trust in these times? There is no faith left among men. I saw Sinbad perish with my own eyes, as did also the passengers on board, and yet you tell me you are that Sinbad. What impudence is this? To look on you, one would take you to be a man of probity, and yet you tell a horrible falsehood, in order to possess yourself of what does not belong to you."

After much discussion, the captain was convinced of the truth of my words, and, having seen me identified by members of the crew, he handed me over my goods, congratulating me upon my escape.

I took out what was most valuable in my bales, and presented them to the Maharajah, who, knowing my misfortune, asked me how I came by such rarities. I acquainted him with the circumstance of their recovery. He was pleased at my good luck, accepted my present, and in return gave me one much more considerable. Thereupon, I took leave of him, and went aboard the same ship, after I had exchanged my goods for the commodities of that country. We passed by several islands, and at last arrived at Bussorah, from whence I came to this city, with the value of one hundred thousand sequins.

Sinbad stopped here, and ordered the musicians to proceed with their concert, which the story had interrupted. The company continued enjoying themselves till the evening, and it was time to retire, when Sinbad sent for a purse of one hundred sequins, and giving it to the porter said, "Take this, Hindbad, return to your home, and come back tomorrow to hear more of my adventures." The porter went away, astonished at the honor done and the present made him, and arrayed in his best apparel returned to Sinbad's house next day. After he had graciously received and feasted his guest, Sinbad continued his narrative:

THE SECOND VOYAGE

I designed, after my first voyage, to spend the rest of my days at Bagdad; but it was not long ere I grew weary of an indolent life, and, therefore, I set out a second time upon a voyage. We embarked on board a good ship, and, after recommending ourselves to God, set sail. We traded from island to island, and exchanged commodities with great profit. One day we landed at an island covered with several sorts of fruit trees, but we could see neither man nor animal. We went to take a little fresh air in the meadows, along the streams that watered them. While some diverted themselves with gathering flowers,

and others fruits, I took my wine and provisions, and sat down near a stream betwixt two high trees, which formed a thick shade. I made a good meal, and afterward fell asleep. I cannot tell how long I slept, but when I awoke the ship was gone.

I was much alarmed at finding the ship gone. I got up and looked around me, but could not see one of the merchants who landed with me. I perceived the ship under sail, but at such a distance that I lost sight of her in a short time. I upbraided myself a hundred times for not being content with the produce of my first voyage, that might have sufficed me all my life. But all this was in vain, and my repentance too late. Not knowing what to do, I climbed up to the top of a lofty tree, whence I looked about on all sides, to see if I could discover anything that could give me hopes. When I gazed over the land I beheld something white; and coming down, I took what provision I had left, and went toward it, the distance being so great that I could not distinguish what it was.

As I approached, I thought it to be a white dome, of a prodigious height and extent; and when I came up to it, I touched it, and found it to be very smooth. I went round to see if it was open on any side, but saw it was not, and that there was no climbing up to the top, as it was so smooth. It was at least fifty paces round.

By this time the sun was about to set, and all of a sudden the sky became as dark as if it had been covered with a thick cloud. I was much astonished at this sudden darkness, but much more when I found it occasioned by a bird of monstrous size, that came flying toward me. I remembered that I had often heard mariners speak of a miraculous bird called a roc, and conceived that the great dome which I so much admired must be its egg. In a short time, the bird alighted, and sat over the egg. As I perceived her coming, I crept close to the egg, so that I had before me one of the legs of the bird, which was as big as the trunk of a tree. I tied myself strongly to it with my turban, in hopes that the roc next morning would carry me with her out of this desert island. After having passed the

night in this condition, the bird flew away as soon as it was daylight, and carried me so high that I could not discern the earth; she afterward descended with so much rapidity that I lost my senses. But when I found myself on the ground, I speedily untied the knot, and had scarcely done so, when the roc, having taken up a serpent of a great length in her bill, flew away.

The spot where it left me was encompassed on all sides by mountains, which seemed to reach above the clouds, and so steep that there was no possibility of getting out of the valley. This was a new perplexity; so that when I compared this place with the desert island from which the roc had brought me, I found that I had gained nothing by the change.

As I walked through this valley, I perceived it was strewn with diamonds, some of which were of a surprising size. I took pleasure in looking upon them. But shortly I saw at a distance some objects that greatly diminished my satisfaction, and which I could not view without terror, namely, a great number of serpents, so monstrous that the least of them was capable of swallowing an elephant. They retired in the daytime to their dens, where they hid themselves from the roc, their enemy, and came out only in the night.

I spent the day in walking about in the valley, resting myself at times in such places as I thought most convenient. When night came on, I went into a cave, where I thought I might repose in safety. I secured the entrance which was low and narrow, with a great stone to preserve me from the serpents; but not so far as to exclude the light. I supped on part of my provisions, but the serpents, which began hissing round me, put me into such extreme fear that you may easily imagine I did not sleep. When day appeared, the serpents retired, and I came out of the cave trembling. I can justly say that I walked upon diamonds without feeling any inclination to touch them. At last I sat down, and notwithstanding my apprehensions, not having closed my eyes during the night, fell asleep, after having eaten a little more of my provision. But I had scarcely

shut my eyes when something that fell by me with a great noise awaked me. This was a large piece of raw meat; and at the same time I saw several others fall down from the rocks in different places.

I had always regarded as fabulous what I had heard sailors and others relate of the valley of diamonds, and of the stratagems employed by merchants to obtain jewels from thence; but now I found that they had stated nothing but the truth. For as a fact, the merchants come to the neighborhood of this valley, when the eagles have young ones, and throwing great joints of meat into the valley, the diamonds, upon whose points they fall, stick to them. The eagles, which are stronger in this country than anywhere else, pounce with great force upon those pieces of meat, and carry them to their nests on the precipices of the rocks to feed their young. The merchants at this time run to their nests, disturb and drive off the eagles by their shouts, and take away the diamonds that stick to the meat.

The happy idea struck me that here was a means of escape from my living tomb; so I collected a number of the largest diamonds, with which I filled my wallet, which I tied to my girdle. Then I fastened one of the joints of meat to the middle of my back by means of my turban cloth, and lay down with my face to the ground.

I had scarcely placed myself in this posture when the eagles came. Each of them seized a piece of meat, and one of the strongest having taken me up, with the piece of meat to which I was fastened, carried me to his nest on the top of the mountain. The merchants began their shouting to frighten the eagles; and when they had obliged them to quit their prey, one of them came to the nest where I was. He was much alarmed when he saw me. But recovering himself, instead of inquiring how I came thither, began to quarrel with me, and asked why I stole his goods.

"You will treat me," replied I, "with more civility, when you know me better. Do not be uneasy; I have diamonds enough

for you and myself, more than all the other merchants together. Whatever they have they owe to chance, but I selected for myself in the bottom of the valley those which you see in this bag."

I had scarcely done speaking, when the other merchants came crowding about us, much astonished to see me. But they were much more surprised when I told them my story. Yet they did not so much admire my stratagem to effect my deliverance as my courage in putting it into execution.

They conducted me to their encampment, and there, having opened my bag, they were surprised at the largeness of my diamonds, and confessed that in all the courts which they had visited they had never seen any of such size and perfection. I prayed the merchant, who owned the nest to which I had been carried (for every merchant had his own), to take as many for his share as he pleased. He contented himself with one, and that too the least of them; and when I pressed him to take more, without fear of doing me injury, he said, "No, I am very well satisfied with this which is valuable enough to save me the trouble of making any more voyages, and will raise as great a fortune as I desire."

I spent the night with the merchants, to whom I related my story a second time, for the satisfaction of those who had not heard it. I could not moderate my joy when I found myself delivered from the danger I have mentioned. I thought myself in a dream, and could scarcely believe myself out of danger. When at length I reached home I gave large presents to the poor, and lived luxuriously upon my hard-earned wealth.

Then Sinbad ended the account of his second voyage, and, having given Hindbad another hundred sequins, asked him to come on the next day to hear his further adventures.

THE THIRD VOYAGE

I soon wearied of the idle, luxurious life I led, and therefore undertook another voyage. Overtaken by a dreadful tempest

in the main ocean, we were driven upon an island which, the captain told us, was inhabited by hairy savages, from whom there was danger of attack. Though they were but dwarfs, yet our misfortune was such that we must make no resistance, for they were more in number than the locusts; and if we happened to kill one of them, they would all fall upon us and destroy us.

It was not long before the captain's words were proved, for an innumerable multitude of frightful savages, about two feet high, covered all over with red hair, came swimming toward us, and encompassed our ship. We advanced into the island on which we were, and came to a palace, elegantly built, and very lofty, with a gate of ebony of two leaves, which we forced open. We entered the court, where we saw before us a large apartment, with a porch, having on one side a heap of human bones, and on the other a vast number of roasting spits. Our fears were not diminished when the gates of the apartment opened with a loud crash, and out came the horrible figure of a black man, as tall as a lofty palm tree. He had but one eye, and that in the middle of his forehead, where it looked as red as a burning coal. His fore-teeth were very long and sharp, and stood out of his mouth, which was as deep as that of a horse. His upper lip hung down upon his breast. His ears resembled those of an elephant, and covered his shoulders; and his nails were as long and crooked as the talons of the greatest birds. At the sight of so frightful a giant, we became insensible, and lay like dead men. When he had considered us well, he advanced toward us, and laying his hand upon me, took me up by the nape of my neck and turned me round as a butcher would do a sheep's head. After having examined me, and perceiving me to be so lean that I had nothing but skin and bone, he let me go. He took up all the rest one by one, and viewed them in the same manner. The captain being the fattest, he held him with one hand, as I would do a sparrow, and thrust a spit through him. He then kindled a great fire and roasted and ate him in his apartment for his supper. Having finished

his repast, he returned to his porch, where he lay and fell asleep, snoring louder than thunder.

We all sat numbed by fear, but the next day, after the giant had gone out, we devised a means of vengeance. And so, when he had again made a supper off one of our number, and lay down to sleep, we prepared to execute the daring design. Therefore nine of us and myself, when we heard him snore, each armed with a spit, the points of which we had made red-hot, approached the monster and thrust the spits into his eye at the same time, so that he was blind. The giant made wild efforts to seize us, but finding that we had hidden he went out roaring in his agony.

We lost no time in fleeing from the palace, and soon reached the shore, where we contrived to construct some rafts upon which to sail away in case of need. But knowing the danger that such a voyage would entail, we waited in the hope that the giant might be dead, since he had ceased to howl. Day had scarcely dawned, however, when we saw our enemy coming toward us, led by two others, nearly as big as himself, and accompanied by hosts of others.

We immediately took to our rafts. Thereupon the giants, enraged at being thus balked, took up great stones, and, running to the shore, entered the water up to the middle, and threw so exactly that they sunk all the rafts but that I was upon. All my companions, except the two with me, were drowned. We rowed with all our might, and got out of the reach of the giants, and tossed about for a day and night until at last we reached an island, whereon grew much excellent fruit.

At night we went to sleep on the seashore; but were awakened by the noise of a serpent of surprising length and thickness, whose scales made a rustling noise as it wound itself along. It swallowed up one of my comrades, notwithstanding his loud cries and the efforts he made to extricate himself from it. Dashing him several times against the ground, it crushed him, and we could hear it gnaw and tear the poor

wretch's bones, though we had fled to a considerable distance. Seeing the danger to which we were exposed, we climbed a tall tree the next night to escape the serpent. But, to our horror, the monster raised itself against the trunk of the tree, and perceiving my companion, who was lower down than I, swallowed him and withdrew.

I remained in the tree till it was day, and then came down, and collected together a great quantity of small wood, brambles, and dry thorns, and tying them up into fagots, made a wide circle with them round the tree, and also tied some of them to the branches over my head. Having done this, when the evening came, I shut myself up within this circle, with the melancholy satisfaction that I had neglected nothing which could preserve me from the cruel destiny with which I was threatened. The serpent failed not to come at the usual hour, and went round the tree, seeking for an opportunity to devour me, but was prevented by the rampart I had made. So it lay till day, like a cat watching in vain for a mouse that has fortunately reached a place of safety. When day appeared it retired, but I dared not to leave my fort until the sun arose.

As I ran toward the sea, determined no longer to prolong my miserable existence, I perceived a ship at a considerable distance. I called as loud as I could, and taking the linen from my turban, displayed it, that they might observe me. This had the desired effect; the crew perceived me, and the captain sent his boat for me. As soon as I came on board, the merchants and seamen flocked about me, to know how I came into that desert island. And after I had related to them all that had befallen me, the oldest among them told me they had several times heard of the giants that dwelt in that island, that they were cannibals, and ate men raw as well as roasted; and as to the serpents, they added, they were in abundance on the island, hiding themselves by day, and coming abroad by night.

After having shown their joy at my escaping so many dangers, they brought me the best of their provisions. The captain, being the man who had deserted me upon my second

voyage, seeing that I was in rags, was so generous as to give me one of his own suits. I soon made myself known to him, whereupon he exclaimed, "God be praised. I rejoice that fortune has rectified my fault. There are your goods, which I always took care to preserve."

I took them from him, thanked him warmly for his honesty, and contrived to deal so well on the voyage that I arrived at Bussorah with another vast fortune. From Bussorah I returned to Bagdad, where I gave a great deal to the poor, and bought another considerable estate in addition to what I already had.

Having thus finished the account of his third voyage, Sinbad sent Hindbad on his way, after he had given him another hundred sequins, and invited him to dinner the next day to hear the continuation of his adventures.

THE FOURTH VOYAGE

It was not long before I again started on a journey. This time I traveled through Persia and arrived at a port, where I took ship. We had not been long at sea when a great storm overtook us, which was so violent that the sails were split into a thousand pieces, and the ship was stranded. Several of the merchants and seamen were drowned, and the cargo was lost.

I had the good fortune, with several of the merchants and mariners, to get upon some planks, and we were carried by the current to an island which lay before us. There we found fruit and spring water, which preserved our lives; and we lay down almost where we had landed and slept.

Next morning, as soon as the sun was up, we walked from the shore, and advancing into the island saw some houses, which we approached. As soon as we drew near, we were encompassed by a great number of natives with very dark skins, who seized us, shared us among them, and carried us to their respective habitations.

I and five of my comrades were carried to one place where they made us sit down, and gave us a certain herb, which they made signs to us to eat. My comrades not taking notice that

the blacks ate none of it themselves, thought only of satisfying their hunger, and ate with greediness. But I, suspecting some trick, would not so much as taste it, which turned out well for me; for in a short time, I perceived my companions had lost their senses, and that when they spoke to me, they knew not what they said.

The natives fed us afterward with rice, prepared with oil of coconuts; and my comrades, who had lost their reason, ate of it greedily. I also partook of it, but very sparingly. They gave us that herb at first on purpose to deprive us of our senses, that we might not be aware of the sad destiny prepared for us. And they supplied us with rice to fatten us; for, being cannibals, their design was to eat us as soon as we grew fat. This accordingly happened, for they devoured my comrades, who were not sensible of their condition; but my senses being entire, you may easily guess that instead of growing fat, as the rest did, I grew leaner every day. The fear of death under which I labored turned all my food into poison. I fell into a languishing distemper, which proved my safety; for the Negroes, having killed and eaten my companions, seeing me to be withered, lean, and sick, deferred my death.

Meanwhile I had much liberty, so that scarcely any notice was taken of what I did, and this gave me an opportunity one day to get at a distance from the houses and to make my escape. An old man, who saw me, and suspected my design, called to me as loud as he could to return; but instead of obeying him, I redoubled my speed, and quickly got out of sight. I traveled as fast as I could, and chose those places which seemed most deserted, living for seven days on the fruit I gathered.

On the eighth day I came near the sea, and saw some white people like myself, gathering pepper, of which there was great plenty in that place. As soon as they saw me they came to meet me, and asked me in Arabic who I was and whence I came. I was overjoyed to hear them speak in my own language, and satisfied their curiosity by giving them an account

of my shipwreck, and how I fell into the hands of the Negroes. Those Negroes, they told me, ate men, and they marveled by what miracle I had escaped their cruelty. I related to them the circumstances I have just mentioned, at which they were greatly surprised.

I stayed with them till they had gathered their quantity of pepper, and then sailed with them to the island from whence they had come. They presented me to their King, who was a good prince. He listened to my story, bade me welcome, and soon had conceived a great friendship for me, which fact made me a person of importance in the capital. None of these people rides with either saddle or bridle, and so, wishing to honor the King, I went to a workman, and gave him a model for making the stock of a saddle. When that was done, I covered it myself with velvet and leather, and embroidered it with gold. I afterward went to a smith, who made me a bit, according to the pattern I showed him, and also some stirrups.

When I had all the trappings completed, I presented them to the King, and put them upon one of his horses. His Majesty mounted immediately, and was so pleased with them that he showed his satisfaction by large presents, and said, "I wish you to marry and think no more of your own land, but stay here as long as you live." I durst not resist the Prince's will, and he gave me one of the ladies of his court, noble, beautiful, and rich. The ceremonies of marriage being over, I went and dwelt with my wife, and for some time we lived together in perfect harmony. I was not, however, content with my exile. Therefore I designed to make my escape upon the first opportunity and to return to Bagdad, which my present circumstances, howsoever advantageous, could not make me forget.

At this time the wife of one of my neighbors, with whom I had contracted a very strict friendship, fell sick, and died. I went to see and comfort him in his affliction, and finding him absorbed in sorrow, I said to him as soon as I saw him, "God preserve you and grant you a long life."

"Alas!" replied he, "your good wishes are in vain, for I must

be buried this day with my wife. This is a law which our ancestors established in this island, and it is always observed inviolably. The living husband is interred with the dead wife, and the living wife with the dead husband. Nothing can save me; everyone must submit to this law."

While he was giving me an account of this barbarous custom, the very relation of which chilled my blood, his kindred, friends, and neighbors came in a body to assist at the funeral. They dressed the body of the woman in her richest apparel, and all her jewels, as if it had been her wedding day; then they placed her in an open coffin, and began their march to the place of burial. The husband walked at the head of the company, and followed the corpse. They proceeded to a high mountain, and when they had reached the place of their destination, they took up a large stone, which covered the mouth of a deep pit, and let down the corpse with all its apparel and jewels. Then the husband, embracing his kindred and friends, suffered himself to be put into another open coffin without resistance, with a pot of water, and seven small loaves, and was let down in the same manner. The mountain was of considerable length, and extended along the seashore, and the pit was very deep. The ceremony being over, the aperture was again covered with the stone, and the company returned.

Not long after this I was destined to share a like fate, for my wife, of whose health I took particular care, fell sick and died. In spite of every effort on my part, the law of the land had to be fulfilled. And so, accompanied by the King and the chief nobles, who had come to honor me at the grave, I was lowered into the tomb with my wife's body and the usual supply of bread and water. I had come to the end of my provisions, and was expecting death, when I heard a puffing noise as of something breathing. I moved toward the place whence the sound came, and heard a scurrying of feet as the creature ran away. I pursued it, and at last perceived what seemed to be a star in the distance. The speck of light grew larger as I approached, and I soon found that it was a hole in the side of the moun-

tain, above the seashore. I cast myself upon the sand overcome with joy, and as I raised my eyes to heaven I perceived a ship at no great distance. I waved my turban linen, which attracted the attention of those on board; whereupon they sent a boat which carried me safely on board. I told the captain that I was a shipwrecked merchant, and he believed my story, and without asking any questions took me with him.

After a long voyage, during which we called at several ports, whereat I made much money, I arrived happily at Bagdad with infinite riches, of which it is needless to trouble you with the detail. Out of gratitude to God for His mercies, I contributed liberally toward the support of several mosques, and the subsistence of the poor, and gave myself up to the society of my kindred and friends, enjoying myself with them in festivities and amusements.

Sinbad then presented another hundred sequins to the porter, and bade him honor him with his presence again next day.

THE FIFTH VOYAGE

The pleasures I enjoyed had again charms enough to make me forget all the troubles and calamities I had undergone, but could not cure me of my inclination to make new voyages. I therefore bought goods and departed with them for the best seaport. There, that I might not be obliged to depend upon a captain, but have a ship at my own command, I remained till one was built at my own charge. When the ship was ready, I went on board with my goods; but not having enough to load her, I agreed to take with me several merchants of different nations with their merchandise.

We sailed with the first fair wind, and after a long voyage, the first place we touched at was a desert island, where we found an egg of a roc, equal in size to the one I previously mentioned. There was a young roc in it just ready to be hatched, and its bill had begun to appear.

The merchants who landed with me broke the egg with hatchets, and pulled out the young roc piecemeal, and roasted it. I had earnestly entreated them not to meddle with the egg, but they would not listen to me.

Scarcely had they finished their repast when there appeared in the air at a considerable distance from us two great clouds. The captain whom I had hired to navigate my ship, knowing by experience what they meant, said they were the male and female roc that belonged to the young one, and pressed us to re-embark with all speed, to prevent the misfortune which he saw would otherwise befall us. We hastened on board, and set sail with all possible expedition.

In the meantime, the two rocs approached the island with a frightful noise, which they redoubled when they saw the egg

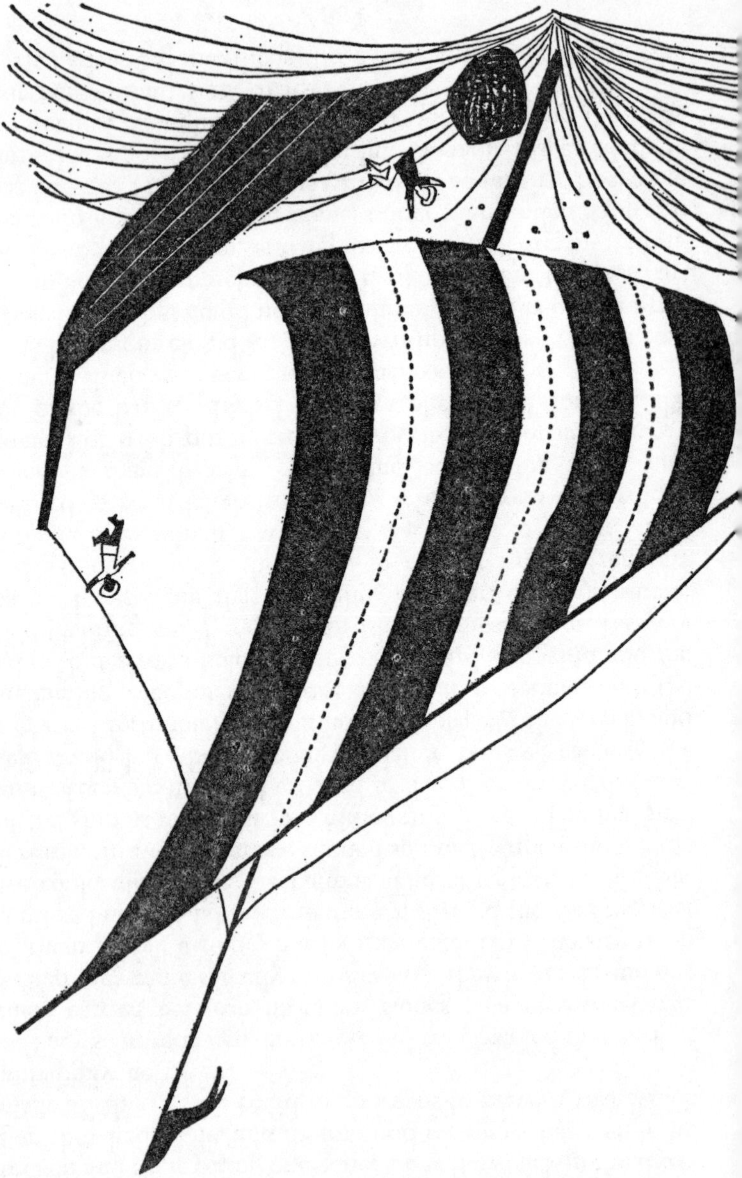

broken and their young one gone. They flew back in the direction they had come, and disappeared for some time, while we made all the sail we could to endeavor to prevent that which unhappily befell us.

They soon returned, however, and we observed that each of them carried between its talons stones of a monstrous size. When they came directly over my ship, they hovered, and one of them let fall a stone, but by the dexterity of the steersman it missed us, and falling into the sea, divided the water so that we could almost see the bottom. The other roc, to our misfortune, threw his massive burden so exactly upon the middle of the ship as to split it into a thousand pieces. The mariners and passengers were all crushed to death, or drowned. I myself would have been among the latter, but as I came to the surface, I fortunately caught hold of a piece of the wreck, and swimming sometimes with one hand, and sometimes with the other, but always holding fast to my board, the wind and the tide favoring me, I came to an island, whose shore was very steep. I overcame that difficulty, however, and got ashore.

I sat down upon the grass, to recover myself from my fatigue, after which I went into the island to explore it. It seemed to be a delightful garden. I found trees everywhere, some of them bearing green, and others ripe fruits, and streams of fresh pure water running in pleasant meanders. I ate of the fruits, which I found excellent, and drank of the water, which was very sweet and good.

When night closed in, I lay down upon the grass in a convenient spot, but could not sleep more than an hour at a time, my mind being apprehensive of danger. I spent the best part of the night in alarm, and reproached myself for my imprudence in not remaining at home, rather than undertaking this last voyage. These reflections carried me so far that I began to form a design against my life; but daylight dispersed these melancholy thoughts. I got up, and walked among the trees, but not without some fears.

As I advanced into the island, I came upon an old man who

appeared very weak and infirm. He was sitting on the bank of a stream, and at first I took him to be one who had been shipwrecked like myself. I went toward him and saluted him, but he only slightly bowed his head. I asked him why he sat so still, but instead of answering me, he made a sign for me to take him upon my back, and carry him over the brook, signifying that it was to gather fruit.

I believed him really to be in need of my assistance. So I took him upon my back, and having carried him over, bade him get down, and for that end stooped, that he might get off with ease. But instead of doing so the old man, who to me appeared quite decrepit, clasped his legs nimbly about my neck, so tightly that I swooned.

Notwithstanding my fainting, the ill-natured old fellow kept fast about my neck, but opened his legs a little to give me time to recover my breath. When I had done so, he thrust one of his feet against my stomach, and struck me so rudely on the side with the other, that he forced me to rise up against my will. Having arisen, he made me walk under the trees, and forced me now and then to stop, to gather and eat fruit such as we found. He never left me all day, and when I lay down to rest at night, laid himself down with me, holding always fast about my neck. Every morning he pushed me to make me awake, and afterward obliged me to get up and walk, and pressed me with his feet. You may judge, then, what trouble I was in, to be loaded with such a burden of which I could not rid myself.

One day I found in my way several dry calabashes that had fallen from a tree. I took a large one, and after cleaning it, pressed into it some juice of grapes, which abounded in the island. Having filled the calabash, I put it by in a convenient place, and going thither again some days after, I tasted it, and found the wine so good that it soon made me forget my sorrow, gave me new vigor, and so exhilarated my spirits that I began to sing and dance as I walked along.

The old man, perceiving the effect which this liquor had

upon me, and that I carried him with more ease than before, made me a sign to give him some of it. I handed him the calabash, and the liquor pleasing his palate, he drank it all off, and was soon so intoxicated that his grip released. Seizing this opportunity, I threw him upon the ground, where he lay without motion. I then took up a great stone, and crushed his head to pieces.

I was extremely glad to be thus freed forever from this troublesome fellow. I now walked toward the beach, where I met the crew of a ship that had cast anchor to take in water. They were surprised to see me, but more so at hearing the particulars of my adventures. "You fell," said they, "into the hands of the Old Man of the Sea, and are the first who ever escaped strangling by his malicious tricks. He never quitted those he had once made himself master of, till he had destroyed them, and he has made this island notorious by the number of men he has slain; so that the merchants and mariners who landed upon it, durst not advance into the island but in numbers at a time." After saying this, they carried me with them to the ship. The captain received me with great kindness when they told him what had befallen me. He put out to sea, and after some days' sail, we arrived at the harbor of a great city, the houses of which were built of hewn stone.

One of the merchants who had taken me into his friendship invited me to go along with him. He gave me a large bag, and having recommended me to some people of the town, who used to gather coconuts, desired them to take me with them. "Go," said he, "follow them, and act as you see them do, but do not separate from them, otherwise you may endanger your life." Having thus spoken, he gave me provisions for the journey, and I went with them.

We came to a thick forest of coco palms, very lofty, with trunks so smooth that it was not possible to climb to the branches that bore the fruit. When we entered the forest we saw a great number of apes of various sizes, who fled as soon as they perceived us, and climbed up to the top of the trees with surprising swiftness.

The merchants in whose company I was gathered stones and threw them at the apes on the trees. I did the same, and the apes out of revenge threw coconuts at us so fast, and with such gestures, as sufficiently showed their anger and resentment. We gathered up the coconuts, and from time to time threw stones to provoke the apes. By this stratagem we filled our bags with coconuts. I soon sold mine, and returned several times to the forest for more. By this means I made a considerable sum.

The vessel in which I had come sailed with some merchants, who loaded her with coconuts. I expected the arrival of another, which anchored soon after for the like loading. I embarked in her all the coconuts I had, and when she was ready to sail, took leave of the merchant who had been so kind to me. But he could not embark with me, because he had not finished his business at the port. We sailed toward the islands where pepper grows in great plenty. From thence we went to the Isle of Comari, where the best species of wood of aloes grows, and whose inhabitants have made it an inviolable law to themselves to drink no wine. I exchanged my coconuts in those islands for pepper and wood of aloes, and went with other merchants pearl-fishing. I hired divers, who brought me up some that were very large and pure. Later I embarked in a vessel that happily arrived at Bussorah. From thence I returned to Bagdad, where I made vast sums from my pepper, wood of aloes, and pearls. I gave the tenth of my gains in alms, as I had done upon my return from my other voyages, and endeavored to dissipate my fatigues by amusements of different kinds.

When he had thus finished his story Sinbad presented Hindbad with a hundred sequins, as before, and entreated him to present himself at the usual hour the next day.

THE SIXTH VOYAGE

The roving spirit being in me, I could not stay long idle. So, after a year's rest, I made ready for my sixth voyage, in spite

of the entreaties of my friends and kinsfolk. This time I traveled through Persia and the Indies before taking ship, and at last embarked, at a distant port, in a vessel that was bound for a long voyage. We had sailed far when one day the captain quitted his post in great grief, and casting away his turban, cried, in a voice of agony, "A rapid current carries the ship along with it, and we shall all perish in less than a quarter of an hour. Pray to God to deliver us from this peril; we cannot escape if He does not take pity on us." At these words he ordered the sails to be lowered. But all the ropes broke, and the ship was carried by the current to the foot of an inaccessible mountain, where she struck and went to pieces, yet in such a manner that we saved our lives, our provisions, and the best of our goods.

The danger being over, the captain said to us, "God has done what pleased Him. Each of us may dig his grave, and bid the world adieu; for we are all in so fatal a place that none shipwrecked here ever returned to his home." His discourse affected us deeply, and we embraced each other, bewailing our unhappy fate.

The mountain at the foot of which we were wrecked formed part of the coast of a very large island. It was incredible what a quantity of goods and riches we found cast ashore. All these objects served only to augment our despair. In all other places, rivers run from their channels into the sea, but here a river of fresh water ran out of the sea into a dark cavern, whose entrance was very high and spacious. What was most remarkable in this place was that the stones of the mountain were of crystal, rubies, or other precious stones. Trees also grew here, most of which were wood of aloes, equal in goodness to those of Comari.

To finish the description of this place, which might well be called a gulf, since nothing ever returned from it, it was not possible for ships to get off when once they approached within a certain distance. If they were driven thither by a wind from the sea, then the wind and the current impelled them; and if

they came into it when a land wind was blowing, which might seem to favor their getting out again, the height of the mountain stopped the wind, and brought a calm, so that the force of the current carried them ashore. To make the misfortune complete, there was no possibility of ascending the mountain, or of escaping by sea.

We were, indeed, in a sorry plight. The number of wrecks and skeletons which were upon the coast confirmed the captain's statement that our chance of escape was very small. Although the spot was fair enough to see, we mourned our lot, and awaited death with such patience as we could command.

At last our provisions began to run short, and one by one the members of the company died, until I was left alone out of the entire number. Those who died first were interred by the survivors, and I paid the last duty to all my companions. Nor are you to wonder at this; for I had husbanded the provisions that fell to my share better than they. In addition I had some of my own, which I did not share with my comrades. Yet when I buried the last, I had so little remaining that I thought I could not long survive. I dug a grave, resolving to lie down in it, because there was no one left to inter me. I must confess to you at the same time that while I was thus employed I could not but reproach myself as the cause of my own ruin, and I repented that I had ever undertaken this last voyage. Nor did I stop at reflections only, but had begun to hasten my own death by tearing my hands with my teeth.

But it pleased God once more to take compassion on me, and put it in my mind to go to the bank of the river which ran into the great cavern. Considering its probable course with great attention, I said to myself: "This river, which runs thus underground, must somewhere have an issue. If I make a raft, and leave myself to the current, it will convey me to some inhabited country, or I shall perish. If I be drowned, I lose nothing, but only change one kind of death for another; and if I get out of this fatal place, I shall not only avoid the sad fate of my comrades, but perhaps find some new occasion of

enriching myself. Who knows but fortune waits, upon my getting off this dangerous shelf, to compensate my shipwreck with usury."

I immediately went to work upon large pieces of timber and cables, for I had considerable choice of them, and tied them together so strongly that I soon made a very solid raft. When I had finished, I loaded it with some bags of rubies, emeralds, ambergris, rock crystal, and bales of rich stuffs, and leaving it to the course of the river, resigned myself to the will of God, comforting myself in the reflection that in any case it little mattered how death came, whether in the form of drowning or starvation.

As soon as I entered the cavern, I lost all light, and the stream carried me I knew not whither. Thus I floated some days in perfect darkness, and once I found the arch so low that it very nearly touched my head, which made me cautious afterward to avoid the like danger. All this while I ate nothing but what was just necessary to support nature. But, notwithstanding my frugality, all my provisions became exhausted, and I lost consciousness. I cannot tell how long I remained insensible. But when I revived, I was surprised to find myself in an extensive plain on the brink of a river, where my raft was tied, amidst a great number of natives. I got up as soon as I saw them, and saluted them. They spoke to me, but I did not understand their language. I was so transported with joy that I cried aloud in Arabic, expressing my gratitude to God.

One of the natives, who understood Arabic, hearing me speak thus, came toward me, and said, "Brother, pray tell us your history, for it must be extraordinary. How did you venture yourself upon this river, and whence did you come?"

I begged of them first to give me something to eat, and assured them I would then satisfy their curiosity. They gave me several sorts of food, and when I had satisfied my hunger I related all that had befallen me, which they listened to with attentive surprise. Then they brought a horse and conducted me to their King, that he might hear so remarkable a story.

We marched till we came to the capital of Serendib, for it was in that island I had landed. The natives presented me to their King. I approached his throne, and saluted him as I used to do the Kings of the Indies; that is to say, I prostrated myself at his feet. The Prince ordered me to arise, received me with an obliging air, and made me sit down near him. He first asked me my name, and I answered, "People call me Sinbad the voyager, because of the many voyages I have taken, and I am a citizen of Bagdad." I then narrated all my adventures without reserve, and observing that he looked on my jewels with pleasure, and viewed the most remarkable among them one after another, I fell prostrate at his feet, and took the liberty to say to him, "Sire, not only my person is at your Majesty's service, but the cargo of the raft, and I would beg of you to dispose of it as your own." He answered me with a smile, "Sinbad, instead of taking from you, I intend to add presents worthy of your acceptance." All the answer I returned was a prayer for the prosperity of that noble-minded Prince and commendations of his generosity and bounty. He charged one of his officers to take care of me, and ordered people to serve me at his own expense. The officer was very faithful in the execution of his commission, and caused all the goods to be carried to the lodgings provided for me.

The Isle of Serendib is situated just under the equinoctial line; so that the days and nights there are always of twelve hours each, and the island is eighty parasangs in length, and as many in breadth.

The capital stands at the end of a fine valley, in the middle of the island, encompassed by mountains the highest in the world. They are seen three days' sail off at sea. Rubies and several sorts of minerals abound, and the rocks are for the most part composed of a metalline stone made use of to cut and polish other precious stones. All kinds of rare plants and trees grow there, especially cedar and coconut. There is also a pearl-fishery in the mouth of its principal river; and in some of its valleys are found diamonds.

Having spent some time in the capital, and having visited all the places of interest around, among which is the place where Adam dwelt after his banishment from paradise, I prayed the King to allow me to return to my own country, and he granted me permission in the most obliging and most honorable manner. He forced a rich present upon me; and when I went to take my leave of him, he gave me one much more considerable, and at the same time charged me with a letter for the Commander of the Faithful, our sovereign, saying to me, "I pray you give this present from me, and this letter to the Caliph, and assure him of my friendship."

The letter from the King of Serendib was written on the skin of a certain animal of great value, because of its being so scarce, and of a yellowish color. The characters of this letter were of azure, and the contents as follows:

"The King of the Indies, before whom march one hundred elephants, who lives in a palace that shines with one hundred thousand rubies, and who has in his treasury twenty thousand crowns enriched with diamonds, to Caliph Haroun al-Raschid.

"Though the present we send you be inconsiderable, receive it however as a brother and a friend, in consideration of the hearty friendship which we bear for you, and of which we are willing to give you proof. We desire the same part in your friendship, considering that we believe it to be our merit, being of the same dignity with yourself. We conjure you this in quality of a brother. Adieu."

The present consisted firstly of one single ruby made into a cup, about half a foot high, an inch thick, and filled with round pearls of half a drachma each. Secondly, the skin of a serpent, whose scales were as large as an ordinary piece of gold, and had the virtue to preserve from sickness those who lay upon it. Thirdly, fifty thousand drachmas of the best wood of aloes, with thirty grains of camphire as big as pistachios. And, fourthly, a female of exceeding beauty, whose apparel was all covered over with jewels.

The ship set sail, and after a very successful voyage we landed at Bussorah, and from thence I went to Bagdad, where I immediately went to deliver the King's letter to the Caliph. And after I had presented myself, the Caliph listened with attention to my description of the Indies, which showed that the King had in no way exaggerated his wealth. And I likewise described the manners and customs of the people, which also interested the Commander of the Faithful.

Having spoken thus, Sinbad signified that the account of his sixth voyage was at an end, and presented Hindbad with another hundred sequins, urging him to return next day to hear the history of his seventh and last voyage.

THE SEVENTH AND LAST VOYAGE

After my sixth voyage I had made up my mind to stay at home. I absolutely laid aside all thoughts of traveling; for, besides that my age now required rest, I was resolved no more to expose myself to such risks as I had encountered. I decided to pass the rest of my days in tranquillity. But one day a messenger came from the Caliph summoning me to the palace, and when I came into the presence chamber the Caliph said, "Sinbad, I stand in need of your service; you must carry my answer and present to the King of Serendib. It is but just I should return his civility."

I tried to escape from this new trial, and narrated all my adventures to the Caliph. As soon as I had finished he said, "I confess that the things you tell me are very extraordinary, yet you must for my sake undertake this voyage which I propose to you. You will only have to go to the Isle of Serendib, and deliver the commission which I give you. After that you are at liberty to return. But you must go; for you know it would not comport with my dignity to be indebted to the King of that island."

Perceiving that the Caliph insisted upon my compliance, I submitted, and told him that I was willing to obey. He was very well pleased, and ordered me one thousand sequins for

the expenses of my journey. I therefore prepared for my departure in a few days. As soon as the Caliph's letter and present were delivered to me, I went to Bussorah, where I embarked, and had a very happy voyage. Having arrived at the Isle of Serendib, I was at once led, with great ceremony, to the palace, where the King, seeing me, exclaimed, "Sinbad, you are welcome. I have many times thought of you since you departed. I bless the day on which we see one another once more." I made my compliment to him, and after having thanked him for his kindness, delivered the Caliph's letter and present, which he received with all imaginable satisfaction.

The Caliph's present was a complete suit of cloth of gold, valued at one thousand sequins; fifty robes of rich stuff; a hundred of white cloth, the finest of Cairo, Suez, and Alexandria; a vessel of agate broader than deep, an inch thick, and half a foot wide, the bottom of which represented in bas-relief a man with one knee on the ground, who held a bow and an arrow ready to discharge at a lion. He sent him also a rich tablet, which, according to tradition, belonged to the great Solomon.

The Caliph's letter was as follows:

"Greeting, in the name of the sovereign guide of the right way, from the dependent on God, Haroun al-Raschid, whom God hath set in the place of vice-regent to His Prophet, after his ancestors of happy memory, to the potent and esteemed Rajah of Serendib.

"We received your letter with joy, and send you this from our imperial residence, the garden of superior wits. We hope, when you look upon it, you will perceive our good intention and be pleased with it. Adieu."

The King of Serendib was highly gratified that the Caliph answered his friendship. A little time after this audience, I, with great difficulty, obtained permission to return, and with a very handsome present I embarked to return to Bagdad, but had not the good fortune to arrive there so speedily as I had hoped. God ordered it otherwise.

Three or four days after my departure, we were attacked by

corsairs, who easily seized upon our ship, and took those of the crew who did not fall in the fight into a far country, and sold us as slaves.

I, being one of the number, fell into the hands of a rich merchant, who, as soon as he bought me, carried me to his house, treated me well, and clad me handsomely for a slave. Some days after, not knowing who I was, he asked me if I understood any trade. I answered that I was no mechanic, but a merchant, and that the corsairs, who sold me, had robbed me of all I possessed. "But tell me," replied he, "can you shoot with a bow?" I answered that the bow was one of my exercises in my youth. He gave me a bow and arrows, and taking me behind him upon an elephant, carried me to a thick forest some leagues from the town. We penetrated a great way into the wood, and when he thought fit to stop, he bade me alight. Then showing me a great tree, he said, "Climb up that, and shoot at the elephants as you see them pass by, for there is a prodigious number of them in this forest. And if any of them fall, come and give me notice." Having spoken thus, he left me victuals, and returned to the town, and I remained in the tree all night.

I saw no elephant during that time, but next morning, as soon as the sun was up, I perceived a great number. I shot several arrows among them, and at last one of the elephants fell, whereupon the rest retired immediately, and left me liberty to go and acquaint my patron of my booty. When I had informed him, he gave me a good meal, commended my dexterity, and praised me highly. We went afterward together to the forest, where we dug a hole for the elephant, my patron designing to return when it was rotten and take the teeth to trade with.

I continued this employment for two months, and killed an elephant every day, getting sometimes into one tree and sometimes into another. One morning, as I looked for the elephants, I perceived with extreme amazement that, instead of passing by me across the forest as usual, they stopped, and came to me with a horrible noise, in such number that the

plain was covered and shook under them. They encompassed the tree in which I was concealed, with their trunks extended, and all fixed their eyes upon me. At this alarming spectacle I remained immovable, and was so much terrified that my bow and arrows fell out of my hand.

My fears were not without cause; for after the elephants had stared upon me for some time, one of the largest of them put his trunk around the foot of the tree, plucked it up, and threw it on the ground. I fell with the tree, and the elephant, taking me up with his trunk, laid me on his back, and, followed by all the others, carried me to a hill, where he deposited me and withdrew with the herd. Imagine my surprise when I got up and saw that the hill was covered with elephants' bones and teeth. I at once guessed that this was the burial ground of the elephants, and admired the instinct of the animals. For I doubted not but that they carried me thither on purpose to tell me that I should forbear to persecute them, since I did it only for their teeth. I did not stay on the hill, but turned toward the city, and, after having traveled a day and a night, I came to my patron. I met no elephant on my way, which made me think they had retired farther into the forest, to leave me at liberty to come back to the hill without any obstacle.

My master was overjoyed to see me. "Ah, poor Sinbad," exclaimed he, "I was in great trouble to know what was become of you. I have been at the forest, where I found a tree newly pulled up, and a bow and arrows on the ground, and after having sought for you in vain, I despaired of ever seeing you more. Pray tell me what befell you, and by what good chance you are still alive."

I satisfied his curiosity, and going both of us next morning to the hill, he found to his great joy that what I had told him was true. We loaded the elephant which had carried us with as many teeth as he could bear; and when I told him what I had found he hastened to reach the hill, and we carried away as much ivory as we could. After we reached home, he said,

"Sinbad, not only are we made rich, but you have also saved many lives, for hitherto a large number of slaves perished in the task of obtaining ivory. Consider yourself no longer a slave, and ask whatever you will from me, for you are evidently chosen by God for some great work."

To this obliging declaration I replied, "Your giving me my liberty is enough to discharge what you owe me, and I desire no other reward for the service I had the good fortune to do to you but leave to return to my own country."

"Very well," said he, "the monsoon will in a little time bring ships for ivory. I will then send you home, and give you wherewith to bear your passage." I thanked him again for my liberty and his good intentions toward me. I stayed with him awaiting the monsoon, and during that time we made so many journeys to the hill that we filled all our warehouses with ivory. The other merchants who traded in it did the same, for it could not be long concealed from them.

The ships arrived at last, and my patron, himself having made choice of the ship wherein I was to embark, loaded half of it with ivory on my account, laid in provisions in abundance for my passage, and besides obliged me to accept a present of some curiosities of the country of great value, for which I returned him a thousand thanks, and then departed, after a sad leave-taking.

We stopped at some islands to take in fresh provisions. Our vessel being come to a port on the mainland in the Indies, we touched there, and not being willing to venture by sea to Bussorah, I landed my proportion of the ivory, resolving to proceed on my journey by land. I made vast sums from my ivory, bought several rarities, which I intended for presents, and when my equipage was ready, set out in company with a large caravan of merchants. I was a long time on the way, and suffered much, but endured all with patience, when I considered that I had nothing to fear from the seas, from pirates, from serpents, or from the other perils to which I had been exposed.

All these fatigues ended at last, and I arrived safe at Bagdad. I went immediately to wait upon the Caliph, and gave him an account of my embassy. That Prince said he had been uneasy, as I was so long in returning, but that he always hoped God would preserve me. When I told him the adventure of the elephants he seemed much surprised, and would never have given any credit to it had he not known my veracity. He deemed this story, and the other tales I had given him, to be so curious that he ordered one of his secretaries to write them in characters of gold and lay them up in his treasury. I retired well satisfied with the honors I received and the presents which he gave me, and ever since I have devoted myself wholly to my family, kindred, and friends.

Sinbad here finished the relation of his seventh and last voyage, and then addressed himself to Hindbad. "Well, friend," said he, "did you ever hear of any person that suffered so much as I have done, or of any mortal that has gone through so many vicissitudes? Is it not reasonable that, after all this, I should enjoy a quiet and pleasant life?"

Hindbad drew near and kissed his hand in token of respect, and said how insignificant were his own troubles compared with those he had heard related. Sinbad gave him another hundred sequins, and told him that every day there would be a place laid for him at his table, and that he could always rely upon the friendship of Sinbad the Sailor.

The Story of the Three Sisters

THERE WAS once a Sultan of Persia named Khoonoo Shah, who often walked in disguise through the city, attended by his trusty Grand Vizier, and met with many adventures. Once, while passing through the poorer part of the town, he heard loud voices proceeding from a certain house, and coming closer he saw through the window three sisters sitting on a sofa conversing together after supper. From what the eldest was saying, he discovered that the subject of the conversation was wishes.

"My wish," she was saying, "is to have the Sultan's baker for my husband, for then I shall eat my fill of that excellent bread called the Sultan's bread. Let us see if your tastes are as good as mine."

The second sister said, "I wish I were the wife of the Sultan's chief cook, for then I could eat all sorts of delicious food. But I should not want any of the Sultan's bread, for I am sure it must be quite common in the palace. So you see that I have better taste than you."

The youngest sister, who was very beautiful and more charming and more witty than the two elder ones, spoke in

her turn. "For my part, sisters," said she, "my desires take a higher flight. I wish to be the Sultan's Queen Consort. I would make him father of a Prince, whose hair should be gold on one side of his head, and silver on the other. When he cried, the tears from his eyes should be pearls; and when he smiled, his vermilion lips should look like a rosebud fresh blown."

The three sisters' wishes, particularly that of the youngest, seemed so singular to the Sultan that he resolved to gratify them. So he charged his Grand Vizier to take note of the house, and bring the three sisters before him the following day.

Accordingly, the Grand Vizier brought the three sisters to the palace, and presented them to the Sultan, who said, "Do you remember the wishes that you expressed last night, when you were all in such a merry mood? Speak the truth, for I must know what those wishes were."

At these unexpected words, the three sisters were much embarrassed, and cast down their eyes and blushed. But fear of offending the Sultan kept them silent. The Sultan, perceiving their confusion, then said, "Have no fear, for I did not send for you to distress you, since I know already what your wishes were. You," he added, turning to the youngest sister, "shall have your desire and become my wife today. And you," he continued, addressing the other two, "shall also be married to my chief baker and my cook."

The three weddings were all celebrated that day, as the Sultan had resolved. The youngest sister's took place with all the rejoicing and splendor befitting the marriage of a Sultan of Persia; and those of the other two sisters in a humbler manner, as befitted the quality and rank of their husbands, the chief baker and the head cook.

The two elder sisters felt strongly the great difference between their marriages and that of their younger sister. Accordingly, they gave themselves up to jealousy, and frequently planned how they might revenge themselves on the Queen.

But they continued to flatter her, and show every sign of affection and respect.

In course of time the Queen gave birth to a young Prince, as bright as the day. But the sisters, to whom the child's care was entrusted, wrapped him up and placed him in a basket and let it float away on a canal that ran near the palace, and announced that the Queen's child was nothing but a little dog. This news made the Sultan very angry.

Meanwhile, the basket containing the little Prince was carried by the stream toward the gardens of the palace. By chance the Keeper of the Sultan's Gardens was walking beside the canal, and perceiving the floating basket, called to a gardener who, with his rake, drew the basket to the side of the canal and handed it to him.

The Keeper of the Gardens was greatly surprised when he saw the child which, though only just born, already had fine features. Although he had been married several years, the Keeper of the Gardens had not been blessed with children. Accordingly, taking the child, he returned to his house, and went at once to his wife's apartment.

"Wife," said he, "as we have no children of our own, God has sent us one. Provide him with a nurse, and take every care of him, for from this moment I acknowledge him as our own son."

The following year the Queen Consort gave birth to a second little Prince, whom the unnatural sisters exposed in the same way in a basket, and set him adrift in the canal, pretending this time that the child proved to be nothing but a cat. Luckily the Keeper of the Gardens happened once again to be walking by the canal side, carried this second child to his wife, and charged her to take as good care of it as of the former.

The Sultan of Persia was this time more angry with the Queen than before, and she would have felt the consequences of his anger if the Grand Vizier had not interceded for her.

The next year the Queen gave birth to a Princess, who

suffered the same fate as her two brothers. But like them she was saved from death by the compassion and charity of the Keeper of the Gardens.

This time the two sisters reported that the third child had turned out to be only a stick of wood, which they produced in proof of their falsehood. Khoonoo Shah could no longer contain himself at this third disappointment. He ordered a small shed to be built near the chief mosque, and here he imprisoned the Queen so that she might be subject to the scorn of all who passed by. This ill-usage she bore with patient resignation.

Meanwhile, the two Princes and the Princess were brought up by the Keeper of the Gardens and his wife, with all the tenderness of a father and mother. As they grew up they all three showed marks of superior dignity, such as belongs to noble birth. All this increased the affection of the Keeper and his wife, who called the eldest Prince, Bahman, and the second, Perviz, both of them being names of former Sultans, and the Princess they called, Periezade, a name that had also been borne by many Princesses.

As soon as the two Princes were old enough, the Keeper of the Gardens provided masters to teach them to read and write. And since the Princess their sister showed a great desire to learn, he employed the same master to teach her also. Her natural quickness soon made her as proficient as her brothers. She learned to sing and to play upon various instruments; and when the Princes were learning to ride, she went through all the exercises with them, learning to ride, to bend the bow, and throw the javelin, and often outdid them in the race, and other contests of agility.

The Keeper of the Gardens was so delighted to find that his adopted children so well repaid the care and expense of their education that he decided to go to even greater expense, and purchased a country seat at a short distance from the city. This he furnished in the richest manner, adding a large park, stocked with fallow deer, so that the Princes and Princess

might divert themselves with hunting when they chose.

When this country seat was finished, the Keeper of the Gardens went and cast himself at the Sultan's feet, and pleading his long service and the infirmities of age, begged permission to resign his charge and retire. The Sultan having granted his request, the Keeper of the Gardens retired with his adopted children to his new country home. His wife had been dead some years, and he himself had lived in his new abode scarcely six months when death came upon him so suddenly that he had no time to give his foster children any account of the manner in which he had saved them from destruction.

The Princes Bahman and Perviz and the Princess Periezade, who knew no other father, paid all the honors in his funeral obsequies which love and filial gratitude required. Satisfied with the abundant fortune he had left them, they lived together in perfect harmony, free from ambition for court favor or the places of honor and dignity which they might easily have obtained.

One day when the two Princes were hunting, and the Princess had remained at home, a devout old woman came to the gate and asked leave to go in to say her prayers, it being then the hour. The Princess ordered her servants to show her into the oratory which had been fitted up in the house, because there was no mosque in the neighborhood. After the good woman had finished her prayers, she was brought into the great hall, before the Princess, who asked her many questions about herself, and ended by asking what she thought of the house and how she liked it.

"Madam," answered the devout woman, "if you give me leave to speak freely, I will take the liberty to tell you that this house would be incomparable if it had three things which are now lacking. The first is the speaking bird, so singular a creature that it draws around it all the singing birds of the neighborhood. The second is the singing tree, the leaves of which are so many mouths, which form a harmonious concert of different voices, that never are silent. The third is the

yellow water, of a gold color, of which a single drop when poured into a vessel properly prepared, immediately fills it and rises up in the middle like a fountain, which continually plays yet never overflows the basin."

"Ah! My good mother," cried the Princess. "How much obliged I am to you for a knowledge of these curious things! I never before heard that there were such wonderful rarities in the world. Pray do me the favor to inform me where they are to be found."

"Madam," replied the good woman, "all these curiosities are to be found in the same spot, near the borderline of this kingdom and India. The road lies before your own house, and whoever you send needs but follow it for twenty days, and on the twentieth he has only to ask the first person he meets where the speaking bird, singing tree, and yellow water are, and he will be informed." After saying this she took her leave and went her way.

The Princess Periezade's thoughts were so filled with her desire to possess these three wonders that when her brothers returned from hunting they were amazed to find her pensive and weighed down as by some secret trouble. At first she would make no answer to their anxious inquiries, but on being further urged, she said, "I always believed that this house which our father built for us was so complete that it lacked nothing. But today I have learned that it wants three rarities, the speaking bird, the singing tree, and the yellow water." Then she explained the peculiar qualities of these three wonders, and asked her brothers to send some trustworthy person in search of them.

"Sister," replied Prince Bahman, "I myself will undertake this search. Only tell me the place, and the way to it, and I will set out tomorrow."

The next morning, having commended his sister to his brother's care, Prince Bahman mounted his horse, and Perviz and the Princess embraced him and wished him a good journey. But in the midst of their adieus the Princess bethought

herself of the perils to which he might be exposed. "Brother," said she, "who knows whether I shall ever see you again! Give up this journey. I would rather never have the speaking bird, singing tree, and yellow water than run the risk of losing you."

"Sister," replied Bahman, smiling at her sudden fears, "my mind is made up, and you cannot dissuade me. However, since I may fail in this undertaking, I will leave you this knife, which has a singular property. If, when you draw it from the sheath, it is clean as now, it will be a sign that I am alive; but if stained with blood, then you may believe me dead."

Thereupon Bahman rode away, and never turned to the right hand or to the left, but went directly forward toward India. On the twentieth day he perceived a very singular old man sitting by the wayside under a tree. His eyebrows were white as snow, as was also his beard which reached down to his feet. The nails of his hands and feet had grown to an enormous length. A broad umbrella covered his head, and his only clothing was a mat thrown around his body. This old man was a dervish, for many years retired from the world, and devoted to meditation, until he had become as above described.

When he had drawn near the dervish, Prince Bahman stopped and alighted according to the directions which the devout woman had given the Princess Periezade, and saluting him, said, "God prolong your days, good father, and grant the accomplishment of your desires."

The dervish returned the Prince's salutation, but spoke so unintelligibly that he could not understand one word that he said. Perceiving that the trouble was caused by the dervish's hair which hung over his mouth, Prince Bahman drew out a pair of scissors that he had about him, and said, "Good dervish, I want to have some talk with you; but your hair prevents my understanding what you say. With your consent, I will cut off some part of it."

The dervish made no objection; and when the Prince had

cut off as much hair as he thought fit, he perceived that the dervish no longer seemed so very old.

"Good dervish," said he, "if I had a glass I would show you how young you look. You are now a man, but before nobody could tell what you were."

"Sir," replied the dervish with a smile, "whoever you are, I am obliged to you for your kind service. Tell me in what way I may show my gratitude."

"Good dervish," replied Prince Bahman, "I am in search of the speaking bird, the singing tree, and the yellow water. I know that these three rarities are not far from here, but cannot tell exactly where they are to be found. If you know the place I beg of you to show me the way."

While the Prince was speaking the dervish changed countenance and cast down his eyes, looking very serious. At last he broke silence. "Sir," he said to Prince Bahman, "I know the way you ask of me, but the dangers are far greater than you may suppose. A number of gentlemen as courageous as yourself have asked me the same question. I can assure you they have all perished, for I have not seen one come back. If you have any regard for your life take my advice and return home."

"Nothing that you could say," replied Prince Bahman, "can persuade me to change my purpose. Since you know the way, I once more beg you to inform me."

The dervish put his hand into a bag which lay beside him and pulled out a bowl. "Since you will not be led by my advice," said he, "take this bowl; when you have mounted your horse throw the bowl before you and follow it to the foot of the mountain. As soon as the bowl stops, alight, leave your horse with the bridle over his neck and he will stand in the same place until you return. As you ascend, you will see on your right and left a great number of large black stones, and will hear on all sides a confusion of voices, which will utter a thousand injurious threats. Do not be afraid; but above all things, do not turn your head to look behind you.

For if you do, you will instantly be changed into a black stone like the others, all of which are young men who have failed in this same enterprise. If you escape this danger, and reach the top of the mountain, you will see a cage, and in that cage is the bird you seek. Ask him which are the singing tree and the yellow water, and he will tell you. I have nothing more to say except to beg you once again not to risk your life."

After these words the Prince mounted his horse, took a respectful leave of the dervish, and threw the bowl before him. The bowl rolled away with such swiftness that Prince Bahman was forced to put his horse to a gallop to avoid losing sight of it. When it stopped at the foot of the mountain the Prince alighted, laid the bridle on his horse's neck, and having first surveyed the mountain and seen the black stones, began to ascend. He had not gone four steps before he heard voices of invisible speakers shouting in tones like thunder, "Stop him!" "Catch him!" "Kill him!" "Thief!" "Assassin!" "Murderer!" while some, in a taunting tone, cried, "No, no, don't hurt him, let the pretty fellow pass! The cage and bird are waiting for him."

In spite of these threatening voices, Prince Bahman continued for some time to ascend with courage and resolution. But the voices became such a terrifying din that at last he was seized with dread, his legs trembled under him, and forgetting the dervish's advice, he turned about to run down the hill, and was instantly changed into a black stone, as was also his horse at the same moment.

From the time of Prince Bahman's departure the Princess Periezade always wore the knife in her girdle, and pulled it out several times a day to know whether her brother was yet alive. On the fatal day that Prince Bahman was turned into stone the Princess, while talking with Prince Perviz, drew out the knife as usual and was horrified at the sight of blood running down the point. "Ah! My dear brother," cried she, "woe's me! I have been the cause of your death, and shall

never see you more. Why did I listen to the idle tales of a silly old woman!"

Prince Perviz was as much distressed by the death of Prince Bahman as the Princess; but as he knew that she still passionately desired the speaking bird, the singing tree, and the yellow water, he interrupted her, saying, "Sister, our regret for our brother is vain and useless, our grief cannot restore him to life. But why should you doubt the truth of what the holy woman told you? Our brother's death is probably due to some error on his part. I am determined myself to take up the search, and shall set out tomorrow."

The Princess did her best to dissuade Prince Perviz, but her remonstrances had no effect upon him. Before starting he gave her a string of a hundred pearls, telling her that if the pearls would not run when she counted them upon the string, but remained fixed, that would be a sure sign that he had met with the same fate as his brother.

On the twentieth day Prince Perviz met the same dervish, in the same place as his brother Bahman had done before, and asked him the same question. The dervish warned him of the same difficulties and urged him as he had urged Prince Bahman, to return home, telling him that a young gentleman who very much resembled him had come on the same enterprise a short time before, and had not yet returned.

"Good dervish," answered Prince Perviz, "the man of whom you speak was my elder brother. I have learned of his death, but I do not know from what cause."

"I can tell you that," replied the dervish, "He was changed into a black stone, like all the others. And you will meet the same fate unless you follow my advice more carefully than your brother did. But once more I beg of you to renounce your purpose."

"Dervish," said Prince Perviz, "I am grateful for your kind caution, but I cannot give up this enterprise. Therefore I beg that you will do me the same favor that you did my brother."

On this the dervish gave a bowl to the Prince, who flung it before his horse and spurring him forward followed in

pursuit. When the bowl stopped at the bottom of the hill, the Prince alighted, and gathering up his courage, started to ascend. But before he had taken six steps he heard a voice just behind him saying in an insulting tone, "Stay, rash youth, that I may punish you for your presumption."

Forgetting the dervish's advice, the Prince clapped his hand upon his sword and whirled about to avenge the insult. But he scarcely had time to see that nobody followed him before he and his horse were changed into black stones.

Meanwhile, the Princess Periezade counted her chaplet several times a day to assure herself that the pearls would still slide. On the day that Prince Perviz was changed to stone she was counting over the pearls as usual, when all at once they became immovably fixed, a sure sign that the Prince her brother was dead. As she had already determined what to do if this should happen, she wasted no time in outward grief, but at once proceeded to disguise herself in her brother's clothes, mounted her horse, and took the same road as her brothers. On the twentieth day she also met the dervish, as her brothers had done, and asked him the same question, and received the same answer, with the same warning against the folly of risking her life in such a search. The Princess replied, "If I understand you correctly, the only obstacles to success are, first, getting up to the cage without being frightened by that terrible din of voices; and, secondly, not to look behind me. As for this last direction, I hope that I shall have enough self-control to obey it. But for the first, I should like to know if it is allowable to use a stratagem against those voices."

"And what stratagem would you employ?" said the dervish.

"I would stop my ears with cotton," answered the Princess, "so that the voices, however loud and terrible, will be unable to perturb my mind and unbalance my reason."

"Good friend," replied the dervish, "you are at liberty to make the experiment, but I would advise you not to expose yourself to such danger."

After thanking the dervish, the Princess mounted her horse,

threw down the bowl which the dervish had given her, and followed it until it stopped at the foot of the mountain. The Princess alighted, stopped her ears with cotton, and boldly began the ascent. She heard the voices, and the higher she went the louder and more numerous they became. But thanks to the cotton, they failed to make any impression on her. Instead she only laughed at the rude speeches and insulting accusations. At last she saw the cage and the bird, while at the same moment the thunder of invisible voices greatly increased. The Princess, encouraged by the sight of the bird she sought, redoubled her speed, and running directly to the cage, and clapping her hands upon it, cried, "Bird, I have you, and you shall not escape me." At the same moment the voices ceased.

While Periezade drew the cotton from her ears, the bird said, "Heroic Princess, since I am destined to be a slave, I would rather be yours than any other person's, since you have won me so courageously. I know who you are, for you are

not what you seem, and I will someday tell you more. Meanwhile, I promise entire obedience to all your commands."

"Bird," said Periezade, "I have been told that there is not far off a golden water, possessing wonderful properties. Before all things, I ask you to tell me where to find it."

The bird showed her the place, which was close by. So she went and filled a little silver flagon which she had with her. Returning to the bird, she said, "Bird, this is not enough. I want also the singing tree; tell me where I may find that."

"Turn around," said the bird, "and you will see behind you a wood, in which you will find this tree. Break off a branch, carry it home and plant it in your garden. It will at once take root and will soon grow into a fine tree."

The Princess went into the wood, and guided by the har-

monious concert which she heard, soon discovered the singing tree. Having broken off a branch, she returned again to the bird and said, "Bird, what you have done for me is not yet enough. My two brothers, while searching for you, were transformed into black stones on the mountainside. Tell me how I may undo this enchantment."

The bird seemed most reluctant to inform the Princess on this point. But when she threatened to take her own life, he told her to sprinkle every stone on her way down the mountain with a drop of the golden water. This she did, and every stone she touched was changed back into a man or a horse ready saddled and bridled. Among them were her two brothers, who greeted her with much rejoicing. After explaining to her brothers and the other noble youths, the means by which she had rescued them, Periezade placed herself at the head of the procession, which day by day lessened its numbers, since the youths who had come from different countries took leave of the Princess one after another as they came to the roads leading to their homes.

As soon as the Princess reached home, she placed the cage in the garden; and no sooner had the bird begun to warble than he was surrounded by nightingales, larks, linnets, goldfinches and every species of bird in the country. And no sooner was the branch of the singing tree planted than it took root and quickly became a large tree, the leaves of which gave as harmonious a concert as those of the parent tree. A large basin of beautiful marble was placed in the garden, into which the Princess poured the yellow water, which swelled and swelled until it overtopped the edges of the basin and formed in the middle a fountain twenty feet high, perpetually falling back without ever overflowing.

Some days later the two Princes, having recovered from the fatigue of their journey, mounted their horses to indulge in their usual diversion of hunting, this time several miles from their own estate.

As it chanced, the Sultan of Persia came in pursuit of game upon the same ground. Taken by surprise at a narrow point in

the way, they hastened to alight and prostrate themselves before the Sultan, who commanded them to rise. Admiring the easy and graceful air with which they rose and stood before him, the Sultan asked who they were and where they lived.

"Sire," said Prince Bahman, "we are the sons of the late Keeper of your Majesty's Gardens, and live in a house which he built shortly before he died."

"I perceive," said the Sultan, "that you love hunting?"

"Sire," replied Prince Bahman, "it is our common exercise, and one which none of your Majesty's subjects who intend to bear arms in your armies can afford to neglect."

The Sultan, charmed with so prudent an answer, invited the two brothers to join him in the hunt. And such skill did they show with their javelins that the delighted monarch invited them to make him a visit. To his great surprise, they begged to be excused; and when pressed for a reason, Prince Bahman explained that they had a younger sister with whom they lived in such perfect union that they never did anything without first consulting her.

"I commend your brotherly affection," answered the Sultan. "Consult your sister by all means—meet me here tomorrow and give me your answer."

The Princes went home, but neglected to tell the Princess Periezade about their adventure in meeting the Sultan and the honor he had done them in asking them to visit him. But they did not fail the next morning to meet him as agreed. They confessed that they had forgotten to tell their sister, and begged to be excused. The Sultan graciously forgave them, but again made them promise to bring an answer on the morrow. The Princes were guilty of the same forgetfulness a second time. And although the Sultan was so good-natured as to excuse them once again for their negligence he nevertheless drew three little golden balls from his purse and dropped them into Prince Bahman's bosom.

"These balls," said he, smiling, "will prevent your forgetting my request a third time; since the noise they will make by falling on the floor when you undress will remind you."

The event happened just as the Sultan foresaw. For when Prince Bahman unloosed his girdle to go to bed, the balls dropped on the floor. He ran into Prince Perviz's chamber, then together they went into the Princess Periezade's apartment, and told her all the circumstances of their meeting the Sultan.

The Princess was much surprised at the news. "It was on my account, I know," she said, "that you refused the Sultan, and I fully appreciate that it was because of your affection for me. But it is dangerous to oppose monarchs in their desires; and if I should dissuade you from visiting him it might anger him, and in the end make myself and both of you miserable. Before we decide anything, let us consult the speaking bird, for he is wise and has promised to help us in all difficulties."

The Princess sent for the cage, and after explaining the circumstances, asked the bird what they ought to do. The bird replied:

"The Princes, your brothers, must accept the Sultan's invitation and then in their turn invite him to come and see your house."

The next morning they again met the Sultan, and Prince Bahman said, "Sire, your Majesty may dispose of us as you please; for we not only easily obtained our sister's consent, but she rebuked us for consulting her in a question of our duty to your Majesty. But if we have offended we hope you will pardon us."

"Do not be uneasy on that score," replied the Sultan. "I highly approve of your conduct, and only hope that you will show me the same deference you show your sister, if I am to have a share of your friendship."

The Sultan gave orders to return at once to his palace. He made the Princes ride one on each side of him; and when they entered the capital, the eyes of the people, who stood in crowds in the street, were fixed on the two young strangers, and they were eager to know who they might be, and many wished that their Sultan had been blessed with two such handsome sons.

Upon reaching the palace the Sultan led the Princes through the principal apartments, and they showed a nice appreciation of the beauty of the rooms and the richness of the furniture and ornaments. Afterward a magnificent repast was served up, and the Sultan made them sit with him, and was so pleased with their wit and judgment that he said to himself, "Were these my own sons, they could not be more accomplished or better informed."

When night approached the two Princes prostrated themselves at the Sultan's feet, and thanked him for the favors he had heaped upon them. Before they went out of the Sultan's presence, Prince Bahman said, "Sire, may we presume to request that you will do us and our sister the honor to visit us the next time that you are hunting in our neighborhood? Our house is not worthy of your presence; but monarchs have sometimes stooped to take shelter in a cottage."

"My children," replied the Sultan, "your house cannot be otherwise than beautiful and worthy of its owners. I will call and see it with pleasure, and no later than tomorrow. Early in the morning I shall be where I first saw you. Meet me there, and you shall be my guides."

When the Princess Periezade learned from her brothers that the Sultan was to call at their house the next day, she said, "We must plan at once to prepare a repast fit for his Majesty; and for that purpose we must consult the speaking bird, for perhaps he can tell us what meats the Sultan likes."

The Princes approved of her plan, and after they had retired she consulted the bird alone.

"Good mistress," said the bird, "you have excellent cooks, let them do the best they can. But above all things let them prepare a dish of cucumbers stuffed with pearls, which must be set before the Sultan as a first course."

"Cucumbers stuffed with pearls?" cried the Princess. "That is an unheard-of dish! Besides, all the pearls that I have would not be enough."

"As for that," said the bird, "go early tomorrow morning to the park and dig at the foot of the first tree on your right,

and you will find there more pearls than you want."

In the morning the Princess followed the bird's instructions, taking the gardener with her. When the gardener had dug to a certain depth at the foot of the first tree on the right, he discovered a gold box about a foot square, which he placed in the hands of the Princess. Upon opening it she found it full of pearls. As soon as she entered the house she called the head cook, and after giving him general instructions about the entertainment for the Sultan, she added:

"Besides all this, you must dress an extraordinary dish to set before the Sultan himself. This dish must be of cucumbers stuffed with these pearls." And at the same time she opened the box and showed the pearls. The chief cook, who had never heard of such a dish, started back in amazement, but finding nothing to say in reply, took the box and retired.

The same day the two Princes met the Sultan at the place appointed, and while Prince Bahman stayed to conduct him to their house, Prince Perviz rode ahead to announce that he was approaching. When the Sultan entered the courtyard and alighted at the portico, the Princess came and threw herself at his feet. The Sultan stooped to raise her, and after he had gazed for some time at her beauty, he said:

"The brothers are worthy of the sister, and she is worthy of them. I am no longer amazed that the brothers would do nothing without their sister's consent." After the Princess had led the Sultan through all the rooms of the house except the hall, and he had duly considered them and admired their variety, he begged to see the garden. So the Princess opened a door which led into the garden, and conducted him to the spot where the singing tree was planted. And there the Sultan heard a concert different from any he had ever heard before. "My daughter," he said to the Princess, "where are the musicians whom I hear? Are they underground or invisible in the air? Such excellent performers should not remain unseen."

"Sire," replied the Princess, smiling, "they are not mu-

sicians, but the leaves of the tree your Majesty sees before you, which makes this music, as you yourself will be convinced if you draw nearer."

The Sultan went nearer, and was so charmed with the sweet harmony that he begged the Princess to tell him the name of the wonderful tree, and when and where she had obtained it.

"Sire," replied the Princess, "this tree has no other name than that of the singing tree, and it is not a native of this country. Its history is connected with the yellow water and the speaking bird, which came to me at the same time, and which your Majesty may see after you have rested yourself, and if it pleases you, I will then relate the history of these rarities."

"My daughter," replied the Sultan, "my fatigue is all forgotten at sight of the wonderful things you have shown me. I am impatient to see the yellow water and to admire the speaking bird."

When the Sultan came to the yellow water, he was so fascinated by the wonderful sight that he could hardly tear his gaze away from it. But after the Princess had described its strange properties, he at last turned reluctantly away, saying, "Well, this is enough for one time. I promise myself the pleasure to come and visit it often. But now let us go and see the speaking bird."

As he went toward the hall, the Sultan perceived a prodigious number of birds in the trees around, filling the air with their warblings, and asked the reason. The Princess explained that they came from all parts to accompany the song of the speaking bird, which the Sultan could now see in a cage in one of the windows of the hall.

As the Sultan and Princess Periezade entered the hall the Princess raised her voice and said, "My slave, here is the Sultan, pay your compliments to him."

The bird immediately ceased singing, and said, "God save the Sultan! Long may he live!"

As the repast was served near the window where the bird was placed, the Sultan replied, as he took his seat, "Bird, I thank you, and am overjoyed to find in you the Sultan of the race of birds."

When the Sultan saw the dish of cucumbers set before him, he reached out his hand and took one, but upon cutting it was extremely surprised to find it stuffed with pearls. "What novelty is this," he asked, "and what is the purpose of stuffing cucumbers with pearls, since pearls cannot be eaten?" He looked at the two Princes and the Princess to ask them the meaning. But at this moment the bird interrupted him and said:

"How can your Majesty be so greatly astonished at cucumbers stuffed with pearls, which you see with your own eyes, when you so easily believed that the Queen, your own wife, was the mother of a dog, a cat, and a stick of wood?"

"I believed those things," replied the ultan, "because the nurses assured me of the facts."

"Those nurses, sire," replied the bird, "were the Queen's two sisters, who were envious of her happiness, and imposed upon your Majesty's credulity to satisfy their desire of revenge. If you question them they will confess their crime. The two brothers and the sister whom you see before you are your own children, who were rescued by the Keeper of your Gardens, and adopted by him."

"Bird," cried the Sultan, "I believe that you have disclosed the truth to me. The attraction which I felt toward the Princes and Princess shows plainly that they must be my own kin. Come, my sons, come, my daughter, let me embrace you, and give you the first marks of a father's love and tenderness."

When the banquet was over, and the Sultan about to depart, he said, "My children, you see in me your father. To-morrow I will bring the Queen, your mother; therefore prepare to receive her."

The Sultan's first act upon returning to his palace was to command the Grand Vizier to seize the Queen's two sisters.

They were taken from their homes, convicted and condemned, and executed within an hour.

Meanwhile, the Sultan Khoonoo Shah, followed by all the lords of his court, went on foot to take the Queen from the strict confinement in which she had languished for so many years. "I have come," said he, with tears in his eyes, "to entreat your pardon for the injustice I have done you. I have already punished your cruel sisters, who so wickedly deceived me; and I hope soon to present to you two accomplished Princes and a lovely Princess. Come and resume your former rank, with all the honors which are your due." Immediately the joyous news was spread throughout the city.

Early next morning the Sultan and the Queen went with all their court to the house built by the Keeper of the Gardens, where the Sultan presented the Princes Bahman and Perviz and the Princess Periezade to their rejoicing mother. The tears flowed plentifully down the cheeks of all present, but especially of the Queen, because of her great joy at having two such Princes for her sons and such a Princess for her daughter.

When the Sultan returned to his capital, he rode with the Princes Bahman and Perviz on his right hand and with the Queen and Princess at his left, preceded and followed by all the officers of his court. Crowds of people came out to meet them, and with shouts of joy ushered them into the city, where all eyes were focused, not only upon the Queen and her two sons and daughter, but also upon the speaking bird which the Princess carried in its cage, while countless other birds, drawn by his sweet notes, followed, flitting from tree to tree, and from one housetop to another.

So the Princes Bahman and Perviz and the Princess Periezade were brought to the palace with fitting pomp; and all night long there were illuminations and rejoicings, not only in the palace and in all parts of the city, but extending throughout the Empire of Persia.

The Story of Prince Ahmed and Periebanou

THERE WAS ONCE a Sultan of India who had three sons and one niece, the ornaments of his court. The eldest of the Princes was called Houssain, the second Ali, the youngest Ahmed, and the Princess his niece, Nouronnihar.

The Princess Nouronnihar, having lost her father while she was still very young, had been brought up by the Sultan. And now that she was grown to womanhood, the Sultan thought of marrying her to some Prince worthy of the alliance. She was very beautiful, and when the Sultan's idea became known, the Princes informed him, singly, that they loved her and would fain marry her. This discovery pained the Sultan, because he knew that there would be jealousy among his sons.

He therefore sent for each separately and spoke with him, urging him to abide permanently by the lady's choice, but none of them would yield without a struggle. As he found them obstinate, he sent for them all together, and said, "My children, since I have not been able to dissuade you from aspiring to marry the Princess your cousin; and as I have no inclination to use my authority, to give her to one in prefer-

ence to his brothers, I trust I have thought of an expedient which will please you all, and preserve harmony among you, if you will but hear me, and follow my advice. I think it would not be amiss if you were to travel separately into different countries, so that you might not meet each other. And as you know I am very curious, and delight in everything that is rare and singular, I promise my niece in marriage to him who shall bring me the most extraordinary rarity."

The three Princes, each hoping that fortune would be favorable to him, consented to this proposal. The Sultan gave them money; and early the next morning they started from the city, disguised as merchants. They departed by the same gate, each attended by a trusty servant, and for one day they journeyed together. Then they halted at a khan, and having agreed to meet in one year's time at the same place, they said farewell, and early the next morning started on their several journeys.

Prince Houssain, the eldest brother, who had heard wonders of the extent, power, riches, and splendor of the Kingdom of Bisnagar, bent his course toward the Indian coast. And after three months' traveling, sometimes over deserts and barren mountains, and sometimes through populous and fertile countries, he arrived at Bisnagar, the capital of the kingdom of that name, and the residence of its Maharajah. He lodged at a khan appointed for foreign merchants. And having learnt that there were four principal divisions where merchants of all sorts kept their shops, in the midst of which stood the Maharahah's palace, surrounded by three courts, and each gate distant two leagues from the other, he went to one of these quarters the next day.

It was large, divided into several streets, all vaulted and shaded from the sun, but yet very light. The shops were all of the same size and proportion; and all who dealt in the same sort of goods, as well as all the artists of the same profession, lived in one street.

Prince Houssain marveled at the variety and richness of

the articles exposed for sale. And as he wandered from street to street he wondered still more; for on all sides he saw the products of every country in the world. Silks, porcelain, and precious stones in abundance indicated the enormous wealth of the people. Another object which Prince Houssain particularly admired was the great number of flower sellers who crowded the streets. For the Indians are such great lovers of flowers that not one will stir without a nosegay in his hand, or a garland on his head. And the merchants keep them in pots in their shops, so that the air of the whole quarter is beautifully perfumed.

Prince Houssain had finished his inspection when a merchant, perceiving him passing with weary steps, asked him to sit down in his shop. Before long a crier came past, carrying a piece of carpet for which he asked forty purses of gold. It was only about six feet square, and the Prince was astonished at the price. "Surely," said he, "there must be something very extraordinary about this carpet, which I cannot see, for it looks ordinary enough."

"You have guessed right, sir," replied the crier, "and will own it when you learn that whoever sits on this piece of carpeting may be transported in an instant whithersoever he desires to be, without being stopped by any obstacle."

The Prince was overjoyed, for he had found a rarity which would secure him the hand of the Princess. "If," said he, "the carpet has this virtue, I will gladly buy it."

"Sir," replied the crier, "I have told you the truth. And it will be an easy matter to convince you. I will spread the carpeting; and when we have both sat down, and you have formed the wish to be transported into your apartment at the khan, if we are not conveyed thither, it shall be no bargain."

On this assurance of the crier, the Prince accepted the conditions, and concluded the bargain. Then having obtained the shopkeeper's leave, they went into his back shop where they both sat down on the carpeting. And as soon as the

Prince had formed his wish to be transported into his apartment at the khan, he in an instant found himself and the crier there. As he wanted not a more convincing proof of the virtue of the carpeting, he counted out to the crier forty purses of gold, and gave him twenty pieces for himself.

In this manner Prince Houssain became the possessor of the carpeting, and was overjoyed at having so speedily found something worth bringing to his father. He could at will have transported himself to the khan where he had parted from his brothers; but, knowing that they would not have returned, he decided to tarry in the city and study the manners and customs of the people. He gained much satisfaction and information from visiting the different buildings and witnessing the various ceremonies which took place.

He thus became the spectator of a solemn festival attended by a multitude of Hindus. This great assembly, encamped in variously colored tents on a plain of vast extent, as far as the eye could reach, formed an imposing sight. And he also presented himself at the court of the Maharajah by whose wealth he was greatly impressed. All these things made his stay at Bisnagar very pleasant. But he desired to be nearer to the Princess Nouronnihar whom he most ardently loved, and he considered that he could rely upon claiming her as his bride. Therefore, although he might have remained in the city much longer, he paid his reckoning at the khan, spread the carpet upon the floor of his room, and he and his attendant were instantly transported to the meeting place.

Prince Ali, the second brother, joined a caravan; and in four months arrived at Shiraz, which was then the capital of the Empire of Persia. And having on the way contracted a friendship with some merchants, he passed for a jeweler, and lodged in the same khan with them.

On the morning after his arrival Prince Ali started to inspect the valuable articles which were exposed for sale in the quarter where the jewelers lodged. He was astonished by all

the wealth which he saw; and he wandered from street to street lost in admiration. But what surprised him most was a crier who walked to and fro carrying an ivory tube in his hand, for which he asked forty purses of gold. Prince Ali thought the man mad, but he was anxious to find out why the tube was so expensive. "Sir," said the crier, when the Prince addressed him, "this tube is furnished with a glass; by looking through it, you will see whatever object you wish to behold."

The crier presented the tube for his inspection. And he, wishing to see his father, looked through it and beheld the Sultan in perfect health, sitting on his throne, in his council chamber. Next he wished to see the Princess Nouronnihar, and immediately he saw her sitting laughing among her companions.

Prince Ali wanted no other proof to persuade him that this tube was the most valuable article, not only in the city of Shiraz, but in all the world; and believed that if he should neglect to purchase it he should never meet with an equally wonderful curiosity. He said to the crier, "I will purchase this

tube from you for the forty purses." He then took him to the khan where he lodged, told him out the money, and became possessor of the magic tube.

Prince Ali was overjoyed with his purchase, and persuaded himself that, as his brothers would not be able to meet with anything so rare and admirable, the Princess Nouronnihar must be the recompense for the fatigue of his travels. While he was waiting for the caravan to start on its return journey, he visited the court of Persia and saw all the wonders in the neighborhood of the city. When all was ready, he joined his friends, and arrived, happily without any accident or trouble, at the meeting place, where he found Prince Houssain. There they tarried, waiting for Prince Ahmed.

Prince Ahmed took the road to Samarcand. The day after his arrival, as he went through the city, he saw a crier who had an artificial apple in his hand for which he demanded

thirty-five purses of gold. "Let me see that apple," said the Prince, "and tell me what virtue or extraordinary property it possesses to be valued at so high a rate."

"Sir," replied the crier, giving it into his hand, "if you look at the mere outside of this apple, it is not very remarkable. But if you consider its properties, and the great use and benefit it is to mankind, you will say it is invaluable, and that he who possesses it is master of a great treasure. It cures all sick persons of the most mortal diseases; and this merely by the patient's smelling it."

"If one may believe you," replied Prince Ahmed, "the virtues of this apple are wonderful, and it is indeed valuable. But what proof have you of what you say?"

"Sir," replied the crier, "the truth is known to the whole city of Samarcand."

While the crier was detailing to Prince Ahmed the virtues of the artificial apple, many persons gathered about them, and confirmed what he declared. And one amongst the rest said he had a friend who was dangerously ill and whose life was despaired of, which might be a favorable opportunity to try the experiment. Thereupon Prince Ahmed told the crier he would give him forty purses for the apple if it cured the sick person merely by smelling it.

The crier said to Prince Ahmed, "Come, sir, let us go and make the experiment, and the apple shall be yours." The experiment succeeded; and the Prince, after he had counted out to the crier forty purses, and had received the apple from him in return, waited with the greatest impatience for the departure of a caravan for the Indies. In the meantime, he saw all that was curious at and about Samarcand. And when a caravan set out, he joined it, and arrived safely at the appointed place where the Princes Houssain and Ali waited for him.

When Prince Ahmed joined his brothers, they embraced with tenderness, and expressed much joy at meeting again. Then Prince Houssain said, "Brothers, let us postpone the

narrative of our travels, and let us at once show each other what we have brought as a curiosity that we may do ourselves justice beforehand, and judge to which of us our father may give the preference. To set the example, I will tell you that the rarity which I have brought from the Kingdom of Bisnagar is the carpeting on which I sit. It looks but ordinary, and makes no show; but it possesses wonderful virtues. Whoever sits on it, and desires to be transported to any place, is immediately carried thither. I made the experiment myself, before I paid the forty purses, which I most readily gave for it. I expect now that you will tell me whether what you have brought is to be compared with this carpet."

Prince Ali spoke next, and said, "I must own that your carpet is very wonderful. Yet I am as well satisfied with my purchase as you can possibly be with yours. Here is an ivory tube which also cost me forty purses. It looks ordinary enough, yet on gazing through it you can behold whatever you desire to see, no matter how far distant it may be. Take it, brother, and try for yourself."

Houssain took the ivory tube from Prince Ali, with the intention of seeing the Princess Nouronnihar. Suddenly Ali and Prince Ahmed, who had kept their eyes fixed upon him, were extremely surprised to see his countenance change in such a manner, as to express extraordinary alarm and affliction. And he cried out, "Alas! Princes, to what purpose have we undertaken such long and fatiguing journeys, with but the hope of being recompensed by the possession of the charming Nouronnihar, when in a few moments that lovely princess will breathe her last. I saw her in her bed, surrounded by her women all in tears, who gave every evidence of expecting her death. Take the tube, behold yourselves the miserable state she is in, and mingle your tears with mine."

Prince Ali took the tube out of Houssain's hand, and after he had seen the same object, with sensible grief presented it to Ahmed, who took it, to behold the melancholy sight which so much concerned them all.

When Prince Ahmed had taken the tube out of Ali's hands, and had seen that the Princess Nouronnihar's end was so near, he addressed himself to his two brothers, saying, "Brothers, the Princess Nouronnihar is indeed at death's door. But provided we lose no time, we may preserve her life." He then took the artificial apple out of his bosom, and resumed: "This apple cost me as much as the carpet or tube, and has healing properties. If a sick person smells it, though in the last agonies, it will restore him to perfect health immediately. I have made the experiment, and can show you its wonderful effect on the person of the Princess Nouronnihar, if we hasten to assist her."

"We cannot make more dispatch," said Prince Houssain, "than by transporting ourselves instantly into her chamber by means of my carpet. Come, lose no time. Sit down; it is large enough to hold us all."

The Princes Ali and Ahmed sat down by Houssain, and as their interest was the same, they all framed the same wish, and were transported instantaneously into the Princess Nouronnihar's chamber.

The presence of the three Princes, who were so little expected, alarmed the Princess' women, who could not comprehend by what enchantment three strange men should be among them; for they did not know them at first.

Prince Ahmed no sooner saw himself in Nouronnihar's chamber, and perceived the Princess dying, than he rose off the carpet, and went to the bedside, and put the apple to her nostrils. The Princess instantly opened her eyes and asked to be dressed, with the same freedom and naturalness as if she had awaked out of a sound sleep. Her women presently informed her that she was obliged to the three Princes her cousins and particularly to Prince Ahmed, for the sudden recovery of her health. She immediately expressed her joy at seeing them, and thanked them all together, but afterward Prince Ahmed in particular. As she desired to dress, the Princes hastened to express the pleasure they felt at her

recovery. A repast was served to them after which they retired.

While the Princess was dressing, the Princes went to throw themselves at their father's feet. But when they came to him, they found he had been previously informed of their unexpected arrival, and by what means the Princess had been so suddenly cured. The Sultan received and embraced them with the greatest joy, both for their return and the wonderful recovery of the Princess his niece who had been given up by the physicians. After the usual compliments, each of the Princes presented the rarity which he had brought: Prince Houssain his carpet, Prince Ali his ivory tube, and Prince Ahmed the artificial apple. And after each had commended his present, as he put it into the Sultan's hands, they begged of him to pronounce their fate, and declare to which of them he would give the Princess Nouronnihar, according to his promise.

The Sultan of the Indies, having heard all that the Princes had to say, remained some time silent, considering what answer he should make. At last he said to them in terms full of wisdom: "I would declare for one of you, my children, if I could do it with justice. But let us consider. It is true, Ahmed, the Princess is beholden to your artificial apple for her cure. But let me ask you, whether you could have been of such service to her if you had not known by Ali's tube the danger she was in, and Houssain's carpet had not brought you to her so soon? Your tube, Ali, informed you and your brothers that you were likely to lose the Princess, and so for it she is greatly obliged to you. You must also grant that the knowledge of her illness would have been of no service without the artificial apple and carpet. And as for you, Houssain, the Princess would be very ungrateful if she did not show her sense of the value of your carpet, which was so necessary a means toward effecting her cure. But consider, it would have been of little use, if you had not been acquainted with her illness by Ali's tube, or if Ahmed had not applied his artificial apple.

"Therefore, as neither the carpet, the ivory tube, nor the artificial apple has the least preference to the other articles, I cannot grant the Princess to any one of you. And the only fruit you have reaped from your travels is the glory of having equally contributed to restore her to health. As this is the case, you see that I must have recourse to other means to determine the choice I ought to make. And as there is time enough between now and night, I will do it today. Go and procure each of you a bow and arrow, repair to the plain where the horses are exercised. I will soon join you, and will give the Princess Nouronnihar to him who shoots the farthest."

The three Princes had no objection to the decision of the Sultan. When they were dismissed from his presence, each provided himself with a bow and arrow, and they went to the plain appointed, followed by a great concourse of people.

The Sultan did not make them wait long for him. As soon as he arrived, Prince Houssain, as the eldest, took his bow and arrow, and shot first. Prince Ali shot next, and far beyond him. And Prince Ahmed last of all. But it so happened that nobody could see where his arrow fell; and notwithstanding all the search made by himself and all the spectators, it was not to be found. Though it was believed that he had shot the farthest, still, as Prince Ahmed's arrow could not be found, the Sultan determined in favor of Prince Ali, and gave orders for preparations to be made for the solemnization of the nuptials, which were celebrated a few days after with great magnificence.

Prince Houssain would not honor the feast with his presence. He could not bear to see the Princess Nouronnihar wed Prince Ali, who, he said, did not deserve her more deeply nor love her more truly than himself. In short, his grief was so extreme that he left the court, and renounced all right of succession to the crown, to turn dervish, and put himself under the discipline of a famous Sheik, who had gained great reputation for his exemplary life.

Prince Ahmed, urged by the same motive, did not assist at

the nuptials of Prince Ali and the Princess Nouronnihar, any more than his brother Houssain. Yet he did not renounce the world as his brother had done. But as he could not imagine what could have become of his arrow, he resolved to search for it, that he might not have anything with which to reproach himself. With this intent he went to the place where the Princes Houssain and Ali's arrows had been gathered up, and proceeding straight forward from thence looked carefully on both sides as he advanced. He went so far that at last he began to think his labor was in vain. Yet he could not help proceeding till he came to some steep craggy rocks, which completely barred the way.

To his great astonishment he perceived an arrow, which he recognized as his own, at the foot of the rocks. "Certainly," said he to himself, "neither I nor any man living can shoot an arrow so far. Perhaps fortune, to make amends for depriving me of what I thought the greatest happiness of my life, may have reserved a greater blessing for my comfort."

There were many cavities in the rocks into one of which the Prince entered, and looking about, beheld an iron door, which he feared was fastened. But pushing against it, it opened, and disclosed a stairway, which he descended with his arrow in his hand. At first he thought he was entering a dark place, but presently he became aware of a strange light quite different from the light of day. Before him was a spacious square, and in the center of it he beheld a magnificent palace. At the same instant, a damsel of majestic air and of remarkable beauty advanced across the square, attended by a troop of ladies, all magnificently dressed.

As soon as Ahmed perceived the damsel, he hastened to pay his respects; and the lovely lady, seeing him, said, "Come near, Prince Ahmed. You are welcome."

Prince Ahmed was surprised at hearing himself addressed by name, but he bowed low, and followed into the great hall. Here she seated herself upon a sofa, and requested the Prince to sit beside her. Then she said, "You are surprised that I

know you, yet you cannot be completely unprepared, as the Koran informs you that the world is inhabited by genii as well as men. I am the daughter of one of the most powerful and distinguished of these genii, and my name is Periebanou. I am no stranger to your loves or your travels, since it was I, myself, who exposed for sale the artificial apple, which you bought at Samarcand, the carpet which Prince Houssain purchased at Bisnagar, and the tube which Prince Ali brought from Shiraz. This is sufficient to let you know that I am not unacquainted with everything that relates to you. You seemed to me worthy of a more happy fate than that of possessing the Princess Nouronnihar. And that you might attain to it, I carried your arrow to the place where you found it. It is in your power to avail yourself of the favorable opportunity which presents itself to make you happy."

Ahmed made no answer to this declaration, but knelt to kiss the hem of her garment. This, however, she would not allow him, and presented her hand, which he kissed a thousand times, and kept it fast locked in his own. "Well, Prince Ahmed," said she, "will you pledge your faith to me, as I do mine to you?"

"Yes, madam," replied the Prince in an ecstasy of joy, "what can I do more fortunate for myself, or with greater pleasure?"

"Then," answered the fairy, "you are my husband, and I am your wife. Our fairy marriages are contracted with no other ceremonies, and yet are more indissoluble than those among men, with all their formalities." The fairy Periebanou then conducted Prince Ahmed round the palace, where he saw much that delighted him. At last she led him to a rich apartment in which the marriage feast was spread. The fairy had ordered a sumptuous repast to be prepared; and the Prince marveled at the variety and delicacy of the dishes, many of which were quite strange to him. While they ate there was music; and after dessert a large number of fairies and genii appeared and danced before them. Day after day new amuse-

ments were provided, each more entrancing than the last. For the fairy's intention was not only to give the Prince convincing proofs of the sincerity of her love, but to let him see that, at his father's court, he could meet with nothing comparable to the happiness he enjoyed with her. She wished to attach him entirely to herself and in this she entirely succeeded.

At the end of six months, Prince Ahmed, who still loved and honored the Sultan his father, felt a great desire to know how he was. He mentioned his wish to the fairy, who, lest this should be an excuse to leave her, begged him to abandon the idea of visiting the capital.

"My Queen," replied the Prince, "since you do not consent that I shall go, I will deny myself the pleasure, and there is nothing to which I would not submit to please you."

These words greatly pleased the fairy; but the Prince grieved lest his father should think him dead.

As the Prince had supposed, the Sultan of the Indies, in the midst of the rejoicings on account of the nuptials of Prince Ali and the Princess Nouronnihar, was sensibly afflicted by the absence of his other two sons. It was not long before he was informed of the resolution Houssain had taken to forsake the world, and the place he had chosen for his retreat. He made the most diligent search for Ahmed, and dispatched couriers to all the provinces of his dominions, with orders to the governors to stop him, and oblige him to return to court. But all the pains he took had not the desired success, and his affliction, instead of diminishing, increased. He consulted the Grand Vizier, saying:

"Vizier, thou knowest I always loved Ahmed the most of all my sons. My grief is so heavy that I shall sink under it, if thou hast not compassion on me. I conjure thee to assist and advise me." The Grand Vizier, considering how to give his sovereign some ease, recollected a sorceress, of whom he had heard wonders, and proposed to send for and consult her. The Sultan consented, and she was introduced into his presence.

The Sultan said to the sorceress, "By thine art and skill canst thou tell me what is become of Prince Ahmed? If he be alive, where he is? And if I may hope ever to see him again?" To this the sorceress replied, "It is impossible, sire, for me to answer the questions immediately, but if you will allow me till tomorrow, I will endeavor to satisfy you." The Sultan granted her the time, and promised to reward her richly.

The sorceress returned the next day, and said, "Sire, I have only been able to discover that Prince Ahmed is alive; but where he is I cannot discover." The Sultan of the Indies was obliged to remain satisfied with this answer, which left him in the same uneasiness as before as to the Prince's situation.

Meanwhile Prince Ahmed had never again asked the fairy Periebanou to allow him to visit his father, but he often spoke to her of the Sultan; and she perceived the desire that was in his mind. One dav she said to him, "Prince, since I am now convinced of the fidelity of your love, I grant you the permission you sought, on one condition: that you will first swear to me that your absence shall not be long. Also, let me give you some advice: Do not inform your father of our marriage, neither of my quality, nor the place of our residence. Beg of him to be satisfied with knowing that you are happy, and the sole end of your visit is to make him easy respecting your fate."

Prince Ahmed was greatly pleased by this. Accompanied by twenty horsemen, he set out on a charger, which was most richly caparisoned, and as beautiful a creature as any in the Sultan of the Indies' stables. It was no great distance to his father's capital; and, when Prince Ahmed arrived, the people received him with acclamations, and followed him in crowds to the palace. The Sultan embraced him with great joy, complaining at the same time, with a fatherly tenderness, of the affliction his long absence had occasioned.

"Sire," replied Prince Ahmed, "when my arrow so mysteriously disappeared, I wanted to find it. Returning alone, I

commenced my search. I sought all about the place where Houssain's and Ali's arrows were found, and where I imagined mine must have fallen, but all my labor was in vain. I proceeded along the plain in a straight line for a league, and found nothing. I was about to give up my search, when I found myself drawn forward against my will. And after having gone four leagues, to that part of the plain where it is bounded by rocks, I perceived an arrow. I ran to the spot, took it up, and knew it to be the same which I had shot. Then I knew that your decision was faulty, and that some power was working for my good. But as to this mystery I beg you will not be offended if I remain silent, and that you will be satisfied to know from my own mouth that I am happy, and content with my fate. Nevertheless, I was grieved lest you should suffer in uncertainty, and I beg you to allow me to come here occasionally to visit you."

"Son, I wish to penetrate no further into your secrets. Your presence has restored to me the joy I have not felt for a long time, and you shall always be welcome when you come."

Prince Ahmed stayed three days in his father's court, and on the fourth returned to the fairy Periebanou who received him with great joy.

A month after Prince Ahmed's return from visiting his father, the fairy said, "Do not you remember the promise you made to your father? I think you should not be longer in renewing your visits. Pay him one tomorrow. And after that, go and visit once a month, without speaking to me, or waiting for my permission. I readily consent to such an arrangement."

Prince Ahmed went the next morning with the same attendants as before, but much more magnificently mounted, equipped, and dressed, and was received by the Sultan with the same joy and satisfaction. For several months he faithfully paid him visits, and always with a richer and more brilliant equipage.

At last the Sultan's favorites, who judged of Prince Ahmed's power by the splendor of his appearance, strove to make the

father jealous of his son. They represented that it was but common prudence to discover where the Prince had retired, and how he could afford to live so magnificently, since he had no revenue assigned for his expenses; that he seemed to come to court only to insult him; and that it was to be feared he might court the people's favor and dethrone him. And they brought many cunning arguments to bear, in support of their words, adding, "It is dangerous to have so powerful a neighbor; for he must live near at hand, since neither horses nor men bear marks of travel."

When the favorites had concluded these insinuations, the Sultan said, "I do not believe my son Ahmed is so wicked as you would persuade me he is. However, I am obliged to you for your advice, and I do not doubt that it proceeds from good intention and loyalty to my person."

The Sultan of the Indies said this in order that his favorites might not know the impression their observations had made on his mind. He was, however, so much alarmed by them that he resolved to have Prince Ahmed watched. To this end he sent for the sorceress, who was introduced by a private door into his closet.

"My son Ahmed," said the Sultan, "comes to my court every month. But I cannot learn from him where he resides, and do not wish to force his secret from him. He is at this time with me, and usually departs without taking leave of me, or of any of my court. You must watch him, so as to find out where he retires to, and bring me information."

The sorceress left the Sultan, and knowing the place where Prince Ahmed found his arrow, went immediately thither, and concealed herself near the rocks, so as not to be seen.

The next morning Prince Ahmed set out by daybreak, without taking leave either of the Sultan or any of his court, according to custom. The sorceress watched him until suddenly he disappeared among the rocks. The steepness of the rocks formed an insurmountable barrier to men, whether on horseback or on foot, so that the sorceress judged that the

Prince retired either into some cavern, or some subterraneous place, the abode of genii or fairies. When she thought the Prince and his attendants must have advanced far into whatever concealment they inhabited, she came out of her hiding place and explored the hollow way where she had lost sight of them, but could find no trace of them. The sorceress, who saw it was in vain for her to search any farther, returned to the Sultan. "Though I have failed this time," she said, "I hope ere long to succeed."

The Sultan was pleased, and said, "Do as you think fit." And to encourage her, he presented her with a diamond of great value, telling her it was only an earnest of the ample recompense she should receive when she had performed this important service. A day or two before the Prince's next visit the sorceress went to the foot of the rock where she had lost sight of him and his attendants, and waited there to execute the project she had formed.

As Prince Ahmed started upon his journey, he saw her lying on the ground, groaning and bewailing the fact that she was far from aid. The Prince pitied her, turned his horse, and said, "Good woman, you are not so far from help as you imagine. I will assist you, and convey you where you shall have all possible care taken of you, and where you shall find a speedy cure. Rise, and let one of my people take you behind him."

At these words the sorceress, who pretended sickness only to explore where the Prince resided, made many efforts to rise, pretending that the violence of her illness prevented her. Then two of the Prince's attendants alighted, and helped her rise. They placed her on a horse behind one of their companions. The Prince turned back to the iron gate, and when he had entered the outer court, he sent to ask Periebanou to see him. The fairy came with all imaginable haste, and the Prince said to her, "My Princess, I desire you would have compassion on this good woman. I found her in the condition you see her, and promised her the assistance she required. I

recommend her to your care, and am persuaded that you, from inclination, as well as my request, will not abandon her."

The fairy, who had her eyes fixed on the pretended sick woman all the time the Prince was speaking, ordered two of her women to take her from the men who supported her, and conduct her into an apartment of the palace, and take as much care of her as they would of herself.

While the two women were executing the fairy's commands, she went up to Prince Ahmed, and whispering in his ear, said, "Prince, this woman is not so sick as she pretends to be; and I am much mistaken if she is not sent thither on purpose to occasion you great trouble. But do not be concerned; I will deliver you out of all snares that shall be laid for you. Go and pursue your journey."

This address of the fairy's did not in the least alarm Prince Ahmed. "My Princess," said he, "as I do not remember I ever did, or designed to do, anybody injury, I cannot believe anyone can have a thought of injuring me. But if they have, I shall not forbear doing good whenever I have an opportunity." So saying, he took leave of the fairy, and set forward again for his father's capital, where he soon arrived, and was received as usual by the Sultan, who constrained himself as much as possible to disguise the anxiety arising from suspicions suggested by his favorites.

In the meantime, the two women to whom Periebanou had given her orders conveyed the sorceress into an elegant apartment, richly furnished. When they had put her into bed, one of the women went out, and returned soon with a china cup in her hand, full of a certain liquid, which she presented to the sorceress, while the other helped her to sit up. "Drink this," said the attendant. "It is the water of the fountain of lions, and a sovereign remedy against fevers. You will find the effect of it in less than an hour's time."

The attendants then left her, and returned at the end of an hour, when they found the sorceress seated on the sofa. When she saw them open the door of the apartment, she

cried out, "O the admirable potion! it has wrought its cure, and I have waited with impatience to desire you to conduct me to your charitable mistress, as I would not lose time, but prosecute my journey."

The two women conducted her through several apartments, all more superb than that wherein she had lain, into a large hall, the most richly and magnificently furnished in all the palace.

Periebanou was seated in this hall, upon a throne of massive gold, enriched with diamonds, rubies, and pearls of an extraordinary size, and attended on each hand by a great number of beautiful fairies, all richly dressed. At the sight of so much splendor, the sorceress was not only dazzled, but so confused that after she had prostrated herself before the throne, she could not open her lips to thank the fairy, as she had proposed. However, Periebanou saved her the trouble, and said, "Good woman, I am glad that you are able to pursue your journey. I will not detain you. But perhaps you may like to see my palace. Follow my women, and they will show it to you."

The old sorceress, who had not power or courage to say a word, prostrated herself once more, with her head on the carpet that covered the foot of the throne. Then she took her leave, and was conducted by the two fairies through the same apartments which were shown to Prince Ahmed at his first arrival. Afterward they conducted her to the iron gate through which she had entered, and let her depart, wishing her a good journey.

After the sorceress had gone a little way, she turned to observe the door, that she might know it again, but all in vain. For it was invisible to her and all other women. Except in this circumstance, she was very well satisfied with her success, and posted away to the Sultan. When she came to the capital, she went by many byways to the private door of the palace, and was at once admitted to the Sultan.

The sorceress related to the Sultan how she had succeeded

in entering the fairy's palace, and told him all the wonders she had seen there. When she had finished her narrative, the sorceress said, "I shudder when I consider the misfortunes which may happen to you, for who can say that the fairy may not inspire him with the unnatural design of dethroning your Majesty, and seizing the crown of the Indies? This is what your Majesty ought to consider as of the utmost importance."

The Sultan of the Indies had been consulting with his favorites, when he was told of the sorceress' arriving. He now ordered her to follow him to them. He acquainted them with what he had learned might happen. Then one of the favorites said, "In order to prevent this, now that the Prince is in your power, you ought to put him under arrest. I will not say take away his life, but make him a close prisoner." This advice all the other favorites unanimously applauded.

The sorceress asked the Sultan leave to speak, which being granted, she said, "If you arrest the Prince, you must also detain his retinue. But they are all genii, and will disappear, by the property they possess of rendering themselves invisible, and transport themselves instantly to the fairy, and give her an account of the insult offered her husband. And can it be supposed she will let it go unrevenged? Could you not find other means which would answer the same purpose, and yet be of advantage to you? Make demands upon his filial love. And if he fail, then you have cause of complaint against him. For example, request the Prince to procure you a tent, which can be carried in a man's hand, but so large as to shelter your whole army. If the Prince brings such a tent, you may make other demands of the same nature, so that at last he may sink under the difficulties and the impossibility of executing them."

When the sorceress had finished her speech, the Sultan asked his favorites if they had anything better to propose; and finding them all silent, determined to follow her advice.

The next day when the Prince came into his father's pres-

ence, the Sultan said, "Son, you are fortunate to have wed a fairy so rich and so worthy of your love. And since I hear that she is powerful, I would ask you to beg of her to do me a great service. You know to what great expense I am put every time I take the field to provide tents for my army. I am persuaded you could easily procure from the fairy a pavilion that might be carried in a man's hand, and which would extend over my whole army, and I am sure you will do this for me."

Prince Ahmed was in the greatest embarrassment as to what answer to make. At last he replied, "I know not how this mystery has been revealed to you. I cannot deny but your information is correct. I have married the fairy you speak of. I love her, and am persuaded she loves me in return. But I can say nothing as to the influence I have over her. However, the demand of a father is a command upon every child. And though it is with the greatest reluctance, I will not fail to ask my wife the favor you desire, but cannot promise you to obtain it. And if I should not have the honor to come again to pay you my respects, it will be the sign that I have not been able to succeed in my request."

"Son," replied the Sultan of the Indies, "I should be sorry that what I ask should oblige you to deprive me of the gratification of seeing you as usual. I find you do not know the power a husband has over a wife. And yours would show that her love to you was very slight, if, with the power she possesses as a fairy, she should refuse so trifling a request as that I have begged you to make."

All these representations could not satisfy Prince Ahmed, and so great was his vexation that he left the court two days sooner than he used to do.

When he returned, the fairy, to whom he always before had appeared with a gay countenance, asked him the cause of the alteration she perceived in his looks. Yielding to her insistence, Ahmed confessed that the Sultan had discovered the secret of his abode, and knew that he was married to her, though he was ignorant of the means by which he had gained

his information. Here the fairy reminded him of the woman he had helped, and added, "But, surely, there must be something more than this to make you so downcast—tell me, I pray?"

Prince Ahmed replied: "My father doubts my allegiance to him, and as a proof of it he demands that I should ask you for a pavilion which may be carried in a man's hand, and which will cover his whole army."

"Prince," replied the fairy, smiling, "what the Sultan requests is a trifle. Upon occasion I can do him more important service. Therefore be persuaded that far from thinking myself importuned, I shall always take real pleasure in performing whatever you can desire." Periebanou then sent for her treasurer, to whom she said, "Noor-Jehaun, bring me the largest pavilion in my treasury." Noor-Jehaun returned presently with a pavilion, which could not only be held, but concealed, in the palm of the hand, and presented it to her mistress, who gave it to Prince Ahmed to examine.

When Prince Ahmed saw the pavilion, which the fairy called the largest in her treasury, he fancied she had a mind to banter him, and his surprise soon appeared in his countenance. When Periebanou perceived his expression, she laughed. "What! Prince," cried she, "do you think I jest with you? You will see that I am in earnest. . . . Noor-Jehaun," said she to her treasurer, "go and set it up, that he may judge whether the Sultan will think it large enough."

The treasurer went out immediately with it from the palace, and set it up. The Prince found it large enough to shelter two armies as numerous as that of his father.

"You see," said the fairy, "that pavilion is larger than your father may have occasion for. But you are to observe that it has one property, that it becomes larger or smaller, according to the extent of the army it has to cover, without applying any hands to it."

The treasurer took down the tent again, reduced it to its original size, brought it and put it into the Prince's hands. He

took it, and without staying longer than till the next day, mounted his horse, and went with the usual attendants to the Sultan his father.

The Sultan was in great surprise at the Prince's speedy return. He took the tent; but after he had admired its smallness, his amazement was so great that he could not recover himself when he had set it up in the great plain before mentioned, and found it large enough to shelter an army twice as large as he could bring into the field.

The Sultan expressed great obligation to the Prince for so noble a present, desiring him to return his thanks to the fairy. And to show what a value he had set upon it, he ordered it to be carefully laid up in his treasury. But within himself he felt greater jealousy than ever of his son. Therefore, more intent than before upon his ruin, he went to consult the sorceress again, who advised him to engage the Prince to bring him some of the water of the fountain of lions.

In the evening, when the Sultan was surrounded as usual by all his court, and the Prince came to pay his respects among the rest, he addressed himself to him in these words: "Son, I have already expressed to you how much I am obliged for the present of the tent you have procured me, which I esteem the most valuable thing in my treasury. But you must do one thing more, which will be no less agreeable to me. I am informed that the fairy, your spouse, makes use of a certain water, called the water of the fountain of lions, which cures all sorts of fevers, even the most dangerous. And as I am perfectly well persuaded my health is dear to you, I do not doubt but you will ask her for a bottle of that water, and bring it to me as a sovereign remedy, which I may use as I have occasion. Do me this important service, and complete the duty of a good son toward a tender father."

Prince Ahmed, who believed that the Sultan his father should have been satisfied with so singular and useful a tent as that which he had brought, and that he should not have imposed any new task upon him which might hazard the

fairy's displeasure, was thunderstruck by this new request. After a long silence, he said, "I beg of your Majesty to be assured that there is nothing I would not undertake to procure what may contribute to the prolonging of your life, but I could wish it might not be by the means of my wife. For this reason I dare not promise to bring the water. All I can do is to assure you I will request it of her. But it will be with as great reluctance as I asked for the tent."

The next morning Prince Ahmed returned to the fairy Periebanou and related to her sincerely and faithfully all that had passed at his father's court. "But, my Princess, I only tell you this as a plain account of what passed between me and my father. I leave you to your own pleasure, whether you will gratify or reject this, his new desire. It shall be as you please."

"No, no," replied the fairy, "I will satisfy him, and whatever advice the sorceress may give him (for I see that he hearkens to her counsel), he shall find no fault with you or me. There is much wickedness in this demand, as you will understand by what I am going to tell you. The fountain of lions is situated in the middle of a court of a great castle, the entrance into which is guarded by four fierce lions, two of which sleep alternately, while the other two are awake. But let not that frighten you. I will supply you with means to pass by them without danger."

The fairy Periebanou was at work with her needle. And as she had by her several clues of thread, she took up one,

and presenting it to Prince Ahmed, said, "First take this clue of thread. I will tell you presently the use of it. In the second place, you must have two horses. One you must ride yourself, and the other you must lead, which must be loaded with a sheep cut into four quarters, that must be killed today. In the third place, you must be provided with a bottle, which I will give you, to fetch the water in. Set out early tomorrow morning, and when you have passed the iron gate, throw before you the clue of thread, which will roll till it reaches the gates of the castle. Follow it, and when it stops, as the gates will be open, you will see the four lions. The two that are awake will, by their roaring, wake the other two. Be not alarmed, but throw each of them a quarter of the sheep, and then clap spurs to your horse, and ride to the fountain. Fill your bottle without alighting, and return with the same expedition. The

lions will be so busy eating they will let you pass unmolested."

Prince Ahmed set out the next morning at the time appointed him by the fairy, and followed her directions punctually. When he arrived at the gates of the castle, he distributed the quarters of the sheep among the four lions, and passing through the midst of them with intrepidity, got to the fountain, filled his bottle, and returned safely. When he had got a little distance from the castle gates, he turned about; and perceiving two of the lions coming after him, he drew his saber, and prepared himself for defense. But as he went forward, he saw one of them turn out of the road at some disance, and showed by his head and tail that he did not come to do him any harm, but only to go before him, and that the other stayed behind to follow. He therefore put his sword again into its scabbard. Guarded in this manner, he arrived at the capital of the Indies. The lions never left him till they had conducted him to the gates of the Sultan's palace; after which they returned the way they had come, though not without alarming the populace, who fled or hid themselves to avoid them, notwithstanding they walked gently and showed no signs of fierceness.

A number of officers came to attend the Prince while he dismounted, and conduct him to the Sultan's apartment, who was at that time conversing with his favorites. He approached the throne, laid the bottle at the Sultan's feet, kissed the carpet which covered the footstool, and rising, said, "I have brought you, sir, the salutary water which your Majesty so much desired. But at the same time I wish you such health as never to have occasion to make use of it."

After the Prince had concluded, the Sultan placed him on his right hand, and said, "Son, I am much obliged to you for this valuable present. But I have one thing more to ask of you, after which I shall expect nothing more from your obedience, nor from your interest with your wife. This request is, to bring me a man not above a foot and a half high, whose beard is thirty feet long, who carries upon his shoulders

a bar of iron of five hundredweight, which he uses as a quarterstaff, and who can speak."

The next day the Prince returned to Periebanou, to whom he related his father's new demand, which, he said, he looked upon to be a thing more impossible than the first two; for, added he, "I cannot imagine there is or can be such a man in the world."

"Do not alarm yourself, Prince," replied the fairy. "You ran a risk in fetching the water of the fountain of lions for your father; but there is no danger in finding this man. It is my brother Schaibar, who is far from being like me, though we both had the same father. He is of so violent a nature that nothing can prevent his giving bloody marks of his resentment for a slight offense, yet, on the other hand, is so liberal as to oblige anyone in whatever he desires. I will send for him. But prepare yourself not to be alarmed at his extraordinary figure."

"What! my Queen," replied Prince Ahmed, "do you say Schaibar is your brother? Let him be ever so ugly or deformed, I shall love and honor him as my nearest relation."

The fairy ordered a gold chafing dish to be set with a fire in it under the porch of her palace. She then took some incense, and when she threw it into the fire, there arose a thick cloud of smoke.

Some moments after, the fairy said to Prince Ahmed, "Prince, there comes my brother, do you see him?" The Prince immediately perceived Schaibar, who looked at the Prince with fierce eyes, and asked Periebanou the name of the stranger. To which she replied, "He is my husband, brother. His name is Ahmed. He is a son of the Sultan of the Indies. On his account I have taken the liberty now to call for you."

At these words, Schaibar, looking at Prince Ahmed with a favorable eye, which however diminished neither his fierceness nor his savage look, said, "It is enough for me that he is your husband to engage me to do for him whatever he desires."

"The Sultan his father," replied Periebanou, "is curious to see you, and I desire he may be your guide to the Sultan's court."

"He needs but lead the way. I will follow him," replied Schaibar.

The next morning Schaibar set out with Prince Ahmed for the Sultan's court. When they arrived at the gates of the capital, the people, as soon as they saw Schaibar, ran and hid themselves in their shops and houses, shutting the doors, while others, taking to their heels, communicated their fears to all they met, who stayed not to look behind them. Schaibar and Prince Ahmed, as they went along, found all the streets and squares desolate, till they came to the palace, where the porters, instead of preventing Schaibar from entering, ran away too; so that the Prince and he advanced without any obstacle to the council hall, where the Sultan was seated on his throne, giving audience.

Schaibar went fiercely up to the throne, without waiting to be presented, and accosted the Sultan in these words: "You have asked for me. What would you have of me?"

The Sultan turned away his head, to avoid the sight of so terrible an object. Schaibar was so provoked at this rude reception that he instantly lifted up his iron bar, and let it fall on the Sultan's head, killing him, before Prince Ahmed could intercede in his behalf.

Schaibar then smote all the favorites who had given the Sultan bad advice, but he spared the Grand Vizier, who was a just man. When this terrible execution was over, Schaibar came out of the council hall into the courtyard with the iron bar upon his shoulder, and looking at the Grand Vizier, said, "I know there is here a certain sorceress, who is a greater enemy of the Prince my brother-in-law than all those base favorites I have chastised. Let her be brought to me immediately." The Grand Vizier instantly sent for her, and as soon as she was brought, Schaibar knocked her down with his iron bar, and killed her also.

After this he said, "I will treat the whole city in the same manner, if they do not immediately acknowledge Prince Ahmed my brother-in-law to be Sultan of the Indies." Then all who were present made the air ring with the repeated acclamations of "Long life to Sultan Ahmed!" Schaibar caused him to be clothed in the royal vestments, installed him on the throne, and after he had made all swear homage and fidelity, returned to his sister Periebanou whom he brought with great pomp, and made her to be declared Sultana of the Indies.

Prince Ali and Princess Nouronnihar were given a considerable province, with its capital, where they spent the rest of their lives. Afterward he sent an officer to Houssain to acquaint him with the change, and make him an offer of any province he might choose. But that Prince thought himself so happy in his solitude that he desired the officer to return his brother thanks for the kindness he offered him, assuring him of his submission; but that the only favor he desired was to be indulged with leave to retire to the place he had chosen for his retreat.

The Story of Ali Baba and the Forty Thieves

IN A TOWN IN PERSIA, there lived two brothers, one named Cassim, the other Ali Baba. Their father left them scarcely anything; but Cassim married a wealthy wife and prospered in life, becoming a famous merchant. Ali Baba, on the other hand, married a woman as poor as himself, and lived by cutting wood, and bringing it upon three asses into the town to sell.

One day, when Ali Baba was in the forest, he saw at a distance a great cloud of dust, which seemed to be approaching. He observed it very attentively, and distinguished a body of horsemen.

Fearing that they might be robbers, he left his asses and climbed into a tree, from which place of concealment he could watch all that passed in safety.

The troop consisted of forty men, all well mounted, who, when they arrived, dismounted and tied up their horses and fed them. They then removed their saddlebags, which seemed heavy, and followed the captain, who approached a rock that stood near Ali Baba's hiding place. When he was come to it, he said, in a loud voice, "Open, Sesame!" As soon as the cap-

tain had uttered these words, a door opened in the rock; and after he had made all his troop enter before him, he followed them, after which the door shut again of itself.

Although the robbers remained some time in the rock, Ali Baba did not dare to move until after they had filed out again, and were out of sight. Then, when he thought that all was safe, he descended, and going up to the door, said, "Open, Sesame!" as the captain had done, and instantly the door flew open.

Ali Baba, who expected a dark dismal cavern, was surprised to see it well lighted and spacious, receiving light from an opening at the top of the rock. He saw all sorts of provisions, rich bales of silk, brocades, and valuable carpeting, piled upon one another; gold and silver ingots in great heaps, and money in bags. The sight of all these riches made him suppose that this cave must have been occupied for ages by robbers, who had succeeded one another.

Ali Baba loaded his asses with gold coin, and then covering the bags with sticks he returned home. Having secured the door of his house, he emptied out the gold before his wife, who was dazzled by its brightness, and told her all, urging upon her the necessity of keeping the secret.

The wife rejoiced at their good fortune, and wished to count all the gold, piece by piece. "Wife," said Ali Baba, "you do not know what you undertake, when you pretend to count the money. You will never have done. I will dig a hole, and bury it. There is no time to be lost."

"You are right, husband," replied she; "but let us know, as nigh as possible, how much we have. I will borrow a small measure and measure it, while you dig the hole."

Away the wife ran to her brother-in-law Cassim, who lived just by, and addressing herself to his wife, desired her to lend her a measure for a little while. The sister-in-law did so, but as she knew Ali Baba's poverty, she was curious to know what sort of grain his wife wanted to measure, and artfully putting some suet at the bottom of the measure, brought it

to her with an excuse, that she was sorry that she had made her stay so long, but that she could not find it sooner.

Ali Baba's wife went home and continued to fill the measure from the heap of gold and empty it till she had done: when she was very well satisfied to find the number of measures amounted to as many as they did, and went to tell her husband, who had almost finished digging the hole. While Ali Baba was burying the gold, his wife, to show her exactness and diligence to her sister-in-law, carried the measure back again, but without taking notice that a piece of gold had stuck to the bottom. "Sister," said she, giving it to her again, "you see that I have not kept your measure long. I am obliged to you for it, and return it with thanks."

As soon as Ali Baba's wife was gone, Cassim's wife looked at the bottom of the measure and was greatly surprised to find a piece of gold stuck to it. Envy immediately possessed her breast. "What!" said she, "has Ali Baba gold so plentiful that he has to measure it?" When Cassim came home, his wife said to him, "I know you think yourself rich, but you are much mistaken. Ali Baba is infinitely richer than you. He does not count his money, but measures it." Cassim desired her to explain the riddle, which she did, by telling him the stratagem she had used to make the discovery, and showed him the piece of money, which was so old that they could not tell in what prince's reign it was coined.

Cassim was also envious when he heard this, and slept so badly that he rose early and went to his brother.

"Ali Baba," said he, "you pretend to be miserably poor, and yet you measure gold. My wife found this at the bottom of the measure you borrowed yesterday."

Ali Baba perceived that Cassim and his wife, through his own wife's folly, knew what they had so much reason to conceal. However, what was done could not be recalled. There-

fore, without showing the least surprise or trouble, he confessed all, and offered him part of his treasure to keep the secret. "I expected as much," replied Cassim haughtily. "But I must know exactly where this treasure is, and how I may visit it myself when I choose. Otherwise I will go and inform against you, and then you will not only get no more, but will lose all you have, and I shall have a share for my information."

Ali Baba told him all he desired, and even the very words he was to use to gain admission into the cave.

Cassim rose the next morning, long before the sun, and set out for the forest with ten mules bearing great chests, which he planned to fill. He was not long before he reached the rock, and found out the place by the tree and other marks which his brother had given him. When he reached the entrance of the cavern, he pronounced the words, "Open, Sesame!" The door immediately opened, and when he was in, closed upon him. He quickly entered, and laid as many bags of gold as he could carry at the door of the cavern, but his thoughts were so full of the great riches he should possess, that he could not think of the necessary word to make it open. Instead of Sesame, he said, "Open, Barley!" and was much amazed to find that the door remained fast shut. He named several sorts of grain, but still the door would not open.

Cassim had never expected such an incident, and was so alarmed at the danger he was in that the more he endeavored to remember the word "Sesame," the more his memory was confounded, and he had as much forgotten it as if he had never heard it mentioned. He threw down the bags he had loaded himself with, and walked distractedly up and down the cave, without having the least regard for the riches about him.

About noon the robbers chanced to visit their cave, and at some distance from it saw Cassim's mules straggling about the rock, with great chests on their backs. Alarmed at this novelty, they galloped full speed to the cave. Cassim, who heard the noise of the horses' feet from the middle of the

cave, never doubted of the arrival of the robbers, and resolved to make one effort to escape from them. To this end he rushed to the door, and no sooner saw it open, than he ran out and struck down the leader, but could not escape the other robbers, who with their sabers soon made an end of him.

The first care of the robbers after this was to examine the cave. They found all the bags which Cassim had brought to the door, to be ready to load his mules, and carried them again to their places, without missing what Ali Baba had taken away the previous day. Then holding a council, they agreed to cut Cassim's body into four quarters, to hang two on one side and two on the other, within the door of the cave, to terrify any person who should attempt the same thing. This done, they mounted their horses, went to beat the roads again, and to attack any caravans they might meet.

In the meantime, Cassim's wife was very uneasy when night came and her husband had not returned. She ran to Ali Baba in alarm, and said, "I believe, brother-in-law, that you know Cassim your brother is gone to the forest, and upon what account. It is now night and he is not returned. I am afraid some misfortune has happened to him." Ali Baba told her that she need not frighten herself, for that certainly Cassim would not think it proper to come into the town till late at night.

Cassim's wife passed a miserable night, and bitterly repented of her curiosity. As soon as daylight appeared, she went to Ali Baba, weeping profusely.

Ali Baba departed immediately with his three asses to seek for Cassim, begging of her first to cease her lamentations. He went to the forest, and when he came near the rock, having seen neither his brother nor the mules on his way, was seriously alarmed at finding some blood spilt near the door, which he took for an ill omen. But when he had pronounced the password, and the door had opened, he was struck with horror at the dismal sight of his brother's remains. He loaded

one of his asses with them, and covered them over with wood. The other two asses he loaded with bags of gold, covering them with wood also as before; and then bidding the door shut, came away. But he took care to stop some time at the edge of the forest, so that he might not reach the town before night. When he came home, he drove the two asses loaded with gold into his little yard, and left the care of unloading them to his wife, while he led the other to his sister-in-law's house.

Ali Baba knocked at the door, which was opened by Morgiana, an intelligent slave, whose tact was to be relied upon. When he came into the court, he unloaded the ass, and taking Morgiana aside, said to her, "Mention what I say to no one. Your master's body is contained in these two bundles, and our business is to bury him as if he had died a natural death. I can trust you to manage this for me."

Ali Baba consoled the widow as best he could, and having deposited the body in the house returned home.

Morgiana went out at the same time to an apothecary, and asked for a sort of lozenge very efficacious in the most dangerous disorders. The apothecary inquired who was ill. She replied with a sigh, "My good master Cassim himself. He can neither eat nor speak." After these words Morgiana carried the lozenges home with her, and the next morning went to the same apothecary's again, and with tears in her eyes, asked for an essence which they used to give to sick people only when at the last extremity. "Alas!" said she, "I am afraid that this remedy will have no better effect than the lozenges; and that I shall lose my good master."

On the other hand, as Ali Baba and his wife were often seen to go between Cassim's and their own house all that day, and to seem melancholy, nobody was surprised in the evening to hear the lamentable shrieks and cries of Cassim's wife and Morgiana, who gave out everywhere that her master was dead. The next morning Morgiana betook herslf early to the stall of a cobbler named Mustapha, and bidding him

good morrow, put a piece of gold into his hand, saying, "Baba Mustapha, you must take your sewing tackle, and come with me. But I must tell you, I shall have to blindfold you when you come to the place."

Baba Mustapha hesitated a little at these words. "Oh! oh!" replied he, "you would have me do something against my conscience, or against my honor?"

"God forbid!" said Morgiana, putting another piece of gold into his hand, "that I should ask anything that is contrary to your honor. Only come along with me, and fear nothing."

Baba Mustapha went with Morgiana, who, after she had bound his eyes with a handkerchief, conveyed him to her deceased master's house, and never unloosed his eyes till he had entered the room, where she had put the corpse together. "Baba Mustapha," said she, "you must make haste and sew these quarters together. And when you have done, I will give you another piece of gold."

After Baba Mustapha had finished his task, she once more blindfolded him, gave him the third piece of gold as she had promised, and recommending secrecy to him, conducted him back again to the place where she had first bound his eyes, pulled off the bandage, and let him go home, but watched him that he returned toward his shop, till he was quite out of sight, for fear that he should have the curiosity to return and follow her. She then went home.

The ceremony of washing and dressing the body was hastily performed by Morgiana and Ali Baba, after which it was sewed up ready to be placed in the mausoleum. While Ali Baba and the other members of the household followed the body, the women of the neighborhood came, according to custom, and joined their mourning with that of the widow, so that the whole quarter was filled with the sound of their weeping. Thus was Cassim's horrible death successfully concealed.

Three or four days after the funeral, Ali Baba removed his goods openly to the widow's house. But the money he had taken from the robbers he conveyed thither by night. When

at length the robbers came again to their retreat in the forest, great was their surprise to find Cassim's body taken away, with some of their bags of gold. "We are certainly discovered," said the captain, "and if we do not find and kill the man who knows our secret, we shall gradually lose all the riches."

The robbers unanimously approved of the captain's speech.

"The only way in which this can be discovered," said the captain, "is by spying on the town. And, lest any treachery may be practiced, I suggest that whoever undertakes the task shall pay dearly if he fails—even with his life."

One of the robbers immediately started up, and said, "I submit to this condition, and think it an honor to expose my life to serve the troop."

The robber's courage was highly commended by the captain and his comrades, and when he had disguised himself so that nobody would know him, he went into the town and walked up and down, till accidentally he came to Baba Mustapha's shop.

Baba Mustapha was seated, with an awl beside him, on the bench, just starting to work. The robber saluted him, and perceiving that he was old, said, "Honest man, you begin to work very early. How is it possible that one of your age can see so well? I question, even if it were somewhat lighter, whether you could see to stitch."

"Why," replied Baba Mustapha, "I sewed a dead body together in a place where I had not so much light as I have now."

"A dead body!" cried the robber, with affected amazement.

"It is so," replied Baba Mustapha. "But I will tell you no more."

"Indeed," answered the robber, "I do not want to learn your secret, but I would fain to see the house in which this strange thing was done." To impress the cobbler he gave him a piece of gold.

"If I were disposed to do you that favor," replied Baba Mustapha, "I assure you I cannot, for I was led both to and from the house blindfolded."

"Well," replied the robber, "you may, however, remember a little of the way that you were led blindfolded. Come, let me bind your eyes at the same place. We will walk together; and as everybody ought to be paid for his trouble, there is another piece of gold for you. Gratify me in what I ask you."

The two pieces of gold were too great a temptation for Baba Mustapha, who said, "I am not sure that I remember the way exactly. But since you desire, I will see what I can do." At these words Baba Mustapha rose up, and led the robber to the place where Morgiana had bound his eyes. "It was here," said Baba Mustapha, "I was blindfolded; and I turned as you see me." The robber, who had his handkerchief ready, tied it over his eyes, walked by him till he stopped, partly leading, and partly guided by him. "I think," said Baba Mustapha, "I went no farther." He had now stopped directly at Cassim's house, where Ali Baba then lived. The thief, before he pulled off the band, marked the door with a piece of chalk which he had already in his hand. Then he asked him if he knew whose house that was, to which Baba Mustapha replied, that, as he did not live in that neighborhood, he could not tell.

The robber, finding he could discover no more from Baba Mustapha, thanked him for the trouble he had taken, and left him to go back to his shop, while he, himself, returned to the forest, persuaded that he should be very well received.

Shortly after the robber and Baba Mustapha had parted, Morgiana went out of Ali Baba's house upon some errand, and upon her return, she saw the mark the robber had made and stopped to observe it. "What can be the meaning of this mark?" said she to herself. "Somebody intends my master no good. However, with whatever intention it was done, it is advisable to guard against the worst." Accordingly, she fetched a piece of chalk, and marked two or three doors on each side, in the same manner.

When the robber reached the camp, he reported the success of his expedition. It was at once decided that they should very quietly enter the city and watch for an opportunity of slaying their enemy. To the utter confusion of the guide,

several of the neighboring doors were found to be marked in a similar manner. "Come," said the captain, "this will not do. We must return, and you must die." They returned to the camp, and the false guide was promptly slain.

Then another volunteer came forward, and he in like manner was led by Baba Mustapha to the spot. He cautiously marked the door with red chalk, in a place not likely to be seen. But the quick eye of Morgiana detected this likewise, and she repeated her previous action, with equal effectiveness, for when the robbers came they could not distinguish the house. Then the captain, in great anger, led his men back to the forest, where the second offender was immediately put to death.

The captain, dissatisfied by this waste of time and loss of men, decided to undertake the task himself. And so having been led to the spot by Baba Mustapha, he walked up and down before the house until it was impressed upon his mind. He then returned to the forest. When he came into the cave, where the troop waited for him, he said, "Now, comrades, nothing can prevent our full revenge." He then told them his contrivance. When they approved of it, he ordered them to go into the villages about, and buy nineteen mules, with thirty-eight large leather jars, one full of oil, and the others empty.

In two days all preparations were made, and the nineteen mules were loaded with thirty-seven robbers in jars, and the jar of oil. The captain, as their driver, set out with them, and reached the town by the dusk of the evening, as he had intended. He led them through the streets till he came to Ali Baba's, at whose door he planned to have knocked; but was prevented, as Ali Baba was sitting there after supper to take a little fresh air. He stopped his mules, and said, "I have brought some oil a great way, to sell at tomorrow's market, but it is now so late that I do not know where to lodge. Will you allow me to pass the night with you, and I shall be very much obliged for your hospitality."

Ali Baba, not recognizing the robber, bade him welcome,

and gave directions for his entertainment, and after they had eaten he retired to rest.

The captain, pretending that he wished to see how his jars stood, slipped into the garden, and passing from one to the other he raised the lids of the jars and spoke: "As soon as I throw some stones out of my window, do not fail to come out, and I will immediately join you." After this he retired to his chamber; and to avoid any suspicion, put the light out soon after, and laid himself down in his clothes, that he might be the more ready to rise.

While Morgiana was preparing the food for breakfast, the lamp went out, and there was no more oil in the house, nor were there any candles. What to do she did not know, for the broth must be made. Abdalla, seeing her very uneasy, said, "Do not fret, but go into the yard, and take some oil out of one of the jars."

Morgiana thanked Abdalla for his advice, took the oil pot, and went into the yard. As she came nigh the first jar, the robber within said softly, "Is it time?"

Morgiana naturally was much surprised at finding a man in a jar instead of the oil she wanted, but she at once made up her mind that no time was to be lost, if a great danger was to be averted, so she passed from jar to jar, answering at each, "Not yet, but presently."

At last she came to the oil jar, and made what haste she could to fill her oil pot, and returned into her kitchen. Here, as soon as she had lighted her lamp, she took a great kettle, went again to the oil jar, filled the kettle, set it on a large wood fire, and as soon as it boiled went and poured enough into every jar to stifle and destroy the robber within.

When this action, worthy of the courage of Morgiana, was executed without any noise, as she had planned, she returned to the kitchen with the empty kettle. She then put out the great fire which she had made to boil the oil. Leaving just enough to make the broth, she put out the lamp also, and remained silent; resolving not to go to rest till she had observed

what might follow through a window of the kitchen, which opened into the yard.

She had not waited long before the captain gave his signal, by throwing the stones. Receiving no response, he repeated it several times, until becoming alarmed he descended into the yard and discovered that all the gang were dead. And by the oil he missed out of the last jar he guessed the means and manner of their death. Enraged to despair at having failed in his design, he forced the lock of a door that led from the yard to the garden, and climbing over the walls, made his escape.

Morgiana then went to bed, happy at the success of her plan.

Ali Baba rose before day, and followed by his slave, went to the baths, entirely ignorant of the important events which had taken place at home. When he returned from the baths, the sun had risen. He was very much surprised to see the oil jars, and that the merchant had not gone with the mules. He asked Morgiana, who opened the door, the reason of it. "My good master," answered she, "God preserve you and all your family. You will be better informed of what you wish to know when you have seen what I have to show you, if you will but give yourself the trouble to follow me."

Ali Baba following her, she requested him to look into the first jar and see if there was any oil. Ali Baba did so, and seeing a man, started back in alarm, and cried out. "Do not be afraid," said Morgiana, "the man you see there can neither do you nor anybody else any harm. He is dead."

"Ah, Morgiana!" said Ali Baba, "what is it you show me? Explain yourself."

"I will," replied Morgiana. "Moderate your astonishment, and do not excite the curiosity of your neighbors. Look into all the jars."

Ali Baba examined all the other jars, one after another. And when he came to that which had been filled with oil, he found it almost empty. He stood for some time motionless, sometimes looking at the jars, and sometimes at Morgiana,

without saying a word, so great was his surprise. At last, when he had recovered himself, he said, "And what is become of the merchant?"

"Merchant!" answered she, "he is as much a merchant as I am. I will tell you who he is, and what has become of him." She then told the whole story from beginning to end; from the marking of the house to the destruction of the robbers.

Ali Baba was overcome by this account, and he cried, "You have saved my life, and in return I give you your liberty—but this shall not be all."

Ali Baba and his slave Abdalla then dug a long deep trench at the farther end of the garden, in which the robbers were buried. Afterward the jars and weapons were hidden, and by degrees Ali Baba managed to sell the mules for which he had no use.

Meanwhile the captain, who had returned to the forest, found life very miserable. The cavern became too frightful to be endured. But, resolved to be revenged upon Ali Baba, he laid new plans, and having taken a shop which happened to be opposite Cassim's, where Ali Baba's son now lived, he transported many rich stuffs thither. And, disguised as a silk mercer, he set up in business, under the name of Cogia Houssain.

Having by chance discovered whose son his opposite neighbor was, he often made him presents and invited him to dinner, and did everything to win his good opinion.

Ali Baba's son, who did not like to be indebted to any man, told his father that he desired to ask him to dinner in return, and requested him to do so. Ali Baba readily complied with his wishes, and it was arranged that on the following day he should bring Cogia Houssain with him to dinner.

At the appointed time Ali Baba's son conducted Cogia Houssain to his father's house. And strange to say, when the robber found himself at the door, he would have liked to withdraw, though he had now gained access to the very man he wanted to kill. But at that moment Ali Baba came forward to

receive him and thank him for his goodness to his son. "And now," said Ali Baba, "you will do me the honor of dining with me."

"Sir," replied Cogia Houssain, "I would gladly, but that I have vowed to abstain from salt, and I scarcely like to sit at your table under such conditions."

"Trouble not yourself about that," answered Ali Baba, "I will go and bid the cook put no salt in the food."

When Ali Baba went to the kitchen to give this order, Morgiana was much surprised, and desired to see this strange man. Therefore she helped Abdalla to carry up the dishes, and directly she saw Cogia Houssain, she recognized him as the captain of the robbers.

Morgiana at once decided to rescue Ali Baba from this fresh danger, and resolved upon a very daring expedient, by which to frustrate the robber's designs; for she guessed that he intended no good. In order to carry out her plan she went to her room and put on the garments of a dancer, hid her face under a mask and fastened a handsome girdle around her waist, from which hung a dagger. Then she said to Abdalla, "Fetch your tabor, that we may divert our master and his guest."

Ali Baba bade her dance, and she commenced to move gracefully about, while Abdalla played on his tabor. Cogia Houssain watched, but feared that he would have no opportunity of executing his fell purpose.

After Morgiana had danced for some time, she seized the dagger in her right hand and danced wildly, pretending to stab herself the while. As she swept round, she buried the dagger deep in Cogia Houssain's breast and killed him.

Ali Baba and his son, shocked at this action, cried out aloud, "Unhappy wretch! what have you done to ruin me and my family?"

"It was to preserve, not to ruin you," answered Morgiana. "For see here," continued she, opening the pretended Cogia Houssain's garment, and showing the dagger, "what an en-

emy you had entertained! Look well at him, and you will find him to be both the fictitious oil merchant and the captain of a gang of forty robbers. Remember, too, that he would eat no salt with you. And what would you have more to persuade you of his wicked design?"

Ali Baba, who immediately felt the new obligation he had to Morgiana for saving his life a second time, embraced her. "Morgiana," said he, "I gave you your liberty, and then promised you that my gratitude should not stop there, but that I would soon give you higher proofs of its sincerity, which I now do by making you my daughter-in-law." Then addressing himself to his son, he said, "I believe, son, that you will not refuse Morgiana for your wife. You see that Cogia Houssain sought your friendship with a treacherous design to take away my life. And, if he had succeeded, there is no doubt but he would have sacrificed you also to his revenge. Consider, that by marrying Morgiana you marry the preserver of my family and your own."

The son, far from showing any dislike, readily consented to the marriage. And a few days afterward, Ali Baba celebrated the nuptials of his son and Morgiana with great solemnity, with a sumptuous feast, and the usual dancing and spectacles.

Ali Baba, fearing that the other two robbers might be alive still, did not visit the cave for a whole year. Finding, however, that they did not seek to disturb him, he then went to the cave, and, having pronounced the words, "Open, Sesame," entered and saw that no one had been there recently. He then knew that he alone in the world knew the secret of the cave; and he rejoiced to think of his good fortune. When he returned to the city he took as much gold as his horse could carry from his inexhaustible storehouse.

Afterward Ali Baba took his son to the cave, taught him the secret, which they handed down to their posterity, who, using their good fortune with moderation, lived in great honor and splendor.

The Story of Aladdin; or, The Wonderful Lamp

ONCE THERE LIVED a tailor, by the name Mustapha, in one of the wealthy cities of China, who was so poor that he could hardly maintain himself and his family, which consisted only of a wife and son.

His son, who was called Aladdin, was a good-for-nothing, and caused his father much trouble, for he used to go out early in the morning, and stay out all day, playing in the streets with idle children of his own age.

When he was old enough to learn a trade, his father took him into his own shop, and taught him how to use his needle, but to no purpose. For as soon as his back turned, Aladdin was gone for that day. Mustapha chastised him, but Aladdin was incorrigible, and his father was so much troubled about him that he became ill, and died in a few months.

Aladdin, no longer restrained by the fear of his father, gave himself entirely over to his idle habits, and was never out of the streets. This course he followed till he was fifteen years old, without giving his mind to any useful pursuit. As he was one day playing in the street, with his vagabond associates, a stranger passing by stood and watched him closely. The

stranger was a sorcerer, known as the African magician, and had been but two days in the city.

The African magician, perceiving that Aladdin was a boy well suited for his purpose, made inquiries about him; and, after he had learned his history, called him aside, and said, "Child, was not your father called Mustapha the tailor?"

"Yes, sir," answered the boy, "but he has been dead a long time."

At these words, the African magician threw his arms about Aladdin's neck, and kissing him, with tears in his eyes, said, "I am your uncle; your worthy father was my own brother. You are so like him that I knew you at first sight." Then he gave Aladdin a handful of small coins, saying, "Go, my son, to your mother, give my love to her, and tell her that I will visit her tomorrow, that I may see where my good brother lived so long, and ended his days."

Aladdin ran to his mother, overjoyed at his uncle's gift. "Mother," said he, "have I an uncle?"

"No, child," replied his mother, "you have no uncle by your father's side, or mine."

"I am just now come," said Aladdin, "from a man who says he is my uncle, my father's brother. He cried and kissed me when I told him my father was dead, and gave me money. Also he bade me give you his love and say that he will come to see you, that he may be shown the house wherein my father lived and died."

"Indeed, child," replied the mother, "your father had a brother, but he has been dead a long time, and I never heard of another."

The next day Aladdin's uncle found him playing in another part of the town, and embracing him as before, put two pieces of gold into his hand, and said to him, "Carry this, child, to your mother, tell her that I will come and see her tonight, and bid her get us something for supper; but first show me the house where you live."

Aladdin showed the magician the house, and carried the

two pieces of gold to his mother. And when he had told her of his uncle's intention, she went out and bought provisions, and borrowed various utensils of her neighbors. She spent the whole day in preparing the supper; and at night, when it was ready, she said to her son, "Perhaps your uncle will not find the way to our house; go and bring him with you if you meet him."

Aladdin was ready to start, when the magician came in loaded with wine, and all sorts of fruits, for dessert. After the African magician had given what he brought into Aladdin's hands, he saluted his mother, and desired her to show him the place where his brother Mustapha used to sit on the sofa. And when she had so done, he bowed his head down, and kissed it, crying out repeatedly with tears in his eyes, "My poor brother! how unhappy am I not to have come soon enough to give you one last embrace." Aladdin's mother desired him to sit down in the same place, but he declined. "No," said he, "I shall not do that; but let me sit opposite to it that although I may not see the master of a family so dear to me I may at least have the pleasure of beholding the place where he used to sit."

When the magician had sat down, he began to enter into discourse with Aladdin's mother. "My good sister," said he, "do not be surprised at your never having seen me all the time you have been married to my brother Mustapha, of happy memory. I have been forty years absent from this country; and during that time have traveled into the Indies, Persia, Arabia, Syria, and Egypt, and afterward crossed over into Africa, where I settled. Being desirous to see my native land once more, and to embrace my brother, I made the necessary preparations, and set out. It was a long and painful journey, but my greatest grief was the news of my brother's death. But it is a comfort for me to find, as it were, my brother in a son, who has his most remarkable features."

The African magician, perceiving that the widow had begun to weep at the remembrance of her husband, changed

the conversation, and turning toward her son, asked him his name, and what business he followed.

At this question the youth hung his head, and was not a little abashed when his mother answered, "Aladdin is an idle fellow. His father, when alive, strove to teach him his trade, but could not succeed. Since his death our son does nothing, but idles away his time in the streets, as you saw him, without considering that he is no longer a child. And if you do not make him ashamed of it, I despair of his ever coming to any good. For my part, I am resolved one of these days to turn him out of doors, and let him provide for himself."

After these words, Aladdin's mother burst into tears. The magician said, "This is not well, nephew; you must think of helping yourself, and getting your livelihood. There are many sorts of trades. If you have any choice, I will endeavor to help you. Or if you have no mind to learn any handicraft, I will take a shop for you, furnish it with all sorts of fine stuffs and linens; and with the money you make of them lay in fresh goods, and then you will live in an honorable way. Tell me freely what you think of my proposal. You shall always find me ready to keep my word."

This plan greatly pleased Aladdin, who hated work. He told the magician he had a greater inclination to that business than to any other, and that he should be much obliged to him for his kindness. "Very well," said the African magician, "I will carry you with me tomorrow, clothe you as handsomely as the best merchants in the city, and afterward we will open a shop."

The widow, who never till then could believe that the magician was her husband's brother, no longer doubted after his promises of kindness to her son. She thanked him for his good intentions; and after having exhorted Aladdin to render himself worthy of his uncle's favor by good behavior, served up supper, and afterward the magician took his leave, and retired.

He came again the next day, as he had promised, and took

Aladdin with him to a merchant, who sold all sorts of clothes, and a variety of fine stuffs. He bade Aladdin choose those he preferred, and paid for them immediately.

Aladdin was much delighted by his new dress, and thanked his uncle warmly. Then the magician replied, "As you are soon to be a merchant, it is proper you should frequent these shops, and be acquainted with them." He then showed him the largest and finest mosques, led him to the khans, and afterward to the Sultan's palace, where he had free access; and at last brought him to his own khan, where, meeting with some merchants he had become acquainted with since his arrival, he introduced his pretended nephew to them.

This entertainment lasted till night. When Aladdin would have taken leave of his uncle to go home, the magician would not let him go by himself, but conducted him to his mother, who, when she saw him so well dressed, was transported with joy, and bestowed a thousand blessings upon the magician.

Early the next morning the magician took Aladdin out, saying that he would show him the country road, and that on the following day he would purchase the shop. He then led him out at one of the gates of the city, to some magnificent palaces, to each of which belonged many beautiful gardens, into which anybody might enter. At every building he came to, he asked Aladdin if he did not think it fine. The youth cried out each time, "Here is a finer house, uncle, than any we have seen yet." By this artifice, the cunning magician led Aladdin some way into the country. But as he meant to carry him farther, to execute his design, he took an opportunity to sit down in one of the gardens on the brink of a fountain of clear water, which discharged itself by a lion's mouth of bronze into a basin, pretending to be tired. "Come, nephew," said he, "you must be weary as well as I; let us rest ourselves, and we shall be better able to pursue our walk."

The magician then pulled from his girdle a handkerchief with cakes and fruit, which he had provided, and laid them

on the edge of the basin. While they were partaking of this short repast the magician spoke gravely to his nephew, urging him to give up his evil companions and to seek the company of wise men from whose society he would benefit. When he had finished his advice they resumed their walk through the gardens. The African magician drew Aladdin beyond the gardens, and crossed the level country, till they reached the mountains.

At last they arrived at a place where two mountains of moderate height, and equal size, were divided to form a narrow valley, which was the place where the magician intended to execute the design that had brought him from Africa to China. "We will go no farther now," said he. "I will show you here some extraordinary things, which you will thank me to have seen. But while I strike a light, gather up all the loose dry sticks you can find, to kindle a fire."

Aladdin collected a great heap. The magician set them on fire; and when they were in a blaze, threw in some incense, and pronounced several magical words which Aladdin did not understand.

At the same time the earth began to tremble and opened just before the magician, uncovering a stone with a brass ring fixed in the middle. Aladdin was so frightened that he would have run away, but the magician caught hold of him, and gave him such a box on the ear that he knocked him down. Aladdin got up trembling, and with tears in his eyes, said, "What have I done, uncle, to be treated in this severe manner?"

"I supply the place of your father," replied the magician, "and you ought to make no reply. But, child," added he, softening, "do not be afraid; for I shall not ask anything of you, but that you obey me punctually, if you would reap the advantages which I intend you. Know, then, that under this stone there is hidden a treasure, destined to be yours, and which will make you richer than the greatest monarch in the

world. No person but yourself is permitted to lift this stone, or enter the cave. Therefore you must punctually execute what I may command, for it is a matter of great consequence both to you and to me."

Aladdin, amazed at all he saw and heard, forgot what was past, and rising, said, "Well, uncle, what is to be done? Command me, I am ready to obey."

"I am overjoyed, child," said the magician, embracing him. "Take hold of the ring, and lift up that stone."

"Indeed, uncle," replied Aladdin, "I am not strong enough; you must help me."

"Then we shall be able to do nothing," replied the magician. "Take hold of the ring, pronounce the names of your father and grandfather, then lift it up, and you will find it will come easily." Aladdin did as the magician bade him, raised the stone with ease, and laid it on one side.

When the stone was pulled up, there appeared a little door, and steps leading down. "Descend into the cave," said the magician, "and you will find three great halls, in each of which you will see four large brass cisterns placed on each side, full of gold and silver. But take care you do not meddle with them. Before you enter the first hall, be sure to tuck up your robe, wrap it about you, and then pass through the second into the third without stopping. Above all things, have a care that you do not touch the walls, even so much as with your clothes; for if you do, you will die instantly. At the end of the third hall, you will find a door which opens into a garden planted with fine trees loaded with fruit. Walk across the garden to five steps that will bring you upon a terrace, where you will see a lighted lamp in a niche before you. Take the lamp down, and extinguish it. When you have thrown away the wick, and poured out the liquor, put it in your girdle and bring it to me. Do not be afraid that the liquor will spoil your clothes, for it is not oil. And the lamp will be dry as soon as the liquid is thrown out."

After these words, the magician drew a ring off his finger,

and put it on one of Aladdin's, telling him that it was a talisman. Then he added, "Go down boldly, and we shall both be rich all our lives."

Aladdin descended, and found the three halls just as the African magician had described. He went through them with all the precaution the fear of death could inspire, crossed the garden without stopping, took down the lamp from the niche, emptied it, and put it in his girdle. As he came down from the terrace, he stopped in the garden to observe the trees, which were loaded with extraordinary fruit, of different colors on each tree. Some bore fruit entirely white, and some clear and transparent as crystal; some pale red, and others deeper; some green, blue, and purple, and others yellow; in short, there was fruit of all colors. The white were pearls; the clear and transparent, diamonds; the deep red, rubies; the paler, balas rubies; the green, emeralds; the blue, turquoises; the purple, amethysts; and the yellow, sapphires. Aladdin was ignorant of their worth, and would have preferred figs and grapes, or any other fruits. But thinking them pretty, he collected as many of each sort as he could carry, and filled his purses and the flaps of his robe.

Aladdin having thus loaded himself with riches he knew not the value of, returned through the three halls with the same precaution and soon arrived at the mouth of the cave, where the magician awaited him with the utmost impatience. As soon as Aladdin saw him, he cried out, "Pray, uncle, lend me your hand, to help me out."

"Give me the lamp first," replied the magician. "It will be troublesome to you."

"Indeed, uncle," answered Aladdin, "I cannot now; but I will as soon as I am up."

The African magician was resolved to have the lamp before he would help him up. And Aladdin, who had encumbered himself so much with his fruit that he could not well get at it, refused to give it to him till he was out of the cave. The magician, provoked by this obstinate refusal, flew into a

passion, threw a little of his incense into the fire, and pronounced two magical words. Immediately the stone moved into its place, with the earth over it in the same manner as it lay upon the arrival of the magician and Aladdin.

This action plainly showed that the magician was not the boy's uncle, but some adventurer who sought to possess the lamp, of which he had read in the magic book. And, moreover, it was but recently that he had learned where the wonderful lamp was concealed. He had also discovered that he must receive the lamp from another's hand, so he chanced to select Aladdin, whose life he reckoned as nought.

When the magician saw that all his hopes were frustrated, he returned the same day to Africa. But on his way he avoided the town, lest Aladdin's absence should be noticed and questions asked. When Aladdin found himself shut in, he cried, and called out to his uncle, to tell him he was ready to give him the lamp. But it was in vain, since his cries could not be heard. He descended to the bottom of the steps, with a design to get into the garden, but the door, which was opened before by enchantment, was now shut by the same means. He then redoubled his cries and tears, sat down on the steps, without any hopes of ever seeing light again, and in a melancholy certainty of passing from the present darkness into that of a speedy death. Clasping his hands with an entire resignation to the will of God, he said, "There is no strength or power but in the great and high God." In joining his hands he rubbed the ring which the magician had put on his finger. Immediately a genie of frightful aspect rose out of the earth, his head reaching the roof of the vault, and said to him, "What wouldst thou have? I am ready to obey thee as thy slave, and the slave of all who may possess the ring on thy finger; I, and the other slaves of that ring."

At another time, Aladdin would have been so frightened at the sight of so extraordinary a figure that he would not have been able to speak. But the danger he was in made him answer without hesitation: "Deliver me from this place." He

had no sooner spoken these words than he found himself on the very spot where the magician had caused the earth to open. Aladdin was greatly astonished. Returning thanks to God to find himself once more in the world, he made the best of his way home.

When he got within his mother's door, the joy to see her and his weakness for want of substance for three days made him faint, and he remained for a long time as though dead. As soon as he recovered, he related to his mother all that had happened, and she was very bitter in her denunciation of the magician. Aladdin then retired to rest, and slept till late the next morning. The first thing he said to his mother was that he wanted something to eat. "Alas! child," said she, "I have not a bit of bread to give you; but I have a little cotton, which I have spun. I will go and sell it, buy bread, and something for our dinner."

"Mother," replied Aladdin, "keep your cotton for another time, and give me the lamp I brought home with me yesterday. I will go and sell it, and the money I shall get for it will serve both for breakfast and dinner, and perhaps supper too."

Aladdin's mother took the lamp, and said to her son, "Here it is, but it is very dirty. If it were a little cleaner I believe it would bring something more." She took some fine sand and water to clean it; but had no sooner begun to rub it, than in an instant a hideous genie of gigantic size appeared before her, and said in a voice like thunder, "What wouldst thou have? I am ready to obey thee as thy slave, and the slave of all those who have that lamp in their hands; I, and the other slaves of the lamp."

Aladdin's mother, terrified at the sight of the genie, fainted. Aladdin, who had seen such a phantom in the cavern, snatched the lamp out of his mother's hand, and said to the genie boldly, "I am hungry, bring me something to eat." The genie disappeared immediately, and in an instant returned with a large silver tray, holding twelve covered dishes of the same metal, which contained the most delicious viands; six

large white bread cakes on two plates, two flagons of wine, and two silver cups. All these he placed upon a carpet, and disappeared. This was done before Aladdin's mother recovered from her swoon.

Aladdin fetched some water, and sprinkled it in her face, to restore her; and it was not long before she came to herself. "Mother," said Aladdin, "do not be alarmed. Here is what will put you in heart, and at the same time satisfy my extreme hunger."

His mother was much surprised to see the repast spread before her. "Child," said she, "to whom are we obliged for this great plenty and liberality? Has the Sultan been made acquainted with our poverty, and had compassion on us?"

"It is no matter, mother," said Aladdin, "let us sit down and eat; for you have as much need of a good breakfast as myself. When we have done, I will tell you." Accordingly both mother and son sat down, and ate with the better relish as the table was so well furnished. But all the time Aladdin's mother could not forbear looking at and admiring the tray and dishes, though she could not judge whether they were silver or any other metal, and the novelty more than the value attracted her attention.

When Aladdin's mother had taken away and set by what was left, she went and sat down by her son on the sofa, saying, "I expect now that you should satisfy my impatience, and tell me exactly what passed between the genie and you while I was in a swoon." Aladdin readily complied with his mother's request.

She was in as great amazement at what her son told her as at the appearance of the genie; and said to him, "But, son, what have we to do with genii? How came that vile genie to address himself to me, and not to you, to whom he had appeared before in the cave?"

"Mother," answered Aladdin, "the genie you saw is not the one who appeared to me, though he resembles him in size. No, they had quite different persons and habits. They belong

to different masters. If you remember, he that I first saw called himself the slave of the ring on my finger. And this one you saw called himself the slave of the lamp you had in your hand. But I believe you did not hear him, for I think you fainted as soon as he began to speak."

"What!" cried the mother, "was your lamp then the occasion of the genie's addressing himself rather to me than to you? Ah! my son, take it out of my sight, and put it where you please. I had rather you would sell it, than run the hazard of being frightened to death again by touching it. And if you would take my advice, you would part also with the ring, and not have anything to do with genii, who, as our prophet has told us, are only devils."

"With your leave, mother," replied Aladdin, "I shall now take care how I sell a lamp which may be so serviceable both to you and me. That false and wicked magician would not have undertaken so tedious a journey if he had not known the value of this wonderful lamp. And since chance has given it to us, let us make a profitable use of it, without making any great show, and exciting the envy and jealousy of our neighbors. However, since the genii frighten you so much, I will take it out of your sight, and put it where I may find it when I want it. The ring I cannot resolve to part with. For without that you would never have seen me again. And though I am alive now, perhaps, if it were gone, I might not be alive some moments hence; therefore I hope you will give me leave to keep it, and to wear it always on my finger." She replied that he might do what he pleased, but for her part, she would have nothing to do with genii, and never say anything more about them.

By the next night they had eaten all the provisions the genie had brought. The following day Aladdin, who could not bear the thoughts of hunger, put one of the silver dishes under his vest, and went out early to sell it. He addressed himself to a peddler whom he met in the streets, and pulling out the plate, asked him if he would buy it. The cunning fellow

took the dish, examined it, and as soon as he found that it was good silver, asked Aladdin at how much he valued it. Aladdin, who knew not its value, and never had been used to such traffic, told him he would trust to his judgment and honor. The peddler was somewhat confounded at this plain dealing. Doubting whether Aladdin understood the material or the full value of what he offered to sell, he took a piece of gold out of his purse and gave it him, though it was but the sixtieth part of the worth of the plate. Aladdin, taking the money very eagerly, retired with so much haste that the man, not content with the exorbitance of his profit, was vexed that he had been so liberal. He was going to run after the boy, to endeavor to get some change out of the piece of gold; but Aladdin had run so fast, and had got so far, that it would have been impossible for him to overtake him.

Before Aladdin went home, he called at a baker's, bought some cakes of bread, changed his money, and on his return gave the rest to his mother, who went and purchased provisions enough to last them some time. After this manner they lived, till Aladdin had sold the twelve dishes singly, as necessity pressed, to the peddler, for the same amount of money. The man, after the first transaction, durst not offer him less, for fear of losing so good a bargain. When he had sold the last dish, he had recourse to the tray, which weighed ten times as much as the dishes, and would have carried it to his old purchaser, except that it was too large and cumbersome. Therefore he was obliged to bring him home to his mother's,

where, after the tray had been weighed and examined, he laid down ten pieces of gold, with which Aladdin was very well satisfied.

When all the money was spent, Aladdin had recourse again to the lamp. He took it in his hand and rubbed it. Immediately the genie appeared, and repeated the same words that he had used before. "I am hungry," said Aladdin, "bring me something to eat." The genie disappeared, and presently returned with a tray, the same number of covered dishes as before, set them down, and vanished.

As soon as Aladdin found that their provisions were expended, he took one of the dishes, and went to look for his merchant. As he was passing by a goldsmith's shop, the goldsmith saw him, called to him, and said, "My lad, I imagine that you carry something which you wish to sell to that fellow with whom I see you speak. But perhaps you do not know that he is the greatest rogue in the city. I will give you the full worth of it; or I will direct you to other merchants who will not cheat you."

The hopes of getting more money for his plate induced Aladdin to pull it from under his vest, and show it to the goldsmith, who at first sight, seeing that it was made of the finest silver, asked him if he had sold such as that to the peddler. When Aladdin told him that he had sold him twelve such, for a piece of gold each, the goldsmith cried, "What a villain!" Then he added, "My son, what is past cannot be recalled. By showing you the value of this plate, which is of the finest silver we use in our shops, I will let you see how much the rogue has cheated you."

The goldsmith took a pair of scales, weighed the dish, and after he had mentioned how much an ounce of fine silver cost, assured him that his plate would fetch by weight sixty pieces of gold, which he offered to pay down immediately.

Aladdin thanked him for his fair dealing, and sold him all his dishes and the tray, and had as much for them as the weight came to.

Though Aladdin and his mother had an inexhaustible treasure in their lamp, and might have had whatever they wished for, yet they lived with the same frugality as before, and it may easily be supposed that the money for which Aladdin had sold the dishes and tray was sufficient to maintain them for some time.

During this interval, Aladdin frequented the shops of the principal merchants, where they sold cloth of gold and silver, linens, silk stuffs, and jewelry, and oftentimes joining in their conversation, acquired a knowledge of the world. By his acquaintance among the jewelers, he came to know that the fruits which he had gathered when he took the lamp were, instead of colored glass, stones of inestimable value. But he had the prudence not to mention this to anyone, not even to his mother.

One day as Aladdin was walking about the town, he heard an order proclaimed, commanding the people to shut up their shops and houses, and keep within doors, while the Princess Buddir al-Buddoor, the Sultan's daughter, went to the baths and returned.

This proclamation inspired Aladdin with curiosity to see the Princess' face. To achieve this he placed himself behind the door of the bath, which was so situated that he could not fail of seeing her face. Aladdin had not waited long before the Princess came. She was attended by a great crowd of ladies and slaves, who walked on each side, and behind her. When she came within three or four paces of the door of the baths, she took off her veil, and gave Aladdin an opportunity of a full view.

The Princess was the most beautiful brunette in the world. Her eyes were large and sparkling; her looks sweet and modest; her nose faultless; her mouth small; her lips vermilion; and her figure perfect. It is not, therefore, surprising that Aladdin was dazzled and enchanted.

After the Princess had passed by, and entered the baths, Aladdin left his hiding place and went home. His mother per-

ceived that he was much more thoughtful and melancholy than usual; and asked what had happened to make him so, or if he was ill. For some time he remained silent, but at length he told her all, saying in conclusion, "I love the Princess, and am resolved to ask her in marriage of the Sultan."

Aladdin's mother listened with surprise to what her son told her. But when he talked of asking the Princess in marriage, she said, "Child, what are you thinking of? You must be mad to talk thus."

"I assure you, mother," replied Aladdin, "that I am in my right senses. I foresaw that you would reproach me with folly and extravagance, but I must tell you once more that I am resolved to demand the Princess of the Sultan in marriage, and your remonstrances shall not prevent me. As for a present worthy of the Sultan's acceptance, those pieces of glass which I brought with me from the subterranean storehouse are in reality jewels of inestimable value, and fit for the greatest monarchs. I know the worth of them by frequenting the shops. And you may take my word that none of the jewelers have stones to be compared with those we have, either for size or beauty, and yet they value theirs at an excessive price. So I am persuaded that they will be received very favorably by the Sultan. You have a large porcelain dish fit to hold them. Fetch it, and let us see how they will look when we have arranged them according to their different colors."

Aladdin's mother brought the china dish, and he took the jewels out of the two purses in which he had kept them, placing them in order acording to his fancy. But the brightness and luster they emitted in the daytime, and the variety of the colors, so dazzled their eyes that they were astonished beyond measure. The sight of all these precious stones, of which she knew not the value, only partially removed the mother's anxiety; but, fearing that Aladdin might do something rash, she promised to go to the palace the next morning. Aladdin rose before daybreak, awakened his mother, pressing her to get

herself dressed to go to the Sultan's palace, and to get admittance, if possible, before the Grand Vizier and the great officers of state went in to take their seats in the divan, where the Sultan held his court daily.

Aladdin's mother took the china dish, in which they had put the jewels the day before, wrapped in two napkins, and set forward for the Sultan's palace. When she came to the gates, the Grand Vizier, and the most distinguished lords of the court, had just gone in. But, notwithstanding the crowd of people, she was able to get into the divan, a spacious hall, the entrance into which was very magnificent. She placed herself just before the Sultan, Grand Vizier, and the great lords, who sat in council on his right and left hand. Several causes were called, according to their order, pleaded and adjudged, until the time came when the divan usually broke up. The Sultan then arose and returned to his apartment, attended by the Grand Vizier.

Aladdin's mother, seeing the Sultan retire, and all the people depart, judged rightly that he would not sit again that day, and resolved to go home. Aladdin was greatly disappointed when he heard of her failure, but she soothed him by saying, "I will go again tomorrow; perhaps the Sultan may not be so busy and will hear me."

The next morning she repaired to the Sultan's palace with the present, as early as the day before, but when she came there, she found the gates of the divan shut, and understood that the council sat but every other day, therefore she must come again the next. She went six times afterward on the days appointed, placed herself always directly before the Sultan, but with as little success as the first morning.

On the sixth day, however, when the divan was broken up, and the Sultan had returned to his own apartment, he said to his Grand Vizier, "I have for some time observed a certain woman, who attends constantly every day that I give audience, with something wrapped up in a napkin. She always stands up from the beginning to the breaking up of the

audience, and affects to place herself just before me. If she comes to our next audience, do not fail to call her, that I may hear what she has to say." The Grand Vizier made answer by lowering his hand, and then lifting it up above his head, signifying his willingness to lose it if he failed.

The next audience day Aladdin's mother went to the divan, and placed herself in front of the Sultan as usual. The Grand Vizier immediately called the chief of the mace-bearers, and pointing to her, bade him tell her to come before the Sultan. The widow promptly followed him; and when she reached the throne she bowed her head to the ground, and waited for the Sultan's command to rise. The Sultan immediately said to her, "Good woman, I have observed you to stand a long time, from the beginning to the rising of the divan. What business brings you here?"

After these words, Aladdin's mother prostrated herself a second time, and said, "Monarch of monarchs, I beg of you to pardon the boldness of my request, and to assure me first of your pardon and forgiveness."

"Well," replied the Sultan, "I will forgive you, be it what it may, and no hurt shall come to you. Speak boldly."

When Aladdin's mother had taken all these precautions, she told him faithfully the errand on which she had come, and made many apologies and explanations in extenuation of her son's love for the Princess.

The Sultan hearkened to this discourse without showing the least anger. But before he gave her any answer he asked her what she had brought tied up in the napkin. She took the china dish, which she had set down at the foot of the throne, untied it, and presented it to the Sultan.

The Sultan's amazement and surprise were inexpressible, when he saw so many large, beautiful, and valuable jewels collected in the dish. He remained for some time motionless with admiration. Then he received the present from Aladdin's mother's hand, crying out in a transport of joy, "How rich, how beautiful!"

After he had admired and handled all the jewels, one after another, he turned to his Grand Vizier, and showing him the dish, said, "Behold, admire, wonder, and confess that your eyes never beheld jewels so rich and beautiful before!" The Vizier was charmed. "Well," continued the Sultan, "what sayest thou to such a present? Is it not worthy of the Princess my daughter? And ought I not to bestow her on one who values her at so great a price?"

"I cannot but own," replied the Grand Vizier, "that the present is worthy of the Princess. But I beg of your Majesty to grant me three months before you come to a final resolution. I hope, before that time, my son, whom you have regarded favorably, will be able to make a nobler present than Aladdin, who is an entire stranger to your Majesty."

The Sultan readily granted this request, and said to the widow, "Good woman, go home, and tell your son that I agree to the proposal you have made me; but I cannot marry the Princess my daughter for the next three months. At the expiration of that time come again."

Aladdin's mother returned home much more gratified than she had expected, since she had met with a favorable answer, and told her son that she was to attend at the court in three months to hear the Sultan's decision.

Aladdin thought himself the most happy of men at hearing this news, and thanked his mother for the pains she had taken in the affair, the good success of which was of so great importance to his peace. When two of the three months had passed, his mother one evening went into the town, and found the shops dressed with foliage, silks, and carpeting, and everyone rejoicing. The streets were crowded with officers in habits of ceremony, mounted on horses richly caparisoned, each attended by a great many footmen. Aladdin's mother asked what was the meaning of all this preparation of public festivity. "Whence came you, good woman," said one, "that you don't know that the Grand Vizier's son is to marry the Princess Buddir al-Buddoor, the Sultan's daughter, tonight? She

will presently return from the baths; and these officers whom you see are to assist at the cavalcade to the palace, where the ceremony is to be solemnized."

The widow hastened home to inform Aladdin. "Child," cried she, "you are undone! The Sultan's fine promises will come to nothing. This night the Grand Vizier's son is to marry the Princess."

At this account Aladdin was thunderstruck, but with a sudden hope he bethought himself of the lamp; vowing to stop the marriage. He therefore went to his chamber, took the lamp, and rubbed it. Immediately the genie appeared, and said to him, "What wouldst thou have?"

"Hear me," said Aladdin; "thou hast hitherto served me well; but now I entrust to thee a matter of great importance. The Sultan's daughter, who was to have been mine, is tonight to wed the son of the Grand Vizier. It shall not be. Bring them both to me ere the marriage takes place."

"Master," replied the genie, "I will obey you."

Aladdin supped with his mother as usual. Then he retired to his own chamber again, and waited for the genie to execute his orders.

At the Sultan's palace the greatest rejoicings prevailed at the wedding festivities, which were kept up until midnight. The bride and bridegroom retired to their apartments. They had scarcely entered the room when the genie seized them, and bore them straight to Aladdin's chamber, much to the terror of both, as they could not see by what means they were transported. "Remove the bridegroom," said Aladdin, "and keep him in close custody until dawn tomorrow, when you shall return with him." Aladdin then tried to soothe the Princess' fears by explaining how ill he had been treated. But he did not succeed overwell, as the Princess knew nothing of the matter.

At dawn the genie appeared with the Vizier's son, who had been kept in a house all night, near at hand, merely by being breathed upon by the genie. He was left motionless and

entranced at the chamber door. At a word from Aladdin the slave of the lamp took the couple and bore them back to the palace.

The genie had only just deposited them in safety when the Sultan tapped at the door to wish them good morning. The Grand Vizier's son, who had almost perished with cold, by standing in his thin undergarment all night, no sooner heard the knocking at the door than he ran into the robing chamber, where he had undressed himself the night before.

The Sultan, having opened the door, went to the bedside, kissed the Princess on the forehead, but was extremely surprised to see her so melancholy. She only cast at him a sorrowful look, expressive of great affliction. He suspected that there was something extraordinary in this silence, and thereupon went immediately to the Sultana's apartment, and told her in what a state he had found the Princess, and how she had received him. "Sire," said the Sultana, "I will go and see her. She will not receive me in the same manner."

The Princess was quite as reserved when her mother came. But when the Sultana pressed her to speak she said, with a deep sigh and many tears, "I am very unhappy." She then narrated all that had taken place.

"Daughter," replied the Sultana, "you must keep all this to yourself, for no one would believe that you were sane if you told this strange tale." The Sultana then questioned the Vizier's son. But he, being proud of the alliance he had made, denied everything, and so the celebrations of the marriage went forward that day with equal splendor.

That night Aladdin again summoned the genie, and had the Princess and the Vizier's son brought to him as before. And on the following morning they were conveyed back to the palace, just in time to receive the visit of the Sultan. The Princess answered his inquiries with tears, and at last told him everything that had happened. The Sultan consulted with the Grand Vizier; and, learning that his son had suffered even worse than the Princess, he ordered the marriage to be

canceled, and all the festivities—which should have lasted for several days more—were stopped throughout the kingdom.

This sudden stopping of the wedding celebrations gave rise to much gossip, but nothing could be discovered. This sudden and unexpected change gave rise in both the city and kingdom to various speculations and inquiries; but no other account could be given of it, except that both the Vizier and his son went out of the palace very much dejected. Nobody but Aladdin knew the secret, and he kept it most cunningly to himself; so that neither the Sultan nor the Grand Vizier, who had forgotten Aladdin and his request, had the slightest suspicion that he was the cause of all the trouble.

Three months had now elapsed since the Sultan had made his promise to Aladdin's mother, and so she again repaired to the palace to hear his decision. The Sultan at once recognized her, and bade the Grand Vizier bring her to him.

"Sire," said the widow, bowing to the ground before him, "I have come, as you directed, at the end of the three months, to plead for my son." The Sultan, when he had fixed a time to answer the request of this good woman, little thought of hearing any more of a marriage; but he was loath to break his word. Therefore he consulted his Vizier, who advised that such conditions should be imposed that no one in Aladdin's position could fulfill them. This suggestion seemed wise, so the Sultan said, "Good woman, it is true Sultans ought to abide by their word, and I am ready to keep mine, by making your son happy in marriage with my daughter. But as I cannot marry her without some further valuable consideration from your son, you may tell him, I will fulfill my promise as soon as he shall send me forty trays of massive gold, full of the same sort of jewels you already have presented me, and carried by the like number of black slaves, who shall be led by as many young and handsome white slaves, all dressed magnificently. On these conditions I am ready to bestow the Princess upon him. Go, and tell him so, and I will wait till you bring me his answer."

Aladdin's mother prostrated herself a second time before the throne, and retired. On her way home, she laughed within herself at her son's foolish imagination. "Where," said she, "can he get all that the Sultan demands?" When she came home, she told her son the message she had been commanded to deliver, adding, "The Sultan expects your answer immediately; but," continued she, laughing, "I believe he may wait long enough."

"Not so long, mother, as you imagine," replied Aladdin. "I am very well pleased. His demand is but a trifle to what I could have done for her. I will at once provide these things."

Aladdin promptly withdrew and summoned the genie, to whom he made known his wants. The genie told him his command should be immediately obeyed, and disappeared. In a very short time the genie returned with forty black slaves, each bearing on his head a heavy tray of pure gold, full of pearls, diamonds, rubies, emeralds, and every sort of precious stone, all larger and more beautiful than those presented to the Sultan. "Mother," said Aladdin, "let us lose no time. Before the Sultan and the divan rise, I would have you return to the palace with this present as the dowry demanded for the Princess, that he may judge by my diligence and exactness of the ardent and sincere desire I have to procure myself the honor of this alliance."

So magnificent was this procession that as it passed through the streets crowds of people came out to look in wonder. The splendor of the dress of the slaves, which glistened with precious stones, made the people think that they were so many Kings or Princes. They walked sedately, Aladdin's mother at their head, toward the palace, and were all so much alike that the spectators marveled.

As the Sultan, who had been informed of their approach, had given orders for them to be admitted, they met with no obstacle, but went into the divan in regular order, one part filing to the right, and the other to the left. After they had all entered, and had formed a semicircle before the Sultan's

throne, the black slaves laid the golden trays on the carpet, prostrated themselves, touching the carpet with their foreheads, and at the same time the white slaves did the same. When they arose, the black slaves uncovered the trays, and then all stood with their arms crossed over their breasts.

In the meantime Aladdin's mother advanced to the foot of the throne, and having paid her respects, said to the Sultan, "Sire, my son feels that this present is much below the Princess Buddir al-Buddoor's worth; but hopes, nevertheless, that your Majesty will accept of it, and make it agreeable to the Princess, and with the greater confidence since he has endeavored to conform to the conditions you were pleased to impose."

The Sultan hesitated no longer. He was overjoyed at the sight of Aladdin's rich present. "Go," said he, "and tell your son that I wait with open arms to embrace him, and the more haste he makes to come and receive the Princess my daughter from my hands, the greater pleasure he will do me." As soon as the tailor's widow had retired, the Sultan put an end to the audience; and rising from his throne, ordered that the Princess' servants should come and carry the trays into their mistress' apartment, whither he went himself to examine them with her at his leisure. The fourscore slaves were conducted into the palace; and the Sultan, telling the Princess of their magnificent appearance, ordered them to be brought before her apartment, that she might see through the lattices he had not exaggerated in his account of them.

In the meantime Aladdin's mother got home, and showed in her air and countenance the good news she brought her son. "My son," said she to him, "rejoice, for you have arrived at the height of your desires. The Sultan has declared that you are worthy to possess the Princess Buddir al-Buddoor, and waits with impatience to embrace you, and conclude your marriage."

Aladdin, enraptured with this news, retired to his chamber, and summoned the slave of the lamp as usual. "Genie," said

he, "I want to bathe immediately, and you must afterward provide me the richest and most magnificent habit ever worn by a monarch." No sooner were the words out of his mouth than the genie rendered him, as well as himself, invisible, and transported him into a saloon of the finest marble of all sorts of colors where he bathed in scented water. And when he returned into the hall he found, instead of his own, a suit the magnificence of which astonished him. The genie helped him to dress, and, when he had done, transported him back to his own chamber, where he asked him if he had any other commands. "Yes," answered Aladdin, "bring me a charger that surpasses in beauty and goodness the best in the Sultan's stables, with a saddle, bridle, and other caparisons worth a King's ransom. I want also twenty slaves, as richly clothed as those who carried the present to the Sultan, to walk by my side and follow me, and twenty more to go before me in two ranks. Besides these, bring my mother six women slaves to attend her, as richly dressed as any of the Princess Buddir al-Buddoor's, each carrying a complete dress fit for any Sultana. I want also ten thousand pieces of gold in ten purses. Go, and make haste."

As soon as Aladdin had given these orders, the genie disappeared, but presently returned with the horse, the forty slaves, ten of whom carried each a purse containing ten thousand pieces of gold, and six women slaves, each carrying on her head a different dress for Aladdin's mother, wrapped up in a piece of silver tissue, and presented them all to Aladdin.

Aladdin took four of the purses, which he presented to his mother, together with the six women slaves who carried the dresses, telling her to spend the money as she wished. The other six he left with the slaves, and bade them cast handfuls among the people as they walked. And after this, when all was ready, he set out for the palace, mounted upon the charger, three of the purse-bearers walking on his right hand, and three on his left. Although Aladdin never was on horseback before, he appeared with such extraordinary grace that

the most experienced horseman would not have taken him for a novice. The streets through which he was to pass were filled with an innumerable concourse of people, who made the air echo with their acclamations, especially every time the six slaves who carried the purses threw handfuls of gold among the populace. The Sultan, much surprised by the magnificence of Aladdin's dress and the splendor of his cortege, received him with joy, and did everything in his power to honor him. After they had feasted, the marriage contract was drawn up and duly signed, and the Sultan was anxious that the nuptials should be completed at once. But Aladdin said, "Sire, I beg of you to grant me sufficient land near your palace on which I may build a home worthy of the Princess, before our wedding takes place. You may judge of my eagerness to claim the Princess by the expedition with which the castle shall be erected."

The Sultan readily granted this request; and, having embraced Aladdin, he allowed him to return home.

Aladdin withdrew with a most courtly bow, and hastened home, amid the cheers of the people, to consult the genie. And as soon as he reached his house he went to his chamber, and took the lamp and rubbed it. Immediately the genie appeared, professed his allegiance, and Aladdin said to him, "Genie, build me a palace fit to receive my spouse the Princess Buddir al-Buddoor. Let it be built of porphyry, jasper, agate, lapis lazuli, and the finest marble of various colors. On the roof of the palace build a large, dome-crowned hall, having four equal fronts. And instead of bricks, let the walls be formed of layers of massive gold and silver, laid alternately; let each front contain six windows. The lattices of these, except one, which must be left unfinished, must be so enriched with diamonds, rubies, and emeralds that they shall exceed everything of the kind ever seen in the world. There must also be an inner and outer court in front of the palace, and a spacious garden; but, above all things, provide and fill an ample treasure house, well supplied with gold and silver. Let

nothing be lacking in the kitchens and storehouses; and let the stables be filled with the best horses. Finally, see that there is a royal staff of servants. Go, execute my orders."

It was about the hour of sunset when Aladdin gave these orders, and the next morning, before break of day, the genie presented himself, and said, "Sir, your palace is finished." At a word from Aladdin the genie carried him to the palace, and led him through all the apartments, all of which, as well as the servants, delighted him. The genie then showed him the treasury, which was opened by a treasurer, where Aladdin saw heaps of purses, of different sizes, piled up to the top of the ceiling and disposed in most excellent order. The genie thence led him to the stables, where he showed him some of the finest horses in the world, and the grooms busy in dressing them. From thence they went to the storehouses, which were filled with all things necessary, both for food and ornament.

When Aladdin had thoroughly examined the palace, he said, "Genie, no one can be better satisfied than I am. There is only one thing wanting; that is, a carpet of fine velvet for the Princess to walk upon from the Sultan's palace here." The genie immediately disappeared, and Aladdin saw what he desired executed in an instant. The genie then returned and carried him home before the gates of the Sultan's palace were opened.

When the Sultan's porters came to open the gates, they were amazed to find a magnificent palace erected, and to see a carpet of velvet spread from the grand entrance. They immediately informed the Grand Vizier, who hastened to tell the Sultan. "It must be Aladdin's palace," exclaimed the Sultan, "which I gave him leave to build. He has done this as a surprise for me, to show what can be done in one night."

When Aladdin had been conveyed home, he requested his mother to go to the Princess Buddir al-Buddoor to inform her that the palace would be ready for her reception that evening. She at once set out, attended by her women slaves. The

widow was sitting with the Princess when the Sultan came in. He was much surprised to see the change that had taken place in her, and was greatly pleased. Aladdin had, meanwhile, set out to his new home, being careful to take the lamp and the ring, both of which had served him in such good stead. Great were the rejoicings, and loud the sounds of music, when the Princess Buddir al-Buddoor set out from the Sultan's palace in the evening. A wonderful procession attended her to the door of Aladdin's palace, where he stood ready to receive her with all honors. He conducted her into a large hall, the wealth of which astonished her beyond measure, and then the festivities were kept up until a late hour.

The next morning, as soon as he was dressed, Aladdin set out to invite the Sultan and his court to come to his palace. The Sultan willingly consented, and attended by his Grand Vizier and all the great lords of his court he accompanied Aladdin. The nearer the Sultan approached Aladdin's palace, the more he was struck with its beauty. But when he came into the hall, and saw the windows, enriched with diamonds, rubies, emeralds—all large, perfect stones—he was so much surprised that he remained some time motionless. "Son," said the Sultan, "this hall is the most worthy of admiration of any in the world. There is only one thing that surprises me, which is to find one of the windows unfinished."

"Sire," answered Aladdin, "the omission was by design, since I wished that your Majesty should have the glory of finishing this hall."

"I take it kindly," replied the Sultan, "and will give orders about it immediately."

When the Sultan rose from the repast that had been prepared, he was informed that the jewelers and goldsmiths attended. Thereupon he returned to the hall, and showed them the window which was unfinished. "I sent for you," said he, "to fit up this window in as great perfection as the rest; and make all the dispatch you can."

The jewelers and goldsmiths examined the three and

twenty windows with great attention, and after they had consulted together, to know what each could furnish, they returned, and presented themselves before the Sultan, whose principal jeweler, undertaking to speak for the rest, said, "Sire, we are all willing to exert our utmost care and industry to obey your Majesty; but among us all we cannot furnish jewels enough for so great a work."

"I have more than are necessary," said the Sultan; "come to my palace and you shall choose what may answer your purpose."

When the Sultan returned to his palace, he ordered his jewels to be brought out, and the jewelers took a great quantity, particularly those Aladdin had made him a present of, which they soon used, without making any great advance in their work. They came again several times for more, and in a month's time had not finished half their work. In short, they used all the jewels the Sultan had, and borrowed of the Vizier, but yet the work was not half done.

Aladdin, who knew that all the Sultan's endeavors to make this window like the rest were in vain, sent for the jewelers and goldsmiths, and not only commanded them to desist from their work, but ordered them to undo what they had begun, and to carry all their jewels back to the Sultan and to the Vizier. They undid in a few hours what they had been six weeks about, and retired, leaving Aladdin alone in the hall. He took the lamp, which he carried about him, rubbed it, and presently the genie appeared. "Genie," said Aladdin, "I ordered thee to leave one of the four and twenty windows of this hall imperfect, and thou hast executed my commands punctually; now I would have thee make it like the rest." The genie immediately disappeared. Aladdin went out of the hall, and returning soon after, found the window, as he wished it to be, like the others.

In the meantime the jewelers and goldsmiths repaired to the palace, and were introduced into the Sultan's presence. The chief jeweler presented the precious stones which he had

brought back. The Sultan asked them if Aladdin had given them any reason for so doing, and they answering that he had given them none, he ordered a horse to be brought, which he mounted, and rode to his son-in-law's palace, with some few attendants on foot. Aladdin met him at the gate, and instead of answering his question, led him to the great hall. Here the Sultan was much surprised to find the window finished just like the others. He fancied at first that he had mistaken the window, but, having examined all the others, he found that it had been completed in a few minutes, whereas the jewelers had spent weeks upon it without finishing the work. "My son," said he, "what a man you are to do such surprising things always in the twinkling of an eye. There is not your equal in the world. The more I know, the more I admire you."

Aladdin did not confine himself in his palace, but took care to show himself once or twice a week in the town, by going sometimes to one mosque, and sometimes to another, to prayers, or to visit the Grand Vizier, or the principal lords of the court. Every time he went out, he caused two slaves, who walked by the side of his horse, to throw handfuls of money among the people as he passed through the streets and squares. This generosity gained him the love and blessings of the people, and it was common for them to swear by his head. Thus he won the affections of the people, and was more beloved than the Sultan himself.

Aladdin had conducted himself in this manner several years, when the African magician recalled him to his recollection in Africa, and, though he thought him dead in the cave, where he had left him, he resolved to find out for certain. After a long and careful course of magical inquiries, he discovered that Aladdin had escaped, and lived in great splendor, all of which he owed to the wonderful lamp.

Directly the magician found this out, he set out in hot haste for the capital of China. And when he arrived, he went to a khan, where he rested after his long journey.

He made inquiries, which revealed to him Aladdin's enormous wealth, and heard of all his charities and of the magnificent palace he had built. The magician, when he saw the palace, knew that none but genii could have erected it, and he was exceedingly annoyed to think how he had been worsted. He returned to the khan, determined to find out where the lamp was kept; and by the magic knowledge he possessed he was enabled to discover what he wanted to know. Then, to his great delight, he learned that the lamp was in the palace—not, as he feared, about Aladdin's person. "Now," said he, "I shall have the lamp, and will be revenged upon this fellow, who shall be degraded to his original mean station in life."

The magician also learned that Aladdin had set out on a hunting expedition, three days before, which was to last for eight days. This knowledge was sufficient to enable the magician to carry out his plans, which he straightway did.

First he went to a coppersmith, from whom he purchased a dozen lamps, which he put into a basket, and then he set out to Aladdin's palace again. As he drew near he called out: "Who will change old lamps for new?" The Princess happened to hear the cries, though she heard not his words. Curious to learn why the people collected around him, she sent one of her women to inquire what he sold.

The slave soon returned, laughing so heartily that the Princess was angry. "Madam," said the slave, laughing still, "this fellow has a basket on his arm, full of fine new lamps, asking to change them for old ones. The children and mob, crowding about him so that he can hardly stir, make all the noise they can in derision of him."

Another female slave, hearing this, said, "Now you speak of lamps, I know not whether the Princess may have observed it, but there is an old one upon a shelf of the Prince's robing room, and whoever owns it will not be sorry to find a new one in its stead."

The Princess, who knew not the value of this lamp, com-

manded a slave to take it, and make the exchange. The slave obeyed, went out of the hall, and no sooner got to the palace gates than he saw the African magician, called to him, and showing him the old lamp, said, "Give me a new lamp for this."

The magician never doubted but this was the lamp he wanted. There could be no other such in this palace, where every utensil was gold or silver. He snatched it eagerly out of the slave's hand, and thrusting it as far as he could into his breast, offered him his basket, and bade him choose which he liked best. The slave picked out one, and carried it to the Princess. But the exchange was no sooner made than the place rang with the shouts of the children, deriding the magician's folly.

The African magician gave everybody leave to laugh as much as he pleased; and as soon as he was out of the square between the two palaces, he hastened down the streets which were the least frequented. Having no more occasion for his lamps or basket, he set all down in an alley where nobody saw him. Then going down another street or two, he walked till he came to one of the city gates, and pursuing his way through the suburbs, at length reached a lonely spot, where he passed the remainder of the day. When night came he pulled the lamp out of his breast and rubbed it. At that summons the genie appeared, and said, "What wouldst thou have? I am ready to obey thee as thy slave, and the slave of all those who have that lamp in their hands, both I and the other slaves of the lamp."

"I command thee," replied the magician, "to transport me immediately and the palace which thou and the other slaves of the lamp have built in this city, with all the people in it, to Africa." The genie made no reply, but immediately transported him and the palace entire, to the spot whither he was desired to convey it.

The Sultan was so surprised at not finding the palace upon

which he was used to gaze that he called the Grand Vizier to him in order that he might give his opinion. The Grand Vizier, who feared and disliked Aladdin, was not slow to advise the Sultan to have him arrested. He would have had him put to death but that the people threatened to rebel if this were done.

The Sultan in his wrath sent for Aladdin, and said to him, "Where is your palace?"

"Indeed," answered Aladdin, "I cannot tell you. But pray, sire, give me forty days, and if at the end of that time I do not restore it to its place, I offer my head as a forfeit."

"Go then," said the Sultan, "but forget not to return in forty days."

Aladdin went out of the Sultan's presence in great humiliation, so that he durst not lift up his eyes. The principal officers of the court, who had all professed themselves his friends, turned their backs to avoid seeing him. He was quite distraught, and wandered about the city vainly asking if anyone had seen his palace.

Having spent three days in this way, he at length went into the country, determined to end his life. As he approached the river in which he intended to drown himself, he slipped and fell, and in falling rubbed the magic ring, which he still wore, but of which he had forgotten the power. Immediately the genie whom he had seen in the cave appeared, and said, "What wouldst thou? I am thy slave; the slave of the ring."

"Genie," said Aladdin, agreeably surprised at this unexpected help, "transport me immediately to the spot whither my palace has been removed." No sooner were these words spoken than Aladdin found himself in Africa, beside his own palace, under the Princess' window.

It so happened that shortly thereafter the Princess Buddir al-Buddoor came to the window, and seeing Aladdin was overcome with joy. "Come," she cried, "to the private door, and hasten to me." Aladdin's joy was no less than that of the Prin-

cess. He tenderly embraced her, and then asked, "Tell me what has become of the lamp that stood on the shelf in my room."

"Alas," replied the Princess, "I foolishly changed it for a new one, not knowing its power, and the next morning found myself in this place, which I am told is Africa."

"Then, since we are in Africa," said Aladdin, "I know that this must be the doing of the African magician. Can you tell me where he keeps the lamp?"

The Princess told him that the magician always carried the lamp in the bosom of his dress, because he had shown it to her. "Then," said Aladdin, "we may yet punish this wicked magician. Let the private door be opened to me directly I return; for the first thing is to secure the lamp."

Aladdin set out and soon descried a wayfarer who was overjoyed to change clothes with him, and went to an apothecary and asked for a certain powder, which was very costly. The apothecary looked askance, but Aladdin showed him a purse full of gold and demanded half a dram, with which he returned quickly to the palace. He entered by the private door. Hastening to the Princess' apartment he said to her, "When the magician comes to visit you, you must be most gracious to him. Entertain him as becomes you, and ere he leaves request him to drink to you. Then give him this cup, in which there is a powder that will send him to sleep. While he sleeps we can secure the lamp, whose slaves will do our bidding, and we shall be restored to China once more."

The Princess most carefully performed all that Aladdin had directed and when the magician came as usual to pay her a visit, he was agreeably surprised to find her waiting to receive him with a smile. At the close of the evening, during which the Princess had tried all she could to please him, she asked him to exchange cups with her, and giving the signal, had the drugged cup brought, which she gave to the magician. He drank it out of compliment to the Princess to the very last drop, when he fell backward lifeless on the sofa, and the Prin-

cess gave the signal which she had arranged with Aladdin.

As soon as Aladdin entered the hall, the Princess rose from her seat, and ran overjoyed to embrace him. But he stopped her, and said, "Princess, it is not yet time. Oblige me by retiring to your apartment; and let me be left alone a moment, while I endeavor to transport you back to China as speedily as you were brought from thence."

When the Princess and her women were gone out of the hall, Aladdin shut the door, and going directly to the dead body of the magician, opened his vest, took out the lamp—which was carefully wrapped up, as the Princess had told him—and unfolding and rubbing it, the genie immediately appeared. "Genie," said Aladdin, "I command thee to transport this palace instantly into China, to the place from whence it was brought hither." Immediately the palace was transported into China, and its removal was only felt by two little shocks—the one when it was lifted up, the other when it was set down, and both within a very short interval of time.

The Sultan, who rose early, looked, as was his wont, in sorrow over the empty space. To his astonishment he perceived that the palace had been replaced, and he was overjoyed. He at once called for his horse and rode over to the palace, to welcome the return of his daughter and Aladdin. Aladdin, who had foreseen this visit, had risen early, and was ready to receive the Sultan in the hall, clothed in a most magnificent garment. He led the Sultan straight to the Princess' apartment, where the happy father fondly embraced his child. "Son," said he, turning to Aladdin, "forgive the harshness of my conduct toward you, which was inspired by paternal affection."

"Sire," replied Aladdin, "you are not to blame; that base magician was alone the cause of all my troubles."

Although the African magician was dead, he had a younger brother, who was equally skillful as a necromancer, and even surpassed him in villainy and pernicious designs. These two brothers did not live together, but each year they communi-

cated by means of their magic arts. Not having received any tidings of his elder brother, the younger one made an astrological inquiry, by which he discovered that the elder had been poisoned. By a further investigation, he discovered that he was buried in the capital of China, near the dwelling of the man who had murdered him, who, he learned, was married to the Sultan's daughter.

He at once set out for the capital of China to avenge his brother's death, and after a long and fatiguing journey reached the city, where he soon discovered that Aladdin was the poisoner whom he sought. He took a lodging in a khan, where he heard of the virtue and piety of a woman called Fatima, who had retired from the world, and of the miracles she wrought. As he fancied that this woman might be serviceable to him in the project he had conceived, he requested to be informed more particularly who that holy woman was, and what sort of miracles she performed.

"What!" said the person whom he addressed, "have you never seen or heard of her? She is the admiration of the whole town, for her fasting, her austerities, and her exemplary life. Except Mondays and Fridays, she never stirs out of her little cell; and on those days on which she comes into the town she does an infinite deal of good. There is not a person but is cured by her laying her hand upon them."

That very night the magician went to Fatima's cell; and having murdered her, he put on her clothes and went to the palace of Aladdin, bent upon revenge.

As soon as the people saw the holy woman, as they imagined him to be, they presently gathered about him in a great crowd. Some begged his blessing, others kissed his hand, and others, more reserved, only the hem of his garment; while others stooped for him to lay his hands upon them; which he did, muttering some words in form of prayer, and, in short, counterfeited so well, that everybody took him for the holy woman.

Though the progress was slow, the magician at length

reached the square in front of the palace. The Princess happening to hear that the holy woman was there, and being desirous of seeing her, sent one of her slaves to bid her enter. The people, seeing the slave approach, fell back to allow him to approach Fatima. "Holy woman," said he, "the Princess wishes to see you."

"The Princess does me too great an honor," replied the false Fatima. "I am ready to obey her command." At the same time he followed the slave to the palace, greatly delighted at the success of his plot.

When they had conversed, the Princess said, "My good mother, I have one thing to request, which you must not refuse me. It is, to stay with me, that you may edify me with your way of living; and that I may learn from your good example."

"Princess," said the counterfeit Fatima, "I beg of you not to ask what I cannot consent to, without neglecting my prayers and devotion."

"That shall be no hindrance to you," answered the Princess. "I have a great many apartments unoccupied. You shall choose which you like best, and have as much liberty to perform your devotions as if you were in your own cell."

The magician, who desired nothing more than to introduce himself into the palace, where it would be a much easier matter for him to execute his designs, said, after a pause, "Princess, whatever resolution a poor wretched woman as I am may have made to renounce the pomp and grandeur of this world, I dare not presume to oppose the will and commands of so pious and charitable a Princess." He accordingly followed her with tottering gait.

Afterward the Princess requested him to dine with her. But he, considering that he should then be obliged to show his face, which he had always taken care to conceal, and fearing that the Princess should find out that he was not Fatima, begged of her earnestly to excuse him, telling her that he never ate anything but bread and dried fruits, and desiring to

eat that slight repast in his own apartment. The Princess granted his request, saying, "You may be as free here, good mother, as if you were in your own cell. I will order you a dinner, but remember I expect you as soon as you have finished your repast."

After the Princess had dined, and the false Fatima had been informed by one of the slaves that she had risen from table, he failed not to wait upon her. "My good mother," said the Princess, "I am overjoyed to have the company of so holy a woman as yourself, who will confer a blessing upon this palace. But now I am speaking of the palace, pray how do you like it? And before I show it all to you, tell me first what you think of this hall?"

Upon this question, the counterfeit Fatima surveyed the hall from one end to the other, and said, "As far as such a solitary being as I am, who am unacquainted with what the world calls beautiful, can judge, this hall is truly admirable and most beautiful. There wants but one thing."

"What is that, good mother?" demanded the Princess. "Tell me, I conjure you. For my part, I always believed, and have heard say, it wanted nothing; but if it does, it shall be supplied."

"Princess," said the false Fatima, with great dissimulation, "forgive me the liberty I have taken. But my opinion is, if it can be of any importance, that if a roc's egg were hung up in the middle of the dome, this hall would have no parallel in the four quarters of the world, and your palace would be the wonder of the universe."

"My good mother," said the Princess, "what bird is a roc, and where may one get an egg?"

"Princess," replied the pretended Fatima, "it is a bird of prodigious size, which inhabits the summit of Mount Caucasus. The architect who built your palace can get you one."

The Princess often thought of the roc's egg, and it annoyed her to think that anything was lacking from her palace. So when Aladdin returned she received him coldly, and said, "I

always believed that our palace was the most superb, magnificent, and complete in the world. But I will tell you now what I find fault with upon examining the hall of four-and-twenty windows. Do not you think with me that it would be complete if a roc's egg were hung up in the midst of the dome?"

"Princess," replied Aladdin, "it is enough that you think there wants such an ornament. You shall see by the diligence used to supply that deficiency that there is nothing which I would not do for your sake."

Aladdin left the Princess Buddir al-Buddoor that moment, and went up into the hall of four-and-twenty windows, where, pulling out of his bosom the lamp which, after the danger he had been exposed to, he always carried about him, he rubbed it, upon which the genie immediately appeared. "Genie," said Aladdin, "there wants a roc's egg to be hung up in the midst of the dome. I command thee, in the name of this lamp, to repair the deficiency." Aladdin had no sooner pronounced these words than the genie gave so loud and terrible a cry that the hall shook, and Aladdin could scarcely stand upright. "What! wretch," said the genie, in a voice that would have made the most undaunted man tremble, "is it not enough that I and my companions have done everything for you, but you, by an unheard-of ingratitude, must command me to bring my master and hang him up in the midst of this dome? This attempt deserves that you, your wife, and your palace, should be immediately reduced to ashes. But you are lucky that this request does not come from yourself. Know, then, that the true author is the brother of the African magician, your enemy, whom you have destroyed as he deserved. He is now in your palace, disguised in the habit of the holy woman Fatima, whom he has murdered. And it is he who has suggested to your wife to make this pernicious demand. His design is to kill you, therefore take care of yourself." After these words the genie disappeared.

Aladdin quickly resolved what to do. He returned to the Princess and pretended to be suddenly taken ill. The Princess,

remembering Fatima's power, at once sent for her, and she came with all speed. In the meantime the Princess explained how the holy woman came into the palace. And when she appeared Aladdin smiled and bade her welcome at so opportune a moment. "Surely, good woman," said he, "you can cure me as you have others."

The counterfeit Fatima advanced toward him, with his hand all the time on a dagger concealed in his girdle under his gown. Aladdin perceived this, and snatched the weapon from his hand, and slew him on the spot.

"My dear husband, what have you done?" cried the Princess in surprise. "You have killed the holy woman."

"No, my Princess," answered Aladdin with emotion, "I have not killed Fatima, but a villain, who would have assassinated me if I had not prevented him. This wicked wretch," added he, uncovering his face, "is brother to the African magician."

Thus was Aladdin delivered from the persecution of two brothers, who were magicians. Within a few years afterward, the Sultan died at a good old age, and as he left no male children the Princess Buddir al-Buddoor succeeded him, and she and Aladdin reigned together many years, and left a numerous and illustrious posterity.

The Story of Abou Hassan; or, The Sleeper Awakened

IN THE REIGN of the Caliph Haroun al-Raschid, there lived at Bagdad a very rich merchant, who had but one son, whom he named Abou Hassan, and educated with great strictness. When his son was thirty years old, the merchant, dying, left him his sole heir, and master of great riches, amassed together by much frugality and close application to business.

Abou Hassan, whose father had always forbidden him to be extravagant, longed to spend money, and resolved to make a reputation for lavish generosity. To this end he divided his riches into two parts. With one half he bought houses in town, and land in the country, with a resolution never to touch the income of his real estate, which was considerable enough to live upon very handsomely, but to lay it all by as he received it. With the other half, which consisted of ready money, he designed to make himself amends for the time he had lost by the severe restraint in which his father had always kept him.

With this intent, Abou Hassan formed a society of youths of his own age and condition, who thought of nothing but how to make time pass agreeably. He gave magnificent enter-

tainments, and spared neither trouble nor expense to make them celebrated throughout the city. So enormous was the outlay that in a year the money he had set apart for the purpose was spent, and he was forced to desist. As soon as he discontinued keeping this table, his friends forsook him. Whenever they saw him they avoided him, and if by chance he met any of them, and went to stop them, they always excused themselves on some pretext or other.

Abou Hassan was more affected by this behavior of his late friends, who had forsaken him so basely and ungratefully, after all the protestations they had made him of inviolable attachment, than by the loss of all the money he had so foolishly squandered. He went, melancholy and thoughtful, his countenance expressive of deep vexation, into his mother's apartment, and sat down on the end of a sofa at a distance from her.

"What is the matter with you, son?" said his mother, seeing him thus depressed. "Why are you so altered, so dejected, and so different from yourself?"

At these words Abou Hassan melted into tears; and in the midst of his sighs exclaimed, "Ah! mother, I see at last how insupportable poverty must be. I am sensible that it deprives us of joy, just as the setting of the sun does of light. As poverty makes us forget all the commendations passed upon us before our fall, it makes us endeavor to conceal ourselves, and spend our nights in tears and sorrow. In short, a poor man is looked upon, both by friends and relations, as a stranger. You know, mother, how I have treated my friends for this year past. I have entertained them with all imaginable generosity, till I have spent all my money, and now they have left me, when they suppose I can treat them no longer. For my real estate, I thank Heaven for having given me grace to keep the oath I made not to encroach upon that. I shall now know how to use what is left. But I will, however, see how far my friends, who deserve not that I should call them so, will carry their ingratitude. I will go to them one after another, and when I

have represented to them what I have done on their account, ask them to make up a sum of money to relieve me, merely to try if I can find any sentiment of gratitude remaining in them."

Not one of his companions was moved by the arguments which the afflicted Abou Hassan used to persuade them; and he had the mortification to find that many of them told him plainly they did not know him.

He returned home full of melancholy, and going into his mother's apartment, said, "Ah! madam, instead of friends I have found none but perfidious, ungrateful wretches, who deserve not my friendship. I renounce them, and promise you I will never see them more." He resolved to be as good as his word, and took every precaution to avoid falling again into the inconvenience which his former prodigality had occasioned; taking an oath never to give an inhabitant of Bagdad any entertainment while he lived. He drew the strongbox into which he had put the rents received from his estates from the recess where he had placed it in reserve, put it in the room of that he had emptied, and resolved to take out every day no more than was sufficient to defray the expense of a single person to sup with him, who, according to the oath he had taken, was not of Bagdad, but a stranger arrived in the city the same day, and who must take his leave of him the following morning.

In accordance with this plan, Abou Hassan took care every morning to provide whatever was necessary, and toward the close of the evening went and sat at the end of Bagdad bridge. And as soon as he saw a stranger, he accosted him civilly and invited him to sup and lodge with him that night; and after having informed him of the law he had imposed upon himself, conducted him to his house. The repast with which Abou Hassan regaled his guests was not costly, but well dressed, with plenty of good wine, and generally lasted till the night was pretty far advanced. Instead of entertaining his guests with the affairs of state, his family, or business, as is too frequent, he conversed on various agreeable subjects. He was naturally of so gay and pleasant a temper that he could give

the most agreeable turns to every subject, and make the most melancholy persons merry. When he sent away his guests the next morning, he always said, "God preserve you from all sorrow wherever you go. When I invited you yesterday to come and sup with me, I informed you of the law I have imposed on myself. Therefore do not take it ill if I tell you that we must never see one another again, nor drink together, either at home or anywhere else, for reasons best known to myself. So God conduct you."

One day when Abou Hassan was waiting at the bridge as usual, the Caliph Haroun al-Raschid, attended by one slave, chanced to come by in the garb of a merchant of Moussul. Abou Hassan, taking him for such, saluted him courteously and said, "Sir, I congratulate you on your happy arrival in Bagdad. I beg you to do me the honor to sup with me, and repose yourself at my house for this night, after the fatigue of your journey." He then told him of his custom of entertaining the first stranger with whom he met. The Caliph found something so odd and singular in Abou Hassan's whim that he was very desirous to know the cause. So he told him that he could not better merit a civility, which he did not expect as a stranger, than by accepting the obliging offer made him; that he had only to lead the way, and he was ready to follow him.

Abou Hassan, little guessing the rank of his guest, treated him as an equal, and gave him the usual good but plain supper of which he himself partook. After they had supped and washed their hands, Abou Hassan placed wine upon the table and requested the Caliph to drink, which he did, expressing himself well pleased with the wine. He also listened with satisfaction to the young man's easy and cultured conversation. And at last, in a burst of confidence, Abou Hassan told the Caliph his history, which interested him greatly. "You are indeed a fortunate man," said he, "to have been warned in time, and I highly commend your conduct."

Thus they sat, drinking and talking of indifferent subjects, till the night was pretty far advanced. Then the Caliph said,

"Before we part, pray tell me if there is any way in which I can be of service to you? Speak freely, and open your mind; for though I am but a merchant, it may be in my power to oblige you myself, or by some friend."

To these offers of the Caliph, Abou Hassan, taking him still for a Moussul merchant, replied, "I am very well persuaded, sir, that it is not out of compliment that you make me these generous tenders. But upon the word of an honest man, I assure you, I have nothing that troubles me, no business, nor desires, and I ask nothing of anybody. I have not the least ambition, as I told you before, and am satisfied with my condition. Therefore, I can only thank you for your obliging proffers, and the honor you have done me in condescending to partake of mv frugal fare. Yet I must tell you," pursued Abou Hassan, "there is one thing that gives me uneasiness, without, however, disturbing my rest. You must know the town of Bagdad is divided into four quarters, in each of which there is a mosque with an imam to perform service at certain hours, at the head of the quarter which assembles there. The imam of the division I live in is a surly curmudgeon, of an austere countenance, and the greatest hypocrite in the world. Four old men of this neighborhood, who are people of the same stamp, meet regularly every day at this imam's house. There they vent their slander, calumny, and malice against me and the whole quarter. Were I but in a position to punish them I would do so. And I wish the Caliph knew of their doings, for he is just and would stop them. Would that I had the Caliph's power for one day. Then I would order the imam to receive four hundred lashes, and each of the four men who abet his actions should receive one hundred, as the reward of their iniquities."

The Caliph immediately decided upon a plan by which he could enable Abou Hassan's wish to be realized. He took the bottle and poured out a glass of wine, drank it off to his host's health; and then filling the other, put into it artfully a little opiate powder, which he had about him, and giving it to Abou

Hassan, said, "You have taken the pains to fill for me all night, and it is the least I can do to save you the trouble once. I beg you to take this glass and drink it for my sake."

Abou Hassan took the glass, and to show his guest with how much pleasure he received the honor, drank it off at once. Directly he swallowed it the powder took effect, and he fell into a sound sleep. The Caliph commanded the slave he had brought with him to take Abou Hassan upon his back, and follow him; but to be sure to observe the house, that he might know it again.

In this manner the Caliph, followed by the slave with his sleeping load, went out of the house, but without shutting the door after him as he had been desired. He went directly to his palace, and by a private door into his own apartment, where the officers of his chamber were in waiting, whom he ordered to undress Abou Hassan and put him into his bed. This they immediately performed.

The Caliph then sent for all the officers and ladies to the palace, and said to them, "I would have all those whose business it is to attend my levee wait tomorrow morning upon the man who lies in my bed, pay the same respect to him as to myself, and obey him in whatever he may command. Let him be refused nothing that he asks, and be addressed and answered as if he were the Commander of the Faithful. In short, I expect that you attend to him as the true Caliph, without regarding me; and disobey him not in the least circumstance."

The officers and ladies, who understood that the Caliph meant to divert himself, answered by low bows, and then withdrew, every one preparing to contribute to the best of his power to perform his respective part adroitly.

The Caliph next sent for the Grand Vizier. "Giafer," said he, "I have sent for you to instruct you, and to prevent your being surprised tomorrow when you come to audience, at seeing this man seated on my throne in the royal robes. Accost him with the same reverence and respect that you pay to my-

self. Observe and punctually execute whatever he bids you do, the same as if I commanded you. He will exercise great liberality, and commission you with the distribution of it. Do all he commands; even if his liberality should extend so far as to empty all the coffers in my treasury. And remember to acquaint all my Emirs and the officers without the palace, to pay him the same honor at audience as to myself, and to carry on the matter so well that he may not perceive the least thing that may interrupt the diversion which I design myself."

After the Grand Vizier had retired, the Caliph went to bed in another apartment, and gave Mesrour, the chief of his eunuchs, the orders which he was to execute, that everything should succeed as he intended, so that he might see how Abou Hassan would use the power and authority of the Caliph for the short time he had desired to have it. Above all, he charged him not to fail to awaken him at the usual hour, before he awakened Abou Hassan, because he wished to be present when he arose.

Mesrour failed not to do as the Caliph had commanded, and as soon as the Caliph went into the room where Abou Hassan lay, he placed himself in a little closet, from whence he could see all that passed. All the officers and ladies, who were to attend Abou Hassan's levee, went in at the same time, and took their posts according to their rank, ready to acquit themselves of their respective duties as if the Caliph himself had been going to rise.

As it was just daybreak, and time to prepare for the morning prayer before sunrise, the officers who stood nearest to the head of the bed put a sponge steeped in vinegar to Abou Hassan's nose, who immediately awoke with a start. He was greatly surprised to find himself in a large room, magnificently furnished, the ceiling of which was finely painted in arabesque, adorned with bases of gold and silver, and the floor covered with a rich silk tapestry. After casting his eyes on the covering of the bed, he perceived it was cloth of gold richly

embossed with pearls and diamonds. And near the bed lay, on a cushion, a habit of tissue embroidered with jewels with a Caliph's turban.

At the sight of these glittering objects, Abou Hassan was in the most inexpressible amazement, and looked upon all he saw as a dream; yet a dream he wished it not to be. "So," said he to himself, "I am Caliph; but," added he, recollecting himself, "it is only a dream, the effect of the wish I entertained my guest with last night"; and then he turned himself about and shut his eyes to sleep. At the same time the slave said, very respectfully, "Commander of the Faithful, it is time for your Majesty to rise to prayers, the morning begins to advance."

At the sound of this voice Abou Hassan sat up and said to himself, "This cannot be a dream." He rubbed his eyes, to make sure that he was awake, and when he opened them, the sun shone full in at the chamber window. And at that instant Mesrour came in, prostrated himself before Abou Hassan, and said, "Commander of the Faithful, your Majesty will excuse me for representing to you that you used not to rise so late, and that the time of prayer is over. If your Majesty has not had a bad night, it is time to ascend your throne and hold a council as usual. All your generals, governors, and other officers of state, wait your presence in the council hall."

By this discourse, Abou Hassan was persuaded that he was neither asleep nor in a dream; but at the same time was not less embarrassed and confused under his uncertainty as to what steps to take. At last, looking earnestly at Mesrour, he said to him in a serious tone, "Whom is it you speak to, and call the Commander of the Faithful? I do not know you, and you must mistake me for somebody else."

Any person but Mesrour would have been puzzled by these questions of Abou Hassan. But he had been so well instructed by the Caliph that he played his part admirably. "My imperial lord and master," said he, "your Majesty only speaks thus to try me. Is not your Majesty the Commander of the Faithful, Monarch of the World from East to West, and Vicar on

Earth to the Prophet sent of God? Mesrour, your poor slave, has not forgotten you, after so many years that he has had the honor and happiness to serve and pay his respects to your Majesty. He would think himself the most unhappy of men if he has incurred your displeasure, and begs of you most humbly to remove his fears; but had rather suppose that you have been disturbed by some troublesome dream."

Abou Hassan burst out laughing at these words, and fell backward upon the bolster, which pleased the Caliph so much that he would have laughed as loudly himself if he had not been afraid of putting a stop to the pleasant scene he had promised himself.

Abou Hassan, when he had tired himself with laughing, sat up again, and speaking to a little boy that stood by him, black as Mesrour, said, "Hark ye, tell me who I am?"

"Sire," answered the little boy modestly, "your Majesty is the Commander of the Believers, and God's Vicar on Earth."

"That is not true, you little blackface," said Abou Hassan. Then he called the lady that stood nearest to him. "Come hither, fair one," said he, holding out his hand, "bite the end of my finger, that I may feel whether I am asleep or awake."

The lady, who knew the Caliph was witnessing all that passed, was overjoyed to have an opportunity of showing her power of diverting him, went with a grave countenance, and putting his finger between her teeth, bit it so hard that she put him to violent pain. Snatching his hand quickly back again, he said, "I find I am awake, and not asleep. But by what miracle have I become Caliph in a night's time? This is certainly the most strange and surprising event in the world!" Then addressing himself to the same lady, he said, "I conjure you, by the protection of God, in whom you trust as well as I, not to hide the truth from me; am I really the Commander of the Faithful?"

"It is so true," answered the lady, "that we who are your slaves are amazed to find that you will not believe yourself to be so."

"You are a deceiver," replied Abou Hassan. "I know very well who I am."

More puzzled than ever, Abou Hassan permitted Mesrour to assist him to rise, and he submitted to be dressed by the slaves without offering any resistance. When this task was completed, the Grand Vizier led him through the double rows of curtains to the council hall, where he was conducted with all the splendor of royal pomp to the throne. Having reached the throne, Mesrour gave him his arm to lean upon, and another officer on the other side did the same, and by their aid Abou Hassan mounted the steps and sat down amidst the acclamations of the officers.

The Caliph had, meanwhile, followed, and taken up his station in a place from which he could see without being seen. What pleased him highly was to see Abou Hassan fill his throne with almost as much gravity as himself.

As soon as Abou Hassan was seated upon the throne the Grand Vizier came forward and, making a low obeisance, said, "Commander of the Faithful, God shower down blessings on your Majesty in this life, receive you into His paradise in the other world, and confound your enemies."

Abou Hassan, who began by this time to believe that he really was Caliph, asked the Grand Vizier what business there was to transact. "Commander of the Faithful," replied the Grand Vizier, "the officers of your council wait without till your Majesty gives them leave to pay their accustomed respects." Abou Hassan immediately ordered the door to be opened so that the officers might enter. And he bowed to them regally as they prostrated themselves before taking their seats.

After this ceremony the business of the day was transacted, the Grand Vizier standing before the throne made his report, and the Caliph, who watched everything, greatly admired the wit with which Abou Hassan called the Cadi to him and said, "Go to a mosque in a certain quarter, wherein there is an old imam. Seize him and four old men, who abet his weakness,

and bastinado them. Give the imam four hundred and each of the others one hundred strokes. After that, mount them all five, clothed in rags, on camels, with their faces to the tails, and lead them through the whole city, with a crier before them, who shall proclaim with a loud voice, 'This is the punishment of all those who are meddlesome.' Command them also to quit the quarter forever." The Cadi bowed to the Grand Vizier and withdrew to execute the order, and in a short time returned to report that his duty was discharged.

The Caliph was highly pleased at the firmness with which this order was given, and perceived that Abou Hassan was resolved not to lose the opportunity of punishing the imam and the other four old hypocrites of his quarter. In the meantime the Grand Vizier went on with his report, and had just finished, when the judge of the police came back from executing his commission. He approached the throne with the usual ceremony, and said, "Commander of the Faithful, I found the imam and his four companions in the mosque, which your Majesty pointed out; and as a proof that I have punctually obeyed your commands, I have brought an instrument signed by the principal inhabitants of the ward." At the same time he pulled a paper out of his bosom, and presented it to the pretended Caliph.

Abou Hassan, then addressing himself to the Grand Vizier, said, "Go to the high treasurer for a purse of a thousand pieces of gold, and carry it to the mother of one Abou Hassan, who lives in the same quarter to which I sent the judge of the police. Go and return immediately."

The Grand Vizier, after laying his hand upon his head, and prostrating himself before the throne, went to the high treasurer, who gave him the money, which he offered a slave to take, and to follow him to Abou Hassan's mother, to whom he gave it, saying only, "The Caliph makes you this present." She received it with the greatest surprise imaginable.

The business of the day being finished, the council withdrew, and Abou Hassan descended from the throne, and was

conducted to the dining hall, where he fared sumptuously while the musicians played and danced before him. And all the while seven very beautiful ladies stood near and fanned him. Abou Hassan was charmed by everything; not least by the beauty of the ladies who attended him. When he looked at them attentively, he said that he believed one of them was enough to give him all the air he wanted, and would have six of the ladies sit at table with him, three on his right hand, and three on his left. The six ladies obeyed. And Abou Hassan, taking notice that out of respect they did not eat, helped them himself, and invited them to eat in the most pressing and obliging terms. Afterward he asked their names, which they told him were Alabaster Neck, Coral Lips, Moon Face, Sunshine, Eyes' Delight, Heart's Delight, and she who fanned him was Sugar Cane. The many soft things he said upon their names showed him to be a man of sprightly wit, and it is not to be conceived how much it increased the esteem which the Caliph (who saw everything) had already conceived for him.

After this repast Abou Hassan was conducted into another hall, where dessert was spread, and where seven other ladies, more beautiful than the others, stood ready to fan him. Abou Hassan, however, would not suffer them to do so, but bade them sit near him that he might enjoy their society. The Caliph was delighted to hear the ready wit with which he amused the ladies, and knew him to be a man of no ordinary merits.

By this time, the day beginning to close, Abou Hassan was conducted into a hall, much more superbly and magnificently furnished, lighted with wax in seven gold lusters, which gave a splendid light. There he saw seven large silver flagons full of the choicest wines, and by them seven crystal glasses of the finest workmanship. Hitherto Abou Hassan had drunk nothing but water, according to the custom observed at Bagdad, from the highest to the lowest, and at the Caliph's court, never to drink wine till the evening.

As soon as Abou Hassan entered the hall, he went to the table, sat down, and was a long time in a kind of ecstasy at the sight which surrounded him, and which was much more beautiful than anything he had beheld before. Taking by the hand the lady who stood on the right next to him, he made her sit down by him, and presenting her with a cake, asked her name. "Commander of the Faithful," said the lady, "I am called Cluster of Pearls."

"No name," replied Abou Hassan, "could have more properly expressed your worth; and indeed your teeth exceed the finest pearls. Cluster of Pearls," added he, "since that is your name, oblige me with a glass of wine from your fair hand." The lady brought him a glass of wine, which she presented to him with a pleasant air. Then Abou Hassan drank with each of the seven ladies. And when he had toasted them severally, Cluster of Pearls went to the buffet, poured out a glass of wine, and putting in a pinch of the same powder the Caliph had used the night before, presented it to Abou Hassan. "Commander of the Faithful," said she, "I beg of your Majesty to take this glass of wine, and before you drink it, do me the favor to hear a song I have composed today, and which I flatter myself will not displease you."

When the lady had concluded, Abou Hassan drank off his glass, and turned his head toward her to give her those praises which he thought she merited, but was prevented by the opiate, which operated so suddenly that his mouth was instantly wide open, and his eyes close shut. And dropping his head on the cushions, he slept as profoundly as the day before when the Caliph had given him the powder. One of the ladies stood ready to catch the glass, which fell out of his hand. And then the Caliph, who enjoyed greater satisfaction in this scene than he had promised himself, and was all along a spectator of what had passed, came into the hall to them, overjoyed at the success of his plan. He ordered Abou Hassan to be dressed in his own clothes, and carried back to his house by the slave

who had brought him, charging him to lay him on a sofa in the same room, without making any noise and to leave the door open when he came away.

Abou Hassan slept till very late the next morning. When the effect of the powder had worn off, he awoke, opened his eyes, and finding himself at home, was in the utmost surprise. "Cluster of Pearls! Morning Star! Coral Lips! Moon Face!" cried he, calling the ladies of the palace by their names, as he remembered them. "Where are you? Come hither."

Abou Hassan called so loudly that his mother, who was in her own apartment, heard him, and running to him because of the noise he made, said, "What ails you, son? What has happened to you?" At these words Abou Hassan lifted up his head, and looking haughtily at his mother, said, "Good woman! who is it you call son?"

"Why, you," answered his mother very mildly. "Are you not Abou Hassan, my son? It is strange that you have forgotten yourself so soon."

"I your son?" replied Abou Hassan. "You know not what you say! I am the Commander of the Faithful! and you cannot make me believe otherwise."

Abou Hassan's mother, who was convinced that he was suffering from a mental disorder, tried to change the conversation. And to do this she related how the imam had been punished on the previous day. Abou Hassan no sooner heard this statement than he cried out, "I am neither thy son nor Abou Hassan, but certainly the Commander of the Believers. I cannot doubt after what you have told me. Know that it was by my order the imam and the four Sheiks were punished and all your arguments cannot convince me of the contrary."

His mother vainly tried to soothe his troubled mind, but her remonstrances only enraged Abou Hassan the more. And he was so provoked at his mother that, regardless of her tears, he took hold of a cane, and ran to his mother in great fury, and in a threatening manner that would have frightened anyone but a mother so partial to him, said, "Tell me directly who I am."

"I do not believe, son," replied she, looking at him tenderly and without fear, "that you are so abandoned by God as not to know your mother, who brought you into the world. You are indeed my son, Abou Hassan, and are much in the wrong to arrogate to yourself the title which belongs only to our sovereign lord the Caliph Haroun al-Raschid, especially after the noble and generous present the monarch made us yesterday."

At these words Abou Hassan grew quite mad. The circumstance of the Caliph's liberality persuaded him more than ever that he was Caliph, remembering that he sent the Vizier. And in his frenzy he beat his mother with the cane, telling her the while that it was he who sent the money.

The poor mother, who could not have thought that her son would have come so soon from words to blows, called out for help so loudly that the neighbors ran in to her assistance. Abou Hassan continued to beat her, at every stroke asking her if he was the Commander of the Faithful, to which she always answered tenderly that he was her son.

At the sound of her cries the neighbors came running in, and upon hearing Abou Hassan proclaim himself as Caliph, they no longer doubted but that he was insane. They therefore seized him, and, having bound him, carried him to the lunatic asylum, where he was lodged in a grated cell, and here they left him to recover his senses. He received fifty strokes of the bastinado daily to help him to remember that he was not the Commander of the Faithful, as he maintained.

By degrees those strong and lively ideas, which Abou Hassan had entertained, of having been clothed in the Caliph's habit, having exercised his authority, and been punctually obeyed and treated like the true Caliph, the assurance of which had persuaded him that he was so, began to wear away. He then made up his mind to think of the whole thing as a dream and to return to his own house in peace.

When Abou Hassan's mother came to see him, she found him so much better that she wept for joy. "Indeed, mother," said he, "I cannot understand what has taken place, but I am

resolved to regard it all as a very vivid dream. And I beg of you to forgive me for all my ill-treatment of you."

"My son!" cried she, transported with pleasure, "my satisfaction and comfort to hear you talk so reasonably are inexpressible, and it gives me much joy; but I must tell you my opinion of this adventure. The stranger whom you brought home the evening before your illness to sup with you went away without shutting your chamber door after him, as you desired, which I believe gave the devil an opportunity to enter and throw you into the horrible illusion you have been in. Therefore, my son, you ought to return God thanks for your deliverance."

"I believe that you are right," said he, "and I beg of you to have me released from this place." His mother waited no second asking, but hurried to the keeper, who, having examined Abou Hassan, released him as she desired.

Abou Hassan took several days' rest after his return, and then resumed his practice of inviting a stranger to supper. The very first time he went to the bridge he perceived the merchant who, as he thought, had caused all his troubles, coming toward him. Abou Hassan turned away to avoid him, but the merchant would not be put off, and came up to him. "Ho, brother Abou Hassan," said he, "is it you?—I greet you! Give me leave to embrace you."

"Not I," replied Abou Hassan, "I do not greet you. I will have neither your greeting nor your embraces. Go along with you!"

The Caliph, who had carefully planned the meeting, since he knew that Abou Hassan had returned home, was not to be diverted from his purpose by this rude behavior. He well knew the law Abou Hassan had imposed on himself, never to have commerce again with a stranger he had once entertained, but pretended to be ignorant of it. "Ah! brother Abou Hassan," said he, embracing him, "I do not intend to part with you thus, since I have had the good fortune to meet with you a second time. You must exercise the same hospitality toward

me again that you showed me a month ago, when I had the honor to drink with you."

Abou Hassan would fain have sent the Caliph away, but his efforts to rid himself of his unwelcome presence were futile, and at last he found himself compelled to allow him to accompany him. "But," said he, "since your last visit entailed so much trouble, I must tell you what happened, and beg of you to spare me a repetition." Abou Hassan then related his adventure, and concluded by making the Caliph promise to form no more good intentions for his future. "I am satisfied," said he, "and will forgive all that is past."

As soon as Abou Hassan entered his house, he called for his mother and for candles, desired his guest to sit down upon a sofa, and then placed himself by him. A little time after, supper was brought up, and they both began to eat without ceremony.

When they had done, Abou Hassan's mother cleared the table, set on a small dessert of fruit, wine, and glasses by her son, then withdrew, and appeared no more.

After they had been drinking for some time the Caliph said, "Have you never thought of getting married?"

"No," replied Abou Hassan, "I prefer to remain free."

"That is not right," continued the Caliph. "I must find you a lady who will be worthy of your love. And I am sure you will like her." Then taking Abou Hassan's glass he put into it a little of the powder, and handed it to his host filled with wine. "Come," said he, "drink the health of the lady I shall provide for you."

Abou Hassan took the glass, laughing, and shaking his head, said, "Be it so. Since you desire it, I cannot be guilty of so great a piece of incivility, nor disoblige a guest of so much merit in such a trifling matter. I will drink the health of the lady you promise me, though I am very well contented as I am, and do not rely on your keeping your word." No sooner had Abou Hassan drunk off his bumper, than he was seized with as deep a sleep as before. And the Caliph ordered the

same slave to take him and carry him to the palace. The slave obeyed, and the Caliph, who did not intend to send back Abou Hassan as before, shut the door after him, as he had promised, and followed.

When they arrived at the palace, the Caliph ordered Abou Hassan to be laid on a sofa in the hall, from whence he had been carried home fast asleep a month before. But first he bade the attendants to put on him the same habit in which he had acted as Caliph, which was done. He then charged all the officers, ladies, and musicians, who were in the hall when he

drank the last glass of wine which had put him to sleep, to be there by daybreak, and to take care to act their part well when the visitor should wake. He then retired to rest, charging Mesrour to awake him before they went into the hall, that he might conceal himself in the closet as before.

Things being thus disposed, and the Caliph's powder having had its effect, Abou Hassan began to awake without opening his eyes. At that instant, the seven bands of singers joined their voices to the sound of hautboys, fifes, flutes, and other instruments, forming a very agreeable concert. Abou Hassan was greatly surprised to hear the delightful harmony. But when he opened his eyes, and saw the ladies and officers about him, whom he thought he recognized, his amazement increased. The hall that he was in seemed to be the same he had seen in his first dream, and he observed the same lusters, and the same furniture and ornaments.

He was, however, too frightened to regain all his faculties at once. "God have mercy upon me," he exclaimed, "for I am possessed of the evil spirit." The lords tried to convince him that he was the victim of an unpleasant dream. "Sir," cried he, "see my back, are these marks, then, imaginary? I tell you I can feel the pain of the blows still. Come hither and bite my ear, that I may feel if I am awake." One of the slaves stepped forward and obeyed, whereupon Abou Hassan screamed, but was still mystified. The band immediately struck

up, and all the attendants began to dance round the sofa on which Abou Hassan sat. Seeing among the ladies some that he recognized, Abou Hassan threw off his royal robes and joined in the dance, jumping and cutting capers with the others. So amused was the Caliph that he put his head into the room and cried out, "Abou Hassan, Abou Hassan, have you mind to cause my death from laughing?"

As soon as the Caliph's voice was heard, everybody was silent, and Abou Hassan, among the rest, who, turning his head to see from whence the voice came, knew the Caliph, and in him recognized the Moussul merchant, but was not in the least daunted. On the contrary, he became convinced that he was awake, and that all that had happened to him had been real, and not a dream. He entered into the Caliph's pleasantry. "Ha! ha!" said he, looking at him with good assurance, "you are a merchant of Moussul, and complain that I would kill you. I see the whole thing now. But nay, tell me what you did to make me insensible, or else I shall always feel that I am half mad."

The Caliph then told him all that had happened during the unnatural sleep, and how it was accomplished. "I have a desire to know how my people live," said he, "and therefore often wander about the city in disguise. It was thus that I came to your house; and hearing you express a wish to have royal power for a day, I decided to grant your wish. I never thought that my acquiescence would lead to so much trouble, but I am prepared to make every return in my power—not only as your due, but because I have proved that you are a man of high qualities. Ask what you will and I shall grant it."

"Commander of the Faithful," replied Abou Hassan, "how great soever my tortures may have been, they are all blotted out of my remembrance, since I understand my sovereign lord and master had a share in them. And since I may make a request, I would ask to be allowed to enjoy the happiness of admiring, all my lifetime, your virtues."

The Caliph was much pleased by this speech, and ordered

Abou Hassan to be given whatever he wanted, and to come to him whenever he wished. Abou Hassan suitably expressed his obligation, and returned home to tell his mother all that had taken place, and how his previous experience had been no empty dream.

The Caliph was much delighted by Abou Hassan, whose society he constantly desired. He also brought him to his wife Zobeide, who was greatly entertained by the history of his adventures. She often expressed a wish to see him, and noticing that whenever he came he had his eyes always fixed upon one of her slaves, called Nouzhatoul-âouadat, resolved to tell the Caliph of it. "Commander of the Faithful," said she one day, "you do not observe that every time Abou Hassan attends you in your visits to me, he never keeps his eyes off Nouzhatoul-âouadat. And she seems to respond to his advances. If you approve of it, we will make a match between them and celebrate their nuptials here in the palace."

"Madam," replied the Caliph, "if Nouzhatoul-âouadat is willing to accept Abou Hassan as a husband I see no obstacle. Let them decide at once, since they are both present."

Abou Hassan threw himself at the Caliph's and Zobeide's feet, to show the appreciation he had of their goodness; and rising up, said, "I cannot receive a wife from better hands, but dare not hope that Nouzhatoul-âouadat will give me her hand as readily as I give her mine."

At these words he looked at the Princess' slave, who showed by her respectful silence, and the sudden blush that arose in her cheeks, that she was disposed to obey the Caliph and her mistress Zobeide.

The rejoicings at the wedding lasted for many days, and both Zobeide and the Caliph gave the newly married couple very handsome presents. Abou Hassan found his wife all that he desired, and she was equally pleased with him—in fact, they suited each other admirably. After the feastings and merrymakings, Abou Hassan and his wife settled down to live in great luxury. They spared no expense on the entertain-

ments they gave, and so extravagantly did they spend money that scarcely a year after the wedding they found themselves penniless.

In their need Abou Hassan said to his wife, "I was sure that you would not fail me in a business which concerns us both; and therefore I must tell you, this want of money has made me think of a plan which will supply us, at least for a time. It consists in a little trick we must play, I upon the Caliph and you upon Zobeide, and as it will, I am sure, divert them both greatly, it will answer advantageously for us. You and I will both die."

"Not I, indeed," interrupted Nouzhatoul-âouadat. "You may die by yourself, if you please, but I am not so weary of this life; and whether you are pleased or not, will not die so soon. If you have nothing else to propose, you may die by yourself; for I assure you I shall not join you."

"You are a woman of such vivacity and wonderful quickness," replied Abou Hassan, "that you scarcely give me time to explain my design. Have but a little patience, and you shall find that you will be ready enough to die such a death as I intend; for surely you could not think I meant a real death?"

"Well," said his wife, "if it is but a sham death you design, I am at your service, and you may depend on my zeal to second you in this manner of dying. But I must tell you truly, I am very unwilling to die as I apprehended you at first to mean."

"Be but silent a little," said Abou Hassan, "and I will tell you what I promise. I will feign myself dead, and you shall lay me out in the middle of my chamber, with my turban upon my face, my feet toward Mecca, as if ready to be carried out to burial. When you have done this, you must lament, and weep bitterly, as is usual in such cases, tear your clothes and hair, or pretend to do it, and go all in tears, with your locks disheveled, to Zobeide. The Princess will of course inquire the cause of your grief. And when you have told her, with words intermixed with sobs, she will pity you, give you money to defray the expense of my funeral, and a piece of rich brocade to

cover my body, that my interment may be the more magnificent, and to make you a new dress in the place of the one you will have torn. As soon as you return, I will rise, lay you in my place, and go and act the same part with the Caliph, who I dare say will be as generous to me as Zobeide will have been to you."

This plan commended itself to Nouzhatoul-âouadat, and she at once acted upon her husband's suggestion and placed him as he desired, pulled off the headdress, and went straight to Zobeide, weeping and mourning. She poured out her woes to the sympathetic Princess, who was deeply grieved when she heard of Abou Hassan's death. After the two women had sorrowed together, the Princess ordered her slaves to give Nouzhatoul-âouadat a purse of gold and a rich piece of brocade to cover the body, and bade her have no fear for the future, that she would take care of her.

As soon as Nouzhatoul-âouadat got out of the Princess' presence, she dried up her tears, and returned with joy to Abou Hassan, to give him an account of her good success. When she came home she burst out laughing on seeing her husband still stretched out in the middle of the floor. She ran to him, bade him rise and see the fruits of his stratagem. He arose, and rejoiced with his wife at the sight of the purse and brocade. Unable to contain herself at the success of her artifice, she cried, "Come, husband, let me act the dead part, and see if you can manage the Caliph as well as I have done Zobeide."

"That is the temper of all women," replied Abou Hassan, "who, we may well say, have always the vanity to believe they can do things better than men, though at the same time what good they do is by their advice. It would be odd indeed, if I who laid this plot myself could not carry it out as well as you. But let us lose no time in idle discourse. Lie down in my place, and witness if I do not come off with as much applause."

Abou Hassan wrapped up his wife as she had done him, and with his turban unrolled, like a man in the greatest afflic-

tion, ran to the Caliph, who was holding a private council. He presented himself at the door, and the officer, knowing he had free access, opened it. He entered holding with one hand his handkerchief before his eyes, to hide the feigned tears, which trickled down his cheeks, and striking his breast with the other, with exclamations expressing extraordinary grief.

The Caliph, surprised at seeing Abou Hassan in such a plight, asked the cause of his grief, and when he heard that Nouzhatoul-âouadat was dead he expressed his grief in becoming words. He also bade the Vizier present Abou Hassan with a purse of gold and some rich cloth, just as Zobeide had done for Nouzhatoul-âouadat. Abou Hassan prostrated himself before the Caliph and thanked him for his kindness. Then taking the gifts, he hurried back to his house, greatly pleased by the success of his scheme.

Nouzhatoul-âouadat, weary with lying so long in one posture, waited not till Abou Hassan bade her rise. But as soon as she heard the door open, sprang up, ran to her husband, and asked him if he had imposed on the Caliph as cleverly as she had done on Zobeide. "You see," said he, showing her the stuff, and shaking the purse, "that I can act a sorrowful husband for a living wife, as well as you can a weeping widow for a husband not dead." Abou Hassan, however, was not without his fears that this double plot might be attended with some ill consequences. He thought it would not be amiss to put his wife on her guard as to what might happen, that they might act in concert. "For," added he, "the better we succeed in embarrassing the Caliph and Zobeide, the more they will be pleased at last, and perhaps may show their satisfaction by greater liberality." This last consideration induced them to carry on their stratagem further.

The Caliph, though he had important affairs to decide, was so impatient to condole with the Princess on the death of her slave that he rose up as soon as Abou Hassan was gone, and went to Zobeide's apartment. "Madam," said he, "allow me to

express my deep sorrow for the loss you have sustained by the death of Nouzhatoul-âouadat."

"Commander of the Faithful," replied Zobeide, "you are mistaken. It is Abou Hassan who is dead, not Nouzhatoul-âouadat."

"Excuse me, madam," said the Caliph, "you are wrong. Abou Hassan is alive and well."

Zobeide was much piqued at this dry answer of the Caliph. "Commander of the Faithful," replied she, "give me leave to repeat to you once more that it is Abou Hassan who is dead, and that my slave Nouzhatoul-âouadat, his widow, is living. All my women, who wept with me, can bear me witness, and tell you also that I made her a present of a hundred pieces of gold and a piece of brocade. The grief which you found me in was on account of the death of her husband. And just at the instant you entered I was going to send you a compliment of condolence."

At these words of Zobeide, the Caliph cried out in a fit of laughter, "This, madam, is a strange piece of obstinacy. But you may depend upon Nouzhatoul-âouadat's being dead."

"I tell you no, sir," replied Zobeide sharply. "It is Abou Hassan that is dead, and you shall never make me believe otherwise."

The Caliph at once ordered the Vizier to go and find out the truth of the matter at Abou Hassan's house. When Mesrour had departed he said to Zobeide, "You will see, in a moment, which of us is right. So convinced am I that I will bet my garden of pleasures against your palace of paintings, though the one is worth much more than the other." They solemnly vowed to abide by the bet, and anxiously awaited Mesrour's return.

While the Caliph and Zobeide were disputing so earnestly, and with so much warmth, Abou Hassan, who foresaw their difference, was very attentive to whatever might happen. As soon as he perceived Mesrour through a window, at which he

sat talking with his wife, and observed that he was coming directly to their apartment, he guessed his commission, and bade his wife make haste to act the dead part once more, as they had agreed, without loss of time. But they were so pressed that Abou Hassan had much ado to wrap up his wife, and lay the piece of brocade which the Caliph had given him upon her, before Mesrour reached the house. This done, he opened the door of his apartment, and with a melancholy, dejected countenance, and his handkerchief before his eyes, went and sat down at the head of the pretended deceased.

This satisfied Mesrour, who hastened back to report the result of his inquiries to the Caliph. The Caliph was highly delighted, and laughed long when he heard the tidings. "You hear, madam," said he, "you have lost your bet."

Zobeide, however, would not accept Mesrour's unsupported testimony. And as she disputed the wager, it was agreed to send her nurse to see whether Abou Hassan was really dead. But as Abou Hassan was watching at the window, he was prepared to take his place on the couch directly he saw the nurse approaching, so that by the time she reached the apartment Nouzhatoul-âouadat had completed the task of laying him out, and stood mourning by his side.

The nurse stayed only to offer her condolences, and then started back to the palace as fast as she could. As soon as she was gone Nouzhatoul-âouadat wiped her eyes and released Abou Hassan. They both went and sat on a sofa against the window, expecting what would be the end of this stratagem, and to be ready to act according as circumstances might require.

The nurse's report only complicated matters, as both the Caliph and the Princess were convinced of the rectitude of their messengers. And as neither would give way they agreed to go together to see for themselves. Accordingly they arose and sallied forth, accompanied by their attendants.

When Abou Hassan perceived them coming he told his

wife, who was very frightened. "What shall we do?" said she. "We are ruined."

"Fear nothing," replied Abou Hassan. "Have you forgotten already what we agreed on? We will both feign ourselves dead, and you shall see all will go well. At the slow rate they are coming we shall be ready before they reach the door." Accordingly Abou Hassan and his wife wrapped up and covered themselves with the pieces of brocade, and waited patiently for their visitors.

Mesrour, who came first, opened the door, and the Caliph and Zobeide, followed by their attendants, entered the room. But they were struck with horror at the spectacle which presented itself to their view, not knowing what to think. At length Zobeide breaking silence, said to the Caliph, "Alas! they are both dead! You have done much," continued she, looking at the Caliph and Mesrour, "to endeavor to make me believe that my dear slave was dead, and I find it true. Grief at the loss of her husband has certainly killed her."

"Say rather, madam," answered the Caliph, prepossessed to the contrary, that Nouzhatoul-âouadat died first, "the afflicted Abou Hassan sank under his grief, and could not survive his dear wife. You ought, therefore, to confess that you have lost your wager, and that your palace of paintings is mine."

"Hold there," answered Zobeide, warmed at being contradicted by the Caliph; "I will maintain you have lost your garden of pleasures. Abou Hassan died first; since my nurse told you, as well as me, that she saw her alive, and weeping for the death of her husband."

"I will give a thousand pieces of gold to him who can tell me which of these two died first," replied the Caliph.

No sooner were these words out of the Caliph's mouth than he heard a voice under Abou Hassan's piece of brocade say, "Commander of the Faithful, I died first; give me the thousand pieces of gold." At the same instant Abou Hassan

threw off the piece of brocade, and springing up, prostrated himself at his feet, while his wife did the same to Zobeide. The Princess at first shrieked out, but recovering herself, expressed great joy to see her dear slave rise again, just when she was almost inconsolable at having seen her dead. "Ah! wicked Nouzhatoul-âouadat," cried she, "what have I suffered for your sake? However, I forgive you from my heart, since you are not dead."

The Caliph, who was very much amused, demanded the reason for the joke. Whereupon Abou Hassan replied, "Commander of the Faithful, I will declare to your Majesty the whole truth, without the least reserve. The extravagant way in which my wife and I lived was beyond our means. And finding that our money was all gone we were at our wits' end. At last, the shame of seeing ourselves reduced to so low a condition, and not daring to tell your Majesty, made us contrive this stratagem, which we hope your Majesty will be pleased to pardon, to relieve our necessities, and to divert you."

The Caliph and Zobeide began to laugh at the thought of Abou Hassan's scheme. The Caliph, who had not ceased laughing at the singularity of the adventure, rising, said to Abou Hassan and his wife, "Follow me; I will give you the thousand pieces of gold I promised, for joy to find you are not dead." Zobeide desired him to let her make her slave a present of the same sum for the same reason. By this means Abou Hassan and his wife, Nouzhatoul-âouadat, preserved the favor of Caliph Haroun al-Raschid and the Princess Zobeide, and by their liberalities were enabled to pursue their pleasures.

The Story of Codadad and His Brothers

THERE ONCE LIVED a Sultan of Harran, who was blessed with every earthly happiness. He was rich, powerful, and virtuous, and was blessed with many wives, who had given him fifty sons, all joint heirs and successors to his throne. He loved them all equally, with the single exception of one son, named Codadad, whom he hated so deeply from the day of his birth that at last he sent him, with his mother Pirouze, to the court of Prince Samer, a distant but friendly monarch.

Prince Samer took great care of young Codadad's education, and taught him to ride, draw the bow, and other accomplishments befitting the son of a Sultan; so that, at the age of eighteen years Codadad was looked upon as quite a prodigy. The young Prince, inspired by courage worthy of his high birth, one day said to his mother:

"Madam, I feel a great longing to achieve glory. Grant me leave to seek it amidst the perils of war. My father, the Sultan of Harran, has many enemies. I have resolved to offer him my services as a stranger, and not reveal who I am until I have performed some glorious action."

Princess Pirouze approved of her son's generous resolution; and Codadad rode forth from Samaria as if going to the chase, without telling his intention to Prince Samer, for fear the latter might prevent him. He was mounted on a white charger, with bit and shoes of gold. His housing was of blue satin embroidered with pearls. The hilt of his scimitar was of one single diamond, its scabbard was of sandalwood set with emeralds and rubies, and on his shoulder he carried his bow and quiver.

Upon arriving at the city of Harran, he offered his services to the Sultan who, charmed with his good looks, received him cordially and asked his name.

"Sire," answered Codadad, "I am the son of an Emir of Grand Cairo and, learning that you were engaged in war, I have come to offer you my services." The Sultan was much pleased, and gave him a command in his army.

The young Prince soon distinguished himself for bravery and rose high in the Sultan's favor. The latter constantly retained him near his person, and as a proof of his confidence committed the other Princes to his care, so that Codadad was made governor over his own brothers.

In their resentment, the Princes conceived an implacable hatred against him. "Has it come to this," said they, "that the Sultan, our father, not only loves a stranger more than us, but makes him our governor to control our every action? It is not to be endured. We must rid ourselves of this foreigner."

"Let us slay him," said one brother.

"No, no," said another, "let us use stratagem. We will ask his permission to go hunting, and instead we will go to some distant city and stay there. When the Sultan discovers our absence he will blame this stranger, whom he set over us, and will perhaps put him to death, or at least banish him."

All the Princes agreed to this, and the plan was at once carried out. After the brothers had been absent three days the Sultan became alarmed, and when he learned from Codadad that he had given them permission to go hunting he could not

restrain his anger. "Indiscreet stranger," said he to Codadad, "why did you let my sons go without accompanying them? Go, seek them immediately and bring them to me or your life shall pay the forfeit."

At these words Codadad felt the pangs of keenest self-reproach. "Alas! My brothers," he said to himself, "what has become of you through my fault? Have I come to the court of Harran only to increase the Sultan's anxiety?" He departed from the city and, like a shepherd who has lost his flock, searched the whole country for his brothers, inquiring at every village whether they had been seen.

After many days of fruitless search, he came upon a vast plain, in the midst of which was a palace of black marble. As he drew near he beheld at a window a most beautiful lady, but with torn garments and disheveled hair. At sight of Codadad she cried out, "Young man, flee away, I pray you. A monster inhabits this palace, who seizes, imprisons, and devours every luckless being who passes this way."

"Madam," answered Codadad, "I have no fear, but who are you and how can I aid you?"

"I am a Princess of Grand Cairo," answered the lady, "I was yesterday traveling to Bagdad when the monster killed my attendants, and brought me to this castle, and now he threatens my life if I will not become his wife. But once more let me beg you to escape while there is yet time."

Hardly had she spoken when the giant appeared. He was of vast size and of dreadful aspect. He rode a huge Tartar horse, and carried a scimitar so heavy that none but himself could wield it. The Prince, although amazed at his gigantic stature, drew his own scimitar and firmly awaited his approach. The giant, uttering a mighty roar and foaming with rage, raised himself in his stirrups and rode headlong at Codadad, swinging his terrible weapon. The Prince avoided the blow by a sudden turn of his horse. The scimitar made a horrible hissing sound through the air. But before the giant had time for a second blow, Codadad struck him on his right arm with such

force that he severed it, and both arm and scimitar fell to earth together, while the giant, writhing under the violence of the blow, lost his stirrup and rolled upon the ground. The Prince alighted and cut off his head.

Thereupon, the lady, who had witnessed the combat, uttered a cry of joy and called to Codadad, "Prince, finish the work you have begun. Take the keys of this castle, which the giant has, and deliver me out of prison."

Searching the clothes of his late enemy, the Prince found the keys, opened the gate of the castle, and entered a court, where he saw the lady coming to meet him. She praised his valor, and extolled him above all the heroes in the world. The Prince returned her compliments abundantly, for she appeared even more lovely close at hand than she had at a distance. But suddenly their conversation was interrupted by dismal cries and groans.

"What do I hear?" said Codadad. "What are these sad sounds that pierce my ears?"

"Prince," said the lady, "those are the lamentations of the many wretched persons chained and imprisoned in the castle dungeons. Let us hasten to give them liberty."

The Prince immediately descended a very steep staircase to the deep, vaulted dungeon in which there were over a hundred prisoners, chained hand and foot.

"Unfortunate travelers," he said, "give thanks to Heaven which has this day delivered you from cruel death. I have slain the giant and have come to set you free."

At these words the prisoners gave a shout of mingled joy and surprise, while Codadad and the lady hastened to remove their fetters. When they had all come out from the dungeon into the court, under the light of day, the Prince's surprise was as great as his joy to see among the prisoners the very men whom he was seeking.

"Princes!" cried he, "is it really you whom I behold? May I hope to restore you to the Sultan your father who is inconsolable over your loss? Are you all here alive?"

The forty-nine Princes all made themselves known to Codadad, and in common with the other prisoners expressed unbounded gratitude for their deliverance. Codadad, with their help, searched the whole castle and found a vast store of hidden treasure, curious silks, gold brocades, Persian carpets, China silks, and an infinite variety of other goods which the giant had taken from the caravans he plundered, and some part of which was the property of the released prisoners. The Prince restored to them their own and divided the rest of the treasure equally among them all. Proceeding from the castle to the stables they found many stolen camels and horses, among them the horses belonging to the Sultan of Harran's sons. The merchants, overjoyed at recovering their goods and camels as well as their liberty, hastened to continue on their various ways. When they were gone Codadad, turning to the lady, said, "If you will tell us, madam, where you wish to go from here, these Princes and I will be glad to attend you. Will you not honor us with the story of your adventures?"

Thereupon the lady began the following recital:

"In the great city of Deryabar there ruled a powerful and good Sultan. He wanted only one thing to make him perfectly happy, and that was—a child. He constantly prayed Heaven for the blessing of a son; but his prayer was granted only in part as the Queen, his wife, gave birth to a daughter. I am that daughter. My father was grieved, but resigned himself to the will of God, and had me educated so that I might become a worthy successor to his crown.

"One day when hunting my father lost his way, and rode deep into the forest until overtaken by night. Making his way toward a faint light which shone from a hut among the trees, he found a gigantic Negro seated on a carpet with a huge pitcher of wine before him, and a whole ox roasting before the fire. More surprising still, there was also a beautiful woman in the hut, who seemed overwhelmed with grief, and at her feet was a little boy who cried without stopping. My father waited outside the hut. Before long the giant, having

emptied the pitcher and eaten about half the ox, seized the unhappy lady by the hair and, drawing his scimitar, was about to strike off her head when my father shot an arrow which pierced the giant's breast, and laid him dead upon the floor.

"My father entered the hut, unbound the lady's hands, and inquired who she was and how she had come to this place. 'My Lord,' she said, 'my husband is a Saracen Prince, ruling over certain seacoast tribes. One day when we were traveling through our dominions, my child and I became separated from the Prince, and this giant surprised us and carried us off to the forest. He was about to kill me because I refused to become his wife.' My father pitied the lady in her distress and told her that he would guide her the next day to the city of Deryabar of which he was Sultan, and that she was welcome to lodge at the palace until her husband came to claim her. The Saracen lady accepted the offer and the next day she accompanied my father, who found all his retinue anxiously waiting at the edge of the wood, after having spent a fruitless night in search of him.

"Upon arriving at the palace my father assigned an apartment to the beautiful Saracen lady, and arranged that her little son should be carefully educated. In course of time the boy grew up, tall and handsome and clever, and my father became much attached to him. All the courtiers perceived this and predicted that the young man might aspire to be my husband. Encouraged by such gossip, the young man forgot the distance between our stations, and boldly asked the Sultan for my hand. My father told him that he had other plans for me. The youth was so angry at this refusal that with basest ingratitude he murdered my father and caused himself to be proclaimed Sultan of Deryabar. Next, he came to my apartment at the head of the conspirators to take my life or oblige me to marry him. The Grand Vizier, however, always loyal to my father, carried me from the palace to a place of safety, until he could find a boat on which we presently set sail from the island.

"We had been but a few days at sea when a furious storm arose and our vessel was dashed to pieces on the rocks. The Grand Vizier and all my attendants were swallowed up by the sea. By what miracle I was saved I know not; but when my senses returned I found myself on shore. I was so overcome with the sense of my utter loneliness that I resolved to cast myself back into the sea, when I heard behind me a great noise of men and horses. Turning about, I saw several armed horsemen, one of whom was conspicuous above the rest in his dress and manner. He was mounted on an Arabian horse, his garments were embroidered in silver, and on his head was a golden crown. He gazed at me earnestly and seeing that I had been weeping he begged me not to give way to despair. 'My palace,' he said, 'is at your service. You shall live with the Queen my mother who will show you every kindness. I do not know who you are; yet I am already deeply interested in your welfare.'

"I thanked the young Sultan for his kindness, and to prove that I was not unworthy of it, I told him of my rank and of my misfortunes. The Prince at once took me to the Queen his mother who soon became extremely fond of me. Presently her son offered me himself and his crown, and our marriage was celebrated with all imaginable splendor.

"In the midst of these celebrations a formidable enemy, the King of Zanguebar, made a night attack on our kingdom with a great number of troops, and nearly captured us both. We escaped, however, and reached the seacoast, where we set sail in a fishing boat. On the third day we were overtaken by a pirate ship, and when it came alongside five or six armed pirates leaped into our boat, bound the Prince and cast him into the sea before my eyes. They then took me on board their own ship and instead of casting lots, they quarreled over me, and fought like madmen. At last they were all killed but one who said to me, 'Now you are mine. I will carry you to Grand Cairo and sell you to a friend of mine, who wants a beautiful slave.'

"We were on our way to Grand Cairo when the giant killed the pirate and took me to his black castle from which you rescued me."

When the Princess finished the story of her adventures Codadad said, "Happily, madam, your troubles are now over. The Sultan of Harran's sons offer you safe escort to their father's court. And if you do not disdain the hand of your rescuer, let me offer it to you, and let all these Princes be witnesses."

The Princess consented and the marriage took place that very day, after which they all set out for the Sultan of Harran's court. After they had traveled several days, and were within one day's journey of Harran, Codadad said:

"Princes, I have too long concealed from you my true history. I am your brother Codadad. The Sultan of Harran is my father, and the Princess Pirouze is my mother."

The Princess Deryabar and all the Princes congratulated Codadad on his birth with every appearance of the keenest joy. But in reality the hatred of the forty-nine brothers was redoubled. They met secretly that night while Codadad and his Princess lay asleep in their tent, and forgetting that they owed him their lives, agreed among themselves to murder him. "We have no other choice," said they, "for the moment that our father learns that this stranger, of whom he is so fond, is our brother, he will proclaim him heir to the throne."

Accordingly, they immediately surrounded the tent in which Codadad slept, stabbed him repeatedly, and left him for dead in the arms of the Princess Deryabar. The Princess rent the air with her frantic cries, tore her hair, and her tears rained down upon her husband's body. But presently, observing that Codadad still breathed, she left the tent to look for help, and met two travelers who willingly agreed to help her. But on returning with her they could nowhere find Codadad, and were forced to conclude that he had been dragged away by some wild beast.

Having at last persuaded the unhappy Princess to tell them

her history, the travelers advised her that it was her duty as a wife to continue at once to the court of the Sultan of Harran.

"He is a good and a just Prince," they said, "you need only tell him how Prince Codadad has been treated by his brothers and he will surely do you justice."

"I will follow your advice," replied the Princess. "It is my duty to avenge Codadad's death; and since you are so generous as to offer to escort me, I am ready to set out."

They halted at the first caravanserai that they reached on the road to Harran, and inquired of the host the latest news at court. "It is," said the host, "in very great perplexity. The Sultan had a son who lived long with him as a stranger, but has disappeared, and none can tell what has become of him. One of the Sultan's wives, named Pirouze, is his mother, and is now at Harran making all possible inquiry, but in vain. Everyone is heartbroken at the loss of this Prince. None of the Sultan's forty-nine other sons can console him for the death of Codadad."

Upon hearing this the two travelers agreed that one of them should remain with the Princess, while the other went on to the city, and obtained an interview with Pirouze. As this latter traveler was approaching the palace, he beheld a lady mounted on a richly caparisoned mule followed by several other mounted ladies, with a great number of guards and black slaves. The traveler asked a bystander whether the lady was one of the Sultan's wives. "Yes," answered the bystander, "and much honored and beloved by the people, because she is the mother of the lost Prince Codadad."

The traveler asked no more questions, but followed Pirouze to a mosque, where public prayers were being offered for the safe return of Codadad. When the prayers were over, the traveler approached one of the slaves and whispered in his ear, "Brother, I have a secret of great importance to impart to the Princess Pirouze. It concerns the Prince Codadad."

"If that be so," said the slave, "follow us to the palace and you shall have an opportunity."

Accordingly, the traveler followed them, and the slave immediately conducted him into the Princess' closet, and after humbly prostrating himself he related all the details of what had passed between Codadad and his brothers. The mother listened with eager attention; but when he came to speak of the murder, she fainted away, and fell back on her sofa as though she herself had been stabbed. When her women had restored her to herself, Pirouze said to the traveler, "Go back to the Princess of Deryabar and assure her from me that the Sultan will receive her as his daughter-in-law. As for yourself, your services shall be richly rewarded."

When the Sultan learned from Pirouze the story of the inhuman manner in which Codadad had been murdered by his brothers, he was transported with anger, and summoning his Grand Vizier, "Hassan," said he, "go immediately, take a thousand of my guards and seize all the Princes, my sons; shut them up in the safest tower, and let this be done at once."

The Grand Vizier, without uttering a word, laid his hand on his head in token of obedience, and hastened away to execute his orders.

When the Grand Vizier presently returned, to announce that all the forty-nine Princes had been seized and imprisoned, the Sultan said:

"I have further commands for you. Go to the caravanserai, where the Princess of Deryabar and the two travelers are lodged, and conduct them with all due honor to my palace."

Upon her arrival, the Princess of Deryabar found the Sultan at the palace gate, waiting to receive her. He took her by the hand and led her to Pirouze's apartment, where all three gave way to their grief, and mingled their tears and sighs. At length the Princess of Deryabar, having somewhat recovered, related the adventure with the giant, and Codadad's subsequent fate, and demanded justice for the treachery of the Princes.

"Assuredly," said the Sultan, "those ungrateful brothers

shall atone for their crimes with their lives. But Codadad's death must first be made public; and although my son's body is missing we shall nevertheless pay him the last solemn tribute."

Summoning his Grand Vizier, he ordered him to have erected a dome of white marble on the plain where the city of Harran stands. Hassan urged on the work with such diligence that the dome was soon finished. Within it was erected a tomb covered with gold brocade. When all was completed the Sultan appointed a day for the celebration of his son's funeral rites. The impressive ceremony was conducted with the greatest pomp and magnificence, after which there were public prayers in all the mosques for a period of eight days.

On the ninth day the Sultan decreed that the forty-nine Princes should be executed. The scaffolds were already being erected when a stay of the execution was ordered, because news had come that some neighboring rulers who had already made war on the Sultan of Harran were again advancing on the city with a greater force than ever. This news occasioned general consternation, and gave everyone fresh cause to lament the loss of Codadad. "Alas!" said the people, "if the brave Codadad were alive we should have small fear of the enemy who is advancing against us."

The Sultan valiantly placed himself at the head of his troops and went out to meet the foe. The struggle was long and fierce, and much blood was shed on both sides. At last, just as victory seemed to favor the enemy, a great body of fresh cavalry appeared on the plain, and fell upon the enemy's flank with such a furious charge that they not only routed them, but followed after and cut most of them in pieces.

The Sultan of Harran, who had closely watched the battle, admired the bravery of this strange body of cavalry whose unhoped-for arrival had changed defeat into victory. But above all, he longed to know the name of the generous hero who had fought with such extraordinary valor. Impatient to

meet and thank him, he hurried forward to meet the stranger, and to his joyful amazement recognized in the brave warrior his lost son Codadad.

"Oh, my son!" cried the Sultan. "Is it possible that you are restored to me! Alas! I despaired of ever seeing you again. But never fear! You shall be amply revenged tomorrow."

"Sire," said Codadad, "how did you learn that I am your son? Have my brothers repented and told you who I am?"

"No," answered the Sultan, "it is the Princess of Deryabar who has told us everything, for she is at the palace demanding justice against your brothers. And with her is your mother, the Princess Pirouze, who came seeking everywhere news of you."

The Sultan and his recovered son hastened back to the palace, where they found Pirouze and her daughter-in-law waiting to congratulate the Sultan upon his victory. But words

cannot express the transports of joy they felt when they saw the young Prince with him. Presently, when their first excitement was calmed, they asked Codadad by what miracle he came to be still alive. He answered that a peasant who chanced to pass the tent and found him senseless and dangerously wounded had strapped him upon his mule and carried him to his house where, with the help of certain wild herbs, he had cured him. "I was on my way back to Harran," continued Codadad, "when I learned that the enemy was marching on the city. So I made myself known to the in-

habitants as I passed along, and gathered a great number of young horsemen in your defense. Luckily, I happened to arrive in time."

When Codadad had finished, the Sultan said, "Let us return thanks to God for having preserved Codadad. But the traitors who sought his life must perish."

"Sire," answered the generous Prince, "even though my brothers are ungrateful, remember that they are your sons

and my brothers. For myself, I freely forgive their offense, and I pray you also to pardon them."

This generosity drew tears from the Sultan. He immediately caused all the people to be assembled, and publicly declared Codadad his heir. He then ordered the imprisoned Princes to be brought forth, loaded down with their chains. Codadad struck off their chains, and embraced them all with so much sincerity and affection that the people were all charmed with his generosity, and the wicked brothers themselves repented and resolved henceforth to give him loyal devotion.

* * * *

The Sultan of the Indies could not fail to admire the prodigious store of interesting stories with which the Sultana had whiled away the time through one thousand and one nights.

He also admired the courage which had inspired her to offer to become his wife; and for her sake his stern vow was relaxed, so that he could not bear to put her to death. "I confess, most lovely Scheherazade," said he, "that your wit has disarmed me. For your sweet sake I renounce my terrible vow to slay a woman every day. And for that reason you shall ever be remembered as the deliverer of the maidens who would have fallen victims to my wrath—which I now know to be unjust." The Sultana cast herself at his feet, and embraced him with the most warm affection and gratitude.

The Grand Vizier was the first who learned these glad tidings, which he caused to be quickly spread through every province and town of the Empire, so that the fair Scheherazade won the blessing of everyone throughout the country. The Sultan lived happily with his lovely Sultana, and their names were loved and respected throughout the wide territory of the Empire of the Indies.